*The*
*Gunpowder and*
*Glory Girls*

**Rosie Archer** was born in Gosport, Hampshire, where she still lives. She has had a variety of jobs including waitress, fruit picker, barmaid, shop assistant and market trader selling second-hand books. Rosie is the author of three other Bomb Girls books as well as a series of gangster sagas under the name June Hampson.

Also by Rosie Archer

THE BOMB GIRLS SERIES

*The Munitions Girls*
*The Canary Girls*
*The Factory Girls*

# The Gunpowder and Glory Girls

## ROSIE ARCHER

Quercus

First published in Great Britain in 2016 by Quercus
This paperback edition published 2016 by

Quercus Editions Ltd
Carmelite House
50 Victoria Embankment
London EC4Y 0DZ

An Hachette UK company

A CIP catalogue record for this book is available
from the British Library

PB ISBN 978 1 78429 784 8
EBOOK ISBN 978 1 78429 785 5

10 9 8 7 6 5 4 3 2 1

Typeset by CC Book Production

Printed and bound in Great Britain by Clays Ltd, St Ives plc

# The Gunpowder and Glory Girls

# Chapter One

*August 1944, Gosport*

'Come on love, it can't be as bad as all that.'

The moment the words had flown from Gladys's mouth, she wished she hadn't uttered them. The stench of cordite and burning wood, the noise of ambulances after the all-clear had sounded and the shouting from ARP men searching through the smoking rubble was enough to distress anyone, let alone this girl. She had long blonde hair and was sitting alone on a broken box, cuddling an orange-coloured cat and crying noisily.

'Shove up.' Gladys parked her bottom alongside her and put her arm around the girl's shoulder. 'You want to tell me what's wrong?'

Gladys should have been on her way to work the night shift at Gosport's armament factory, where she had been promoted to overseer, but there was no way she could ignore this girl looking so lost and forlorn; it just wasn't in her nature.

The girl stared at her and her grip tightened on the cat, which was visibly frightened by all the hustle and bustle. Gladys saw the livid bruise on the side of her face, then the red marks around the girl's thin wrists. She had obviously suffered some trauma.

Gladys's night shift at Priddy's could wait for a while. She was early as usual and no doubt the women would be late getting back to their machines because of the raid. Ol' Hitler and his V1s and V2s were a damn nuisance, disrupting things. She took a handkerchief from the pocket of her cardigan and gave it to the girl, who sniffed and muttered her thanks as she accepted it.

'What's your name, love?' Gladys tried again.

'Gwendolynne.' She lifted her head. She was a looker all right, thought Gladys. The girl dabbed at her eyes and the cat gave an angry, drawn-out growl of a meow. 'But I'm called Goldie, because of my hair.' She brushed a long lock off her face and another bruise became visible.

'Didn't think that colour came out of a bottle.' Gladys was conscious of her own peroxide-blonde hair, now orange and brittle at the front where her fringe wasn't covered by the turban she wore at Priddy's. The damage was caused by TNT, the powerful explosive she worked with.

Goldie sniffed. 'My gran's gone. The houses at the top of this street have copped the doodlebug. Mogs is all that's left.' She suddenly buried her teary face in the cat's fur.

'Oh, I'm sorry, love.' Would the horrors of this war never end?

'I needed to stay with her . . .' Fresh tears fell as she looked up. Gladys decided it was time to take charge of things.

'Look, love, that's my place over there.' She pointed to number fourteen, a terraced house unscathed by the bombing. 'I think you could do with a cup of tea. I know I could.' She rose and waited while Goldie hoisted the feisty cat to her chest and stood up beside her. Apart from the cat and her handbag, the girl had nothing else with her.

Together they threaded their way through a small crowd of WVS women busily stacking a table with blankets in a hastily erected tent. A large tea urn, used to give succour to the homeless and those in shock, was already in operation. Several people sat on chairs with blankets around their shoulders, hugging mugs, with dazed expressions on their faces.

Dust filled the air and Gladys averted her eyes as two ambulance men passed by, carrying a stretcher with a fully covered figure lying on it. She knew that person would be going to the mortuary and not the hospital.

When our boys had landed on the French beaches, Gladys

remembered, everyone was filled with hope, but Hitler was still sending those terrible, whining rockets that suddenly cut out and dropped, dashing everything in their paths to smithereens.

'Here we are,' said Gladys, pulling the string through the letter box and unlocking her front door.

The house was empty now, but she still left her key hanging on a string for visitors. She didn't like living alone.

Em, her best friend, had gone to live in Lyme Regis. Em's son-in-law Joel had been offered a managerial position at the care home, Yew Trees, so the whole family had left Gosport.

Gladys missed them all so much, but funnily enough it was her canary she grieved for more than anything – apart from her beloved daughter, Pixie, who had been killed in a raid. The little yellow bird had been given to her years ago by some man she'd been going with, whose name she'd long forgotten. The canary had chirped its way into her heart and when one morning she'd got up for work to find the dear little bird had passed away in the night, she'd been heartbroken.

'Come along in,' Gladys said, showing the girl along the passage and into the kitchen. 'Sit down while I put on the kettle.'

In the scullery she bustled about with cups and saucers,

putting them on a tray along with a plate of the last of her precious Bourbon biscuits.

While the kettle boiled, she peeked back into the kitchen. The girl was now sitting on the old frayed armchair beneath the window, still with the cat clutched tightly.

'You can let him down, he won't come to any harm here,' Gladys said. She watched as Mogs made another bid for freedom from the girl's arms and this time made it. He sat down in front of the black-leaded range and began washing himself. Gladys poured milk into a saucer, took it into the kitchen and put it near the fender on the rag rug.

'While I make the tea, are you going to tell me who's been hurting you?'

Goldie looked down at her wrists as though surprised someone had noticed the discoloured flesh. Now there were fresh tears in her eyes.

'I was tied up.' Her voice was very quiet, as though she didn't really want to say anything. The older woman had to stop herself from gasping at the girl's words.

The kettle began to wail so Gladys finished making the tea, deliberating whether to use fresh tea leaves or simply top up the pot. She then brought in the tray and set it on the table. She hoped the tea would be strong enough, because she'd only put one miserly half a teaspoon of leaves on top of the dregs left from earlier. With only two ounces of tea per person every week she had to be very careful. Gladys lived on tea. Damn the war, she thought. Would rationing ever end? She waited until Goldie spoke again. Because of her bruising she didn't think it right to urge the girl to tell her story.

'It's Fred, my stepbrother. I've managed to get away from him. I thought if I got to Gran's house, I could stay there out of his way . . .' Now the tears came thick and fast and her words were jumbled and rushed.

'Hang on a bit,' Gladys interrupted. 'I think you'd better start at the beginning.' She poured out the girl's tea and stirred in two precious spoonfuls of sugar, thinking Goldie might be in shock. She didn't take sugar herself.

'Drink this, love, nothing like a cuppa to make a person feel better.' She pushed the cup and saucer towards Goldie and sat down on a kitchen chair facing the girl. Immediately she was seated, the cat jumped up onto Gladys's lap and settled down.

'Well I never,' she said, happily smoothing the silky fur. The sound of purring filled the room and Goldie began to speak.

'A few months ago my mother met a man – his son is Fred, who's in his twenties. There's also a girl aged fifteen, his daughter, named Dorothy, who everyone calls Doll.' Goldie once more pushed back strands of her long hair from her face, this time tucking them behind an ear. 'My dad was killed in France last year.' Gladys saw the terrible sadness in her eyes as she spoke of the loss of her father. 'My gran thought my mum was wrong to get involved with another man so soon. That's the gran who lived here in Alma Street.' Gladys nodded. 'She said she didn't even want to meet "that family", as she called them.'

'Doll is spoilt.' She looked straight into Gladys's eyes. 'I'm not just saying that. They do everything for her, especially Fred, who's always buying her little treats. He's more like her father, telling her what to do, what to wear, who to be friends with. He controls her completely.'

'Doesn't her father have any say in the matter?' Gladys couldn't help interrupting.

'He doesn't care who looks after Doll as long as it isn't him.'

Gladys shook her head. What an awful state of affairs, she thought. 'But what about your mum, doesn't she worry about you?'

'She's so caught up with her husband and their new life together I think she's forgotten I exist. I did write to her.' Goldie looked very sad. 'She hasn't replied to my letter.'

Goldie went very quiet. Gladys felt bad about reminding her of her mother's abandonment, so she asked, 'This Fred, what does he do for a living?'

'He runs a club in Southsea and Doll dances on the stage. Actually, she's a really good dancer. But she's not allowed to talk to anyone who works there, especially not the other girls who are older and . . . and . . .' Gladys saw the blush rise from her neck up and over her face, 'go with men there.' She rubbed her hand across her eyes and Gladys could see she was tired, but she let Goldie go on talking. She wondered how old the girl was, perhaps about eighteen?

'Fred touched me at every available moment.' Gladys saw she was embarrassed talking about this, as she wouldn't look her in the eyes. But she went on. 'He'd get me in a corner and put his hand up my skirt. He'd come into the bathroom when I was washing; there was no lock on the door, you see. He was always going through my clothes, touching my underwear. I tried not to be alone with him. Once he came into my bedroom when everyone was asleep and he was putting his hands on me.' Goldie's face hardened. 'He left when I said I'd scream. He laughed and told me that next time he'd gag me so I couldn't call out. He said he was going to "have me" and there was no escaping my fate.' She shivered, as though talking about it brought back her fears.

'Didn't you tell anyone?' Gladys couldn't help butting in, passing Goldie another handkerchief. She used it to wipe her nose.

'Of course I did.' For a moment she looked indignant.

'But Mum accused me of being jealous and trying to stop her getting married and moving down to the seaside in Cornwall. That's where Mum's gone; her and her new husband have a live-in job.'

Goldie drank the last of her tea and Gladys began to pour more. The cat jumped down, disturbed by the sudden movement, and began licking itself. When Gladys was once more settled in the chair, Mogs jumped back onto her lap.

'Mum left the three of us together in the house.' Goldie shuddered. 'I came home from work today – I work in a laundry – and found Doll was spending the night with a schoolfriend who Fred fancies and there were three friends of his in the kitchen, drinking home-made elderberry wine and whisky.' Goldie paused to explain, 'Mum made lots of different wines when she could get the ingredients. Mostly she gave bottles away as Christmas presents. Anyway, there were empty bottles on the table and the place stank of cigarettes. When I went to open a window I saw it was nailed shut. I must have looked surprised, because Fred started laughing. He said I was going to get what was coming to me. His mates started laughing as well and I knew I was going to be . . . going to be . . .' she took a deep breath, 'passed round like a thing, like I had no say in the matter.' The girl had put the handkerchief to her face and was sobbing as though her heart was going to break.

9

Gladys got up from the chair, letting Mogs slide to the floor, and went over to Goldie, putting her arms around her.

'Cry if you want,' she said. The girl's shoulders heaved as she sobbed. After a while Goldie quietened; as Gladys sat down again, she carried on.

'Fred got hold of me and started pulling at my clothes and hitting me, but I managed to run upstairs. He wouldn't let his mates touch me, he said he wanted to be first. But he got one to come up and hold my arms while he tied my wrists together. I was scared stiff, screaming at him. Then he tied a blindfold around my eyes.

'He said I had to calm down a bit so he went downstairs with his mate. It took me ages to get that blindfold off – chewing on a piece of the material that was hanging down – so that it slid from my eyes. I found he'd taken the key so that he could lock the door from the outside.

'I knew I had to get away. My window was cracked and the frame had moved when a bomb had exploded across the way. He couldn't lock that, but he'd banged in a nail. I pulled the nail out; once I'd got it loosened it wasn't so bad.' She showed Gladys her bloodied fingertips and broken nails. 'But first I managed to get the string off my wrists by sawing at it with a nail file from my handbag.

'I could hear them drinking and laughing downstairs and I was terrified that Fred would come up and discover I'd got free. I managed to climb out of the window and onto the flat roof below, then I jumped down and ran along the alley at the back of the houses. I only had my handbag and precious little money in my purse with me. I just wanted to get away from them.' She drank some more tea. 'I thought if I could get to Gran's place she'd let me stay with her, then I wouldn't have to go back to that house.' She sighed. 'I had enough money for the ferry and I walked here from Gosport town.

'But when I got here the V1 had arrived first. The ARP warden said there was nobody left in the three houses at the top of the street. He was lovely, he got a lady to give me some tea. Then I saw Mogs, Gran's cat, sitting on top of a wall.'

As if he understood that they were talking about him, Mogs yawned, showing sharp white teeth. Then he stretched, his paws out in front of him, his claws digging in the rug. Jumping up once more onto Gladys's lap, he circled then curled into a ball.

'Now,' Goldie sighed, 'I don't know what to do.' She shook her head. 'I don't want to go back to Southsea; besides, I don't have enough money for the ferry.' She paused. 'I know Fred will come after me because I made him look stupid in front of his mates. I'm frightened of him.' She couldn't hold herself together any longer and put her face in her hands again. Gladys watched her for a while. She hated to see her so distraught. Then the girl mumbled, 'Oh, I loved my gran. I just don't know what to do or where to go.'

She took the girl's hands away and looked into her swollen face. She'd already made her decision.

'I have to go to work now, but you're more than welcome to stay here. There's a bed, made up, upstairs in the front bedroom. There's a hot-water bottle under the sink.' She waved a hand towards the scullery. 'Put it in the bed to air it. I'm sorry about your gran, I can't do anything about her, but when I come home in the morning, we'll talk again. Hopefully you'll feel better after a night's sleep. Fred won't find you here. You'll be safe.'

Goldie stared at her. 'You'd do that for me?' She was incredulous. 'You'd let me stay here?'

Gladys nodded as she gently pushed the sleeping Mogs to the floor and got up. The orange cat, now wide awake, was now twisting itself in and out of Gladys's legs.

'You can't possibly know how relieved and thankful I am.' Goldie gave a huge sigh. 'Thank you.' She looked at the cat. 'Gran said Mogs hated everyone, but he seems to have taken a real shine to you.'

Gladys bent down and patted the cat. 'Good,' she said. 'Because I've taken a real shine to the pair of you.'

# Chapter Two

Gladys opened her locker and took out her navy-blue dunga-rees. The air in the room smelled of sweat and stale perfume. It was noisy, all the girls talking at once while they changed their clothes.

A bomb had exploded in the creek behind the armament factory. It had blown a wooden footbridge to smithereens and a couple of moored boats had disintegrated. Happily, no one had been injured and it was far enough away from the buildings not to cause any problems. She'd been right in thinking there would be a late start tonight.

Pam came over and searched her. It was a criminal offence to take in any hazardous materials that might cause a spark, because of the risk of explosion inside the factory. Even hairgrips had to be removed. Jewellery as well, except for wedding rings, which were allowed to be worn, but only if covered with a strip of sticking plaster.

Gladys pulled on the hated boots provided for all the workers. Ordinary shoes, especially those with metal tips and Blakeys on the heels, were highly dangerous.

Then she tied on the white turban that made her head itch. Although she didn't like the headgear, she appreciated that without it all of her hair would become yellowed and frizzy, just like her fringe. The colour white denoted the station in which she worked. There were different colours for different stations.

Hiding tobacco and matches for a crafty smoke during breaks often meant instant dismissal. One woman in a different factory, it had been reported in the newspapers, had been sent to prison for the offence.

She rolled up one sleeve and examined her arm. The TNT floating in the air caused the workers' skin to yellow and gave them the nickname 'Canaries'. Gladys had worked at Priddy's for so long that her skin was very tanned, making her look as though much of her time was spent outdoors.

Some of the workers became ill with liver and chest complaints and jaundice. Sometimes their periods ceased. Hadn't her own periods stopped recently? Maybe, she thought, it was because she was getting older, going through an early 'change of life'. Gladys was well aware she was nearer forty than thirty. Or perhaps they'd stopped due to delayed shock caused by the terrible burns on her back she'd received when one of Priddy's workers had dropped a grenade. She knew she was lucky to be alive. Gladys had spent time in the marvellous Queen Victoria Hospital at East Grinstead, where they had treated her so well that very few scars remained.

Sores and itching skin were common complaints, caused by the dangerous chemicals the workers handled. If one felt particularly ill, a few days spent in a different department was usually the answer. The workers were also the recipients of a pint of milk every day to help keep them fit.

Gladys walked along the stone-floored corridors to the manager's office, to see if there were special orders needing to be relayed to the night workers.

She thought about Goldie and how frightened the girl was. As she remembered the cat, a smile lit her face. It would be nice having company about the place, she thought. Goldie would be safe staying at Alma Street. She would need work though, to pay her way. Goldie had said she worked in a Portsmouth laundry, but Gladys doubted the girl would want to continue with that job. After all, she'd have to cross on the ferry twice a day and Fred might be waiting for her at her workplace.

She decided she would ask the manager, Mr Scrivenor, if there was a vacancy at Priddy's. They always needed workers to help build bombs. Hitler mustn't be allowed to win this war. Goldie might be glad of the higher wages that were paid to the women working in the Ordnance Factory. She could expect between £2 and £4 a week. With overtime and bonuses, Gladys had received almost £7 in her wage packet last week. That was a lot of money, but it was wartime and food prices seemed to rise all the time. Goods were rationed, but cheapness didn't come into it. She knocked on the door.

'Come in.'

'Good evening, Mr Scrivenor, is there anything I should tell the girls on the night shift?'

Gladys liked Rupert Scrivenor. He was a fair man and a kind boss, always ready to listen to the girls when they had problems. He was immaculately dressed, as always, in a suit and white shirt with just a little of the cuffs showing beneath his sleeves.

'No, Gladys.' That was another thing that made him popular – he always remembered the workers' names. When he walked through the factory he would stop and chat and ask after their families. Everyone respected Rupert Scrivenor. 'We're getting back to normal after the latest rocket attack, which delayed production. Luckily the bomb didn't hit us.'

Priddy's was named after Jane Priddy who in 1770 sold the land to the Board of Ordnance as a powder depot to serve the navy's fleet. In 1775, Nelson's gunpowder was stored there, and now 4,000 people, men and women, worked there supplying explosives. With green-painted roofs to foil the enemy aircraft, Priddy's stood just outside the heart of Gosport, hidden in woodland and backing onto Forton Creek, where the munitions could be loaded onto ships. A strip of water separated Portsmouth from Gosport and small ferry boats like black beetles carried passengers back and forth. Nelson's flagship, the *Victory*, was moored at Portsmouth's dockyard.

At break-times, when she worked the day shift, Gladys loved sitting in the sun and eating her packed lunch. The wind blowing the scents of wild flowers helped to disguise the muddy smell of the creek, and the stink of the gunpowder.

'Sir, I have a friend staying with me who needs work . . .'

Rupert Scrivenor stared at her. 'And you wondered if there's a job here?'

Gladys knew she was blushing. 'Yes, sir.'

'This friend, can you vouch for her?'

Gladys didn't know Goldie at all, not really. But her sixth sense told her the girl was trustworthy. She believed her story. How awful to be scared to go home when home should be the one place a person could feel safe.

'Yes,' she replied.

'Then tell her to come along and have a chat with me.'

Gladys thanked him, left the office and went first to her own workshop. There she'd give the women their instructions, make a note of any absentees and attend to any problems her girls might have about work. All that sorted, she could then go to the detonator shop where she'd be 'filling in' for a girl who was sick. Sprinkling detonators with mercury was extremely dangerous and the girls were paid an extra two shillings and sixpence a week to do it. She'd already asked if any of her girls wanted the job, but they'd all declined.

'Hello, Marie.' The big, beefy woman was already at work with the other women at the long bench. The wireless was playing but the girls weren't singing along. This was exacting work and they had to keep their wits about them. Gladys looked at Marie's arms, though not a great deal of her skin was visible. 'I see your rash has cleared up.' Marie nodded, took off her mask and put down her heavy face shield.

Gladys knew Marie had been working with mercury powder for a long time and it had made her skin red and itchy. Marie had been moved to a different workshop, but as soon as the rash cleared she was back again. She had a large family, her husband had been killed on the beaches in France and she needed the extra money.

'You ain't forgot how to do this job, have you?' Marie laughed. Her teeth were rotten; that was another hazard of breathing in the chemicals.

'What, me?' Gladys laughed. 'I been here so long, I

reckon I could run this place single-handed.' A couple of the women laughed. Gladys was well liked. She pressed her mask into place.

Marie grinned and passed her a tub. Gladys had to work behind a steel shield with a Perspex window. She also had to wear a cotton-wool mask, which she hated because it rubbed against her lips and made her mouth sore.

She took the tub over to a container called a hopper that had an opening at its base for the mercury to be released. A tray of detonators lay ready for her to sprinkle the powder on top, one at a time; she then had to slide them along the table, carefully, for the next worker to do her part of the job.

'After break I'll be cleaning detonators with you,' Gladys said to Marie. The mask also made her voice sound funny.

There were eight women powdering the detonators and four cleaning them. Although Gladys didn't like doing this job, she would at least be working at something different after her day off tomorrow. This was the last of her night shift and then she'd be back on days, unlike Marie who was permanently on nights, because it paid more.

'Have you seen Marlene lately?' Marie asked.

Last week Gladys had been for a drink with Marlene, who had the most gorgeous red hair.

'Yes, we went down the Fox. But she couldn't stay long; she had to get home for an early night. She's doing well, selling gold at the markets, but of course she has to get up at three every morning.'

'It's a hard life, the markets,' said Marie. 'She still with that copper?'

'Mac MacKenzie, the detective? Yes, she's head over heels in love with him.'

'He's a nice man.'

Gladys agreed with Marie. She didn't want to go on chatting about people they both knew, because it made her feel sad that Marlene was the only good mate she had left now that Em had gone to live in Lyme Regis. On the wireless Harry James and his orchestra were playing 'I'll Get By' and it seemed to her that all the music was sad. If it wasn't for her job at Priddy's, she would be even more lonely.

Then she thought about Goldie and how unhappy that poor girl was. Gladys determined she would look after her and make sure that beast of a Fred didn't find her. She immediately began to feel better.

'Do you know anything about cats?' she asked.

'They spray on your furniture, make the house smell and leave hairs all over the cushions,' said Iris, a woman working at the side of her.

'I'm sorry I asked,' said Gladys. Iris had a downturned mouth and looked miserable.

'I've got a cat,' said Marie. 'My Fluffy is beautiful. I brush her long fur and I treat her to a bit of cod when I can get it from the fishmonger.'

'Your Fluffy eats better than me, then,' said Iris.

Gladys thought she might see if she could get some fish for Mogs. Fish wasn't on ration, but you couldn't always buy it.

Last night she'd taken over from another woman in a different workshop who claimed she was sick and had gone home. Gladys had sat by herself with an oilcan with a big spout and had had to carefully drip a substance used as a moulding compound onto little cartridges. She'd needed a steady hand, as a single drip in the wrong place meant the cartridge would be a reject. She'd had no one to talk to there, so it was better here where she was at least able to chat.

Marie said, 'It's funny, we all do our bit working on parts of this and that but we never see the end product.' Gladys knew what she meant. The sum total of all their work was the bombs of varying sizes that were loaded onto the boats in the creek, but no one worker built a shell from start to finish.

'I don't mind what I do, as long as we defeat that damned Hitler,' said Gladys, but already she was looking forward to their first tea break of the night.

'Have you seen the bloke in that new club down the ferry?' asked Iris. When Iris smiled she looked almost pretty. Unfortunately she didn't smile much.

Gladys said, 'Nice place, that Rainbow Club. You mean that Londoner?'

'Yeah, him with the curly hair. I wouldn't mind a bit of that.' This came from another woman cleaning detonators, Jill. Gladys didn't know much about Jill except that her husband had run off with a bus conductress. 'Mind you, those twins of his are a handful. I saw one pinch sweets from Woolies'.'

'Don't think they're his kids, though,' Iris broke in.

Gladys didn't say anything. She'd been in the Rainbow Club with Marlene, who'd told her that Mac and William Hill, the owner of the club, were mates from way back. Apparently Will wasn't always on the right side of the law, but they had an understanding. Will had sent over drinks to Marlene and when he'd stopped by their table, Gladys had felt all fluttery when he spoke to her.

Gladys didn't answer Jill, but she remembered Will's brown eyes that reminded her of melted chocolate. No, they weren't his kids, but Violet, the twins' mother, was often in Gosport and Gladys had liked the small blonde woman very much when she'd been introduced to her.

At five in the morning the buzzer sounded and Gladys was glad to be going home. She breathed a huge sigh of relief at leaving the mask and the shield behind her.

She checked on the girls in her station, visited other

workrooms and made sure everything was all right. Several girls wanted time off and she arranged others to stand in for them. There'd been no problems to write up on her report card, so she was able to take her clipboard along to Rupert Scrivenor's office for him to sign and then she could leave without a long discussion.

The women were searched again before leaving. It was noisy and smelly in the locker room; women were everywhere, getting undressed and dressing to leave. Gladys was tired and wanted her bed.

Outside, the day was beginning. The blackout had been relaxed and it was lovely, she thought, to see the sun come up with the blinds open. Even nicer now they could have the electric lights on inside Priddy's and not bother with the blackout blinds.

There were some ports of entry along the south coast that still had to observe the restrictions to lighting. She'd hated having to remember to keep the blackout curtains tightly closed at home.

Women were stopping outside the gates to light up cigarettes. She waved to the gatekeeper and stepped aside as a cyclist almost ran her down. A great many of the workers, both male and female, depended on bicycles to get to work. Many, like Gladys, walked. She used to walk with Em and her daughter Lizzie, but now she walked alone.

Cheer up, she told herself, she could soon be walking to Priddy's with Goldie, that's if the girl wanted the job, of course.

She was surprised when she unlocked her front door to be greeted by the smell of cooking and the sound of a newscaster talking from the wireless.

Goldie poked her head around the scullery door. 'I guessed to the second when you'd get home,' she said. She came into the kitchen just as Gladys was taking off her cardigan. 'I hope it's all right, I've made you some breakfast.' She was wearing Gladys's pinny. Gladys was now wriggling her feet out of her shoes. Her bunion was giving her gyp and she longed to put her feet in her old pom-pom slippers.

Gladys opened her eyes wide. 'But I never had anything in to make a meal with,' she said. Goldie brought in a plate and put it on the table.

'I found powdered egg and bread, so you've got scrambled eggs on toast.'

Gladys frowned. Goldie laughed. 'I promise you'll like the way I made the eggs, all fluffy, just like real ones,' she said. She set the plate down and Gladys felt her mouth water at the sight. Two slices of golden toast topped with egg and a couple of fried tomatoes on the side. 'Them grey bits in the egg is pepper; taste it and you'll be begging me to make it again,' Goldie said. 'I'll just go and bring in the teapot.'

Gladys, hungry, sat down at the table. It was then she saw that Goldie had cleared up, swept the lino and polished all available surfaces.

'You've been busy,' she said.

'Well, you've been so kind to me and Mogs,' Goldie pointed out.

'Where is the cat?' Goldie was pouring her a cup of tea. Gladys looked under the table.

'No idea,' said Goldie. 'I expect he's found somewhere to snuggle down.' She paused before she said, 'I hope you don't mind, but it's better that he stays indoors until he's used to his new home – I've put a bit of marge on his paws. I found a big roasting tin with rust on it in the cupboard beneath the stairs. I felt sure you didn't use it any more . . .' She looked expectantly at Gladys who knew exactly the tin she meant and had been meaning to throw it out. 'Anyway,' she continued, 'I put some earth from the garden in it to make a litter tray.' She blushed. 'I don't expect you to clean out the tray, of course. I'll do it.'

Gladys said, 'I hope Mogs uses it, then. I don't want to find little presents in corners!' Secretly she already missed the cat and hoped he hadn't run away.

She began to eat her breakfast. 'This is lovely,' Gladys said. However did the girl manage to produce such fluffy scrambled egg? 'It's really tasty.' Every time she'd tried to cook with the powder it tasted like cardboard. In no time at all she'd finished and patted her full belly while Goldie laughed at her. The wireless was still on and the music made the house seem homelier than it had in ages. Gladys was tired, but very happy to come home to Goldie.

'Oh, I forgot,' she said. 'If you fancy working at Priddy's with me, our manager will be happy to see you.'

Goldie put the teapot down – she'd begun to pour out more tea – and threw her arms around Gladys's neck.

'That's wonderful,' she said. 'I was scared about returning to the laundry because Fred knows where it is. I'll be able to pay you for my keep.' She suddenly looked sad. 'I can stay with you, can't I?'

'Of course you can. I'll be very glad to have you,' laughed Gladys. 'It's my day off today, and after I've had a sleep we'll sort out everything, okay?'

She thought how quickly she had picked up the American slang words, just as most of the girls had. She took the breakfast plate and cutlery into the scullery then left them on the draining board to wash when she'd had a well-earned sleep.

'I think I'll go up to Gran's house, what's left of it, and see if there's anything in the rubble. Maybe there's a few photos?'

'Good idea,' called Gladys down the stairs, though she

doubted Goldie would find anything at all. 'I'll only sleep a few hours.' She pushed open her bedroom door, deciding that when she woke she'd help Goldie sort out her room and find her a couple of nighties to sleep in. Maybe they could go down the market, sort through the second-hand stall and she could buy the girl clothes to wear. After all, she only had the ones she stood up in. She'd need more shoes and perhaps it would be a good idea for Gladys to give her some money, to buy herself any personal articles she needed. Gladys sighed. She hadn't always been the best mother to Pixie. Now it seemed she was being given a second chance with Goldie. This girl needed her. She decided she'd better find out if Goldie had her ration book.

Gladys had a strip-wash, pouring cold water into the basin from the jug on the washstand. After she'd scrubbed her teeth she put on her silky nightdress. She never wore flannelette nightgowns.

She brushed her hair, rubbed some Pond's cream on her face and then pulled back the quilt to climb into bed.

An orange, whiskered face turned towards her, amber eyes sleepily blinking.

'So you found the bed, did you, Mogs?' The cat began to purr. Gladys got in carefully and pulled it into her arms. 'I think I'm going to like having the both of you around,' she said.

# Chapter Three

Jamie Kennet tore open the letter from Goldie. He'd been surprised she'd moved to Gosport, worried at first that he'd had no letters from her for a while. He'd been told that the postal service took only a few days to deliver communications from England, but he knew that wasn't always true. She wrote regularly, as did he; he hated it when there were no letters for days then perhaps three at once. Her letters kept him sane. When he held the page to his face he swore he could smell her scent on the paper. Or was it simply wishful thinking?

The tank battalion was just south of Brouay and the French breeze was stiff, but it had been a dry day. He eagerly read her words then put the missive in his top pocket.

'We're moving out tonight,' called Eli, his mate. 'Entire crew's on the move.'

'Suppose there'll be hold-ups,' replied Jamie. There'd been

no letter for Eli. He was supposed to be marrying his girl on the next leave home, but her letters had stopped coming.

Jamie jumped down from the turret he'd been leaning against. He brushed his blond hair back from his forehead. The 6th Royal Tank Regiment was making its way through France after the retreating Germans. He felt worn out from the physical effort of staying alive and the mental strain of knowing he could be blown to smithereens at any moment, either inside the tank or out. Survival was on his mind constantly. Jamie knew it was all a matter of daily luck who lived and who died. Booby traps were everywhere, left by the Germans to target the troops. Mines too, were carefully hidden from sight.

Unlike the corpses. Dead Germans littered the earth. Some were hastily buried, barely covered by the sods of the glorious countryside. Dead farm animals also stank up the area.

Yet, despite all this, France was quite beautiful, especially this prosperous farmland, thought Jamie. He patted the letter in his pocket and thanked God for Goldie. She didn't often talk about her family. He'd met Fred and Doll on his last leave. Both were despicable, he thought. The young girl was a spoiled brat and he hadn't trusted that awful stepbrother, who somehow seemed to have managed to wriggle out of being called up in the services.

He'd gone along with a couple of his mates to that club the bloke managed, but it was nothing more than a glorified knocking shop. Considering Fred allowed his sister to dance on the stage, he wondered what on earth was going on in his head. Fifteen years old and dancing her little heart out while the next turn was obviously some harridan touting for a bedfellow. Still, it wasn't his problem, he had problems enough of his own to worry about. He hoped with all his heart that Fred left Goldie alone. He'd seen the way the bloke had leered at her.

Eli was on guard tonight. Each crew kept one member on lookout, just for safety. Last night mortars fell. Not many, but enough to keep them on their toes. German suicide attacks were few now but the air attacks were pretty fierce. Several planes flew low, using their machine guns. All the artillery around might have been their target. A heavy stench of cordite and smoke had spread a long way. None of them had slept much; the firing went on for ages. The foxhole wasn't big enough, not with three of them sleeping in it.

Jamie decided to write back to Goldie.

'When you gonna marry her?' Eli shouted.

'Soon as I bleeding can,' Jamie sang out to his mate. All the women had eyes for Eli. He was taller than Jamie and though he hated to admit it, broader and better-looking. Eli was a good bloke. 'Got to get engaged first, though,' Jamie shouted. 'I got a lovely ring; it used to belong to my gran. My mum likes Goldie. We went to the same school. Lost touch afterwards; I played the field a bit.' He looked towards Eli and winked. 'But we met up again at a birthday party and I knew straight away I didn't want nobody else.'

Jamie suddenly remembered Eli hadn't had a letter from his girl.

'Sorry, mate,' he said. 'There could be a hundred reasons why you haven't heard from your Carol.'

'Well, I wish she'd drop me a line and tell me,' Eli yelled.

Fred slapped the woman around the face. She fell back against the metal filing cabinet. A trickle of blood appeared on her skin where the corner of the drawer had dug into her hip. She'd not long come off the dance floor and was wearing see-through harem pants. Her top was threaded with sequins and shiny buttons and he noted that a lot of them were hanging by threads. A long net scarf draped over her shoulder didn't leave much to anyone's imagination. Chipped nail varnish. He shuddered. Rene was a bit long in the tooth for the Dance of the Seven Veils, but she made up her money by sleeping with the punters. She smelled of stale rose perfume and old sweat.

'Oww!'

'That was nothing to what you'll get if you don't up my money. This is fuckin' rubbish!'

He threw the two pounds' worth of change at her and she tried to turn her face away as the money in the envelope hit her cheek then fell to the floor.

'I can't help it if the punters won't pay what I ask.'

'I've told you, you stupid cow, ask for the cash before you let 'em touch you, not bloody afterwards. Pick up that dosh.'

Rene scrabbled around picking up the money that had scattered over the filthy office floor. Then she handed it back to Fred, who stuffed it in his inside pocket. Rene looked petrified.

'Doll needs new clothes now she's left school and I want the best for her,' he growled. 'I got other debts to pay, you know.'

Fred had been looking after his sister for as long as he could remember, paying for her keep since he was fifteen and had his first job selling newspapers on a street corner in the town. Their mother had been useless. She spent the naval allotment on herself, going dancing and buying clothes. There was never enough food indoors, yet she always had a fag in her mouth. If their father had been at home instead of serving in the Royal Navy, Fred was sure he would have left her years ago, seeing how she treated them. The years passed and Della was lucky she lasted as long as she did, the way she drank. It was only after she'd walked in front of a bus that their dad had been able to leave the navy and be there for them.

Their father made a better job of it than Della, but being told what to do in the services was easier for him than looking after a couple of nearly grown-up offspring.

With no job, a war on and the remains of his money disappearing fast, their father had been really lucky to meet Goldie's mother. She was a war widow with a girl prettier than Jean Harlow, Fred's favourite film star, with long blonde hair that was the most beautiful colour he'd ever seen. The woman's husband had been newly killed in action in France. She seemed to bring luck with her, for simultaneously the wedding and a job in Cornwall happened. The fly in the ointment was that the live-in estate job didn't include three kids, even if they were grown-ups.

Not that Fred minded being the man of the house. Hadn't he fallen on his feet becoming the manager of the Blue Club? Sure, it was a dump, but he was going to make it into something to be proud of, even if he had to buy it first.

Alf Swinnerton needed money. He'd got into trouble with the big boys in London and owed them plenty. Fred already had schemes running that would enable him to buy the Blue from Alf.

He was also going to get even with Goldie. His mates

had laughed when they realized the girl had run away. He'd promised them a bit of tail, sweet young tail.

Hadn't he said, 'After me, you can be first'?

But the bitch had bolted.

He'd brought them here and let them have their pick of the girls. Only the girls weren't as fresh as they'd once been and it was a let-down for the lads. His reputation suffered because of Goldie. Oh, he'd get even with the bitch, when he found her. They were all the same, bitches: give them an inch and they took a yard, just like Rene here.

'I reckon you been pocketing the money.'

She stared at him, scared he was going to hit her again.

'I wouldn't do that. You're good to me, make sure I don't come to harm on the streets.'

'Sure I do, Rene, but you ain't on the streets tonight, you're in my club, and by the end of the night I want double this amount or I'll be cutting off me nose to spite me face, because I'll mark you an' you won't be able to work.' He pushed his face close to hers. 'Got it?'

'But . . . But . . .'

'But nothing, bitch. I don't care how you do it, I just want the money.'

Rene's eyes slid to the floor. Her red lipstick had soaked into the creases around her mouth. She nodded.

'Get out there and watch Doll. She's going to do another

turn on the stage. She wanted a dress to fit her nicely to do the Lindy hop. She got it off one of the other girls. I got to wait in here for a phone call an' I can't check on her. I ain't seen the frock on her; if she's showing any bits of flesh I'll hold you responsible for that an' all . . .'

Rene looked at him, gulped, and the words came out in a rush. 'If you don't mind me sayin', she shouldn't be in this place—'

'She lives to fuckin' dance. I got a stage,' he shrugged his shoulders, 'so she can dance on it. You just look after her. I don't want no toerags talking to her, and keep the other tarts away.'

Rene nodded. Then she looked down at her hip, where the blood had dried. She rubbed at it. It caked and disappeared as she smoothed the flimsy material between her fingers. A bruise had bloomed.

He stared at her. Rene was a decent sort, really.

'What are you waiting for? You ain't earning money in here, are you?' She turned towards the door as he spoke again: 'Sammy's partnering her tonight. Tell him to watch where he puts his hands. I don't want his dirty mitts touching my little sister.'

With Gladys tucked up in bed, Goldie turned down the sound on the wireless. 'Paper Doll' was playing softly as she washed up the breakfast things, then looked at the old gas stove. She gave it a quick wipe. It could do with a really good scrub to get all the grease off. Gladys, Goldie realized, didn't bother too much with scrubbing things down. As long as everything looked clean, that seemed good enough for her.

She was glad her benefactor had liked her breakfast. Goldie enjoyed cooking and making things out of next to nothing. Which was just as well, since food was hard to get hold of, unless it was bought under the counter – but then it cost the earth. She still had a few pennies left, hardly any money really, but would go out later and see what she could pick up for dinner.

But on the draining board wrapped in paper was a lovely bit of cod. Gladys had bought it for Mogs, she'd said. The wet fish shop hadn't been open when Gladys came home from work but apparently she'd banged on the shop door until the fishmonger opened up just for her. Goldie was learning that Gladys had a way of getting what she wanted, because everyone liked her.

There was much too much fish there for the cat to eat. By the time the cod was finished up, it would have gone bad. Goldie would cook some of it for her and Gladys. She discovered some potatoes; the eyes were sprouting but they'd be all right if she cut them out. Then she rummaged around on the shelves and found three onions and some fresh peas wrapped in newspaper, which looked as if they'd come from someone's garden. That was enough for a fish pie if she could use some more of that egg powder and find a bit of parsley in the jungle-like garden. She washed the fish, put a net covering over it, and it went in the cupboard out of the way of Mogs, except for a nice tail piece that she boiled for him. Not that she'd seen him since last night, when he'd slunk upstairs.

Mogs seemed to have taken a fancy to Gladys. Her gran had said Mogs was a one-woman cat. She was right about that, she thought, looking at the long scratches on her arms and hands from where she'd clutched the animal close to her while sitting in the road amongst the rubble. A tear formed as she thought about her gran.

She'd go up to the flattened house and see if there was anything she could salvage. Gran had loved her. She'd loved the old lady as well. It had been so sad when Gran had said to Goldie's mother, 'You've got a heart of stone, my daughter; your husband is hardly cold in his grave and you're in bed with another man. I don't agree with it, and what's more you can stay away from this house until you come to your senses.' Goldie knew her gran wouldn't change her mind.

But her mum had married anyway. Goldie wasn't surprised her mum had left the area. She was so besotted with her new husband that she had no time for anyone else, not even her own daughter.

Gran's house in Alma Street was the one place where Goldie could go and be safe. Her gran might have been strict and had some funny ideas, but she had loved Goldie.

Gladys was a bit like her gran. Not strict, exactly. But she liked things done her way and she was a lovely lady. She'd got her an interview for a job, hadn't she?

Goldie had got on well with the girls in the laundry. She also knew what it was like working in a factory as she'd done a short spell in the Portsmouth corset works. Surely it wouldn't be much different working in the munitions yard? She'd write another letter to Jamie.

She wouldn't tell him about Fred, though. She couldn't lie to him. It wasn't right to lie to the man you loved. As Jamie never asked about Fred or Doll, there was no need to write and give him cause to worry about her safety. It might be better to allow him to think changing her job to the munitions yard meant it was easier for her to live in Gosport.

She wondered if she'd be able to sleep tonight. Last night she had kept waking up, frightened. What Fred had intended to do to her was on her mind. He was going to let those awful men have their way with her as well. She looked at the bruises on her wrists. There was something wrong with Fred. He wasn't right in the head, she was sure of that.

It was wrong the way he wouldn't let Doll out of his sight. Theirs wasn't a healthy relationship, not like other brothers and sisters. She really was like a doll to him. Goldie shivered. She thought about Fred and Doll's father. He acted as though his children were an encumbrance. He didn't seem to mind a bit that Fred took charge of Doll. Goldie often wondered what had made her mother fall in love with him. From the first moment they met, her mother and Doll and Fred's father were inseparable.

She knew it would be a long time before she'd stop being scared that Fred would find her. But she also had to think of a way to get Doll out from Fred's clutches.

# Chapter Four

'This is Betty and Myra.' Gladys introduced the two women sitting at the wooden bench. 'They know what they're doing, so if you need help, just ask.' In front of them were pieces of silk, scales, boxes and other items that Goldie had never seen before in her life.

Nervously, she smiled at the two women. Betty was about her age and Myra was a bit older, quite a big lady whose bottom overflowed on the seating.

'She'll be all right here, Glad,' said Myra. 'Sit down, love.' Goldie squeezed in beside them. 'You going down the Connaught tonight, Gladys?' Myra poked her fingers up beneath her turban and scratched her head.

'If Goldie ain't blown us all up,' Gladys laughed. 'If you arrive at the hall before us, save us a seat at your table.'

That morning they'd discussed going to the dance hall.

Gladys had forced Goldie to take a pound note, because she knew she had no money left.

They'd gone together to Gosport market and managed to pick up a few bits and pieces for Goldie to wear, but it was expensive starting from scratch when she urgently needed things like shoes, a hairbrush, toothbrush, Gibbs dentifrice and other personal objects, before even thinking about clothes.

'You'll have to pay your way with drinks and you might need some stockings or something, if you can get them.'

Goldie had laughed. 'Wouldn't it be nice to be able to buy proper nylons instead of having to draw a line up the back of our legs?'

Gladys agreed with her, then said, 'Several ships have come in recently and the sailors like to spend their money on us girls ashore. We might even get some nylons for free!'

Goldie was looking forward to going dancing.

Gladys had taken her to the Fox, a pub in Gosport town where she'd been made to feel very welcome by the friendly manager, Sam. In the few days of being with Gladys, Goldie had felt happier than she'd been for a long time.

There were a few friends from the laundry that she missed, but she knew she had to let them go. If she kept in contact, Fred could easily discover her whereabouts. She hated looking over her shoulder all the time, fearful he was around every corner.

Now she looked up at Gladys and smiled at her. She really didn't know what she would have done if she hadn't been taken in by this small, bossy, curvy woman with bleached-blonde hair. She wondered how old Gladys was. She could be any age between thirty and forty-five. She had a few wrinkles, but Goldie thought they added to her attractiveness. Like she'd had problems in her life and conquered the lot of them. When she was all dolled up with her eyelashes on, she looked pretty good, and the blokes thought so too. It was towards Gladys that the men gravitated and she was always bought the first drink.

'I thought we could go down that new club after the Connaught,' said Betty.

'That's 'cos you fancy the owner,' Myra said, still scratching her head. Goldie caught Gladys's eye again. The curly-haired bloke kept coming up in conversation at home.

Gladys said, 'Shut up about Will—'

Before she could finish Myra said, 'Not you an' all! I'll admit he's an eyeful. He's got half the women in Gosport after him!'

'Not me,' Gladys interrupted. 'I got a man. He lives next door and his name's Siddy.'

'He's too old for you. He's got one foot in the grave and the other on a banana skin,' said Myra.

'My Siddy is good to me,' said Gladys. 'I can depend on

him. Often I'll come home to find a nice chop on the table that he's managed to wangle out of the butcher, or a bit of tea or sugar. Now shut up, the lot of you, I got to tell this girl what to do. We do come to Priddy's to work, you know. There's a war to win.' Both Myra and Betty lowered their eyes and went quiet.

Goldie had met Siddy and liked him. He was Gladys's landlord but lived at number twelve, next door. He often took her out for a drink or a drive in the country in his two-door Ford CX, when he had petrol. He was tall and thin, like a hairpin, thought Goldie, but he really cared about Gladys. He might have been a looker when he was younger but now he had a comb-over, was always in his slippers and braces and wore a cardigan with pockets. But Gladys said he never raised his voice to her.

'Are you paying attention?'

Goldie realized Gladys was talking to her.

'Yes,' she said, and tried to take in what Gladys was saying.

'This cordite has to be made into charges.' Gladys held up a piece of silk shaped like a long bean. 'You'll need these filled with cordite. It's all got to be weighed carefully.' She put a small core on the scales along with the bags. 'Each bag is a different weight. You make them into a bundle, see?' She worked methodically, carefully. 'Keep your wits about you. You don't have to stop nattering but you might find it easier

43

if you get used to doing it before joining in with the chit-chat. Then the bundle goes into that box with its detonator.' She looked at Goldie. Goldie looked first at Myra and then at Betty, both of whose fingers seemed to fly as the filled bundles went into the boxes.

Goldie began her first shift at Priddy's.

'Do I look all right?' Goldie asked Myra. 'I've had to borrow this dress from Gladys. I managed to get hold of some clothes down the market, but not anything suitable for tonight.'

'She got bombed out, didn't you, love?' Gladys swiftly chipped in.

Quickly Goldie realized she'd nearly let the cat out of the bag about the reason for not having any clothes. Gladys had jumped in with the lie. Gladys knew that if Fred came asking after her he wouldn't associate the girl who was bombed out with Goldie. Gratefully she looked at Gladys, who winked back at her. She was also glad that her bruises were fading fast. They were just shadows now. She'd dreaded anyone asking about them.

Goldie took a sip of watered-down orange juice and listened as Myra told her she looked just fine in a box-pleated grey dress with a sweetheart neckline. She'd drawn a line up the back of her legs with an eyebrow pencil. Gladys was wearing her last pair of silk stockings, which had been given to her by an American sailor.

'I wish I had hair like yours,' said Betty, who had put her own dark locks up in a victory roll.

'Trouble is it's too long to do anything with, except tie it back or let it hang loose.' She thought of the itchy turban she wore at work, but before she had time to say anything else a young sailor asked her to dance. She looked at his bell-bottomed trousers with the neat creases and his tight navy-blue top with the wide collar and got up, setting her drink back on the table.

'Did your boat dock today?' Goldie had watched the ships entering the dockyard waters as she'd eaten her sandwiches at lunchtime. The strip of water between Gosport and Portsmouth was always busy with all sorts of craft. She'd sat on the wall, glad to be out of the stink that the picric acid made, while drinking tea from her flask. It had been nice in the sunshine with all the other girls chattering.

'How did you know that?' His blue eyes were wide with curiosity.

She tapped the side of her nose. He might be an English sailor fighting for his country, but loose lips sank ships.

'Be like Dad and keep Mum,' she laughed. It was a slow dance and he was holding her close. Not so close that it was uncomfortable. Some of the blokes crushed the girls' bodies, as though accepting an offer to dance meant they could put their hands all over them. This lad seemed shy.

'I haven't been in the navy long,' he said.

Goldie thought he didn't look old enough to be in the services at all. 'Haven't you?'

He shook his head. 'My mum didn't want me to go on the ships. My brother went down on the *Royal Oak*.'

'I can understand that,' she said. The tragedy had been the worst possible start to the war. In 1939 the *Royal Oak* had been sunk by a German U-boat in Scapa Flow off the Orkney Islands. 'How old was he?'

The band was playing another slow dance. Mr Prout the conductor, wearing his usual white gloves, was waving his baton and the music was wafting over them. Lots of the girls had cuddled up close to their partners and the lighting had been turned down low. She could smell the Brylcreem on her partner's hair.

'He was eighteen.'

'You don't look eighteen,' said Goldie. 'How old are you?'

He pulled away from her and stared into her eyes. His voice was fierce. 'I've got to get them damn Germans back for what they did. My mum ain't never going to get over it. To drown like that must be terrible.'

He hadn't answered her. Goldie knew then that he'd

probably lied about his age to get in the navy. She pressed him: 'How old are you?'

'Sixteen.'

'Oh.' Goldie felt so sorry for him, thinking he had to avenge his brother's death. He was so young.

'Oh, don't worry,' he said. 'I'm on the *Glen Avon*, it's an auxiliary anti-aircraft vessel. The blokes on it are brilliant, I'll be fine. Mum wanted me to go on to university but I can always do evening classes when the war's over.'

'Yes, I suppose you can. Have you got a girlfriend?'

He nodded. 'She lives just up the road from my mum.'

The music stopped and the dancers began to wander back to their seats. The young sailor took Goldie back to her table.

'Thanks for the dance,' he said.

'You're very welcome,' Goldie answered, and suddenly, for no reason, leaned forward and kissed him on the cheek. 'Good luck,' she called as he walked away with a grin on his face.

'What did you do that for?' asked Betty. She blew a stream of smoke to join all the other cigarette smoke in the hall.

'I've got a feeling he's going to need all the luck he can get,' said Goldie.

Gladys looked at her. 'So will you, later. The manager's told me I've got to put you in the gunpowder room before the month is out; least, that's what we call it. You'll come out of there a glorious shade of yellow.'

'Will I be a glorious gunpowder girl?'

The women laughed at her, but it was Gladys who said, 'No, you'll be a bloody Canary Girl, like the rest of us!'

Goldie loved dancing with the servicemen. She and Jamie had talked about the way they would behave while they were separated by the war. She'd told him she didn't expect him to be a monk and to enjoy himself when he could. He'd said he wanted her to have a few laughs with the girls and go dancing because he knew how much she loved it. They both promised that they would never hurt each other by getting involved with anyone. They trusted each other completely.

'Honey, will you dance with me?'

Goldie watched as Gladys gave the American a big smile and walked onto the packed dance floor.

'Cor, he's a bit of all right,' said Betty.

'Did you see them gorgeous brown eyes?' Myra pretended to swoon.

Goldie watched as first he whispered something to Gladys, then they began dancing to the tune the band was playing, 'It Don't Mean A Thing if You Ain't Got That Swing'.

'I never knew she could dance like that.' Goldie was amazed as Gladys was flung about to the fast music. She was quick and light on her feet and anyone could see she loved the intricate steps. Gladys was kicking up her heels, having a whale of a time.

'Our Gladys sure can dance,' said Myra. It wasn't long before the crowd had made a big space on the floor and the American and Gladys were being cheered on, dancing and laughing, while the crowd clapped and whistled. The American picked her up, his hands around her waist, and swung her first one way and then the other, setting Gladys down just long enough for her to jump back into his arms so he could allow her to lean backwards while he held her securely. 'I bet she's glad that dress of hers has a flared skirt,' continued Myra. 'She couldn't dance like that in a straight one.' Then, 'Look at them stocking tops, the saucy minx!'

When the music ended the American took Gladys's arm and led her towards the side door.

The next dance was the Dashing White Sergeant, and almost everyone got up on the floor because it was a dance that they could all join in.

Afterwards Goldie fell down on her chair, laughing. She took big swallows of her orange after she'd got her breath back, then decided to get some more drinks in. She made her way over towards the table in the corner that served as a bar and, while she waited to be served, idly gazed out of the window.

A couple were just visible in a darkened corner in an

embrace that almost made Goldie blush. As the woman moved her head Goldie saw it was Gladys. It looked like the American was almost eating her alive!

'Would you like a tray? I said, would you like a tray?'

Goldie realized the elderly lady behind the bar was talking to her.

'Yes, yes please,' she stuttered and began lifting the drinks she'd ordered onto the round metal tray.

Her knees shaking, she managed to take the glasses back to the table without mishap.

'Thanks,' said Myra. 'Did you get one for Gladys?'

Goldie nodded. 'She's outside,' she said. She put her hand to her mouth. Maybe she shouldn't have said that?

Myra laughed. 'She'll be doing her bit for the war effort,' she said. She took a small bottle of brandy out of her handbag and dripped alcohol into each of the glasses. 'This'll liven up our drinks a bit. Didn't you know our Gladys likes to send the boys away with something good to remember?'

# Chapter Five

As Goldie climbed the steps leading up to the Rainbow Club she had to hold on tightly to Gladys. Gladys stumbled and the three packs of nylons, a present from the American, fell from her pocket. Goldie picked them up and made her put them in her handbag. The little drops of brandy dripped into their glasses of orange at the Connaught had made them all quite tipsy.

The club opposite the ferry was well lit up and packed with people. The double doors were wide open, inviting customers inside. Goldie gasped at the opulence before her.

A red deep-pile carpet led to a polished wooden bar with an array of bottles placed against a mirrored wall at the rear. Chandeliers hung with tiny bulbs glittered above their heads. Through an open door, Goldie could see a roulette wheel and card tables in a room that was obviously used for gaming. There was a small stage with microphones, and in front of it were little wrought-iron tables and chairs all painted gold, upon which men sat watching a girl dancing with such sinewy movements that it made Goldie blush to watch her. The girl was about eighteen with long dark hair and a body to die for. She was clothed in so little that Goldie's blush deepened even further.

Through the windows, the strip of water between Portsmouth and Gosport was a panorama of lights glowing from the boats bobbing in the darkness of the waves.

The Rainbow was obviously a popular place and Goldie hastily scanned faces in case one belonged to Fred. Would she never get over her fear of the man? She tried not to think about him.

'How on earth can the owner furnish this place like this when the war has stolen away everything beautiful the English people have for the fight against Hitler?' Goldie couldn't help herself; the words just flew from her mouth. Maybe the drink helped them.

'Because I'm a businessman, an entrepreneur and can give the country back a bit of glamour to help them forget there's a war on.'

Goldie whirled around and came face to face with a broad-shouldered, curly-haired, good-looking man who towered above her. He was probably well into his forties, with the bearing of a military man. The sharp suit he was wearing gave him a businesslike air.

'Good evening, ladies,' he went on. 'My name is William Hill, Will to my friends. Now you have the advantage over me – you know I'm the owner, but I don't know who you are.' He looked at each of them in turn, allowing his gaze to linger. When it rested on Gladys, a smile lit up his face, showing white, even teeth.

'Jesus Christ!' said Myra. 'Clark Gable with curls!' Goldie saw she was actually blushing.

'That's Myra,' said Goldie, as everyone else seemed to have lost their tongues. 'Betty is the dark-haired one. My name's Goldie and this is Gladys. I believe you already know her.'

She realized she needn't have pointed out Gladys because the man couldn't take his eyes off her.

But just then a fellow in a trilby hat and a light-coloured raincoat called from a doorway at the rear of the bar, 'Boss, you need to hear this.'

Will glanced towards the man and a look of annoyance passed over his face. He said, 'I hope you enjoy the evening, ladies, afraid I'm needed. First drink is on the house.' He raised a hand, caught the eye of a pretty girl serving behind the bar and motioned to Goldie, Gladys, Betty and Myra.

He walked swiftly towards the polished bar, lifted the hatch, then disappeared through the doorway.

'What d'you think of him, then?' Betty was looking at Goldie.

'What does it matter what anyone thinks when he couldn't unglue his eyes from Madam here?' Goldie nodded towards Gladys.

'I don't know how she does it, old bat that she is!'

Gladys poked Myra in the ribs. 'Not so much of the "old bat", if you don't mind. Let's get our drinks.'

Behind the bar were several young women dressed in French maid costumes who took every chance to bend down to the bottom shelves to pick up bottles, showing frilly knickers and suspender belts holding up black stockings.

'You'd think they'd put more stuff on the top shelves, instead of showing their bums like that,' said Myra.

'Well, if you was dressed like that and had to bend down, your big bum would blot out all the shelves.' Gladys was leaning with her elbows on the bar, waiting for one of the girls to serve her.

'I don't know how you gets all your blokes, it ain't as if you're a looker.'

'Thank you, Myra,' said Gladys, now tapping her red-painted nails on the polished wood.

The pretty barmaid began to take the order and Goldie took a moment to look round. It didn't seem right to have such a glamorous place as this in Gosport. It was more suited to London, she thought.

Gladys was talking. 'It ain't nothing to do with looks what gets the men. Often really beautiful girls don't have nothing to say to a feller. Sometimes they're so preoccupied with themselves that they got no time to think about what a feller needs.'

'We all know what fellers need!' broke in Betty with a belly laugh. Her hair had come undone. She blew at the strands covering her face. Goldie repinned it and Betty looked grateful. She was very tipsy.

'No,' said Gladys. 'Blokes ain't much different to us; cut them and they bleed. Thank you, love,' she said to the girl. 'Your boss said these were on the house.' The girl nodded, swinging her dark hair away from her face as she put the drinks on a tray.

Gladys carried on, 'Blokes like to be listened to, looked after and made to feel special. They can sense that in a woman as soon as they meet her. Looks ain't got nothing to do with it.' She picked up the tray and carried it over to an alcove where a recently vacated table and chairs gave them a good view of the dance floor.

As the women made themselves comfortable, Gladys passed the drinks around. 'This is good gin,' she said. 'Wonder where he gets his supplies?' She took another sip.

Goldie had spotted a blonde middle-aged woman with two boys, one each side of her, sitting in an alcove. She was dressed in a flowery skirt and white blouse with frills down the centre. One of the dark-haired boys was asleep, cuddled up against the woman, and the other was hungrily dipping into a bag of crisps.

'Look, there's them twins. You reckon they're his kids?' Goldie asked.

'No,' Gladys said. 'I found out they're his mate's boys. His mate Charlie is on the run from the army: a deserter, a bit of a skiver by all accounts. Will ain't got no kids and he likes having them about. Reg and Ronnie, they are. Little buggers, I've heard.'

'Is he involved with the woman?' At that moment the woman recognized Gladys and put up a hand in welcome, she pointed to the sleeping boy at her side, grinned and shrugged. Gladys waved back.

She laughed, 'Violet? No. I did hear he had a fling with the sister, Rose, but that was a while ago, just after his wife died. It's over and done with now.'

'You know a lot about him.'

Gladys blushed at her words, then shrugged. Goldie carried on.

'And is he a gangster like they say he is?' She'd never met

a gangster before. She'd seen them in films, but Will was better-looking than Humphrey Bogart.

'Don't know,' Gladys said. Myra had lit another cigarette and was being very generous with its smoke. Gladys waved it away. 'Gangsters don't wear notices around their necks, you know. But I believe he did a stint in the air force; that's where he got that gammy leg.'

'I never noticed no limp,' said Goldie.

'Well, look closer next time,' said Gladys, taking another sip of her drink. 'Them kids should be in bed,' she said, looking at the boys again. 'I'm going to get another drink and then I'm going home.'

Goldie watched as she got up, picked up the tray, pushed her way through the noisy crowd at the bar then came back with drinks for them all. Myra and Betty were still nattering. Goldie reached for her gin and orange, smiling her thanks at Gladys.

The place was full of cigarette smoke, which was getting in her throat and stinging her eyes. Suddenly Goldie wished the place was quieter. Another girl was dancing on the stage and looking very fed up, like she'd rather be at home with a cup of cocoa.

Goldie realized that after the day at work and the dancing, she was tired. She was looking forward to doing something different at Priddy's the next day. She hoped it wasn't as tedious as the work she'd done today. She didn't feel tipsy any more, just very, very tired.

She smiled to herself. A letter had come from Jamie while she'd been at work. When she received three or even more in one post she had to put them in the order of his writing them. She hated the irregularity of the post. She'd put the letter under her pillow, promising herself she'd read it when she got home to bed. A feeling of warmth spread through her. Oh, how she wished Jamie was home again.

'What d'you mean, this is all there is?' Will stared at the boxes, opened and broken, piled haphazardly in the big wooden lock-up shed at the back of the club. A lorry, the engine still warm, emptied of its contents and stinking of petrol, was nearby.

'We unloaded the boat and this is all there was.' The skinny bloke, Baz Bowen, looked shifty and scratched his chin.

'What d'you mean, you unloaded?' Will had raised his voice now.

'From the ship,' broke in another man, his grey beard and full head of hair making him look like a discoloured Father Christmas. 'Somebody must have taken the rest of the gear before we got there.'

'Somebody must have taken the rest of the gear,' mimicked Will.

'Careful, boss, these are good blokes.' An elderly man put a hand on Will's arm. 'If Baz says the stuff wasn't there, somebody must have taken it.'

Will gave a long-drawn-out sigh. Obviously someone must have tipped off some toerag that the *Star of Ceylon* was docking with his goods in the hold, and had beaten his blokes to the stuff, unloading supplies of sugar, tea, jams, preserves, bacon, tinned fruits: indeed, most of the stuff he'd brought in from abroad to sell on the black market. He sighed again.

Who would dare to steal from him? Down here on the south coast hardly anyone knew of him, yet. In London it was a different matter. Nobody crossed William Hill, or Billy Hill as he was known in the Smoke. This was the second time in a month that his goods had been stolen.

So, too, had his house been broken into. Someone had got into the safe in his bedroom in the Alverstoke house and stolen a few bits of jewellery that hadn't yet been passed on to a fence. The stuff was part of a haul from the Hatton Garden raid he'd planned and undertaken in the spring. If the thief had got in a few days earlier he'd have cleared a huge fortune.

As it was, a couple of rings, some pearls and a pair of gold cufflinks were all the thief had managed. One of the rings was worth a lot of money, so he wasn't pleased at its disappearance. Like most men of means, Will never kept money indoors. He was glad he'd put the house on the market and now slept at the apartment at his club. Someone was targeting him and he didn't like it. It had to be someone in the know, had to be.

The war had been good for him; his black-market dealings and his ability to provide deserters with papers and passports had made him a lot of money. Hadn't he provided that stupid fool Charlie Kray with forged papers? And still the dunce hid in the loft at his London home. Violet and the boys should leave him. He shook his head; Violet was too soft-hearted for that.

They'd been good mates, once, him and Charlie, but over the years the man had taken to booze and become unreliable. He wondered if Charlie had anything to do with his missing goods? No, the bloke was off his rocker these days. That's why Will had taken Reggie and Ronnie under his wing. Those boys would go far in the underworld one day, he'd make sure of that.

Someone in his employ had a big mouth and light fingers. He thought he could trust his boys, but obviously he'd made a mistake. That needed sorting out, as did the thief of his goods.

'Keep your mouths shut about this,' Will said. Then he left the men standing in the shed and climbed the metal stairs at the back of the club to his office at the top of the building.

So far this club was doing well. There'd been a lot of big spenders at the gaming tables; big losers would be a better description. The club was in a prime position to catch the sailors eager to spend money as soon as they docked. They spent it on the girls and the tables, then came back the following night to try to win their money back. Even he'd been surprised at the many movers and shakers in the community who liked a flutter. All these 'sprats to catch mackerels' were paying off. One free drink meant the customer would buy more.

The girls drew in the punters like flies to the proverbial. Rooms at the back provided an area where the girls would do more than dance for the clients. Not everyone knew about the prostitution, only the privileged few, and they kept their mouths shut. After all, owning a brothel was against the law, and his mate Mac could only close his eyes to so much of what Will got up to. But it was nothing to him to provide a few parties so the locals could come and have a good time for free. He knew they'd come back and spend money. That's how come he was a businessman – and a damned good one. He frowned. That's why he had to catch the menace who was stealing from him.

He patted his inside pocket. His flick knife felt slim and hard against his chest. He'd been fourteen when he'd first killed another youth, in a fight over a girl. He hadn't been the first to draw a knife, so it was kill or be killed, and he'd got away with it. But Will didn't like violence. There were better ways to make sure he stayed at the top of the tree.

He went over to his desk, took out a bottle of whisky and poured himself a generous measure. Tonight he needed a pick-me-up. Someone was making a fool of him. He shook his head. He couldn't have that, could he?

# Chapter Six

Summer turned quickly to autumn, but Goldie still looked over her shoulder when walking around Gosport, in case Fred was about. She was ashamed she'd done nothing about getting Doll away from her creep of a brother.

She still grieved for her grandmother. Gladys had helped her pay for the funeral at Ann's Hill Cemetery.

When Goldie wasn't at work, Gladys made sure they spent as much time as possible enjoying themselves down at the Fox, at the pictures or at dances, to help her over her grief.

She met Saul Simpson when she started her new job. Gladys passed her over to the manager of the Yellow Room who would show Goldie what her new job at Priddy's entailed.

'Everyone calls me Solly,' said the tall, slim, blond-haired man with the devastatingly blue eyes. 'Whatever problems you have, you speak to me.'

Goldie took to him immediately. She asked him why he hadn't been called up and he made her laugh when he cupped a hand to his ear and said, 'What?'

She repeated, 'Why aren't you in the services?' Once more he pressed a hand to his ear and asked her, 'What?' She realized he had been rejected due to hearing difficulties and was teasing her. He was excellent at reading lips and Gladys had told her that all the girls in the Yellow Room fancied him. She followed him down a corridor, then he opened a stout wooden door and they went inside. Goldie opened her mouth in amazement, and then quickly closed it as he explained.

'Lyddite is a bright-yellow powder. It arrives at Priddy's in wooden tubs. This room, as you can see, is completely yellow.' He pointed to the ceiling, to the windows, to the walls. 'It travels everywhere, so the workers get covered as well. Protect your mouth and nose with a scarf, because it'll make you sneeze and you'll get a bitter taste at the back of your throat.' He paused and stared at her. Goldie knew she was looking horrified. 'The powder has to be boiled after it's been sifted like flour, to get the lumps out.' He smiled at her. 'Then, when it's melted and can be poured, it goes into these shell cases.' He showed her the cases on a conveyor belt.

Goldie smiled at the four women sitting at the bench she'd been assigned to. Each woman grinned back at her.

Numerous other benches had women pouring the substance into shells.

The wireless was playing jazz music and the concentration on the women's faces as they poured the liquid was evident. The hands and faces of the workers varied from a dark tan to bright yellow.

Solly picked up an object and showed it to her. 'This beeswax mould has to be inserted before the liquid has time to harden.' He turned the mould in his hand so she could look at it properly. 'An explosive is put in, then you screw on a cap.' He looked deep into her eyes, which she knew showed how absolutely terrified she was of working with these materials. 'Don't screw the cap into the detonator, otherwise you'll be blown to Kingdom Come!'

Goldie's fear, as she watched the other women skilfully using the materials to help destroy Hitler, suddenly deserted her.

'Other than that, this job is as safe as houses?'

Solly grinned. 'I think you and me are going to get on fine.'

'I really am going to be a Canary Girl now, aren't I?' she laughed.

Rene climbed the stairs at the back of the Blue. Through the open door she could see Fred in his office, lounging on a chair with his feet up on the table. He was examining a ring and had a small pile of other jewellery in front of him. She guessed immediately why she'd been summoned. He wanted her to work the tweedle, a con trick.

She wondered why she didn't get on a bus and stay on it until it arrived in Stratford-upon-Avon, then she could go back to her mum's house, put her arms around her and beg to be allowed to stay.

She caught sight of herself in the cracked mirror on the wall outside Fred's office. I look like an old bag, she thought. Inwardly she smiled. Wasn't that exactly what she was now? She sighed. She'd left home on the train, an excited girl of nineteen, got to Portsmouth and after a week her money was gone. She had to stand on the Guildhall steps and wait for a punter to ask, 'How much?'

Then she'd gone with him into Victoria Park, done the business and when he'd buttoned his flies and gone, she went back to the steps. From a virgin to a prossie, just like that.

She was making good money in them days. She got herself a flat, decked it out prettily, and when the war started, she began making more money from the lads on shore leave.

Then came the night she got done over by a weasel of a bloke with a knife. He didn't mark her where anyone could see, but it scared the hell out of her. With her nerve gone, she stayed in her flat until a knock on the door announced Fred.

'I'm not a punter,' he'd said. 'I heard you'd been attacked while you was minding your own business and I've got a proposition for you.'

Silly cow that she was, she'd invited him in. He'd brought her flowers. No one had ever given her flowers before.

'You're a beautiful girl, Rene. But you need someone to look after you.'

She'd fallen for him by the time he'd drunk two cups of tea. He'd told her he had a sister to look after, was in the process of buying a club in Southsea and that if she joined him, he'd look after her. No one would ever harm her again, he said.

No one else did, he made sure of that. Of course, she found out later that the man who had attacked her was one of Fred's henchmen.

Fred gave her the back of his hand often, and she endured it because she loved him.

He could be lovely when he wanted, bringing her gifts of jewellery. Later, she discovered the jewellery was from hauls his goons had stolen.

She paid the price for the presents and for his protection. It wasn't long before he'd had all the money she'd saved, and by sending one of his men along to keep an eye on the punters when she worked the streets, Fred took most of her earnings too.

His bitch of a sister wore pretty things that Rene lay on her back to pay for. But Rene was cross with herself for thinking of Doll as a bitch. The girl could have been a nice kid, if it wasn't for her brother. If Fred could have put Doll in a matchbox and kept her in his pocket, he would have done.

Rene wasn't alone in prostituting herself for him. There were other girls.

'You're my main girl, Rene. You know you are. You know I love you.'

In a way, she really thought he did. He talked to her. He taught her things. Like the tweedle.

'Nice diamond, this one, Rene.'

'Where'd it come from?' He passed her the ring and it glittered in the light from the window like shooting stars on a black night.

'You don't need to know that.'

'It's from that Hatton Garden robbery.' She put the ring on and splayed her fingers, admiring it. There'd been pictures in the papers of the stolen goods and she remembered the ring.

He stared at her. 'Shut your mouth, you know nothing about that.' He ran his fingers through his Brylcreemed hair.

Only she did. She knew he hadn't taken part in the robbery: a London gangster was the mastermind behind that, but she'd overheard Fred talking to one of his men. Some of the proceeds had come into Fred's possession as a debt repayment from a local tea leaf, so Fred said. Fred didn't want the jewellery; he wanted the cash.

'Where d'you want me to take it?' She slid the ring from her finger and looked at it again.

'Jeweller's in Gosport, near the Ferry.'

'Won't he realize it's on the "stolen" list?' Rene knew jewellers and pawnbrokers were issued with details of stolen goods by the police in an effort to nab thieves.

'He will, but he's greedy. I want five hundred but I'll take four-fifty. It's worth a thousand.'

She nodded. How wonderful to be given a ring that cost so much money. The bloke must have to really care for the woman to spend that much on her. She sighed, knowing it would never happen to her. Her sweetener would come next.

'Get this done and you and me'll go shopping in the town,' he said, tipping her chin towards him and kissing her. Rene felt the tingle run through her body and settle at her spine. 'We'll buy some pretties for Doll while we're about it. I heard Dolcis has had some new shoes come in.'

Yes, there it was, a sweetener for her, but more presents for Doll as well. Already the little cow had practically taken over the small room at the back of the stage, the one that was supposed to be Rene's dressing room. Now she had to share it. The other girls were herded like cattle into a cell-like room at the side of the stage. Of course, Doll wasn't allowed to speak to them, nor they to her, and it was Rene who had to make sure that rule was upheld. Doll was too good for the likes of the other dancers. Not that they wanted to speak to the stuck-up little bitch anyway! It was Fred's fault no one liked her.

After he'd pulled away from Rene, she reluctantly gave him back the ring, which he put into a small silk bag. From his pocket, he took another similar bag.

'Is it a good copy?'

'See for yourself,' he said, handing her the second ring.

Rene took it out and stared at it. 'It's a good copy,' she admitted. It, too, glittered in the shaft of sunlight. She put it on her finger. Even though this ring was pasted glass, it still looked the business.

He took a pound note out of his wallet and handed it to her. 'Go over to Harry's, he's got some nail stuff and a few lipsticks. Tell him I sent you and he'll give you the pick of what he's got.' Harry was the one-legged ex-soldier who stood opposite the Blue with his tray of women's fripperies, used nail varnishes, lipsticks, cheap perfumes, stockings that sometimes had ladders in them. No one ever asked how he came by his goods for sale.

'Don't forget to wear one of your wigs this afternoon,' Fred said. During her stage act Rene rang the changes by swapping wigs.

'Yeah, I will,' she said. 'The ring'll look better with me nails done nicely too.'

He held out his hand for the second ring. She pocketed the pound note and promised to be ready at one o'clock.

They were on the ferry to Gosport at half past one and walking through the busy market to Hutchings' the Jewellers shortly afterwards. The sky was grey and rain looked sure to fall before they returned to Portsmouth.

'Have you ever found out where your stepsister went?'

Fred had told her Goldie had run off. Rene had heard rumours of the real reason the girl had left the area in a hurry, but preferred to think Fred hadn't been involved.

'No, but I will.' His voice was darkly ominous.

'Do you think she's gone to visit your dad and her mum?'

He glared at her. 'More fool her, if she has. They only care about themselves.'

At the Dive café opposite the bus station, Fred put his hand in his pocket and drew out the two rings. He slipped the original one on Rene's finger and she put the fake one in her pocket.

'Don't for Christ's sake get 'em mixed up,' he said. 'I'll wait here in the café.' He grabbed her arm roughly. 'And don't think you can leg it. I'll be after you like a shot.'

'Would I do a thing like that to you?' Rene's voice was soft.

'No, you wouldn't, because if you did I'd mark your face so no one would ever give you a second look.'

'Yet you still trust me enough to do the tweedle?' She wondered how the ruse had come by its strange name. Perhaps it had something to do with Tweedledum and Tweedledee, she thought; maybe about the two being almost identical?

'Yeah. I loves yer, don't I?' He gave her a quick kiss, slapped her bottom and Rene walked over to the jeweller's. Next to the shop was a bomb site where one of the new V2s had fallen. She'd read in the *Evening News* that eight people had been killed waiting to get their hair cut at the hairdresser's that used to be there.

Bloody Hitler, she thought. Even his own men hated him. After a plot to kill him, the perpetrators had been sentenced to death. Hadn't they been strung by their necks with piano wire and hung from meat hooks? She couldn't imagine a more painful way to die.

The smell of polish was welcome as Rene opened the door and walked up to the counter of the jeweller's shop. She knew she looked pretty good in her coat with the fox-fur collar, her black high heels and dark wig.

The man was out the back; she could see him through the

open door, sitting at a table fixing a strap to a wristwatch. A woman, possibly of a similar age to herself but wearing spectacles, was serving in the shop. As with most shops, the stock was limited.

'I understand you buy jewellery?' Rene asked as soon as the door closed on the customer.

'I'll call Mr Hutchings.' The woman walked along the back of the counter and spoke to the elderly man, who rose from the chair and came into the showroom.

'I've got a ring that belonged to my mother.' Rene pushed her hand practically beneath the man's nose. 'Unhappily I've been bombed out and need to settle in another home, so I want to sell this.' She took off the ring and handed it to him. He looked her up and down, then took a small eyeglass from his top waistcoat pocket. Rene, having played this game before, knew the magnifying glass was a jewellers' loupe and enabled him to spot imperfections in jewels and read hallmarks clearly. He began to examine the ring.

'My mother, God bless her, died last year. It's all I've got to remember her by, but I need the money.' She took out a handkerchief from her sleeve and began to dab at her eyes.

The man spent a long time peering at the ring that glittered in his fingers.

The blatant lie was partly for the assistant's sake. Hutchings fenced goods. He would greedily and happily hand over money that was well below the ring's value. But he had to think he was duping her.

Rene looked around the shop. Alarm clocks, watches and small figurines adorned the shelves. A black velvet cushion below the glass counter had wedding rings embedded in it. Decorative jewellery not worth the shelves it sat on glittered in glass cases. Once upon a time, before the war, jewellers' shops meant something. Then, they were full of exciting and expensive trinkets. The war had changed that. Ordinary people had no money for pretty things when food and shelter were the items of necessity.

Mind you, she thought, Fred had had a bit of luck 'coming across' a ship carrying black-market supplies, which he promptly misappropriated and delivered to his store at the back of the Blue. He'd been telling her about an MTB he'd picked up for a song so that he could get out into the Solent to bring back more goodies, because he knew a man who knew another man. She asked him what an MTB was and he'd laughed at her.

'Motor torpedo boat. Double diagonal teak and thirty foot long. Few good years left in her yet,' he'd said. She hadn't really bothered overmuch about what he was doing at night out in a boat on the Solent, but she'd appreciated the bag of food he'd given her. Tinned pineapple, tinned peaches, sugar, tea and some bacon. She'd had a feast that night.

'I'll go four hundred and seventy-five pounds,' Hutchings said.

The voice of the man drew her from her reverie. She dabbed afresh at her eyes. 'Oh, I thought it was worth much more.'

'Not to me,' he said. 'I've got a shop full of expensive stuff.'

She stared at him and sniffed once more. 'Done,' she said.

Still holding the ring, he went outside to the small room where he opened a locked cupboard in the wall, putting the ring on his little finger for safekeeping. She saw him count out the money on the table and then bring it in along with the ring, which he transferred to the countertop. He counted out the money again, in front of her. The assistant looked on.

Suddenly, Rene gave a cry: 'Oh, I can't sell it, it's the only thing I've got left—'

She grabbed the ring and hurried towards the door, but just before she opened it she turned quickly back to the jeweller. 'I'm sorry, I'm being too sentimental. I really need the money.'

She stepped back to the counter, shamefaced.

'We all feel like that, my dear,' he said gently, folding the money and handing it to her as she gave him back the ring.

'Thank you,' she said, and two minutes later she was

sitting next to Fred in the Dive café. Beneath the table she passed him the money and the ring. She'd exchanged the diamond ring for the fake one in her pocket as she'd gone to open the door.

'Any problems?'

She shook her head. She didn't normally wear her wigs for long and this one was making her scalp itch. She longed to take it off and shake free her own hair.

'Let's get out of here,' he said. 'Before Hutchings spots the difference.' Then, 'Didn't I promise you a pair of shoes?'

'Hutchings won't be happy when he discovers he's paid a fortune for a paste and glass brass ring,' Rene said.

'Not your problem, my love,' Fred said. She could hear him softly singing 'You Are My Sunshine' as they walked along the High Street.

# Chapter Seven

'I tell you I saw Fred in the town, he was going into Dolcis with this tarty woman on his arm. I'm not sure, but I think it was his doxy from the club.'

Gladys sighed. 'Did he see you?'

'Don't think so.' Goldie was shaking. Gladys hated to see her so scared of the bloke. It had been Goldie's day off and she'd gone down to the market to buy fruit and veg and some fish for Mogs.

The weather had turned suddenly colder today and Gladys had lit a fire in the kitchen range using some of her precious coal. She could do with another load of logs to help eke out the nutty slack. Mogs was curled up like a furry doughnut on the rag rug in the warm. The fire was crackling and the lump of wood Gladys had topped the coal with made the room smell like a pine forest.

'I know he was looking for me.'

'Stop it! He surely didn't expect to find you in a shoe shop! I know he did a terrible thing to you, but you'll make yourself really ill if you imagine you're seeing him round every corner.'

'I must try to get that young girl away from him.'

She kept on saying that, thought Gladys, but as yet young Doll was still living with her brother. Gladys decided they had to make it a priority before anything unsavoury happened to the fifteen-year-old, if it hadn't already.

Goldie was still grumbling and shaking when the siren went. Moaning Minnie began to scream her warning of approaching enemy aircraft.

'Oh, no,' said Gladys. 'Isn't it ever going to end?' She got up from the old, comfortable armchair where she'd just that moment sat down and pushed her way past the table in the centre of the room. In the scullery she filled the kettle, switched on the gas and quickly made two flasks of strong tea using fresh tea leaves. If she was going to be blown to smithereens, she was going with a decent cuppa inside her.

After the kettle had boiled, she got down on her hands and knees and switched off the gas tap beneath the copper. Then she went towards the front door where the electricity meter was, high up on the wall. Gladys flicked the 'off' switch and the house was plunged into darkness. The firelight made it easy for her to go back into the scullery and bring in the flasks to put them in the Morrison shelter. She always felt better when the utilities were turned off during an air raid.

The Morrison shelter in the kitchen was permanently ready for use, lined with pillows and quilts. She also kept a torch in there, along with a small box containing her important papers: birth certificate, medical certificate, Post Office Savings book and family photographs.

Fear took hold of her as planes began to drone in the distance. Goldie had drawn the curtains and made sure the blackout blinds were tightly shut. Suddenly there was a 'swish' of a noise, followed moments later by a huge explosion. The small house shook. Goldie grabbed her and together they tumbled into the shelter. But immediately Gladys fell in, she was out again and snatching the cowering cat, holding it tight to her body as she scrambled back into the metal cage.

Despite the blackout curtains, vivid white flashes showed through.

'That's the searchlights,' said Goldie. Bullets were raining down and being answered by ground fire. It seemed as if the shelling was incredibly fierce and low over Gosport.

'Too near to be comfortable,' Gladys said to Goldie. It sounded as if the planes were coming over in swarms, their loads pouring down on unfortunate targets. 'Heaven knows what terrible destruction is happening,' she said.

She could smell the cordite now: smoke was seeping into the house.

Gladys pushed open the door of the shelter and scrambled out, yet again. She closed it securely behind her so that Mogs wouldn't escape, then went over to the window.

She peeked through the curtain and saw the sky, brilliant with coloured beams going in all directions. The noise was terrible and there was no mistaking the crunch of bombs.

Then came the sound she had been dreading. An ominous whining that suddenly cut out. V1s or possibly V2s, the scourge she hated. Gladys held her breath. The terrible crash shook the house once more, causing yet more plaster to fall from the ceiling. It was near, too near, and Gladys scuttled back into the relative safety of the Morrison.

'Want a cuppa?'

Goldie was trying to make her feel better. Gladys shook her head. It wasn't often she refused tea. In fact, sometimes a cup of tea was the only thing that kept her going. She clutched at Mogs and put her face next to his. His whiskers prickled her cheek and she could smell the fishy breath of him. He was purring and her heart lifted.

A banging at the door made her stare at Goldie in alarm.

'Who comes calling in the middle of an air raid?' Gladys nevertheless scrambled out and was on her feet in moments.

Before she reached the front door, another scent assailed

her senses. This time it was a heavenly meaty smell that made her stomach rumble.

She opened the front door just as a flash lit the sky, illuminating her next-door neighbour with a tea-towel-covered dish in his hands. Siddy had to come to her front door because his was the only house in the street that had no back door and no garden; the house next to him had a huge garden. Siddy reckoned that at some point the bit of land had been sold to his neighbour. Gladys had the back alley from the street for access.

'Siddy! Don't you know there's a war on? Get in here.' She practically pulled him inside the house and shut the door quickly.

His comb-over had come adrift and long strands of lank hair hung down the side of his thin face.

'I didn't want to put this down on the pavement, that's why I didn't use the key. It's cooked to perfection now and I can't keep it warm with the utilities off,' he said. Then, because he knew she was looking at him as though he was daft, he continued, 'A mate gave me a rabbit last night and I've had it on slow with carrots and onions, but this bombing has interrupted supper. Why don't the three of us eat it now? We might be blown to smithereens any minute and then I'll have made it for nothing!'

Gladys let out a belly laugh. 'I love you, you daft man!'

She continued, 'I hope you got eyes like a cat to see to eat, the lights are off.'

'Course I have,' he replied.

She followed him and the gorgeous smell up the passage and into the kitchen, where he put the dish on the table.

'Give us that torch,' she said to Goldie, and kept her fingers over the glass so that a very thin beam gave her just enough light to lay the table with cutlery and dishes. She told Goldie to get out of the shelter and come and eat her supper.

In the glow from the fire, the three of them relished every mouthful of meat in scrumptious gravy. Mogs sat cheerfully at their feet eating bony morsels he'd begged prettily for, by standing on his hind legs and pawing their knees.

'If we had a bit of music it would make this little party complete,' said Siddy. He sat back in his chair and patted his stomach. 'That was grand,' he added. Then, 'I don't know about you two, but I'm fed up with the bombing. He's throwing V2s at us now, you know.'

Gladys started laughing. Siddy and Goldie stared. 'Here we are sitting eating a meal, like it was any normal time. All around us bombs are falling and bits of plaster are coming off the ceiling into me dinner and Siddy says, "He's throwing V2s at us." You're priceless, my love.' Gladys leaned across the table and kissed his cheek.

Goldie smiled at her. 'Anyway, the Germans are on the run. My feller says our allies are pushing them back. Apparently we're ready to take the Siegfried Line.'

'Is he allowed to tell you that?' Siddy looked mystified.

'He writes me stuff that gets crossed out, but a lot gets through. I heard they found Nazi death camps in Poland, inside electrified barbed-wire fences. People arrived in cattle trucks to be systematically murdered and their ashes used as fertilizer.'

Gladys dabbed at her eyes with the corner of the tea towel. Goldie's words were making her soft heart ache and her tears fall.

'I just can't understand how they could be so cruel,' Goldie said.

'I can,' said Siddy. He sat at the table staring into space, as though his memories had caught up with him.

Gladys could hear that the noise from the shelling had lessened. It had been nice sitting eating and chatting as though it was any normal mealtime. 'That was a really lovely meal,' she said to Siddy. She got up, fetched some cups from the shelf then poured out tea from a flask. 'Waste not, want not,' she said. Siddy was a funny bugger, she thought. Kind and thoughtful. She loved the little treats he cooked her. He was lonely. That he loved her was a foregone conclusion. She often spent the night in his bed, where they would cuddle and chat, but she was well aware she didn't love him in that hot, breathy, rapturous way, like lovers. She couldn't remember the last time she and Siddy had had sex. He wasn't like most men, with hands like an octopus. Did she care for him? Yes. But love, proper love, like on the films, like in *Gone with the Wind*, she never felt that with Siddy.

And then it was all over.

The all-clear sounded and gradually the noise of people talking, running feet, filtered in from the street.

'You want any more tea?'

Goldie shook her head at Gladys.

Gladys saw Goldie look towards Siddy for more information about the cruelty of Germans, but he'd already left the table, busying himself taking the dirty dishes out to the scullery.

'Now we can have the electric on again I want to write a letter to Jamie,' said Goldie. 'And I've made up my mind. I want you to come to Southsea with me and talk some sense into Doll. One of the reasons I left it so long before I did anything was because she was still at school. But she should have left by now. I wouldn't mind betting that Fred is letting her dance in that horrible club whenever she wants. She's a good little dancer, but she should have a proper job. She can't go out without him in tow and he watches her like a hawk. He tells her what to wear and who to talk to—'

'That's not healthy,' Gladys broke in. She didn't want Goldie telling her all over again about Fred. She could hear Siddy washing up in the scullery. 'I'm going to look round this house,' she said, 'make sure there's no proper damage after the shelling, then take a walk up the street. Some of those bombs fell pretty close.'

'You haven't answered me, Gladys. I daren't go alone to Southsea because I'm scared of Fred. Will you come with me?'

Gladys answered, 'All right, if I have to. But what do we do with her if she says she'll leave that controlling brother of hers?'

'The front room's doing nothing . . .' Goldie was smiling.

Gladys stood with her hands on her hips. 'Jesus Christ, my life and home ain't me own.' She waltzed into the scullery and disentangled Siddy from the tea towel he was using to wipe the dishes. She picked up one of the flasks. 'No sense in wasting good strong tea.' She grabbed Siddy's arm. 'Let's sit and chat for a bit while the fire's still burning. Nosing down the street can wait. Goldie's going to her room to write to her man.'

*Goldie my love,*

*It didn't rain last night, but was very cold this morning. There were many bombers overhead last night. We've been told to proceed to*

Caen, a fifteen-mile journey, but there's a problem with the tank. The fitters are working on it. I shall be glad to rejoin the unit. I haven't had a letter from you for some time and I'm worried. I hope it's only a postal hold-up. Don't understand why the unit doesn't make the effort to send on our mail. Sometimes I think it's only your letters that keep me going.

We're on a main road. There's lots of refugees with horse-drawn carts piled high with all sorts of household items: beds, mattresses, pots and pans, usually with children holding other children or animals sitting on top. Bicycles seem good modes of transport. They can carry huge loads. Sometimes the refugees have to walk. They lug large suitcases and look so tired.

The vehicle is moving! Fitters are happy and so are we. It's too late to move tonight, so we're going first thing in the morning.

Most of the local menfolk raise their caps as we pass. The women wave; there's a lot of handshaking. The children run alongside and ask for 'bonbons'. They look undernourished.

In every letter I tell you I love you. Goldie, you better believe it. When this war is over and I'm home beside you, we will never be parted again. I think of happier times. Remember when we sat beneath the apple trees in the orchard at Glenning's farm? You wore a white dress with flowers the same colour as the fruit on the trees. Your lovely hair was spread out on the grass – don't you ever cut it all off! The insects were buzzing in the heat of the afternoon and I kissed you for the very first time – a proper kiss, not like the little pecks we'd given each other as children. I realized then there wouldn't be anyone else for me. All the girlfriends I'd had before you and I got back together meant nothing. And when you said you loved me, I was over the moon. Believe me, Goldie darling, I will never hurt you and when I come home, even if it's only on leave – for who knows how long this war will last? – I want us to get engaged. Please say yes, my darling?

Jamie X

PS I forgot to tell you the reason Eli never had any more letters from Carol. A V2 hit the picture house where she'd gone with her mum to see Jane Russell in 'The Outlaw'. It was awful when he got the bad news, and even worse when a delayed letter came from her the next day.

# Chapter Eight

Solly was waiting for Goldie as she reached Priddy's outside gate.

'What are you doing here?'

He handed her a bunch of Michaelmas daisies. 'Sorry they aren't posh flowers. My dad grew them on his allotment. I've been waiting for you. I've only just realized you live in Alma Street and I live in Inverness Road.'

Goldie was aware it was the next street along. 'I don't mind walking with you tonight. Gladys is working the evening shift.' Actually, she hated walking the streets in the dark. The fear that Fred might appear was still niggling at her. 'Normally me and Gladys wait for each other, you see.' She took the blue flowers and smiled at him. 'Thank you, they're lovely.'

'They've been in my locker all day,' he said. 'How are you getting on at Priddy's? I mean, I know you don't particularly like the Yellow Room.'

Goldie knew that he sometimes felt shy and didn't know how to talk to her, which was why he was always making jokes. All the women fancied him. He was good at his job and treated them with respect, unlike some of the other male workers.

'I like the wage packet and the girls are nice enough. The work is hard, though.'

He was looking at her as though he wanted to ask her something, but didn't know how to go about it. He blurted out, 'Do you fancy going for a drink?'

Goldie was tired. But she would be alone in the house apart from Mogs, so she said, 'All right. But only as friends, I already have a boyfriend.'

He beamed at her. 'How refreshing to hear a girl say straight out that she doesn't intend to cheat on her man. So many women only think about having a good time while their fellers are fighting for our country.'

'Well, so long as you understand.' She looked into his face and he smiled down at her.

'Quite. How about the Alma?'

That was the pub at the bottom of her street. 'Fine.'

When they got inside, Goldie was surprised to see the place was packed. However, she saw a couple of chairs near a table and immediately claimed them. 'You buy the first round and I'll get the second.'

Solly laughed. 'Great, that means I get to have two drinks with you.'

While he was at the bar, she looked around and decided it was a nice place.

It was very clean, although smoky from cigarettes and very busy. There were posters on the walls advising the customers to take heed and help win the war. There was a picture of a hay wain and the words, 'Lend a Hand on the Land'. Another showed a woman's hat with a feather and the slogan 'Keep it Under Your Hat'. Yet another was a picture of an ARP man in his tin hat and uniform, begging for air raid wardens. The one she liked best was of a girl in a turban, wearing dungarees and flexing her arm muscles while saying, 'We Can Do It'. That poster reminded her of the girls at Priddy's.

'It's packed tonight because they had barrels of beer delivered this morning,' Solly said. He put a half-pint of amber-coloured liquid down in front of her and another on the table for himself. 'Is this all right?' He looked worried. 'I should have asked you. Maybe you'd prefer a gin and orange?'

'Stop worrying, this is fine.' She took a mouthful. It tasted of summer to her and she remembered going hop picking with her mum and her friend and staying in a wooden shack. They were lovely times.

She began to tell Solly about her childhood. It hurt so much to think that now her mother had remarried she'd forgotten Goldie existed, or at least that was how it felt. She didn't tell Solly everything, of course not. Goldie had written to her mother, thinking she might be worried about the beating the south coast was taking. There'd been no reply so far.

Solly listened to her, really listened, and Goldie found she was nattering on about all sorts of things and soon they were laughing heartily together.

He told her he lived with his parents. His mother had been forty-two when he was born and it was quite a shock, as his parents had resigned themselves to never having children. The downside of it was now that his mother was unwell, forgetful at times. She still managed to look after the house and cook, but sometimes forgot about the saucepans on the gas stove. His dad was very agile, although older than his mother by about ten years, and wouldn't let anyone look after her except himself. Goldie realized Solly loved his parents very much.

He said he'd been engaged a couple of years back, but broke off the engagement when he realized the girl wasn't prepared to live in the family home. Solly had resigned himself to caring for his parents. Though he liked being with women – and there was certainly no shortage of girls hanging around him – he'd decided to play the field until the right one came along.

'So if you simply want to be mates, that's fine by me,' he said.

The barmaid rang the ship's bell at the rear of the bar for last orders. Goldie couldn't believe how long they'd been sitting chatting, laughing and drinking. All night they'd taken turns to buy drinks. But Goldie felt sure he wanted to take their relationship further, even though he'd said he'd leave things up to her. Another thought lodged itself in her mind.

'I never realized the time had gone so quickly. I've really enjoyed your company,' said Goldie. 'But I'd better get a move on. Gladys is working overtime, but not an all-nighter, and I promised to have a meal ready for her.' She got up and stumbled against the table.

'Steady,' Solly said. 'It's a bit of luck you've only a few steps to your house. I'll walk you to your front door.'

Out in the fresh air, Goldie felt better. And happier, when she remembered there was bubble and squeak she intended to fry up with some sausages. It wouldn't take her long to prepare the meal. She also wanted to write to Jamie.

Solly held her arm as they walked up the street and outside number fourteen she drew the key through the letter box and opened the door.

'I'm not inviting you in,' she laughed, but he leaned forward and planted a quick kiss on her cheek.

'I don't expect you to. See you tomorrow at work.'

She stood on the doorstep and watched him walk away. It was almost as if he knew she'd watch until he reached the corner at the bottom of the street, as he stopped there, turned and waved.

After taking off her coat, she put a few knobs of coal on the range to revive the fire. Then she prepared the food and had a strip wash in the scullery. She washed up Mogs's dishes and cooked him a little bit of fish. Gladys cared for Mogs so much she made sure he never ran out of his favourite meal. Dressed in her long, warm nightdress with her dressing gown over the top, Goldie switched the wireless on. It was nice listening to the dance music as she sat down in the armchair and began her letter to Jamie.

When she heard the key in the door she quickly brewed up the pot of tea, mindful not to use too much of the fresh tea leaves. Her words came out in a rush.

'I've been thinking about going over to Southsea and finding Doll, but I've been worried that us two women might not be able to handle ourselves against Fred; that's if he's there . . .'

Gladys hastily took off her coat and threw it over the back of a chair.

'Cor, wait 'til I get in, girl.' She smiled at Goldie. 'My feet are killing me,' she added. 'Now, what are you on about?'

'I haven't told him all the ins and outs,' said Goldie, 'but

93

I'm sure he'd come with us. I'm going to ask Solly to help us persuade Doll to leave Fred.'

'How many times have I told you not to go in there with those slags?'

Fred pulled Doll from the room, which stank of cheap perfume. With his hand on the back of her neck, he frog-marched her out and practically flung her through another open door. If it hadn't been for Rene standing with one leg on a chair, adjusting her fishnet stockings, she would have tumbled to the floor.

'Oy! Watch it, this is my last pair,' yelled Rene, but she managed to save Doll as the unfortunate girl stumbled. With her other hand she grabbed her gin and orange before it slid off her dressing table and onto the floor.

'I was only talking to Eva!' But it was a waste of her breath, as Fred had slammed the door on the two of them. Doll turned her big eyes on Rene, who was now dusting herself down and looking for snags in her precious stockings. 'All we was talking about was nail polish. She was going to let me try some of that deep red one that punter got for her.'

'You know how he feels about you fraternizing with the girls . . .'

'I'm not allowed to do anything,' Doll said. 'I'm a prisoner. It was bad enough when I was at school and he took me there and brought me home, but now it's even worse.' She watched Rene go to a drawer in a table that stood against the wall. She took out a bottle of pink nail varnish and threw it to her. Doll caught it. 'This is a pretty colour.' She immediately unscrewed the top and began to paint her nails using the little brush. The smell of acetate filled the small room.

'He won't mind if you use that colour. You know he doesn't like you wearing anything the least bit tarty . . .'

'Glamorous, you mean. Can I keep it?'

'Yes, it's not my colour.' She held her hands out in front of her and Doll sighed with pleasure at the deep vermilion colour of Rene's nails. It was always the same. She could have whatever she wanted from Fred, as long as it was what he wanted too.

Like the outfit he made her wear. She had on ballet slippers, thick dancing tights, a long pink skirt that reached her calves and a pink top that was round-necked and long-sleeved.

She wore it because if she didn't, her brother wouldn't let her anywhere near the stage in this broken-down club that she hated with all her heart. She loathed the drunks, the punters with their raincoats over their knees, their leering faces. But what else could she do but go along with what Fred dictated?

She needed to dance, it was her life. He hadn't allowed her to go to proper dancing lessons because he would have had to stay and keep an eye on her. To leave her alone in a dance studio with other would-be dancers was unthinkable to him. She knew nothing about correct steps, body language or any of those things. But that didn't matter, because she had a natural grace that allowed her to blend with the music. The feeling of ecstasy that she got as she moved on the stage filled her with joy. So, as long as Fred allowed her to dance, she would do as he bade her. She supposed he only wanted what was best for her.

Doll had once thought that when she left Portsmouth Grammar School she'd be able to go to work, or even on to university. But that was out of the question. Fred wanted her close to him.

So she made him pay for it in the only way she could. She smiled at the gold watch on her wrist. She'd asked him for it because she knew it was something he wouldn't refuse her. Like her bed, which was a brand-new divan, an expensive item of furniture, not a piece of Utility rubbish. She'd also got him to employ Mrs Jenks who came in daily at their house in Southsea to clean and prepare food. Doll didn't intend to start cooking and cleaning, not when her brother could afford someone else to do it. He kept her a prisoner, so she might as well be jailed in style.

She suddenly thought of Goldie. Goldie was all right, though Fred didn't like Doll getting friendly with her either.

He called her a tramp. But that didn't ring true, not when Goldie only had one boyfriend and he was in a tank regiment in France. But then Doll came home after staying the night with Gloria and the place was in a mess. Fred said Goldie'd run off with some bloke. It was all very strange, especially as Goldie never took any clothes with her.

Fred never knew she left school the next day earlier than usual, telling her teacher she didn't feel well. She went to the laundry and asked if she could see Goldie, but they told her she hadn't turned up for work that day. Then she went back to the school gates and waited until Fred came to meet her. After that he'd even stopped her best friend, well, her only friend, Gloria, from coming around. But Fred did let her dance in the club. He owned it now. He'd finally got the money together to buy the Blue.

But unlike the other girls she wasn't allowed to fraternize with the punters. She remained in Fred's office, listened to the wireless or read. Sometimes she was able to spend time with Rene, which she liked best of all, because Rene talked to her. Other times Fred took her home and locked her in the house. Rene knew all this, but there was nothing she could do. When she had tried to protest on behalf of Doll, Fred knocked her about.

Oh, how she wished she could dance on a proper stage wearing pretty clothes. Just dance and dance so she could forget everything. She couldn't even run away; where would she go?

She'd thought about trying to escape; selling her expensive presents so she would have money. But after being told what to do and what to say by Fred, her confidence was so low she was too terrified to do it. Oh, she could be mouthy at times, but that was just a cover-up.

Now she rifled through Rene's meagre stage outfits on hangers in the cupboard. Some of them were none too clean, but she appreciated that sequins didn't like to be washed. She held the harem pants up against herself, then went over to Rene and stared at her glittery top.

'I love your outfit,' she said.

The fishnet stockings and suspenders met up with skimpy satin knickers, tight around Rene's bottom. Above her bare midriff, a sparkly bra barely covered her ample breasts.

'You know what else I like?' Doll didn't wait for an answer but carried on, 'I admire you for sticking up for yourself when you strip off your clothes on stage. You never take off your knickers.'

She knew Fred had hit her once for refusing to do what she was paid for, but Rene stuck to her guns.

'Your brother knows I'm his best stripper,' she said. Rene gave Doll a smile. 'So there's not much he can do about it.' She looked suddenly sad. 'I wish I had the guts to tell him

I don't want the punters pawing at me any more. But he reckons it's a job and that when they touch me it doesn't change anything about how he feels about me.'

Doll didn't like to see her so sad. 'I think he cares for you.'

Rene gave her a beaming smile, 'You think so?' Doll nodded. Rene picked up a lipstick that was a deep red, leaned towards the mirror and touched up her lips. 'What d'you think of your photo outside the club?' She'd changed the subject and Doll was glad Rene seemed happier now.

'I hate it.' In temper, the girl banged her fist on the dressing table and the half-drunk gin and orange slid off the edge and onto the floor. Doll looked at it then turned away. She wouldn't pick up the broken glass. Why should she?

Fred had posted a picture of her in a glass case without an inch of her flesh showing. It said, 'Come and See the Virgin Dance'.

'You're a bit like the taste of honey,' Rene said. 'Get the punters in.'

Rene abandoned the lipstick and put her arm around her. Rene was the only person Doll could talk to.

'So all you other dancers have to flaunt yourselves and sleep with the punters?'

'You got it, Doll. It's called earning a living.'

'You could get a different job . . .' At least he didn't keep Rene locked up, she thought.

'Doll, what would I do?' Rene sighed deeply. 'This is all I know. I'm not like you with your schooling—'

'What good did my schooling do? He wouldn't let me go away to university. Anyway, I don't care about that, I want to dance.'

'I know you do, pet. So you, like me, go on taking what Fred dishes out, so that you get what you want, right?'

Doll thought about it. 'Yes.' Then she asked, 'But what d'you get out of it?'

'Fred. Can't you see I love him?' Rene said.

# Chapter Nine

'Fancy a cuppa, Gladys?' The hand on her shoulder made her jump.

'Jesus, you scared me,' she said turning to Mac. 'Yeah, that'd be nice. But I'm not coming to the cop shop for one.'

'I was thinking more of the Dive.'

She grinned at the tall red-headed detective, then took his arm as they wandered through the market. The smells wafting from the various stalls were lovely. Bath salts by the scoopful. Gladys suspected they were dyed soda crystals. She'd bought some once and the crystals had gone white, leaving a layer of pink water at the bottom of the jar. There were different-coloured soaps that might be suspect to wash with. Branded toiletries were still very much in short supply. There were autumn blooms and potted plants from Evelyn's Flowers. Even the smell from the second-hand clothes stall and the ozone smell coming off the wet fish counter made

Gladys happy. She'd walked through the town on her day off, looking for early Christmas presents.

Gladys thought back to last Christmas, which she'd spent working at Priddy's. The overtime was nice, but a poor substitute for being at home with loved ones. Last year she'd been alone, but this year was different and she was determined that she would do her best for Goldie and Mogs. She looked down at her brown carrier bag with the piece of cod wrapped in paper inside.

'The Dive'll do me fine,' she said. 'I got new-to-me shoes on and they pinch me bunion something terrible.'

She saw him look down at the red high heels she'd fought a woman for at a jumble sale at Bury Hall.

It was only a short walk to the café opposite the bus station and the warmth hit her as soon as she stepped down into the smoky tunnel beneath the Market Tavern. The café was the home of the strongest cuppa in Gosport and the haunt of bus drivers, factory workers and ferry staff.

'Two cuppas, please, Tom,' said Mac and urged her to go on through to find a seat. It wasn't long before Mac followed her, carrying two cups with a saucer perched over each and a currant bun lying on top.

Gladys purred with delight. Tom's currant buns filled with marg were a real treat.

'Thanks Mac,' she said. 'How's Marlene?'

'Didn't you see her in the market? She's doing fine.'

Gladys felt a surge of guilt. 'I didn't go up as far as the post office. I only had time to buy some fish for the cat before I met you.'

'Go and say hello before you go home, she'd like that.' She watched him bite into the softness of the bun.

'I will,' she replied. Marlene used to work at Priddy's, but it was only a stopgap until she made enough money to get her beloved stall up and running. She was selling gold jewellery now. Gladys had known Marlene since she was a young girl. 'And you? I expect you're busy with toerags stealing and breaking and entering now that Christmas is near?'

'Too right, but we got smuggling going on and black-marketeers running riot. Crime never stops in Gosport.' He put his cup down and stared at her. He was a lovely man and had beautiful white teeth.

Gladys sipped her tea; it was just as she liked it. She licked her lips with pleasure. 'How's your mate and his club? I heard he's from London and a proper gangster?' Gladys had found the right opening to talk about Will.

'If so, I know nothing about it.' Gladys knew he had to say that. After all, he was a detective.

She tried again. 'How come you know him so well?' Mac continued drinking his tea. 'Is he married?'

Mac smiled over the rim of his cup. 'No, he's not married.

His wife died of a lingering illness a couple of years back. He doesn't like to talk about her. He's one of the good blokes; he loved his wife and didn't mess about with other women. He's surrounded by pretty girls now, so I guess if he feels the need, they're readily available.' He took a bite of his bun.

'So you've known him a long time?' Gladys didn't need to know anything else about his marital status.

'We played together as kids. Right little buggers we were. Stealing apples; going around the greengrocers' asking for pecked fruit. Will practically lived at our house. His mum and dad were always going at it hammer and tongs. We went through the infant school together, then the junior, then the seniors. He was a clever so-and-so. Sharper than me, used to let me copy his homework.' His eyes grew misty. 'He saved my life.'

Gladys wanted to know more.

'We used to skate on this pond at Seven Dials when it was frozen over. One day, the ice cracked and I went under.' She saw him grip the handle of his cup so hard she thought he was going to break it. 'I remember the fear as though it was yesterday,' he said. 'Will thought quickly. He lay on the frozen surface and as I was sliding under the ice, he grabbed at me and pulled me out.' His eyes had glazed over with the memory. 'We both lay on the ice, out of it with the cold.

Luckily a passer-by got us to the park-keeper's cottage and we thawed out. I'd have died if Will hadn't saved me.'

'He sounds like a right nice bloke.' Gladys wanted him to go on talking about the club owner.

'He is. It's a funny thing, but that was like the end of our childhood. He got into trouble when he messed up some bloke; he was only fourteen and had a knife, right handy he was with that blade. We sort of lost touch. I joined the police force, he went into the services. He's made a lot of money in London, but that's nothing to do with me, not my patch.'

She was silent, mulling over his words.

'What services?'

'Air force. He flew Spitfires. At the end of July 1940, the Germans planned a big attack that they reckoned would destroy our coastal airfields. It was called *Adlerangriff*, Eagle Attack. There was a delay and the actual fighting began during the second week of August. Will's squadron found itself repelling the onslaughts. The Germans crushed radio stations in Kent and Sussex. Forty-seven German aircraft were shot down when Will's squadron caught up with the raiders in a spectacular dogfight over Hampshire. Unfortunately, the leader of his squadron was shot down. Will went after the attacker, got him, but not before the German had winged Will's plane. He managed to get out and parachute to safety but his leg was a mess. He was awarded a bravery medal, not that he'll ever talk about it, but as he could no longer fly a plane he was chucked out of the RAF.' Mac was staring at her. 'Why are you asking me all this?'

'Just wanted to know a bit about the man,' she said.

'He's dangerous. That's all you need to know. He thought he would lose his leg, but a limp is all that there is to remind him. Though I dare say, like the rest of us, his nightmares never go away.'

Gladys was quiet, mulling over all Mac had told her. He and Marlene were very dear friends. She decided to trust him with what she knew of Fred and his club, the Blue, and was surprised when Mac said, 'He's a bloke we keep our eyes on. But what you're talking about are domestic problems, so not really our business. He's got a screw loose, I'm sure of that. Try not to get on the wrong side of him. However, if you say this sister of his dances well, why not ask Will to give her a try-out?'

Gladys sat back on her seat staring at him.

'I don't want to get the girl on the game.' She was indignant. Her voice rose and the couple sitting opposite them looked over in alarm.

Mac laughed. 'His girls aren't on the game, unless they do it in their own time. There are prostitutes, and a punter can have one after a quiet word with Will, but he's a bit particular that nothing goes on in his clubs.' He paused, 'Anyway, that's one of the reasons I wanted to see you. He's having a party around Christmas time and has asked me to invite some friends. He doesn't know many of the Gosport people, only as customers . . .'

'Ooh! Can I bring Goldie?'

'Bring who you like. Knowing Will, there'll be plenty to eat and drink. Just don't ask him where it's come from!'

'Not your business, eh?' Gladys laughed. Excited, she was already planning what to wear. Then a thought struck her. 'Are you sure I can come? After all, I don't know the bloke . . .'

'You're priceless, Gladys! He specially asked me to invite you.'

She looked at him and frowned. 'Really?'

Mac gathered himself together and picked up the cups and saucers. 'Look, I've got to get back to the station. Later, I'd like to tell Will you'll be at the party. Will you say yes?'

Gladys rose from her seat. 'I can't let him down, can I?'

*Goldie darling,*

*We arrived at HQ early today, with three other tanks as reinforcements. Jerry was in this place less than a week ago and everyone yelled and waved as we trundled in. The tricolour hangs from every building. There's no mistaking the warmth of these people and it makes me feel glad to be helping to restore their faith in human nature, after what's happened here.*

The French resistance fighters shave the heads of the women who slept with the Germans. They punish collaborators by daily executions in the town square.

There are Jerries in the forests of Brotonne and the infantry are rounding them up.

We will be here for a few days, as the bridge across the Seine, about six miles away, was blown up and until access is restored we can't cross.

Tonight the 'Passion Wagon' will take us into town. The lads are hoping the girls will be grateful and the bars full of wine. We have done well for food, plenty of salad stuff and eggs scrounged from the civilians. The lads barter with cigarettes. I have heard no artillery fire for days.

Dad says Uncle Billy is eager to offload his house near the South Parade Pier in Southsea. He's selling it cheap because he intends to move to Kent as soon as he can and marry that nurse. Remember the V1 bomb that shook its foundations? It needs money spending on it, but it's near the beach. I think it would be a good start to married life for us. Shall I tell him we'll take it?

I'm surprised you are living in Gosport, but that Gladys sounds a very good sort. Please take care in the armament yard. I think of you, darling, the first moment I wake and the last minute before I sleep.

Jamie

X BOLTOP (Better on lips than on paper)

The thin man sat at the bar drinking, seemingly uninterested in the girl on the stage, who was removing bedraggled ostrich-feathered fans from her body, then tantalizing the audience by replacing them before any flesh showed. The music was too loud, the girl too skinny.

Fred, sitting next to Baz Bowen, knew he had to give Diane her marching orders. She was scaring the punters away instead of bringing them in.

'Are you sure that the ship carrying the supplies is docking at Southampton around three in the morning?'

The man grunted. 'Course I'm sure. I'm helping unload, aren't I?'

Fred stared at Baz Bowen through the haze of cigarette smoke. 'Fair enough, same slice of the action as before.' That wasn't a question, he was telling Baz he wasn't prepared to pay him more for the information. William Hill's trafficked goods were going to find their way into Fred's MTB instead of Hill's boat, and then sail round the coastline to Portsmouth.

'He's got good gear . . .'

'It's all good when the punters can't get enough to eat,' said Fred.

He peeled off some notes and gave them to Baz. 'This is to make sure Hill's boys go for a cuppa while you unload.' He thought that the ship, bringing wounded lads back from

Africa to the hospital near Southampton for a well-earned rest, was good cover for Hill's supplies of tinned salmon, sugar, beer and sweets that he sold on the black market.

'What's the name of the ship?'

'*Princess Leonie*. A requisitioned cruise ship.'

'Right, don't let any of Hill's men have an inkling of what's going to happen to his supplies.'

'What d'you take me for?'

Fred looked at him and raised his eyebrows. Baz Bowen was a snout. A grass, the lowest of the low.

'A good mate,' he lied.

# Chapter Ten

'I'm sorry, Gladys.'

Gladys bit her tongue. He'd tried his best, she knew that. She felt let down and hurt – why didn't Siddy fancy her enough for them to make love properly?

'It's all right. Maybe next time,' she said and kissed him on the end of his nose; there were tears in his eyes, magnified by his spectacles. She said 'next time', but she knew it would be the same as all the other times he tried to make love to her.

She knew he closed his eyes to her dalliances with men at dances and the servicemen she met down at the Fox. If she couldn't have a bit of loving with him, he said he didn't mind if she found solace elsewhere.

Gladys liked to be loved.

'I'll get up and make a cup of tea, shall I?' Siddy had already stretched his long, thin legs out of the tangle of sheets.

'Bugger the tea!' Siddy sat bolt upright at her outburst, then he crawled back into bed and pulled the covers up. 'Talk to me!' Gladys demanded.

She wanted to know what the matter was. Gladys didn't want him wandering down to his kitchen leaving her in bed all frustrated and upset. She wasn't angry, no, not at all, but maybe by talking about their incompatibility in bed she could right any wrongs that made it impossible for Siddy to perform.

It wasn't because he didn't love her. She knew he did. And she always came running back to him when her little flings ended. Didn't that prove she loved him?

She turned and faced him then put her arms around him. There was a stain on the front of his vest where he'd spilled some tea. She dropped her arms and put her finger on the mark, and when he looked down she flicked her finger up and tapped him gently on the nose.

'Gotcha!' she said. He laughed. She knew he liked her teasing him. 'I think, Siddy, we got to talk about this.' She scrabbled in the sheets and found what she was looking for. After slipping her silk nightdress over her head, she smoothed the creases out. If they were going to have a discussion, she needed to cover herself.

It was then that she heard him weeping.

'Siddy, oh, Siddy, I didn't mean to upset you . . .'

'I should have told you ages ago . . .'

She frowned as he wiped his eyes with the back of his hand. 'Whatever do you mean?'

'I'm just not good at this . . .'

'Is it me? Don't you fancy me?'

He leaned in towards her and buried his head in her breasts. 'It was never you,' he mumbled. She put her arms around him again. It was like holding a child, she thought. 'I never said anything because I thought you'd think less of me,' he said.

'I'm going to stay here with you until you explain yourself and if you don't know now that you can say whatever you like to me without fear of reproach, then you really don't know me at all.'

He stared at her, then said, 'Lie down with your head on the pillow, Glad, and let me lie next to you. Promise me you'll try not to interrupt?'

'All right,' she said. 'Let me make myself comfortable.'

The range downstairs in the kitchen was directly beneath the bedroom, so it was warm and cosy. There was a chest of drawers along the wall by the window that still had blackout curtains across it, and a wardrobe near the door. Siddy's bed was an iron-framed monstrosity with brass balls at each corner, but it was very comfortable, with feather pillows and a feather patchwork quilt. 'I'm ready,' Gladys said.

'In 1936 I was working in a factory in Germany. I was in the office and there were four of us, all pals; we used to go out in the evenings to various clubs and bars that catered for the more adventurous young men.'

'What d'you mean by that, Siddy?' She knew she wasn't supposed to interrupt, but she needed to understand. He took her hand and squeezed it.

'None of us were married and Helmut was living with another man he cared for deeply . . .'

'What, like they was married?'

He whispered, 'Yes, exactly that. Of course it was all secret. In these clubs you could meet other men . . .'

'Pansies?'

He sighed. She felt him move his head like he was nodding.

'We listened to jazz, drank, some danced together. It was a nice atmosphere, because in the real world outside those clubs, men fraternizing with men was illegal—'

'Are you telling me you was a pansy too?' Gladys's heart was racing.

'I don't know what I was, Glad. I was simply a young bloke experimenting with life. I'd had a few girlfriends, none I wanted to settle down with, and I found there were some men I could actually talk to. In the summer on the beach I'd look at a pretty girl and think, I'd like to, you know . . . with her. But then I'd spy a young man coming out of the sea with droplets of water glistening in his hair and on his chest and I'd think, "what a beautiful boy". It was all terribly confusing.

'Anyway, one night the doors burst open and the police came in, arresting everyone in sight. Those Nazis didn't mess about; we were rounded up like animals and taken in the back of a lorry to a place called Lübeck. We were classed as mentally ill and sent to prison. I was offered the "cure" of castration, or therapy in a psychiatric facility.'

Gladys gasped.

'Of course, I chose aversion therapy. By now I was separated from my friends, but I heard Helmut had been given a lobotomy . . .'

'What's that?'

Gladys had never heard that word before. She was stunned by Siddy's story of what had happened to him. If he hadn't been one of the most truthful people she knew, she would have accused him of spinning her a tall tale.

'The surgeon drills the prefrontal area of the brain, by going through the eye socket with an instrument that looks like an ice pick.' Gladys grabbed Siddy's hand and cried out. He continued, 'Unfortunately, lobotomies don't always do what they're supposed to, but instead can disable the patient for life.' He paused. 'Are you all right?' She was trembling. She felt sick. 'Look, I don't have to tell you about this, not if it upsets you,' he said, stroking her hair.

Gladys said quietly, 'Go on.' She swallowed down her nausea.

'I was given drugs, Thorazine and apomorphine. They made me sick. I had convulsions. I was made to lie in a bed in my own faeces, piss and vomit. An electric probe was placed on my genitals. They showed me pictures of beautiful young men and when I said I thought they were good-looking, or desirable, I was given an electric shock after being called all sorts of filthy names. Then I was shown pictures of beautiful women and if I said they were nice, I was rewarded with no shocks.

'I was shown pictures of same-sex couples having inter-course and then I was electrically shocked for looking at them. I was told I was depraved. The electric shocks were excruciating, and the Thorazine and apomorphine made me vomit all the time. I began having seizures and sometimes I had no idea what day it was, where I was, or who I was. Eventually, the treatment stopped.' She heard him give a huge sigh. He put his head on the pillow and looked into her eyes. Never before had she seen such pain emanating from someone.

'In 1939 I was sent back here, to England. It was only after I was free of that place that I found out that my other two friends hadn't survived their therapy sessions.

'I came to Portsmouth by boat and was lucky enough

to find employment with a firm of solicitors. I had a small office to work in, alone, as an accountant, and my life consisted of living in a tiny flat. Weekends I spent walking on Southsea Common. A legacy from an aunt enabled me to buy houses in Gosport, and I wanted a change from Portsmouth. Numbers twelve and fourteen Alma Street I rented out and I lived, as you know, in the house at Brockhurst.

'Fits of deep depression and the inability to make friends with people made me reclusive. I didn't need to work, I had money coming in from these houses and from the legacy. Gradually I began to live again and I bought the car. Despite the rationing, sometimes I was able to get hold of a few gallons of petrol and drive out into the countryside.'

'Then I come along . . .'

Gladys could feel his revelations had drained him. It was about time to inject a bit of lightness into this terrible story he'd unfolded.

'I have no idea how to say I'm sorry, or that I understand what you went through,' she said. 'I can see why you didn't want to talk about it.'

Gladys leant up on one elbow and looked down at him. It was as if in the retelling he'd aged twenty years. His wispy comb-over had fallen across one side of his face and his bony cheeks were sunken and pale. He looked like a living cadaver, she thought. And then she suddenly realized that she cared very, very deeply for this man, who'd been through so much and had only now shared his pain with her.

She shook her head. 'I'm glad you told me, Siddy,' she said. 'All this time you've been loving me the best way you can. Well, I'll tell you something: your love knocks spots off some of the blokes who've tried it on with me.' She paused and gave him a small smile. 'An' we both know there's been a few of them.'

Gladys didn't know what else to say. Siddy had gone through hell at the hands of the Nazis. She couldn't cry for him; the cruelty he'd endured was beyond her tears. But now she understood why he was the way he was, she loved him all the more. To her, his sexuality didn't matter. There wasn't so much love in the world that she couldn't take it when it was given and give some back.

Siddy cuddled her close and whispered, 'I've wanted to kill myself. Your friendship and the way you've allowed me to be part of your life has kept me from doing it.' She tried to say something, but Siddy hushed her and continued. 'When you came along it was like being in a deep, dark coal-hole and seeing a shining light appear. You're full of life, full of cheek and I do love you despite . . .'

Gladys looked into his eyes. 'We're all right, we understand each other.' She paused. 'You know, I reckon you'd do anything for me, wouldn't you, Siddy?'

He nodded. 'I reckon so,' he said.

'Right,' she said. 'Go and put the kettle on. I think we could both do with a nice cuppa, then a good cuddle.'

# *Chapter Eleven*

'You only need to be with me and Gladys. You don't have to do anything.'

Goldie handed Solly a cheese and onion sandwich, more onion than cheese, from her OXO-tin lunchbox and continued, 'She's sixteen now and should be doing what young girls her age do – going to dances with her mates and going out with lads. Her brother won't let her do any of those things. She's kept like a prisoner. Well, she was when I lived with them and I don't suppose anything's changed.'

*Music While You Work* was providing continuous wireless music in Priddy's as the women toiled, and was a great morale booster. The sound floated through the open windows as Goldie and Solly sat on a low wall overlooking the creek. It was cold, but preferable to the stink of cordite inside the factory. Solly bit into the sandwich and Goldie smiled winsomely at him.

'Please?' Goldie scratched at her arm. A rash had appeared that the nurse had called dermatitis. Goldie had been given some cream for it and it seemed to be shifting itself.

She'd been filling detonators all morning. It was dangerous work and a high concentration of explosives was needed. She'd already been ticked off by Gladys as she came round checking on the women and their work. Goldie had been talking to the woman opposite and talking wasn't allowed in that section. Gladys had written her name on her clipboard. Goldie realized there was no favouritism where war work was concerned.

'All right.' Solly said. 'It'll make a change from packing smoke bombs.'

'Is that what you've been doing this morning?'

'Yes, one of the girls called in sick, so I took her place. I've been pouring gunpowder into a big machine, then the machine lets out enough powder to fill the bomb case. It isn't hard but it's boring.'

Goldie threw her arms around him. 'You won't be bored tonight,' she said.

'Mind me sandwich!' he yelled. But he was laughing as he said it.

Goldie was still frightened that Fred might be looking for her, but she needed to put the safety of Doll above her own fear.

'I can get hold of a car . . .'

'That would be brilliant,' said Goldie. Petrol was only available on coupons to business people. Ordinary car owners had to go without. 'Doll could have personal stuff that she wants to bring and it might be too much for us to carry if we went across to Southsea on the ferry. That's if we can persuade her to leave Fred.' Goldie decided she'd give Solly some money towards the petrol.

'Surely there's no question of her not wanting to come with us?'

Goldie sighed. 'It's often found that prisoners don't want to leave their jailers. Don't forget, she's been spoiled all her life by him. Maybe she won't take kindly to coming to a place where she's got to pull her weight. There's no way Gladys is going to wait on her hand and foot like she's used to.'

'But surely freedom must mean something?' He pushed his fingers through his blond hair.

'All she wants to do is dance.'

'Where's she going to dance in Gosport? I can't imagine her dancing up the aisles in Priddy's. Anyway, she's not old enough to work there.'

'You know, it depends what job she's doing.' Goldie paused before saying, 'I think Gladys and Mac – he's a detective at Gosport nick – have put their heads together and come up with something.'

He stared at her. 'So the police are involved?'

'Oh, no! Mac says it's a domestic situation and the coppers don't want to know.' She paused. 'Just like when some bloke is strangling his wife and the coppers come out and tell him off. They're not interested in family squabbles.'

'Until someone's killed.'

'Well, I hope it's not going to come to that,' Goldie said. 'If the girl wants to have a normal life, she's welcome to come and live with Gladys. Let's face it, Gladys would be like a mum to her, as well as a friend.' Her eyes grew misty, remembering how Gladys had taken her in and given her and Mogs a home.

'Tonight?'

Solly's voice brought Goldie back to the present. She put her hand on his arm.

'Tonight,' she whispered.

The bell rang to call the workers back from their break. Goldie gathered together her flask and Oxo tin and she and Solly walked back to the locker rooms to be searched before being let into the building once more.

Later that evening Goldie knocked on the door at Fulsham Avenue in Southsea. It was horrible being outside the house she'd escaped from. Since it was in darkness, she guessed no one was home. She'd never had a key and there was no string through the letter box like Gladys's house.

'Looks like we'll have to go to the club,' said Gladys. She stood next to Goldie, rubbing her hands together to bring some life into them. The streets wore a fine sheen of early frost and the air smelled of the sea.

'Do you know where the Blue is?' Solly asked. He stamped his feet on the path.

'Yes, it's in one of the back streets in Southsea. I forget the name of the road, but I can show you the way if we drive along the seafront.'

Back at the car Solly wiped the windscreen. Goldie looked across the stretch of water towards the Isle of Wight. She knew the island was there, even though it was too dark to see it. Down towards South Parade Pier she asked him to turn off along a long road that seemed to be full of bed and breakfasts. Then there was a junction in the road and just past that the Blue was lit up with red lights around the entrance.

Goldie shouted, 'There it is.' Then her heart started beating fiercely. She didn't want to see Fred.

'I can't go in,' she said.

Gladys said, 'You have to. This girl, Doll, doesn't know who we are.'

Goldie saw noticeboards on the pavement. 'Oh, it makes me feel ill to see how he's using his sister to entice men in to spend money.' Pictures of Doll's pretty face smiled out at them in the cold night air.

There were more people here. Men, mostly, Goldie noticed, hanging about and chatting on the corner of the street.

'It's not a bit like Will's place in Gosport, is it?' piped up Gladys. 'It looks very down at heel.'

'I need to park somewhere near,' said Solly. He turned down a street and pulled in next to the pavement. 'We can drive out at the end of this street if we're chased off,' he said.

Goldie stared at him, but was glad he'd thought about that. It was a short walk to the club and Goldie gripped Solly's arm as they climbed the steps to the foyer. She moved aside as a very drunk man wove his way past her, almost missing his footing going down the steps.

'Stinks in here,' said Gladys. Goldie agreed; the air smelled of stale beer, cigarette smoke and the stench of old damp carpet. 'He'd get a better class of customer if he tidied the place up.'

There was a girl behind a small, glass-windowed counter. 'You can't just walk in, you need to pay.' When she told them the entrance fee Gladys nearly choked, but she opened her handbag and paid for all three of them. Goldie noticed the girl had goose pimples on her flesh. All she wore was a thin dress that showed a good deal of her skin.

'I'll pay you back,' Solly told Gladys.

'Don't be stupid, Solly. You've provided the transport,' Gladys answered.

'I'm scared,' said Goldie.

'Well, I'm not,' Gladys answered. She marched up to a girl who was opening a door ahead of them.

'We're looking for Fred, the manager—' She didn't get to finish before the girl said, 'He's the owner now. But he's not here tonight, he's out on business.' She stared at the three of them, then said, 'Rene's here. She's at the side of the stage while Fred's sister's doing her act. Do you want me to go and get her? Have you come about a job?'

Goldie said, 'No, we'll go and surprise her.' She felt braver now the girl hadn't recognized her, but thought the girl must be new to the club. She flicked her long hair back and said, 'Come on.'

It wasn't difficult to find Rene. They followed the sounds of the men in the audience yelling, 'Get 'em off!'

'Poor little kid,' said Gladys. 'She must have a strong disposition to dance on that stage while those apes out there are shouting for her to get her kit off . . .'

'Which of course she won't do, as it's not allowed by her brother. Anyway, showing all her bits and pieces isn't right at her age,' said Solly.

Goldie said, 'You've got to admire the kid, though, she really can dance.'

Just then Rene caught sight of them in the wings. 'What are you lot doing back here?' Then she recognized Goldie. 'I bet this isn't just a social visit?' She suddenly threw herself into her arms. 'Wherever have you been? Nobody knew where you'd disappeared to.'

She didn't wait for an answer, but eyed Goldie up and down. 'You look ever so well,' she said. 'But why are you here?'

'Don't talk about it now,' Gladys butted in. 'Someone might overhear.' Then, 'Does she always have to listen to those ignorant men?' She nodded towards the stage where, seemingly oblivious to their insults, the girl danced in sinuous, slow-moving steps, completely at one with the music.

Goldie looked at Gladys who nodded her head at the spectacle before them.

'Not when Fred's here. He keeps them in order.'

'If you've come to see your brother, Goldie, he's off on business,' Rene said.

Goldie looked at Gladys. It was obvious that Rene didn't know the true reason for Goldie's sudden disappearance from home. She put her fingers to her lips, warning Gladys to keep silent for now.

The three elderly men, one at the piano, one on the drums and one playing a saxophone, stopped their music and Doll waved to the audience, some of whom she'd obviously won over with her dancing. The other drunken louts were still fumbling at Fred's girls' clothing as they sat on the men's laps, oblivious to Doll's departure from the stage.

'Goldie!'

The girl ran towards them and threw her arms about her. 'Where have you been?'

'Is there somewhere we can go and talk?' Goldie was scared that at any moment Fred would appear. She looked about her fearfully.

'My room.' Rene began pulling Doll along the corridor.

'I hope I can sit down, my feet are killing me,' Gladys complained.

Goldie noticed that Doll hadn't taken her eyes off Solly.

A girl with flame-coloured hair and a grass skirt that looked as though a lawnmower had attacked it walked past them. 'Trudy,' said Rene, 'go and strut your stuff, I'll be in my dressing room.' The girl waved and Goldie heard cheers as she went onto the stage.

When they were all in the stuffy room, Gladys shouted for them to be quiet. Then she introduced Solly and herself to Rene.

Goldie wanted to get out of the place before Fred returned.

Gladys related how she'd found Goldie and Mogs that night. Goldie told Rene the real reason she'd suddenly disappeared.

Rene had tears in her eyes. 'I know he's a bastard, but I'd never have believed he'd have done something like that to you, love.'

Doll sat on the floor. She'd picked up her shoulder bag from the chair and was idly looking through it. She was deep in thought. She didn't speak, but she looked upset at Goldie's revelations.

'Look, Doll, I want you to leave this place and come with me.'

The girl's eyes narrowed at Goldie. 'Fred won't let me go.'

'He's not here. And it's what you want that matters,' said Solly.

'He'll come after me.'

'He'll have to find you first,' Gladys said.

Goldie could see Doll was wavering. She wasn't stupid and she was carefully weighing up her prospects. The girl stared at Solly, who Goldie could see was clearly embarrassed, as she watched his every movement.

'What d'you think, Rene?' Gladys asked.

'I think you should go.' Rene looked at the girl. 'This is no place for you.'

'But Fred lets me dance . . .'

Goldie said, 'What if we told you Gladys can make it possible for you to dance on a proper stage in a posh club?'

Doll's eyes lit up. 'Really?'

Gladys nodded. She hadn't actually asked Will about Doll dancing, but Mac had assured her his friend would love the girl on stage in his club. 'Not only that, but your new boss will give you costumes, proper costumes.' Goldie watched her bend and touch the hem of the girl's long skirt. 'Not like these. Ones with spangles and velvet . . .'

Goldie saw Doll waver. 'Honestly?'

Goldie nodded. She thought the girl was won over and was surprised when Doll suddenly said, 'No, I'm not coming, I'm not leaving my brother.'

There was shocked silence for a moment, then Gladys suddenly shouted, 'Reason ain't working, try force, Solly!'

Solly moved towards the girl and swung her up into his arms. As he did so her shoulder bag hit the side of his head. 'Don't you dare scream,' he said menacingly, 'else I'll drop you outside on the cold frosty pavement!'

Goldie could see Rene's hand close over her mouth to stop her laughing as Solly strode out of the door and down the corridor with the wriggling girl in his arms.

'Thanks for everything,' said Goldie. 'I don't have to beg you not to tell Fred . . .'

'He'll go mad when he comes back and finds her missing, but he'll get no joy from me.'

Goldie saw the sudden fear on Rene's face. 'Look, if things get really bad, I work at Priddy's Armament Factory.

Come to me, promise?' She didn't have to ask Rene not to breathe a word about her workplace to Fred; she knew she'd keep the secret. Rene had fresh tears in her eyes as she hugged first Goldie then Gladys.

'I know you'll take care of her,' she said. 'She's a good girl really.'

When Gladys and Goldie reached the car, Solly was standing on the pavement with his arms tight about Doll.

'I had to wait for you; if I let her go she'll run—'

'No I won't,' piped up Doll.

'What do you mean?' Solly demanded, looking down at her.

'I only said I wouldn't come because I wanted to see what else you'd bribe me with.' She stood in the cold, laughing now at their amazed faces.

Gladys took a step forward. 'You little . . .' Goldie grabbed her, in case Gladys lashed out at the girl.

'C'mon, open this door, I'm getting cold,' Doll demanded.

Solly opened the front passenger door, and Doll immediately slid into the front seat. 'You two can sit in the back,' she said.

'Cheeky little madam,' said Gladys, opening the rear door. Then she asked, 'Do you want to go home to pick up clothes?'

'No. I never want to see that rubbish again,' She pushed

her sleeve back and showed them her gold watch. 'This is worth a bit.' Then she said, 'And these,' and swept back her long dark hair to show gold drop earrings. Around her neck was a gold chain with a pearl at her throat. 'I can sell it all and buy new.'

'Blimey, I hope that lot's not stolen.' Gladys looked more closely at the watch. 'Worth a bit, that.'

'Course it's not stolen, I picked all these things out in the shops.'

Goldie raised her eyes heavenwards as though to say, 'We've got a live one here.'

Doll gazed out of the windows, watching everything they passed. But there was silence in the car as Solly drove back to Gosport.

# Chapter Twelve

'It's not very big, is it?'

'It's big enough,' Gladys was beginning to think she had a problem on her hands with Doll. Now here she was, grumbling about the size of Gladys's house.

For a moment Gladys almost wished she had stayed silent, like she'd been in the car.

'I'm only saying . . .' the girl said. Gladys raised her eyes heavenwards before she pulled out the string from the letter box and opened the front door.

'I'm going home, if you don't need me?' said Solly. 'I have to return the car and I'm on early shift tomorrow.'

'Oh, don't you live here?' Doll looked at him expectantly.

'No, he doesn't,' snapped Gladys. She turned to Solly. 'Thanks, lad. I'm so glad you came with us.' She stepped aside and Goldie pulled Doll inside the house while Solly sat in the car. Gladys waved until the vehicle disappeared.

'He's a nice lad,' Gladys said, taking off her coat and throwing it over the back of a chair. 'I've not met your Jamie, but it's clear to me Solly thinks the world of you, Goldie.' Mogs was curled up asleep on the chair beneath the window.

'I like him, but that's as far as it goes. I intend to marry my Jamie when he comes home.'

'Is he as good-looking as Solly?'

Gladys looked at Doll. 'Looks don't come into it when you fall in love,' she said. She went into the front room. Goldie had put the kettle on in the scullery and Doll was wandering about picking up ornaments, then setting them back down again.

Gladys, upstairs now, had collected bedding for the sofa bed downstairs. She came down with her arms full of blankets and advanced upon Doll. 'Take this and make up your bed in the front room.'

Doll stood there with her arms full, amazement on her face.

'Go on, else you'll be sleeping on the floor.' Gladys gave her a push.

'Don't you do all that?' Doll asked.

Goldie, coming in from the scullery with a tray in her hands, looked at Gladys whose mouth had dropped open.

'This ain't a bleeding hotel!'

'I don't make up beds.' Doll said. 'Jean came in every day and did all that.'

'Well, I ain't got no Jean, so in this house you make your own bed.'

'C'mon, I'll show you,' said Goldie. She'd put the tray on the table.

'No!' Goldie jumped as Gladys shouted. 'We're not waiting on her. She's got to learn.'

Goldie stood aside while Doll pushed past her and went down the passage towards the front room, her face like thunder. Bedding trailed along the floor.

'Don't you think you're being a bit hard on the girl?'

'No. She's already shown us she can be a conniving little thing.'

'True,' said Goldie and went back into the scullery for the teapot.

Gladys poked the fire in the grate and soon the small room was warm.

'Wait till she finds out she's got to get a job.'

Goldie looked at Gladys and smiled. 'I'll enjoy hearing what she's got to say about that!' She put the cups and saucers on the table. 'I thought she was going to dance at the Rainbow? Won't that be her job?'

'Not all the time. Will most likely'll give her a few evenings, but I doubt if her wages will cover her keep and necessities. I could get her in at Priddy's . . .'

'She's underage.'

'She's cleverer than a lot of the women working there, Goldie. The little minx has already shown us that. I'll vouch for her. Anyway, as you know, there's quite a few underage youngsters working in factories, and Scrivenor'll take her if he thinks she's seventeen. We need as many able-bodied, sensible workers as we can get to win this war against that damn Hitler.'

'She'll need clothes,' Goldie said quickly. 'She can't wear what she's got on forever.' Thoughtfully, she added, 'She's a pretty little thing; what with those bee-stung lips and wide eyes she looks just like a doll, doesn't she?'

Gladys nodded and poured out tea. 'You'll have to sort her out, you're more her size than I am.' She pushed a cuppa over to Goldie. Both Goldie and Doll were slimmer and taller than Gladys.

'I'll see what I can do. But most of my stuff is your cast-offs. Remember, I turned up here without a stitch to my back as well?'

Gladys was thoughtful as she poured in milk. 'We'll have to take her shopping, then. She reckons on selling her gold jewellery. She won't get much for it. It's food people want, not jewellery. Besides, she should keep what's hers. Has she got her ration book and her medical card?'

Most women kept those documents in their handbags as much for information purposes as for safety. Identification was important if you got caught in an air raid. Gladys said, 'We'll find out when she comes back.'

After a while, as the two women sat drinking their tea and chatting, Doll appeared. Gladys wanted to go and see what her bed-making skills were like, but instead she asked, 'Want a cuppa, love?'

'Don't worry, I'll pour it,' said Doll, rattling a cup and saucer. 'I guess you won't wait on me.'

'Cheeky madam,' laughed Gladys. She was warming to the girl. 'Have you got your ration book and your medical card?'

'Of course, they're in my bag.' She looked at Gladys as if she was daft. 'Don't you know you should always carry those things with you?'

Gladys sighed. 'We're supposed to carry gas masks, but we don't.'

'My brother will knock Rene about for letting me go,' Doll said. 'I don't feel at all happy about that.'

'I think she'll be able to look after herself,' said Goldie.

'You don't know what he's like,' said the girl. 'But I'm not going back, not ever. D'you know this is one of the first conversations I've ever had outside of the club or school?'

Gladys looked at Goldie. Surely that's not possible, she

thought. Could Fred really be that possessive? Suddenly, the girl looked ready to cry.

'He'll come after me.'

Gladys remembered how terrified Goldie had been that Fred would discover her whereabouts.

'He's got to find you first,' she said.

Goldie got up from the table. 'I'm going to do the sarnies for work tomorrow.' She looked at Doll. 'We work at the armament factory. If you're going to live here, you'll need to work an' all.' She looked meaningfully at Gladys. 'She'll help all she can.'

Gladys nodded. 'Tomorrow both of us finish early, so we should be home by three in the afternoon.' She paused. 'If you like, we'll go shopping and see what we can find to rig you out. We'll also go down the Rainbow and see about you dancing, like we promised.' She'd hardly got the last word out before she was almost knocked from the chair as the girl jumped up and threw her arms around her, shouting, 'Thank you, thank you!'

*Hello darling,*

*It's been raining heavily all day. Will probably continue all night and we only just had time to erect bivvies before the wind started.*

*Our blankets are wet, so are our clothes. Feel very fed up, very cold. I tried to dry my clothes in the air outlet from the tank. When* the engine is running the air is hot. Got two letters from you so very happy.

There are rumours we are to attack Le Havre. Officers have gone on ahead, so rumours could be true.

<u>Later.</u>

Our planes dropped their bombs in quick succession. It was a truly terrible sight. Dense smoke, the smell of burning and cordite almost choking us. We were about 2,000 yards from the port. We found out later that 5,000 tons of bombs had been dropped, most of them from Lancasters.

The sky was aglow with flashes and searchlights that cut through the darkness with their beams. There were heavy explosions from the harbour. Battleships were also shelling the port.

The enemy spilled from the woods, where they had been hiding. Later people began running about, whether to hide or to go back to their houses was unclear. Le Havre has been liberated.

Heard from Dad. Uncle Billy has left for Kent. I'm so happy you like the idea of living near the South Parade Pier. Dad has paid the deposit, says it's a pre-wedding present. Imagine, a house of our own! I love you so much.

Always,

Your Jamie


'Somebody here knows something he's not telling me.' Will banged his hand down on the desk, causing papers to jump off and onto the floor. A whisky glass toppled and smashed.

A small man with a hunched back leapt up to pick up the debris.

'Leave it, Dodson! That's not important. What is, is one of you is a fuckin' Judas!' His eyes narrowed. The minion picking up the shattered glass dropped it again, as a red bloom blossomed on his hand.

Will stared at the men around him. Trust, he thought, his trust in these men had been violated. One of them had informed on him to the people responsible for stealing the property he had brought back from Tangier. The tobacco, cigarettes, sweets, preserves and tinned salmon had been taken from the liner used as a troopship bringing back injured men. Stolen from under his nose.

He himself had sailed around the coast to Southampton Water and boarded the *Princess Leonie* at the docks. He'd checked that his goods were packed safely in the hold. He'd paid off the skipper and wished the injured soldiers farewell and good luck, as they departed for the next step of their journey to Netley. The Royal Victoria Hospital wasn't simply a hospital, but also a training depot for nurses and doctors. On the coast, in sumptuous grounds, the injured would be given the best possible attention.

He'd stood and watched the brave souls being stretchered

off. Some were calm, some even chatty. Some poor buggers didn't know what day it was. When his shattered knee had been fixed, he thanked God that the powers that be insisted his days in the air force were over. He missed the camaraderie and he was glad he'd done his bit for England, but he was happy the forces would no longer have him.

His goods had disappeared by the time he went to supervise unloading at the boatyard in Gosport's Ferrol Road. Incredible, but true. Overnight he'd lost so much money he didn't want to think about it. One or more of his men were reneging on their loyalty to him. What could he do about it? Not one of the men in this room knew anything, or so they said. They all looked at one another with suspicion.

Will knew the only way to find out who was deceiving him was to stay with his load from the time the troopship landed in England, to the time he himself unloaded the stock.

He began to form a plan in his mind. He would say nothing to anyone. And when he discovered the perpetrators, they'd wish they'd never been born. For discover them he would.

'Close this time,' Fred said, clapping Rene on the shoulder. 'But the goods are in my lock-up . . .'

'I don't know why you don't buy the stuff yourself and do exactly what that blasted gangster does. Bring it in by water.

The goods can't cost all that much; everyone knows with income tax English goods cost more, but the same stuff brought from the country of origin is cheaper.'

'Costs me bugger all to steal the stuff.'

Rene looked at him. She knew she was sailing close to the wind, telling Fred what to do. Any minute now he'd lash out at her. She pulled her thin dressing gown around her. She was dreading the moment when he asked about Doll.

It was three o'clock in the morning, her so-called dressing room was freezing and she was worn out with worry. Oh, she guessed the girl was being well looked after; after all, it was her stepsister she'd gone off with, and that woman Gladys seemed a good sort.

'How much money did we make tonight?' Fred picked up the cash box.

'Not enough. Punters don't want to come out in the cold.' She heard him shake the box that she knew contained very little after she'd paid off the girls, the band and the cleaners. She heard him swear. It wasn't her fault, but Fred would make out it was. He put his hand back on her shoulder. His fingers dug in, hurting her.

'You been slipping some in your handbag?'

'Don't be silly.' She tried to make light of his words. Her handbag was on the dressing table. He left her side to pick it up and empty the contents over the tabletop, and most of her make-up rolled on the floor. 'Look what you've done,' she said. 'Only gone and broken my new lipstick.'

'I'll break your neck if I ever find you stealing from me,' he said. 'Pick up that rubbish.'

Rene scrabbled on the floor, stuffing her compact, comb and other treasures back in her bag.

'Where's Doll?'

It had come. The question she feared.

'She's gone.'

'I can see that, you cow. Where is she?' He was expecting her to say Doll had gone home.

Rene took a deep breath. She'd practised what she was going to tell him. 'She's run off.'

He turned and stared at her. 'What do you mean, "run off?"'

'I don't know where she is. When I came off after my turn, she was gone.'

His slate-grey eyes had narrowed. 'Gone where?'

'Don't know. I looked everywhere, all over the place, even out on the streets.'

'She wouldn't simply go of her own accord.'

'Well, she did. Maybe she went home.'

'She's not allowed out on her own.'

His fist connected with the side of her face and almost took her off her feet with its force. She wondered why she hadn't gone with Doll, or at least done a runner. After all, she knew he would hit her. But she thought that after the initial shock of realizing Doll wasn't coming back, Fred would turn to her. Maybe he'd even confess he loved her . . .

The second blow made her stagger backwards.

Her high heels twisted and her balance failed her as she fell. There was a sudden sharp pain as the corner of the dressing table bit into her skull. Then the pain stopped almost as suddenly as it had started. She felt like she had after drinking too much gin: befuddled, slow.

'Get up,' Fred was saying. But her limbs had turned to jelly.

He was bending over her, looking at his fingers that had touched her head. She saw the brightness of the blood on his hand. And she saw something else: tears in his eyes. Then his voice, but far away, 'Rene, I didn't mean it. Rene – speak to me.'

As she stared at him, the man she had loved for a long, long time allowed a tear to escape and fall on her cheek. A burst of happiness bloomed inside her as she heard him telling her he loved her. And then the darkness came down.

# Chapter Thirteen

'Rommel's dead! And guess what? He took poison because Hitler said if he committed suicide he'd make sure he had a hero's funeral. Hitler found out that Rommel knew of the plot to kill him.' Solly was buzzing with the news. 'The Nazis said Rommel died from injuries after his car was attacked by our bombers. All the lies are coming out . . .'

'I just wish this war was over,' said Gladys, her arm tucked through Solly's. She was almost running to keep up with his long-legged strides, terrified of slipping on the ice. She was feeling a bit off today.

'Wait for us. Solly, slow down,' Goldie demanded as despite holding onto his other arm, her feet slipped and he had to grab her to stop her falling.

'I want to get home, then washed and changed and out down the pub,' he said. 'What's the use of having a half-day if you don't spend it wisely?'

'We promised to take Doll shopping. Though Lord knows what we'll be able to buy her; there's nothing around worth wearing and what there is costs the earth.'

The sky was grey with unshed snow and the pavements slippery with frost that didn't seem to want to budge. The rain that had fallen overnight had frozen before it had soaked away. Gladys couldn't wait to get home in the warm.

'Have you sorted out a job for her, Gladys?' Solly asked.

'Yes, I had a long talk with Scrivenor this morning. We still need workers, especially now our troops and allies are pushing forward through France . . .'

'Don't forget we've landed in Greece,' butted in Goldie. 'On the news it said twenty million people are homeless, due to our bombing.'

'Well, they shouldn't have started the blasted war,' said Gladys.

'I'll love and leave you now,' said Solly when they reached Alma Street. He disentangled himself from them.

He strode on ahead and Gladys and Goldie walked carefully up the street to number fourteen.

'A nice cup of tea wouldn't go amiss,' said Gladys. 'I hope she's got the kettle on.' She pulled the string through the letter box and opened the door.

'It's a bit parky in here,' said Goldie. She hung her coat on the nail just inside the front door.

'I can't hear anything.' Gladys's coat joined Goldie's and she walked along the passage into the kitchen. 'She's let the range go out.'

Goldie went through to the scullery and lit the gas. In the sink and on the draining board were all the cups and plates, unwashed from the night before.

'Little bugger could have done the washing-up,' she said.

Gladys poked her head around the door. 'Fancy her going out and leaving that lot. You'd have thought she'd have pulled her weight a bit; she's not even tidied up.'

'To be honest, I thought she might have got a bit of something for us to eat before we went out to get her some clothes to wear.'

Gladys clumped up the stairs. 'Everything's just as we left it,' she shouted, noting the unmade beds before she descended again. She walked back along the passage and opened the front-room door.

'Goldie, get in here,' she yelled. Goldie came running.

'Hello,' said Doll. She peeked sleepily over the top of the sheet and stared at Goldie and Gladys.

Gladys saw that Goldie's mouth was open until she gulped and said, 'You've been in bed all morning?'

Doll yawned. 'You woke me up,' she said accusingly.

Gladys launched herself at Doll, arms flailing. 'Get up, you lazy little so-and-so! This ain't no hotel! We been out working an' you been lying in bed! You could at least have made us a cuppa.'

Goldie grabbed hold of Gladys. 'Stop it! She don't know any better.'

Doll had leapt out of bed and was shivering in the corner of the room. 'What have I done wrong?' Her eyes were full of tears.

Goldie said, 'You've got to pull your weight.'

'But nobody told me . . .'

'You shouldn't need telling.' Gladys advanced on the girl again, but Goldie held her back.

'Get dressed,' she said. On the bottom of the sofa bed was a pile of clothes. A pair of trousers with wide legs, a pink jumper that was too tight on Goldie, and Doll's own underwear that Gladys had dried overnight for her on the fireguard. 'Come on,' Goldie said to Gladys, pulling her from the room. 'I think we all need a cup of tea.'

'Does this mean you won't take me shopping?'

Goldie had to restrain Gladys from marching back into the front room.

Fred rolled the body in the piece of carpet, then left the dressing room, locked the door and went in search of Doll. Diligently, he looked in every room backstage: the kitchen, the outside lavatories, the gaming room and the scruffy rooms used by the girls to bed men. Doll wasn't in the Blue.

Doll's school coat was on the back of his office door. He took it off the hook and buried his face in the cloth, eager for the scent of her. If Doll had gone home by taxi, surely she'd have worn her coat? To have left it hanging behind the door meant that she had no intention of ever wearing it again. He collapsed onto the chair behind his desk and, ignoring the pile of unopened letters that he knew were bills, he started to cry. It was true, then, she'd gone.

He'd lost his beloved Doll and he'd killed the only person who truly cared about him.

Time after time, Rene had wanted nothing from him except a kind word, a kiss or a smile, and he'd ignored her, her feelings and her attempts to show him she cared. What had he given her for standing by him? Nothing. She had put her freedom on the line by helping him steal from punters and jewellers. And what had he done for her? He'd ended her life, as though snuffing out a candle.

And now Doll had left him.

He threw the coat across the room.

Perhaps it was a joke? Maybe when he got home his sister would be fast asleep in bed? Yes, he persuaded himself that Doll had gone home after all. She'd got tired of waiting for him in the cold empty club and left Rene to tell him she'd gone. Hope rose in his heart.

He remembered the day Doll had been born as if it was yesterday.

His mother, drunk as usual, had gone into labour and he'd come home from school and found her writhing around in agony on the kitchen floor. He'd wanted to fetch a neighbour, but she'd screamed at him not to leave her. His father wasn't due home, he was at sea, and Fred had been scared stiff by the screams of pain coming from her. She gripped his schoolboy hand so hard she'd made his flesh bleed. Even today the line of curved scars from her fingernails showed on his skin.

After what seemed an eternity of her grunting and yelling and swearing, she called out, 'It's coming!'

And a head appeared, followed by shoulders, all covered in a white wax-like substance that made him want to throw up. Then out she slid, into his boy's hands. A little girl who began crying, still attached to her mother by a curious wrinkled cord. He'd looked at it distastefully.

'You have to cut it!'

Horrified, he found the scissors and cut through the skin and gristle, leaving a short length as his mother decreed. There were no bandages in the house. He covered the cord with three plasters, stood back and surveyed the little girl.

Tiny fists ready to punch the world into shape, quivering and shaking. Fred knew he loved that baby more than anything or anyone else in the whole wide world.

'That's Dorothy,' said his mother. 'After my mother.'

Fred thought she looked like a tiny doll. So Doll she was.

He bathed her and put her in a drawer lined with a piece of blanket. Then he took the newspaper-wrapped bundle of bloodied stuff out to the garden and buried it, just as his mother dictated.

He made tea while the child slept. Every so often he returned to the drawer to make sure she wasn't a dream.

At nine years old, Fred was already Doll's willing slave. He decided he would love her, guide her and never let her out of his sight.

But now she had disappeared.

Fred carried the carpet bundle down to the pickup lorry that was garaged at the rear of the Blue and put it in the back. His MTB was moored at Eastney. The boatyard was locked, but boat owners held keys.

The night, or what was left of it, was misty and cold. He walked up the gangway between the moored boats, carrying the carpet bundle. The moon was the only light and he was glad of it, as frost had turned to ice and underfoot was treacherous. Shackles swung noisily in the breeze. He liked the sounds boats made with the waves lapping their sides as they bounced against the buoys.

He was surprised that Rene weighed so little.

He put her down so that he could unlock the latch that secured the cabin and then, still using the moon as light, he carried his bundle into the boat's interior.

The double diagonal teak flooring had been recently varnished. The boat was old but serviceable and he kept it in shape as best he could. It was a fast boat with a low noise threshold. It had been a debt repayment and he had at one time thought he could make it into a houseboat, after he had stripped out the interior. That hadn't happened because the boat had become operational in securing stolen goods.

Fred untied the boat and steered her out from the moorings. He cruised slowly into the sea between the Isle of Wight and Portsmouth. Red and green lights showed him the correct channel to navigate and it wasn't long before he was off the shores of Warsash. He halted by a marker and tied his vessel to the floating buoy.

Then he hoisted the roll of carpet and attached it to the base of the buoy with rope. He knew the body wouldn't be seen from the shore and other boats sailing by wouldn't give the marker a second glance. He was banking on the carpet's weight keeping the corpse below the surface of the sea and marine creatures eating away at her flesh. He hadn't liked the idea of simply dumping the body at sea; who knows where it might have washed up?

With the corpse taken care of, Fred sailed back to Eastney. When he returned to his car he realized his face was wet with tears.

It was early in the morning when he arrived at the empty house.

He searched every room.

Doll had taken nothing. She must have had help, for it wasn't something she'd do of her own volition.

He sat down in an armchair and drank a shot of whisky, trying to make sense of how, in one night, he could have lost the only two people he had ever really cared about.

When the weak winter morning sun rose he was still sitting there, but the bottle was empty. As empty as he felt.

Even the baggy trousers didn't disguise the legwork as Doll danced on the stage of the Rainbow.

'What did I tell you? She's good, she's a natural.' Gladys looked into Will's eyes and felt as though she was being pulled down into a dark sea that would swallow her whole.

He smiled. 'You're right, the girl can dance. Her body expresses her feelings. She has a freshness about her that makes the suggestive movements of my so-called exotic dancers look dated and common.' He paused. 'What I'm worried about is her age. She's a bit young to be in this environment.'

'She's seventeen.' Gladys crossed her fingers behind her back. 'She wants to dance, she can dance. What's the problem?'

'Can she handle the blokes?'

Gladys didn't want to get into telling him that she was well used to blokes shouting suggestively and had the ability to close her ears and dance as if their taunts meant nothing. Doll had been dancing in one of the roughest clubs in Portsmouth; Gladys felt sure she'd be safer at the Rainbow.

'Why? Do you let your girls get accosted by thugs?'

Will smiled. 'No. This is a good establishment.'

'What if I said she'd be collected after work the nights she was on stage?'

He thought for a while then nodded. 'Done. Three nights a week, with the possibility of more if the punters like her.'

'Will I do?' Doll strolled over to the bar and put her arm through Gladys's. Beads of sweat shone on her forehead.

'You'll do,' Will said, then pointing to the twins who were seated at a table playing Snakes and Ladders, 'Go and chat to them for a while. I need to talk to your aunt.'

Doll stared at him, frowned but then sauntered over to the dark-haired boys.

So, thought Gladys, Will thought she was Doll's aunt. It wasn't the time or place to tell him otherwise; she'd do that later. She'd kept her promise to the girl and got her a job where she could wear pretty clothes and dance. Sure, she'd jumped the gun, but she knew as soon as Will saw what the girl could do, he'd hire her.

'Another thing,' Gladys began. 'Nothing too revealing for her costume, but something glittery. She likes sequins.'

Will had walked to the back of the bar and was pouring a gin and orange she suspected was for her. She was pleased he'd remembered her drink.

'Of course not.' He returned to the booth and pushed the drink towards her. The main bar had recently been cleaned and she could smell polish.

'Are you married, Gladys?' She shook her head.

'Are you with anyone?' Again, she shook her head. In her mind, being with someone meant living and sleeping with them. She dismissed Siddy. 'Look, Gladys, I wanted to speak to you a few weeks back but I was interrupted by work matters.'

Gladys couldn't help herself. 'Why me?'

'I don't know, there's something about you that makes a man feel . . .' he paused, 'comfortable, like he could really confide in you.'

That wasn't what she wanted to hear, especially when a pert young blonde in a tight skirt wiggled her way over to their table to empty the ashtray.

'Surely you'd feel happier talking to a younger woman?' Gladys glared at the blonde, who in tipping out the fag ends had accidentally on purpose let some ash fall into Gladys's lap.

'Oh, I'm sorry.' She didn't look at all sorry. Gladys smiled sweetly at her.

'It's all right, dear, accidents happen when you're not used to a job.'

She brushed the ash away. The girl glared and stomped off. Gladys saw that Will was smothering a laugh.

'See what I mean?' he said. 'Nothing fazes you.'

She looked at Will. 'The fact is, I'm at least . . . er, five years older than most of your pretty little things.' She was well over ten years older, but she wasn't about to tell him that, was she? 'I've been around the block once or twice – ' and all the other times, she thought, 'but I'm not sure I'm the best woman for you.'

'But that's exactly it, Gladys. You're a woman, not a girl.'

She stared at him. He ran well-manicured fingers through his dark curls and she took a deep breath of his masculine cologne. She could imagine herself in bed with him, wearing a virginal white satin nightdress. She wouldn't be naked, oh no, for she'd like to disguise the lumps and bumps that had appeared with age. With the covers over them he'd not notice the tiny thread veins that had suddenly arrived on her puffy ankles, nor the way her upper arms had developed flesh that sagged. In bed, them silly giggly girls wouldn't hold a candle to what she could do to make Will enjoy himself.

She took a deep breath and his cologne seemed to choke her as she was brought quickly back from her musings by a feeling of sickness and a churning in her insides. She rose hastily from the table, calling as she did so, 'Doll, come with me, quickly now!'

Doll came running. Gladys grabbed her handbag and darted a glance at Will, who looked very disconcerted at this turn of events.

'I must leave . . .' She put her hand to her mouth. The back of her neck felt clammy as she hastily made for the exit.

She didn't bother to turn around for she guessed he was watching her still, with a look of amazement on his handsome face as she half ran, half stumbled out of the club's door.

When she reached the alley opposite Woolworths she turned into it with Doll close on her heels.

She vomited into the drain. Doll pulled back her hair so she wouldn't be sick over it and after a while Gladys breathed deeply, put her hand to her head and said, 'I feel better now. Imagine what a fool I'd have looked being sick all over that lovely man.'

Doll stared at her, a look of curiosity on her face, then, 'There's a number three bus just about to leave,' she said, putting her arm around Gladys's shoulder. 'Let's get you home.'

## Chapter Fourteen

'I think it was that bit of Dutch eel I ate from the Devonia Fish shop,' said Gladys. 'Though I swear that place does the best fish and chips in Gosport.'

'Well, you're better now and that's what matters.' Goldie had been rifling through the bags of clothes that Gladys had bought for Doll. 'Ooh, this is lovely.'

She held up a blue dress with box pleats and a sweetheart neckline. 'This must have cost a fortune.'

Gladys shrugged. 'Actually, no. It's a tiny size and Fleure's had had it on their rail for ages. The manageress was glad to see the back of it. She had some other small sizes out the back and did me a good deal. I got Doll some slacks to wear to work – though she's fallen in love with the ones you lent her. I also got her a couple of woollies. You know she had no idea what size she was? She said Fred did all the buying of her clothes. She was like a little kid in a toyshop when I said she could choose between them dresses.' Gladys pointed to two other warm frocks hanging over the back of a kitchen chair. 'She couldn't make up her mind, so I had to buy them both, didn't I? Mind you, I couldn't get her new shoes. For one thing they was too dear, and another is she's only got little feet. Talk about Doll by name and Doll by nature.'

'Well, she can't keep my best ones.' Goldie was quite huffy. Gladys knew Goldie had never wanted the girl to borrow her shoes. They'd cost a lot of money and had very high heels, higher than the wartime regulation height of two inches.

'No, Goldie, but she couldn't go out in the cold in them ballet slipper things she had on, could she?'

'So, what's she got?'

Gladys delved into a brown carrier bag and pulled out a pair of slip-on high heels, all white sequins. 'Before you say anything, these were in a second-hand shop. She fell in love with them. I know they're ridiculous, but she's never had anything that she's chosen for herself, so I bought them. And these.' She pulled out a pair of brown shoes with small heels. One shoe was a slightly different colour to the other. 'They'd been on show in the window and the sun has faded one.' Goldie looked at it, then back at Gladys.

'I suppose these were cheap as well?'

Gladys nodded. 'The girl in the shop reckons a bit of brown Cherry Blossom and they'll both be the same colour in next to no time.'

'Didn't Doll think to pawn some of that gold she's wearing to help you pay for the stuff?'

'Don't be like that, love. So she's got some pretty trinkets. Let her keep them. She'll pay me back.'

Goldie sniffed and looked around. 'And where is the little madam?'

'She's at Priddy's.' Gladys began to put the clothes back in the carrier bags. 'I asked Scrivenor about a job for her and he wanted to see her first.'

'Is that wise? She's likely to give him some lip.'

'I don't think she will. She seemed overjoyed at being allowed to go to the munitions yard on her own. You got to remember, this is all new to her.'

Goldie sniffed again and went out to the scullery. Gladys heard the pop of the gas as it was lit beneath the kettle. A cuppa was just what she wanted. She heard the rustle of the carrier bag and saw Mogs's tail disappearing to sleep on the shoes inside. Ah well, she thought, he won't hurt them.

The screaming of Moaning Minnie startled her.

'I thought we were nearly done with the raids,' Gladys yelled. The piercing sound of the siren cut deep into the early evening.

'Bugger it, I'm making a flask even if it kills me,' shouted Goldie.

Gladys picked up the carrier bag containing the shoes and cat and stuffed them into the Morrison shelter, shutting the door so the cat would be safe inside and couldn't escape.

'Doll's going to be out in this lot, she'll be scared stiff!'

'She'll get in a shelter,' yelled Goldie. 'She's not stupid.'

'She'll be scared,' repeated Gladys. 'I'm going to look for her. She should be on her way home by now.'

'Don't be silly. It's too dangerous for you to go outside, get in the Morrison.'

'Turn off the utilities,' cried Gladys, taking no notice of Goldie's warning and grabbing her coat from the back of the chair, dashing down the hallway and opening the front door, then running out into the crowd of people hurrying towards the public shelter.

As she dodged through the people, she thought about Doll. At first the girl had been horrified about working with so many other women. Doll had flatly refused to work at Priddy's and had got quite heated about it. In the night Gladys had heard her wandering about downstairs because, like Gladys, she couldn't sleep. But Gladys didn't go to her.

In the morning Doll was a changed person.

'I'm sorry, I can't expect you to keep me for nothing. If you've asked the manager about a job for me, I'll do it. We can come to some arrangement about me paying rent, and I'll be able to pay you back for the clothes.'

'What made you change your mind, missy?'

'You did. But I'm not used to working. I just left school and Fred didn't want me to mix with other girls my own age. He bought stuff when I needed it. But everything was of his choosing. Old-fashioned stuff like what you'd wear—'

Gladys coughed. Doll tried to make good what she'd said. 'I mean, he wouldn't buy me any of that – new, what do they call it? Teenage stuff – like they wear in the American films. I wanted a pair of jeans so I could roll the bottoms up, but he wouldn't let me have them.'

'Why don't we see if we can get hold of a pair with your first wage packet?'

Gladys's answer was a hug that nearly threw her off her feet. 'There's something else I'd like to ask you,' Doll said shyly.

Gladys looked at her expectantly.

'Fred wouldn't let me wear make-up. I'd really like to put on some lipstick and a bit of mascara . . .'

'Oh love, at your age I was piling it on.' Gladys stopped talking and looked at her. 'I don't think you ought to do that, it gives the blokes the wrong idea, and I speak from experience.' She put her fingers beneath Doll's chin and tipped her face up. After a while she said, 'Cherry lipstick, don't plaster it on. Black mascara, yes, plaster that on. Pond's cream every night. Make sure you wash off every scrap of make-up before you puts the Pond's cream on.' She fingered Doll's dark hair, which was in an untidy long bob with a straggly fringe. In a moment of madness, Gladys sat Doll down and trimmed her hair so the ends were neat and her fringe straight. Then she searched in her drawstring make-up bag, neatly outlined her lips in a coral red colour and told her to look in the mirror.

'I'm transformed!'

Doll by name, doll by nature. Gladys knew she'd made the pretty duckling into a beautiful swan. She felt immensely proud of herself. The girl was overjoyed.

'Can I keep the lipstick?'

'Sorry, love, we'll have to share it. Lipsticks are like gold dust.'

She felt she was making headway with Doll until she went into the scullery and saw the big bowl of wet washing that had stood there not only all night, but half the day as well. The sheets and wet clothing smelled fusty.

'I thought I asked you to put this stuff through the mangle?'

Doll didn't even bother to look shamefaced. The huge monstrosity stood outside on the concrete path. 'I forgot,' said Doll.

'It all stinks where the stuff's been lying in its own water! It needs to be washed again. It can't be dried in that condition.' Gladys was angry.

'I'm sorry,' said Doll at last.

'Well, we'll see how sorry you are, you can wash it through again.'

Gladys had stomped off upstairs. She was furious with Doll and with herself, for letting her temper get the better of her.

But that was then and this was now. Now the silly girl was out in this lot and could get herself killed.

Gladys reckoned Doll would have left Priddy's and should be on her way home, somewhere between Weevil Lane and the Criterion picture house.

RAF planes were flying overhead. The steady roar of their engines made her ears ache. There were searchlights making paths through the dusky sky and it was so noisy she tried to run with her hands over her ears.

Suddenly, there was a sucking sound, a sensation that took her breath away. Then a huge explosion, followed by the roar of motors catching up with the rocket that had landed.

There was screaming coming from people still out on Forton Road. It was one of those pilotless newfangled planes, she thought. The ones that went faster than the speed of sound, though how they could manage that, Gladys had no idea. Then, through the dust of a huge smoke cloud and the debris flying, she saw a man lifted off his feet and flung like a rag doll into the hedges at the side of St Vincent Naval Training Barracks. Another man ran towards him and bent down. Gladys saw him look at the broken body, then move away to be violently sick against the buckled iron railings.

A huge crater had appeared ahead that must be about sixty feet wide, she thought. These bombs were the new V2s. Scrivenor had got his workers together and told them about the 46-foot-long monsters that had fully loaded warheads. He told them all that Hitler was trying to knock out anything and everything in the coastal path along the south of England. Hitler was convinced it was where our munitions yards lay, together with our shipyards and factories.

Fear for Doll's safety was making Gladys feel crazy. The tears were rolling down her face as she skirted around the still-smoking crater, which must have been at least sixteen feet deep. A dead and mutilated dog lay by the side of what was left of the main road.

And then, through the noise, she thought she heard her name being called. Gladys stopped moving and stared about her through the stinking air that made her eyes feel as though they were filled with grit.

'Gladys.'

She hadn't been mistaken.

Sitting in a shop doorway was Doll. Both she and the grocer's shop were miraculously unscathed. Doll jumped to her feet and ran into Gladys's arms. Gladys breathed a sigh of relief to feel the thin body pressed against her own.

'You came to find me, you came to find me . . .'

Gladys pushed her away, holding her at arm's length to check Doll was indeed all right. Satisfied the girl was unharmed, she pulled her back again into an embrace.

A strange vibration started up. What appeared to be a long thin plane on fire above the rooftops was heading towards them.

'Oh, bugger, here comes another doodlebug,' said Gladys.

Both of them hurled themselves back into the shop's doorway.

'I don't want to die,' wailed Doll.

'I don't want you to die either,' shouted Gladys as she leaned across Doll, shielding her as best she could. 'You ain't sorted out that smelly washing yet!'

*Hello my love,*

*We have three prisoners! We found a Jerry hiding in a foxhole. He's our first prisoner. Civilians have been standing outside farms and houses waving white flags. Some are children. Very dangerous, considering the Jerries are everywhere and the fighting is pretty bad. We've done a good job of reconnaissance, the colonel congratulated* us. We've killed many Germans. We caught two of them very eager to surrender. They were running after our tank! The commander thought it extremely funny. Tonight, I managed to speak with the three prisoners. They assured us many of them wanted to surrender, but they daren't because their officers threatened to shoot them. Some of the Germans hung back waiting for our tanks so they had an excuse to surrender. They told us there is a great deal of friction between the SS and the German army. They believe Hitler is leading them to disaster. The army is apparently involved in plots to get rid of Hitler. The three prisoners are chatty. Two are married with children, one is only a boy. Eli found him crying.

Our house is being painted! Dad got hold of some white paint and has started painting the kitchen. He says it will be nice and clean for when we move in. He spends a lot of time fixing it up. I think he likes to escape from Mum and her tales of what's going on at the WI.

I think of you all the time and kiss your photograph both night and morning.

I miss you so much.

Your Jamie

X

# Chapter Fifteen

'Send a tray of drinks over to that table, Chris.' Will waved his arm in the direction of his mate Mac MacKenzie, who was surrounded by women and a younger, blond man. A stranger to Will, though he supposed he was a friend of Gladys's, perhaps a workmate. 'Tell them it's with my compliments.' There was an older man sitting next to Gladys. He didn't look as though he was enjoying the evening at the Rainbow, but there was no denying his affection for Gladys – he couldn't keep his eyes off her.

The waitress in her silvery outfit gave Will a dazzling smile and went to do his bidding. He watched Chris's pert arse as she wiggled away in her high heels and he smiled. There was no denying the young women who worked for him were every man's fantasy.

The club was full to bursting and most customers had complied with his partywear dress code. Coloured hats sat on grizzled heads. Flashy ties were combined with dark suits, but the women had excelled themselves. The war had left the country with little, but the frocks dazzled and the dance floor was ablaze with colour.

'Chris,' he called. The girl turned. 'Replenish the buffet table; get Carol to help you.' She gave him another warm smile, lifted the flap set in the bar and disappeared into the kitchen to find Carol and the chef.

For a few moments, he stood happily admiring his kingdom.

His mate Mac was a lucky dog. That Marlene was a stunner with her cascade of autumn-red hair. They seemed so happy together, living in that tumbledown house of Mac's that he was forever fixing up. Marlene had a little girl, the apple of his friend's eye. You only had to mention the child and Mac would dive into his wallet to bring out photos.

The young girl, Doll, who danced at his club, was a sight for sore eyes. Of course he didn't believe for one moment she was seventeen. Barely sixteen, he guessed. His other girls exuded sex. But when Doll danced it was pure class, and it gave his club a bit of kudos. After all, the Rainbow was a classy joint.

He'd discovered more of Doll's background than Gladys had told him. She'd apparently rescued Doll from some dive of a place in Southsea. He knew of Fred Leach, her brother, and he wasn't impressed by the lying cheat. Will heard a lot from his gossiping girls.

He found he was humming along to the music. The musicians were playing Glenn Miller tunes. Such a shame, he thought, that Miller's plane had gone down in the Channel: a bloody waste of a brilliant talent.

He thought about his experiences in the Channel a few days before. He'd worn a rough overcoat and cheese-cutter cap and mixed in with the sailors on the *Sea Queen*, whose skipper he'd paid to bring in stores from Tangier. He'd already been on the boat when his own men had met the ship at Southampton and followed the craft past the Hamble. There'd been no stopover at Netley and eventually the *Sea Queen* had docked at Portsmouth, where his men unloaded his stock onto his boat and sailed across to Gosport and the boatyard's pontoon at the bottom of Ferrol Road.

He'd watched his boys unload his goods from the small craft to one of his vehicles. A chest of tea had accidentally fallen and broken open. Most of the tea was returned to the chest, but naturally enough some loose tea also fell into blue sugar bags and was set aside. He'd watched and laughed at the petty thieving of the tea, which he closed his eyes to. Perks of the trade, it was called.

The next morning he checked off his goods at the yard at the back of the Rainbow. Apart from the tea, there was nothing missing. Since he'd shared his secret with no one, he'd already decided that not one of his men had recognized him. Hanging about at Portsmouth, he'd kept to the shadows and spoken to no one. Was this the answer, then? Had he to accompany his men and goods every time to see they arrived safely? Or had the thief simply allowed this shipment of goods to be delivered to its rightful owner? He'd find out, eventually, who was playing a game with him. And when he did . . .

But now Gladys was laughing, raising her glass to him. He waved back at her. Chris was setting more drinks on the table. Gladys was still laughing, that full-throated belly laugh that cut through the noise in the club and made him smile.

He'd heard her talking to the girl with the long blonde hair. Goldie? They weren't going to give each other Christmas presents this year. He'd overheard the conversation, the words, 'clothes for Doll'. He gathered the two women had spent their money on outfits for the young girl. But that was Gladys, wasn't it? She was a kind woman.

He had a surprise for the little family of women. He'd assembled three bags of Christmas goodies. Wine, chocolate, biscuits, tins of ham and fruit. Just a few treats he thought that Gladys might like.

She was a proper woman, was Gladys. Not afraid to eat. A fully rounded woman. Actually, he was sure she'd put on a bit of weight just recently. His dream of the two of them, sitting in bed after they'd had sex, came to him. He'd have made her a cup of tea and she would have lit his cigarette. Then they'd talk about this and that. Her life and his. She was the kind of woman who had sensible things to say and he'd listen to her. Comfortable, that's what he'd be, with Gladys.

'Sorry.'

People were up on the floor dancing. A young couple had accidentally knocked against him. He grinned at them then strolled across to Gladys's table, careful of the dancers.

'Would you like to dance?'

She seemed surprised, but nevertheless got up and fitted herself into his arms.

'I have to know if you're actually going to finish this waltz with me, or are you going to run off like Cinderella again?' He looked down into her face.

She'd coloured up. 'I'm sorry about that,' she said. 'I wasn't well that day.'

He hadn't realized how tiny she was against him. He was a whole head and shoulders taller than her.

'I forgive you,' he said. 'As long as you promise me you're having a good time?'

'Oh, yes.' She looked up at him. 'Can I ask if Doll is dancing to your satisfaction?'

He nodded. 'She's a good girl; goes mad about the clothes.' He ran a hand through his dark curls. 'But because of her age and her build she definitely looks better in Grecian styles. She's making friends. I make sure she's ready when the young man,' he looked back at the table, 'arrives for her.'

'Solly,' Gladys said. He nodded. He didn't want to infer there was anything between Solly and Doll, but there was definitely some chemistry on her side. Gladys seemed happy with his answer. He was just thinking how well she fitted into his body and how her steps matched his when she asked, 'You ever get anyone asking about her?'

'No.' So there definitely was something going on that he had been kept in the dark about. 'Should there be?'

She shook herself free of him and took his hand. 'Can we go somewhere quiet?'

He took her through the kitchen and upstairs to his own premises, a large flat within the Rainbow's upstairs rooms.

'No sense in me buying another house when there's space here for me to live,' he said, unlocking the door. He pushed her towards a leather sofa and went over to a cocktail cabinet. When he turned back to her with a gin and orange in his hand, she had made herself comfortable. He handed her the glass and went back for the whisky he'd poured for himself.

'I know you gave her a job, and took Doll on trust, so I think you should know the whole story.' She took a drink from the glass, then began to talk.

He sat opposite her and listened without interrupting. When Gladys had finished he said, 'It sounds as if the bloke has something wrong with him. That's not only my opinion, but that of mates of mine who've had dealings with him. I'm glad you've told me everything because I can keep a better eye on her, without her knowing, of course. I can't afford to have trouble on my doorstep.' Gladys looked upset. He badly wanted to take her in his arms, but didn't want to scare her off. 'Drink up and we'll go and find your friends. This Fred will definitely be looking for his sister. If you have problems, for goodness sake come to me.'

She drank the rest of her drink and rose from the sofa. He could smell her perfume. 'I'm sorry to dump all this on you,' she said. 'Apart from Mac, who doesn't have any dealings with the girl, Solly and Goldie are the only people who know . . .'

'You've every right to be frightened that the toerag will discover her whereabouts from . . . Rene.' He'd had to wrack his brains to remember the woman's name. Gladys looked as if she might cry. He couldn't help himself. He pulled her close and said softly, 'Leave it with me.'

\*

Fred opened his eyes. He had the grand-daddy of all head-aches. The empty brandy bottle was rolling across the table and he only just managed to catch it before it fell to the office floor.

The banging on the door had woken him.

'What is it?' He screwed up his face at the stench of his own breath.

'Bert says he's not doing any cleaning because he hasn't been paid, and someone's been sick in the lavatory.'

Fred held onto the desk and managed to rise. Every step he took across the floor hurt his head; every tread was like a bolt of thunder behind his eyes. He opened the door to Amy.

'Jesus, you look awful.'

He looked at her chubby face and bright blue eyes and suddenly wondered what a pretty little thing like her was doing in a dump like this. However, it was his dump and Amy needed him.

'I feel worse than I look.'

'What about Bert?'

Fred felt in his pocket for his wallet and took out a pound note. 'Give him this and tell him I'll sort him out later.' She looked hungrily at the money. He took out another note and gave it to her. 'Don't tell the others.'

As she bent forward to take the money, he caught a whiff

of stale perfume. His stomach roiled. He moved away from her and spilled his guts into the waste paper bin.

'Ugh! I suppose you want Bert to clean that up an' all?'

'Get out of here, you cheeky bitch.' He wiped his hand across his chin and was amazed at the length of his stubble. How long had he been holed up in this room drinking himself senseless? 'What day is it?'

'15th of December.'

He looked towards the window and saw it was dark outside. 'Shit.'

It was nearly Christmas. He should be raking in money from blokes spending their wages on his girls, but instead he was drinking his own profits. He'd even missed an opportunity of hijacking one of William Hill's ships. 'I'm going home to see if there's any news of Doll and to have a bath. When I return I want to see this club overflowing with punters.'

'Rene's not in again. Who's going to tell the girls what to do?'

Of course Rene wasn't in, she was dead and he'd killed her, hadn't he?

He looked at Amy. 'You,' he said. 'Consider yourself promoted.'

She looked pleased. 'But what if Rene comes in later?' He knew the girls respected Rene. She could also put the fear of God into them if necessary.

'Somehow, I don't think she will,' he said. 'Now buzz off.'

He went over to the mirror on the wall and stared at his reflection. He looked awful. But this was the end of wallowing in self-pity. He had to accept the fact that his little sister had flown the coop. When he came back after cleaning himself up, he'd get all his staff together and find out who saw Doll last. It was something he should have done before, instead of turning to the bottle. Someone must have witnessed her leaving the Blue.

## Chapter Sixteen

'Do you mind me waiting for you to finish your shift so we can walk home together?'

Goldie looked at Solly and then smiled. 'Of course not. Now you're picking up Doll from the club it's almost like you're one of the family.'

He put his hand beneath her elbow and they began to walk down Weevil Lane, towards Forton Road.

'It was a good night at the Rainbow, wasn't it?'

'Definitely. Though Siddy didn't enjoy himself much,' said Goldie. 'I told Gladys he should have stayed at home.'

'I think she wanted him to come along as a small payback for all the things he does for her.'

'You're probably right.' Goldie twisted her hair up and stuffed it inside her coat to stop it flying about in the wind. 'He even does a bit of shopping for her when he knows she'll be on late turns. Anyway, where did you learn to dance like that?'

'Here and there,' he said. He didn't want to get into talking about the girls he'd taken dancing at Lee Tower ballroom.

Goldie suddenly stopped in her tracks. 'You've had Doll working in your shop today, haven't you?'

'Yes,' he said. 'She's been loading shells onto a lathe, then pouring coolant over them as they've had their bases mechanically smoothed.' Goldie had done that before; it was a monotonous job, as was most of the work there.

'How's she doing?'

'Remarkably well. She's quick-witted and seems to be getting on fine with the other women. She kicked up a fuss about having to wear a turban, though.'

'Well, she would. She's young, doesn't like her hair getting messed up.'

'Be a hell of a lot more messed up if it got caught up in the machines. The turbans aren't only to help keep hair from turning yellow. I got one girl, Marie Jenner, who won't wear anything on her head. I can't make her. She's got that Veronica Lake peekaboo long hairstyle. But you don't want to hear about my problems. Doll's working well.'

'If you'd told me that some time back, I'd never have believed you.'

'Well, you'd better believe me,' he said. 'If I had a few more girls like her I wouldn't be worrying at all.'

Chatting about this and that and their day at Priddy's, they soon reached Alma Street.

'Oh, well, another day tomorrow,' said Goldie.

'What are you doing tomorrow night?'

'Not a lot. Probably the same as tonight. Cook the dinner when I get in, finish knitting a cardigan I've been making from some woollies I got from a jumble sale and unpicked . . .'

'Come to the pictures with me. *Double Indemnity*'s on.'

She was looking at him as if he had two heads.

'Oh, why do you have to go and spoil it! You already know I have a boyfriend.'

'Goldie, I asked you to come to the pictures, not marry me.'

A couple of girls passed them, giggling. Goldie sighed and didn't begin talking until the girls were out of earshot.

'I told you all about Jamie. I'd feel I was betraying him if I went out with you.'

'Yet we all went to the Rainbow Club and you didn't mind dancing with me?'

'That was different. We were all together. In the pictures it would be dark and just us.' He turned away from her and began walking along the pavement. Then he walked quickly back and said, 'If you feel you can't trust yourself to be alone with me, I must mean more to you than either of us thought.' Then he turned on his heel again and was soon swallowed up in the darkness.

'So, how d'you like working at Priddy's?' Gladys had been waiting at the gate for Doll. She'd been passing the time talking to Harry, who checked the workers in and out. Goldie had left the munitions yard on an earlier shift and Gladys and Doll had worked later.

That's a good sign, Gladys thought, as Doll waved good-bye to two young women before she hugged Gladys.

'First, I was shown how to drive this truck thing that had a scoop-like whatsit on the front and I went around moving bales of cotton stuff from one place to another. Then I had to operate a lathe that I loaded a big bomb on and started pouring this watery coolant on it so it didn't get over-heated while the bottom of the bomb thingy was smoothed flat . . .'

'Hang on a bit,' laughed Gladys. 'Stop for breath, for goodness sake. All I wanted to know was whether you liked working today!'

Doll tucked her arm through Gladys's and they began walking down Weevil Lane. Gladys was happy that the girl seemed to have settled down to the job.

'I'm now working with these two girls. One's called Daisy, she's ever so funny. The other one's married and her husband's abroad but she goes out a lot when she can find someone to mind her kiddie. But I really like Daisy.'

Gladys was suddenly halted by Doll swinging herself round and hugging her again.

'If it hadn't been for you, I'd still have been a sort of prisoner doing what Fred wanted. I certainly wouldn't be wearing these lovely shoes.' She wriggled her feet and held up one with the sequins on.

'Quite inappropriate for this weather,' said Gladys.

'I know, but aren't they lovely?'

Gladys smiled. 'It wasn't only me. Goldie was determined to rescue you.'

'But you took me in. I've got such a lot to be thankful to you for.'

Gladys felt quite humbled by all the gushing gratitude. 'Come on, love, let's get home. Goldie will have the dinner on by now and if I'm not mistaken you're dancing tonight, aren't you?'

'I am,' said Doll. Then she grew thoughtful. 'I've been worrying about Rene. I didn't appreciate it at the time, but she was good to me. I hope Fred didn't hurt her because she helped me leave.'

'Surely he wouldn't have done anything bad? I thought you said him and her have a thing going on . . .'

'It doesn't stop him being quite cruel to her at times.'

Gladys patted Doll's arm, then she pulled her coat tighter about herself. The weather was sharply cold with flurries of snow. This morning she'd fainted as she'd been going along the line with her clipboard. She'd been lucky not to have hurt herself. It was probably because she'd not wanted any breakfast. She'd felt a bit sick. Still, when she got in she'd have a nice wash all over and sit in front of the range with Mogs on her lap. She'd managed to get some sausages yesterday that looked half decent. Siddy had come round with a few Brussels sprouts from his mate's allotment, and mashed up with some spuds they'd go down a treat, a sort of bubble and squeak. Siddy had also baked her an apple pie. He had an apple tree in his garden and late summer he'd put the apples up in the loft, laying them out like soldiers in a line, not touching. She patted Doll's arm again.

'Don't you worry about Rene, I'm sure she can look after herself.'

Gladys thought about Rene. Rough and ready she might be, but she wouldn't confess anything to Fred that might enable him to discover Doll's whereabouts, would she?

'Will Solly always pick me up in his mate's car?'

'I hope so, as long as there's petrol.' Will had told her not to worry about fuel. He could provide some agricultural petrol that was dyed pink, but when strained through a gas mask the colour disappeared. 'If he can't get hold of the car, he'll still wait for you to finish at the Rainbow.' Gladys looked at Doll. 'Why?'

'Oh, nothing.'

'I haven't just come up the Solent in a bucket!' Gladys was curious. 'He's a nice bloke.'

'Yes, I know, but he doesn't see me.'

'Whatever do you mean?' Gladys could have kicked herself. The little madam had her eye on Solly!

'I don't suppose you've ever had a boyfriend, have you?' Gladys asked gently.

'No!' Doll's voice was loud. 'Fred kept me away from the opposite sex.'

'What about at school? Was there anyone . . . ?'

Doll laughed. 'You got to be joking. My brother took me and picked me up. There was this blond boy, David, who used to wait for me outside classrooms and he gave me a set of film star cigarette cards.' Gladys saw Doll frown. 'Fred tore them up.'

There was silence until Gladys said, 'Then he told you to keep away from boys?'

Doll nodded.

'Solly's not a boy, but I think he has his eye on Goldie. Or would do if she would give him half a chance, but she's promised to her Jamie. It's not that he doesn't "see" you, love, but his heart's elsewhere. You need someone more your own age . . .'

Though how the girl was going to find anyone her own age working at the Rainbow, where everything was about sex and not love and the men were leeches in disguise, Gladys had no idea. The reason Solly picked her up was to keep her safe and out of the hands of older, more experienced men who might misinterpret her dancing in the club as an open invitation to their advances.

Thank goodness Will also kept an eye on her. Every time Doll set foot in the place, she was being shown all the wrong ways to get noticed by a man. From the waitresses who sat on the knees of unknown men, to the other dancers who encouraged men to put money inside their scanty clothing as they wriggled suggestively on the dance floor.

The environment was all about lust, not love. It was the wrong place for an impressionable girl to grow up. Yet it was the only place where she could dance, and until now dancing had been Doll's priority. It rather looked, thought Gladys, as though Doll's priorities were changing.

'There's a few nice lads working at Priddy's,' said Gladys. She was now well aware that Doll needed to come out with her and Goldie when they went dancing. Doll was growing up, and fast! 'It's a pity there's not so many lads about now. They're all in the services, fighting to win this damn war. But we won't meet any fellas staying indoors, will we?'

# Chapter Seventeen

Goldie let herself into the house and picked up the post from the mat. She noted the forces envelopes amongst the other letters and her heart lifted. She quickly scanned the post dates and saw they were identical. She smiled. Jamie must have written twice on the same day. She left them on the table to read later and took off her coat and boots to begin the chores before Gladys and Doll came home.

First she bent down and picked up Mogs, who was trying to trip her up by weaving himself in and out of her legs, and gave him a big cuddle. Then she put down the purring cat and lit the gas beneath the kettle. She riddled the range, and it wasn't long before she had a good fire going. Sausages and bubble and squeak, with apple pie for afters, sounded good to her. The apple pie came from Siddy. She wondered if Gladys had ever thought about settling down with him. He was kindness itself where she was concerned.

She tidied up downstairs, then went upstairs and closed the bedroom curtains to keep the cold out. She took the stone hot-water bottle from her bed. Gladys had already deposited hers in the scullery, ready to be refilled. Satisfied everything was tidy, Goldie went back downstairs and emptied the hot-water bottle into the sink.

Doll's room at the front of the house was a tip, but Goldie stopped herself from tidying it – the girl had to learn to put her own clothes away. She smiled to herself. Doll was different now, no longer as selfish as she used to be. Who would have thought she would have been happy to start work at Priddy's? No doubt she'd tell them all about it when she got home.

Goldie swung her long hair away from her face as she searched in the unmade bed for Doll's hot-water bottle. One of the first things she did upon leaving the factory was untie her hair. She hated wearing the protective turban, but better that than getting her long hair caught in one of the machines. She drew the curtains and closed the bedroom door behind her.

Mogs was weaving himself in and out of her legs again.

'I suppose you want feeding?' She made noises at him as she dished him up some cooked cod ends that Gladys had wheedled from the fishmonger and watched as he began to eat.

The house was warming up now. After she'd prepared the dinner, she made herself a cup of tea and moved Mogs to the back of the old chair so there was room for her as well. She sat down to read her long-awaited letters from Jamie.

> *Dear Goldie,*
> *First I must apologize for writing to you like this, but you should know the truth, for the news won't come directly to you.*

Goldie stopped reading and turned the page over. This wasn't Jamie's handwriting! Her eyes flew to the end of the letter. Eli. Jamie's friend had written to her. Why? Her heart was beating fast as she turned back and continued reading.

> *You love Jamie and deep down I believe he loved you. For some time now Jamie and I had been at loggerheads. I had better start at the beginning.*
> *Yesterday we reached the forests of Reichwald. We had no idea what was before us, and even in the daylight the journey was terrible. There were snipers hiding. Our Churchill tanks kept the gunfire at bay and it was dark before the infantry was able to dig in beside the tank. About eight of us saw the flashes, along with the noise of the enemy weapons. We were on guard for the rest of the night and heard tanks, not ours, and snipers' bullets. In the morning I learned that Jamie and two other men had been killed in the first flurry of gunfire from the Jerry patrol.*

I'm sorry to be the bearer of such bad news. It's possible your feelings are going to be difficult to come to terms with. I hope you will find it in your heart to forgive him, for he died fighting for our freedom. Whatever he had done, in the end he was not a coward. His family will no doubt contact you.

I'm not in England, so can do nothing physically to help my sister Rebecca, though I have sent her money. I am extremely angry at what has happened to her but I believed him when he said he would put things right by marrying her.

We fought when I found out the truth from Rebecca. I'm sorry, or glad perhaps, to say I gave him a right pasting. I know he won't have told you anything. I don't even know what I'm expecting you to do, but my sister can't cope and our parents have turned her away from the family home. She's sixteen now, unable to work as the baby is tiny. She's always been highly strung. The landlady thought I was her husband, so wrote to me asking for rent for her room at Eastern Road in Southsea. I can only think the woman had gone through Rebecca's things to get hold of my address, our names being the same.

She wrote that Rebecca had taken an overdose and she had nursed her back to health. The child cries constantly.

I repeat, I believe he loved you, even to the end. I wish I didn't feel so helpless.

Eli

Goldie allowed the letter to fall. She was numb. Before she gave vent to her feelings, she knew she had to read the second letter. It was impossible to think he was dead. What did this talk about Rebecca mean? She'd read Eli's letter, but couldn't take in its message. She swallowed back her tears and began to read.

*My darling Goldie,*

*This is the hardest letter I will ever have to write.*

*I have been so stupid. This letter will hurt you. It hurts me to write it, because I love you so very much.*

*I first met Rebecca when I was home on leave, about eighteen months ago, and I spent a few days at Eli's house. Again, about a year ago, I visited with Eli. You said I deserved to go out with the lads and get drunk and try to forget the horrors of the war. I loved you for being so considerate.*

*Rebecca, Eli's sister, had been writing to me. Eli advised against this, as his parents are strict and religious. Unknown to Eli, I exchanged a few letters with her. I saw no harm in it as she was fifteen, just a child.*

*While at Eli's, she followed me around, and I guess I was flattered by her attention. Eli's father is a church minister and was extremely protective of Rebecca. She had never had a boyfriend.*

*One day, the three of us had arranged a visit to Portsdown Hill. Eli and I had been drinking heavily the night before and Eli begged*

*off with a hangover. Rebecca and I went together. Her parents had*
*trusted me to look after her. I'm sorry to say, I behaved abominably.*
*I let my feelings get the better of me while we were horsing about.*
*I was physically sick later at what had happened; I should have*
*had more respect for Eli's father's hospitality and resisted Rebecca's*
*childish attentions. Above all, I'd destroyed your trust in me.*
*Rebecca became pregnant.*

Goldie dropped the letter. She was breathing heavily and felt sick. Despite this, she bent down, picked up the page and made herself continue reading.

*Rebecca wrote and told me about the baby. I said it wasn't mine.*
*All I could think about was that admitting paternity would mean*
*I would lose you. Rebecca kept her secret from her parents for as*
*long as she could. I can't begin to think of the hell she was going*
*through. Eventually she had to tell her mother, and her father made*
*her leave the house. He said she would ruin his standing with the*
*church and he could not have the child anywhere near him because*
*of the shame it would bring the family.*

*When Eli discovered what had happened, we fought. Through*
*my own stupidity I've lost my best friend.*

*The child is a boy. Eli sent money for the rent of a room.*

*Rebecca can't cope. Having no one to turn to, she took an overdose*
*of tablets. Her landlady, Mrs Brooks, alerted by the little boy's constant*

*screams, discovered her in time. That made me realize how selfish I had been. Mrs Brooks was led to believe Rebecca was married to a serviceman, else she would never have let her rent a room.*

*I can't let this girl go on living like this. The little boy is my own flesh and blood. My darling, I can't marry you. I hope you can understand my reasons for breaking up with you. I have to do the right thing and try to repair some of the damage I've caused.*

*I'm frightened she will try to kill herself again. If she does, but survives, the authorities might put her in a hospital for the insane and the boy in a home. I wish I could be there to help sort out this mess of my own making, but I can't because of this godawful war.*

*I'm going to ask Rebecca to marry me. I respect you enough to know you wouldn't want a life with me built on a lie. Eli is sure his parents will agree to the marriage. Eli and I may never resolve our differences. Maybe time will tell.*

*I will always love you. I've thrown away our future together. I am so sorry.*

*Jamie*

Goldie sat at the table with her head in her hands. She was too stunned to cry. She drank the tea she had poured, hardly aware it was cold. All she could think of was that Jamie was dead. He had betrayed her, but why, oh why did he have to die?

Her mind went back to the shore leaves Jamie had

taken when he'd been unable to see her. She realized it was quite possible that it was then he had been with Rebecca. Recriminations were useless. Jamie was dead. Dead.

'Whatever's the matter?'

Goldie hadn't noticed that her friends had arrived home from work.

Gladys was taking off her coat and scarf and Doll was putting her beloved glittery shoes beneath the chair. Goldie pushed back her hair and tried to compose herself with a huge sniff and a watery smile. It didn't work, and she burst into tears.

'Put the kettle on to freshen up that tea,' snapped Gladys immediately, looking at Goldie's cup then coming to her side. Doll threw her coat over the back of the kitchen chair and for once didn't question Gladys's instructions. She tossed back her dark hair and left the kitchen.

'It's not often a letter from Jamie makes you unhappy.' Gladys put her hand on Goldie's shoulder. She looked into Goldie's face and studied her. 'Doll, bring in the washing as well.' Goldie knew she wanted Doll out of the way.

A letter was pushed towards Gladys. 'Don't say anything until you've read both of them,' Goldie said.

The time ticked by. Goldie knew that if she sat watching Gladys read she might not be able to keep herself together, so she rose and went out into the scullery. Doll was still in the garden, unpegging the washing that had been put out in the morning before everyone went to work. She automatically finished the job of brewing the tea.

'Brr!' said Doll, her cheeks pink with the cold as she put the basket of washing on the draining board. Goldie could tell she wanted to know what was wrong, but didn't ask.

'I'll hang that on the fireguard,' said Goldie. She felt as though she was in a dream. She took the basket through to the kitchen and started to place the washing around the metal monstrosity. It would air off overnight with the fire's heat. She could hear Doll clattering the cups and saucers in the scullery.

'Jesus!'

Goldie heard the oath as Gladys looked up from the last page of one of the letters. The disbelief in her eyes glittered brightly. 'I think we need that tea,' she said.

'Read the other one,' Goldie said. 'It will explain more.'

'What's the matter?' Doll was curious and had returned to the kitchen with the tea tray.

'Jamie's dead,' said Goldie. Tears stung her eyes. It seemed worse now that she'd put it into words.

'Tea always makes a person feel better,' said Doll. 'The cup that cheers.' Gladys glared at Doll. Goldie knew the girl was sympathetic, but because of her tender years had no idea of how to help.

'What are you going to do?' Gladys questioned Goldie. She looked towards Doll.

'She might as well read it,' said Goldie. Gladys passed Doll a letter.

'What can I do?' Goldie asked. 'There's a girl with a baby who might do away with herself.' Through the fog of her unhappiness she was jealous that the young girl had Jamie's child, something that she would now never have.

'It's not your problem,' Doll said, as she looked up after reading Jamie's letter. She folded it and left it on the table.

Goldie tried not to think about the baby and the many nights she'd prayed to have children with Jamie. All her emotions were mixed up. It felt as though her head was full of cotton wool and her heart was like a huge stone set in her chest.

Doll stirred a tiny bit of sugar into Goldie's cup. 'I'd have thought you'd be screaming the house down about that bastard.'

'Maybe I would if he was here, but he's not. I'm the lucky one. I could have discovered this after I'd married him. But read the other letter.'

Doll looked up at her when she'd finished reading. 'At least he was going to do the right thing.'

'I loved him.' Goldie wiped her fingers across her eyes. 'I still love him.'

Gladys's face was chalk-white. 'Don't you dare cry over that toerag!' She handed Goldie the tea towel that was hanging over the back of the chair. Goldie dabbed at her eyes and took a deep breath before asking, 'What are we going to do about Rebecca?'

Gladys ignored her and looked at the clock on the mantelpiece.

The clock ticked. It sounded like a time bomb, about to go off at any second.

Doll said. 'He got what he deserved. What goes around, comes around.'

'Don't talk rubbish,' said Gladys. 'And don't speak ill of the dead.'

At the word 'dead' the dam burst in Goldie. She held the tea towel to her face and sobbed until she could cry no longer.

Gladys and Doll allowed her to give vent to her feelings. After a while Doll went over to Goldie. Putting her arms about her, she said, 'I'm so sorry.'

Goldie knew she must look a terrible sight. She wiped her eyes and put the tea towel down. What did it matter what she looked like? She put out a hand and clutched at Gladys's fingers and felt the reassuring grasp of friendship. Gladys, ever practical, said, 'I think we should get something to eat down us. We've all had a hard day and it's a shame to let good food go to waste. It's already too late to go making decisions now, right?'

'I just keep wondering how he managed to keep it all from me.'

'You trusted him, that's how.' Gladys rose from the table and went out to the scullery. Goldie heard the pop of the gas and it wasn't long before she smelled the fragrance of sausages frying.

'I believed him when he said it was all right for us to have fun with other people, as long as we didn't get involved. I kept to my side of the bargain.' She pushed her empty cup over to Doll who was putting the dirty crockery on the tray to take outside to the sink. 'I've been a bloody fool.'

'No, you haven't,' shouted Gladys. 'He's paid for his mistake. You're an honest woman, who should be proud of herself. Look how Solly worships the ground you walk on.'

Goldie was surprised to see Doll's face fall at Gladys's words.

'I can't think about blokes,' she shouted back. 'I don't think I ever will again.'

'No, maybe not now, but you mustn't let this spoil your life. If you let it, it will.' Goldie opened her mouth to answer, but Gladys went on shouting from the scullery. 'We're here; so is a girl with a baby, Jamie's baby. From the sound of it, she needs help. Even if you hate her guts for sleeping with the bloke you loved, you can't deny that little boy a bit of help. I can't turn my back and I don't believe you can either. Jamie was the one who made mistakes but even he knew the difference between right and wrong . . .' She poked her head round the kitchen door and said, 'Come on out here and sort out the hot-water bottles. Don't sit there moping.' Then she disappeared again.

Goldie got up and went out to refill the kettle. She was glad her friends had read the letters. Sitting about and grieving wasn't going to help.

'But what could we do for that poor girl?' Goldie knew then that she couldn't shut Rebecca and the child out of her thoughts.

Doll was drying the cups and hanging them on the shelf hooks. Gladys was turning the bubble and squeak in the frying pan to get it nicely browned and crispy. The sausages were on a pan beneath the grill and the comforting smells were making Goldie feel better.

Gladys took a rolled paper spill from the jam jar on the side and lit the oven, turning it low so the apple pie wouldn't burn. 'I wish we could have some custard with this,' she said. 'But there's not enough milk and even if I eke the milk out with water, we can't spare the sugar.'

'What about that tin of Carnation milk? We could use that,' Doll said.

'Yes, good idea,' said Gladys. She turned the potato and Brussels sprouts again.

'Yummy,' said Doll.

'I'll have a word with Solly tomorrow and see if he can borrow that car again,' said Gladys. 'I'll gladly pay for petrol if he can get it, and perhaps we could go to Eastern Road and have a word with Rebecca and see if we can help in any way. I'm not crossing on the ferry in this icy weather,' she added. 'Oh, he'll already have the car because Doll's down at the Rainbow. We can drop her off.' She looked round at Doll. 'You got them plates out?' Doll nodded at the three plates on the draining board. Goldie watched as Gladys dished up their dinner, then remembered there were no knives and forks on the table so went into the kitchen and took the cutlery from the drawer. She heard Gladys shout, 'You can write to Eli then and put his mind at rest. How does that sound?'

'Good idea,' Goldie shouted back, then went back into the scullery where Gladys was dishing up. The big kettle was boiling. It didn't take Goldie long to fill the hot-water bottles and after wrapping each of them in a towel, it took her even less time to slip a bottle into each of the three beds before she sat down to eat. She knew sleep wouldn't come easily that night, maybe not for many nights to come, but Gladys and Doll were with her and that was a good feeling.

# Chapter Eighteen

'I'm glad we persuaded you to bring us; it looks treacherous out there.' The car was parked in a small street that was quite dark, brightened only by the white of the icy pavements. There was a broken street lamp with a bicycle tyre hanging from its post. On the corner was a gloomy pub, with a group of youths outside who were staring with hostility at the car. 'They should be in the services,' continued Gladys. 'And not standing about scaring people.'

Goldie said, 'They look too young to be called up. They're probably nice boys.'

'Humph,' said Gladys, then asked Solly, 'Are we here?'

'Eastern Road. There's number twelve.' He peered through the windscreen, then pointed to a terraced house and pulled over outside the paint-peeled door. He turned off the car's engine.

Gladys could hear a baby screaming. 'Must be the place,'

she said and opened the door, then carefully stepped out onto the icy pavement. She banged on the door. There was a fox's head door knocker but it was broken. She stepped back and looked at the window. The curtains were drawn. She thumped on the door again.

A skinny woman with plaits wound around her head finally answered the banging.

'You from the council?' Her voice had a nasal drawl, pure Pompey accent. With the opening of the door came a blast of air, thick with the smell of cabbages.

'No,' said Solly, who had joined Gladys. Goldie slammed the car's door and came and stood the other side of Gladys.

'We've come to see Rebecca,' he said. 'Are you Mrs Brooks, her landlady?'

The woman nodded, then started to laugh. She wiped her hand across the front of her grubby wraparound pinny and said, 'You're a bit late, ain't yer?'

Goldie said, 'We couldn't get here any earlier tonight, we all work.'

The woman started laughing again. Then she paused and said, 'Wouldn't have made any difference how early you got here, you'd still have been too late.'

'Isn't she here, then?' Solly asked.

'She is in body, but not in spirit.'

Gladys said, 'Don't tell me . . .'

'Yes,' said the woman. 'She's made a proper job of it this time.'

'But I can hear the baby. It is her baby, isn't it?' Goldie interrupted.

'I didn't say she took the little 'un with her, did I?' Even in the dull light coming from the passage behind the woman, Gladys could see that her teeth were rotten, and she smelled so strongly of body odour that it threatened to make Gladys heave.

'Oh, dear,' began Goldie. 'When?'

'Yesterday morning.'

Gladys held onto Goldie and shivered. Her shivering had nothing to do with the cold. The woman suddenly realized they were talking on the doorstep and the warmth would be leaving her house.

'You'd better come in,' she said grudgingly. 'The heat's going out.' She stepped aside so they could all pass. She carried on talking as she urged them to continue walking down the passage, into a room that contained a fire that looked as if it was dying; a three-piece suite; and a table covered with odds and ends of dirty crockery, newspapers, a bottle of milk and a sugar bowl. She closed the door behind them but it didn't shut out the noise of the child crying. 'I banged on her door, but she didn't answer. The kid was crying, you see. I went in and I could tell immediately that she was a goner.'

The woman continued, 'Did it properly this time. Tablets.' She sniffed. 'You want to see her?'

Solly looked at Gladys, then held onto her as she appeared about to faint. She took a deep breath of the fetid air as the landlady continued, 'She's laid out in the front room.'

Gladys seemed to regain her strength, for she said, 'Yes, please.' It crossed her mind that Jamie hadn't been in time to let Rebecca know he intended to marry her. What a damn shame, she thought. She looked at Goldie and knew the girl was thinking the same thing. Mrs Brooks was still talking.

'I thought she was married, you see? They're removing her tomorrow. And taking the baby an' all.'

She started to walk back the way they'd come along the passage. Strangely, the child had stopped crying. Gladys wondered who was looking after it. Perhaps someone had picked the baby up or possibly it had cried itself back to sleep. She suddenly felt so very sad for the poor motherless and fatherless mite.

'So you thought we'd come to take the child, did you?' Solly sounded businesslike.

'Her father don't want nothin' to do with it. Him in the church an' all.' Gladys could hear the disgust in her voice. 'He said it was a child of sin.'

'It's a baby.' Gladys almost shouted the words. The woman flicked a switch and electric light flooded the room. Gladys looked at Goldie and she could see the pain in her eyes. She could tell the girl was thinking about Jamie and all the hurt he'd caused.

The coffin sat on a large table in the centre of the room. It was open and inside was the body of a girl, barely more than a child. She wore a white gown buttoned to the neck that was practically the same shade as the silk lining the coffin. Her blonde hair was brushed over one shoulder. Gladys thought that in life she had been a pretty little thing.

'Parachute silk. Even the undertakers feel the pinch in wartime,' the woman said. 'She looks peaceful now. That's something she never did all the time she was with me. Always crying, she was.'

Gladys stared at the waxy face. The undertaker had coloured the girl's lips and put a blush to her cheeks. Her thin arms ended in clasped hands over her stomach. Her nails were bitten to the quick. She looked about twelve years old.

'Oh, God,' uttered Gladys. She closed her eyes and whispered the Lord's Prayer. When she finished she broke the silence in the room by asking, 'Who's paying for the funeral?'

'Her brother. I've got his address. He's in the tank regiment. Do you want to look in her room?'

'No,' said Goldie.

'Yes,' said Solly. Gladys saw the look of confusion between

Solly and Goldie, but she followed the woman out into the hall and then up the stairs. She tried to imagine what Goldie was thinking and feeling. Gladys thought she was tremendously brave. None of them had expected the girl to have committed suicide. Her heart went out to Goldie.

'She didn't have much,' the woman said, flooding the small room with light. The child in the cot opened his eyes and his tiny hands quivered. Gladys could smell the child's stench. 'The stuff belongs to me,' the woman said. The shabby brown wooden bed and chest of drawers, a small table and a chair were all the furniture the room contained. 'I shall be glad when he's gone.' She waved a hand towards the cot. 'I can't be 'aving the constant screaming. My ol' man's gone to the pub an' I have to stay in, in case someone comes.' She looked pained to be missing a good time. There was a knock on the downstairs front door.

'Better answer that.' Mrs Brooks left the room, taking with her the sweaty smell.

Gladys looked down at the scuffed lino. She was trying to make some sense out of everything. Then she looked back at the child, wrapped in a scruffy shawl that had probably once been white, and a chip of ice broke off from Gladys's heart and melted. She couldn't take her eyes from the stinking child who had nothing and nobody and who would go into an overfull home of unwanted children to be bullied and teased. He might never be adopted. He might never be fostered. And even if he was, would his new parents love him as that little girl would have loved him had she been loved herself? Gladys went over to the cot and looked down at the little boy. He'd been left to cry for too long and it wasn't right. His little face was covered in snot. That woman wanted shooting, Gladys thought. She so wanted to pick up the child and hold him to her body to give him some kind of comfort, however small.

Goldie was standing behind her now and interrupted her thoughts. 'Caused a lot of problems, didn't he, Jamie?'

'You knew him for years and yet never knew him at all. This child's going to be thrown on the scrapheap.' Gladys was angry. 'A loving dad won't feature in his future and neither will a loving mum. It's difficult to love a kid that isn't your own flesh and blood.'

The screaming had ceased, but the child was snuffling, moving his head from side to side. He opened his eyes and his gaze at the pair of them was straight and strong. Gladys again had to stop herself from picking him up. If she did, she knew she'd run out to the car with him and never let that awful woman near him again.

'It doesn't have to be like that,' Goldie said quietly. She looked at Gladys as though she knew what the older woman was thinking. 'That little boy is all that's left of my Jamie.'

Downstairs, Mrs Brooks coughed. It was as though she was reminding them that she didn't have all night to stand about with them. The front door closed with a bang.

Gladys stared at Goldie. 'He's not our responsibility.' She glanced towards the waving fists in the cot and the snuffles that accompanied them.

'How about if I want him to be?' There was a long silence as Goldie stared at Gladys without blinking.

Gladys knew exactly what she meant. Quietly she said, 'How about if I want him to be our problem as well?'

'Two heads are better than one,' said Goldie. 'Could we?' A sudden hopeful look had entered her eyes.

Gladys knew that between them they could give this little scrap of humanity all the love and protection he needed. It was a crazy, impetuous idea, but one that could benefit the child. The landlady came back into the room.

'Provident man, wanted his weekly money.' Cold air now accompanied her stale smell.

'Is there a pram or a carrycot?' Goldie asked.

The woman laughed. 'That chit of a girl didn't have two halfpennies to rub together. She 'ad nothing to feed herself with, an' she was in no state to work. She stopped in this room an' I couldn't even get her to go an' register his birth.' She nodded towards the cot. 'She only went as far as the corner shop. Why d'you ask?'

'I imagine Rebecca left you with unpaid rent?'

Gladys knew immediately what Goldie was doing. She was going to pay the landlady to keep her mouth shut. She marvelled at Goldie's ingenuity.

'Yes, she did. And she borrowed money from me.' The woman looked up at the ceiling. 'I don't suppose I'll ever see that again.' She licked her lips and stared at Goldie. 'And it's not as though I couldn't do with it. Anyway, why d'you ask?'

'Because I'm the wife of the man who got that young girl downstairs in the family way. We can't have no kiddies. He's in France and he wants that little boy. I want that little boy.'

Mrs Brooks stepped back in amazement. Solly turned away. Gladys thought that he was shocked at Goldie's lies.

'But the council people are coming . . .'

'They won't give you what's owed you, will they? And of course there's the expense you've had, looking after him these last few days. Will they compensate you for that?' Gladys stared at her with admiration; Solly stood there aghast.

'It would be better for 'im,' the woman nodded again towards the cot, 'to be brought up by his proper father. I know for a fact kids picks up all kinds of nasty habits in them homes.' She looked slyly first at Solly, then at each of them in turn. 'But I 'ave been out of pocket . . .'

'Quite so,' said Solly, as though finding his voice. He didn't look at all happy. Gladys glared at him, defying him to say more.

The woman looked at Goldie. 'You'd forgive your old man for sowing his oats elsewhere?'

'We all make mistakes.' Amazement slid across the woman's face.

'But what can I tell the council people?' She moved from one foot to the other. Gladys could practically smell the greed emanating from her.

'Tell them the truth. Tell them he'll be given a good home by his natural father.'

'They might want details.'

'I'll give you my address. You can get in touch with the girl's brother and he'll confirm everything.' Gladys could see the woman weighing up the possibility of more money in her pocket. She looked at Solly. His face was an inscrutable mask.

'You gonna take him tonight?' Mrs Brooks asked.

'Is that all right with you?'

'I'll be glad to see the noisy little bugger go. I can join my hubby down the pub.' She moved her mouth into a semblance of a smile that just showed more bad teeth.

'You want to gather up his bits and pieces?'

The landlady laughed. 'You got to be kiddin'. What bits? Apart from a few nappies in soak that I ain't got around to washing, there ain't a thing. He ain't even got a bleedin' name yet.'

'But he must be a few months old!' Gladys couldn't help herself. Babies were supposed to be registered. 'No birth certificate?'

'I told you that Rebecca didn't go no further than the shop.' She looked at Goldie. Her eyes narrowed. 'The rent owed is a pound.'

Gladys thought about asking to see a rent book, but laughed inwardly at the fuss that would cause. They all knew the woman was screwing them and there wasn't a thing they could do about it if they wanted to get the kiddie away to safety.

'What!' Goldie almost exploded at the woman's words.

'That's cheap, that is. Included heat, lighting and food,' the woman stressed.

Gladys fumbled in her handbag and took out her purse.

'Then there's stamps for the letters to France for her brother, babysitting and—'

'Let's call it a fiver, shall we?' Gladys and Goldie looked at Solly, who was taking the white note from his wallet. He stepped forward and pressed the money into the woman's eager hand. 'Let's say, if you think of anything else, you did it out of the kindness of your heart? We'll need her ration book, birth certificate and anything else she had.'

Mrs Brooks looked shifty. 'I got her ration book down-stairs. She wanted me to look after it.'

'Perhaps she meant you to hand it back to the authorities?' Solly's sarcasm was lost on the landlady, who was tucking the five-pound note into her pinny's pocket. Gladys looked at Solly with admiration. Gladys had no doubt the woman would use the dead girl's coupons.

'Her bits and pieces are in one of the drawers.' The woman pointed to the chest of drawers. Solly began searching through the few oddments of Rebecca's clothes. Gladys noted he was pushing his fingers right to the back of the open drawers.

Then, remembering the woman had a coffin in her front room, Gladys asked, 'What time's the service tomorrow?'

'Eleven o'clock. Will you be there? St Mary's Church.'

'We'll see,' said Gladys. 'It would be the right thing to do, see Rebecca off.'

Goldie went to the cot, bent down and picked up the now sleeping child. She wrinkled her nose at the smell and Gladys saw the stain of faeces on the shawl. Nevertheless, Goldie held the child tightly against herself, almost as if she would never allow him to be parted from her again.

Solly was already through the door and stepping down the stairs. Gladys allowed Goldie to pass her then she too, went down. The woman followed.

Solly had to remind Mrs Brooks about Rebecca's ration book.

Gladys breathed deeply of the Portsmouth air when she closed the door of number twelve behind them.

# Chapter Nineteen

There had been silence in the car on the way back, broken only by the snuffling from the child. Several times Gladys had opened her mouth to speak, but thought better of it. She guessed each of them was thinking about the extraordinary thing that had just happened. Their first stop would be the Rainbow, to pick up Doll.

In the near-darkness, as Solly turned to Goldie, Gladys saw his face brighten. 'Well, you told a pretty convincing lie,' he said.

'She had to make that awful woman believe her, didn't she?' Gladys had managed to wind the window down, but wasn't sure what was worse, the child's smell or the freezing cold air coming in. 'She didn't press for the address, though, did she?'

'I wouldn't have written down the correct one,' said Goldie. 'Should that woman get in touch with Eli, somehow

214

I think he'd find it preferable that his sister's child be looked after by us rather than being shifted into a home.'

'Do you think the authorities will come looking for us?' Solly asked.

'Shouldn't think so. This is wartime and no doubt there are other children being brought up by people who aren't their natural parents,' replied Gladys. She had heard tales of babies and small children being the only survivors of households that had been bombed out. Many of these little ones found themselves being taken to safety and growing up within families who weren't blood relatives.

Solly halted the car outside the club. Doll, who was standing on the steps waiting with Will at her side, waved to them. Will came down the steps and opened the front door of the car so that Doll could climb inside. He gave Gladys a smile that made her heart flutter, before turning and going back up to the club.

'Cor! What's that smell?' Doll's words coincided with the baby's cry. 'Is that a baby?'

'Yes,' said Gladys.

'Who does it belong to?' Doll turned round from the front seat to peer into the back.

'Us,' said Gladys and Goldie together.

For a moment there was silence, then Solly said, 'They get madder every day, don't they?' He smiled briefly at Doll, then looked back at the road. 'First Gladys takes in Goldie and Mogs, then you, and now whoever-he-is. Next time you come home she might have a blinkin' elephant indoors.' Suddenly, the car was full of laughter.

Doll was leaning over and trying to pull the shawl from the baby's face. 'He's lovely, got lots of hair and a dirty nose. What's his name?' Already, she seemed to have accepted the latest addition to number fourteen Alma Street.

'Told you, he hasn't got a name. Gladys will sort it all out,' said Solly. 'But he's a lucky boy. He's a wanted baby.' Then he laughed. 'And I want the smelly little tyke out of this car as soon as possible!'

As soon as they were in the kitchen at Alma Street and Goldie had divested herself of her boots and coat, she said, 'There's more to looking after his lordship than we bargained for. Obviously he's starving.'

By now his hungry screams echoed through the house and Gladys said, 'I'll cut up some old towels as nappies and after he's clean and fed we'll sort out who's going to look after him during the day. Don't forget, we're both supposed to be working.'

'Fed? We ain't got anything to feed him with!' Doll said. 'He looks too little to be eating proper food.' She'd been sent out to the scullery to find the big enamel bowl and to heat water. 'We got no clothes for him, neither,' she shouted back above the child's screams.

'I bet there was stuff there that that awful woman didn't pass on to us.' Gladys looked angry. 'She'll sell it. We don't even know how old he is.'

'According to the letters, he must be about ten weeks?' Goldie looked at Solly for confirmation.

He shrugged. 'What do I know about babies?' Then he said, 'Mrs Symonds at number eight looks after kiddies while their mothers work. She might be able to help.'

'Solly, you're an angel in disguise,' said Goldie. She looked at the enamel bowl on the table. Doll had wiped it free from dust and spiders, because it usually hung outside on the garden wall. There was clean, cold water in the bottom of it. Doll went back for the kettle and Gladys took it from her and poured hot water into the cold. Then she rolled up her sleeve and put her elbow in to test it wasn't too hot.

The baby hadn't stopped screaming. He was rolled up, still in his shawl, on the armchair. His little hands were waving. Goldie said, 'He's got a good pair of lungs on him!'

'Well, get him undressed. He needs this bath more than I need a cup of tea, and that's saying something,' said Gladys.

Doll realized that was her cue to take the kettle out to the scullery and make a pot of tea.

'You going to bathe him or shall I?'

217

'Oh, Gladys, you've had more experience than me, I'd be scared of dropping him, but I'll take these disgusting rags off him.' Goldie picked up the child and began to unravel him. Already her heart had been swallowed up by the little one.

'Oh, look, he's red raw!'

'He hasn't had a nappy change since I don't know when,' said Gladys. Goldie peered at the child's flaming skin. 'That awful woman,' she said. She dropped the offending soiled garments on the floor in a pile. 'Doll, wrap all this in newspaper and stick it in the dustbin.'

'Shouldn't we wash—'

'You want to wash that lot, Doll?' The girl shook her head.

Gladys said, 'You're doing fine. You won't drop the poor little mite. I'll go and beg some stuff off Mrs Symonds. She knows me.'

As soon as the front door banged shut, Goldie had time to look at the baby in her arms. She'd wiped most of the muck off his face and Doll had produced some Lux soap. Solly and Doll were watching her.

The child was very blond and his features were even. He was thin and his little body shook as Goldie washed his head before she placed him in the water and carefully cleaned him.

'We got any cream for his little bum?' she asked. It pained

her to think she had to touch the sores on his skin. It would surely hurt him.

'Vaseline,' said Doll.

'That's as good as any,' Goldie said. The child had stopped crying and was watching her. Doll passed her a clean towel. She wrapped him up while Doll carried the bowl of dirty water out to the scullery. Solly was looking at her with admiration.

The front door opened then closed again and in came Gladys with a brown carrier bag.

'I didn't know what to tell her,' she said breathlessly, bringing cold air in with her. 'I could hardly tell her the truth, could I? I don't want people sniggering about you behind your back because of Jamie,' she said to Goldie. 'I told her it was a cousin's child and they'd been bombed out. She was all right with that. Mind you, it'll be all round Gosport that we got an addition to the family. I said you're his new mum!'

'Oh,' said Goldie, hugging the baby tight against her body. 'I thought we was looking after him together?' She didn't mind being his new mum at all, but she'd had no experience of children.

'Of course we are, you daft thing, but you're a better age to be a mother. I'm more a granny type.'

Goldie felt reassured.

Gladys delved into the bag. 'I could hardly say we found

him under a gooseberry bush, could I?' She laughed. 'Now, what have we here?'

Solly said, 'You want me to explain things to the manager at work? Not everything, but enough to explain your absences from work tomorrow? You'll need to register the mite and hand in his mother's ration book. Then he needs one, and a medical card and stuff . . .'

Gladys put her hand to her head. 'Oh, my God,' she said. 'He needs a name!'

Silence filled the kitchen. 'For Eli's sake he'll have his mother's surname.'

Everyone nodded at Gladys's words.

'Why not go the whole hog and call him Eli?'

Gladys, Goldie and Doll turned towards Solly. Then they looked at each other and smiles began to blossom. Just as Goldie looked down at the child in her arms, he began to grizzle.

'Eli's hungry,' said Doll. They all laughed and Gladys took out a tin of National dried baby's milk and a banana-shaped bottle from the brown bag. Solly said, 'I've got to go.' He looked at the clock on the mantelpiece, then at the range. 'I'll bank up the fire before I leave, though.' He got on with the chore and Gladys disappeared into the scullery. Doll delved into the bag and pulled out a long cotton nightgown and a matinee jacket, knitted mittens and bootees. 'Look how small they are,' she said. Then she found some muslin squares and a few towelling napkins and put them on the arm of the chair within Goldie's reach.

'What were you looking for in Rebecca's room?' Goldie asked Solly.

'Anything that the child might like or find useful in future, perhaps a memento of Rebecca that could be kept for him. I didn't trust that Mrs Brooks. I think she'd already ransacked the room.' He looked up from where he knelt in front of the fireplace.

'Did you find anything?'

'Yes, this.' He foraged in his pocket and pulled out a locket on a gold chain. With his thumbnail he clicked it open and showed Goldie a picture of the child's mother. 'See how young she is.' He handed it to Goldie.

'That's a lovely keepsake for Eli,' Goldie said. 'I'm surprised it was still there, though; isn't it gold?'

'Yes, but it was tucked right at the back of a drawer with these.' Now he held a letter and Rebecca's birth certificate. There were also three other letters tied with a piece of red ribbon.

Goldie recognized Jamie's writing. She had no intention of reading something so personal of Rebecca's. She felt sure the letters tied with red ribbon were love letters. Hadn't Jamie already confessed to writing to her? The proof of his betrayal was this beautiful child she held in her arms. She didn't need to be hurt afresh by reading something that wasn't meant for her, especially if the letters showed Jamie's nastiness, denying the child was his.

Doll leaned across and snatched the crumpled paper from Solly's fingers. He passed the other items to Gladys.

'It says he wants nothing to do with her or the brat she's carrying.'

'We knew that, Doll.' Solly took the letter away from her. She pouted.

Goldie had dressed the little boy in clean white clothes.

'My, doesn't he look lovely,' said Gladys, advancing on the child with a bottle of milk that she passed to Goldie. 'C'mon, Mum, do your stuff.'

Goldie smiled at her. A look of love and understanding flowed between them. Goldie made the little boy comfortable and held the teat to his mouth.

The room was quiet except for the sound of contented sucking. Gladys broke the silence by saying, 'Doll, go and take out the big drawer from the chest in my bedroom, empty it, line it with a pillow, then put it on a chair in Goldie's room next to the bed.' She looked at Goldie, who grinned at her. 'And for Gawd's sake make a pot of tea!'

# Chapter Twenty

Darling,

I hate this war and all that goes with it. Today we saw Fort de Breendonk, a German Gestapo torture camp near Antwerp. There was a drawbridge across a moat, the building itself gloomy. Barbed wire covered everything. The inmates, Jews, lived in darkness inside the concrete buildings.

I saw wooden pillars standing about six or seven feet apart in front of a concrete wall. Apparently, men were strapped to the pillars then shot. Bullet holes in the wall behind confirmed this. We were told hundreds of Belgians were killed this way. There was also a gallows for hanging. The place had been ransacked by the Germans, trying to destroy anything that would incriminate them.

The cold here is excruciating, the only warm place is bed. It stopped raining around four this afternoon, but everything was wet because of the wind. I am certain I have a cold coming. We are *moving on tomorrow. Might be Belgium, but anybody's guess as we're never told.*

*Have you been to see 'our' house?*

*I love you,*

*Jamie*

This letter had been written before Jamie's confession. Goldie cursed the postal system for the letters that went astray or were held up, causing untold hurt to newly bereaved parents and loved ones. After all, Rebecca might still be alive had she received Jamie's letter begging her forgiveness.

She looked at the clock on the mantelpiece. Rebecca's funeral would be over by now. She and Gladys had decided not to attend. It was more important that they looked to the living, not the dead. Gladys had left early with Rebecca's identity papers to visit Fareham Register Office.

The little boy had slept through the night and was still asleep. Goldie allowed a smile to cross her lips. It was almost as though he was worn out with all his crying.

She hadn't slept a wink all night. As she had stood over little Eli's makeshift bed smiling down at him, during the early hours of the morning, Goldie knew they had done the right thing in bringing back the child. He was all she had left of Jamie. The joy and contentment of watching the sleeping child made her unhappiness at Jamie's infidelity and subsequent death pall by comparison.

Sooner or later she must visit Jamie's family. She felt sure that after the shock of the death of their son, the fact that there was a living grandchild would be a great comfort to them. Jamie's parents would contact her; they had been happy their son had chosen to marry her. But she would wait until they could cope with their own grief before telling them about Rebecca and little Eli.

A whimper reached her ears. Goldie, her smile broader, left the living room and went upstairs.

Goldie picked up her cup and drained it of the tea she'd made earlier. In a little while she'd go along and pick up Eli from Mrs Symonds at number eight. Ada Symonds was a stickler for timekeeping. Mogs jumped up on her lap and she scratched his ear. He started to purr.

The trouble was, she hated being parted from the little boy.

There was no denying Ada Symonds was a good child-minder. Six children claimed her attention, three of them babies, two nearly ready for school and the eldest at St John's Primary. Goldie took Eli there in the mornings and brought him back in the afternoon. But she wanted more of him than a couple of hours, a bath before bedtime and listening to his even breathing as he slept in the carrycot next to her bed.

Solly had purchased the carrycot from Margie's market stall in the town. He had paid over the odds for it but prams, pushchairs, cots, indeed all kiddies' paraphernalia, were at a premium during wartime.

Goldie smiled, thinking how in such a short time he had bonded with the little boy. Even on Sundays she had to share Eli with Solly, who now seemed to be an almost permanent fixture in the house.

Mrs Symonds's strict routine had borne fruit. She'd taken Eli with his stick-thin arms and legs and in next to no time plumped him to a decent weight. He was now a smiling, contented baby. But all day long, as Goldie worked at her lathe at Priddy's, her thoughts were on the child.

Later, with little Eli gurgling in his carrycot, perched on the old comfortable armchair beneath the window, she started to prepare the dinner.

Soon the potatoes were simmering on the gas stove, and three of the smallest chops she'd ever seen were nestling in the oven, along with another of Siddy's apple pies. Goldie began to tackle the ironing. Mogs sat curled up in front of the range while Goldie explained to Gladys what was on her mind.

'The thing is, I don't think a child should be passed

around like a pass-the-parcel. I think either you or I should be looking after him full-time.'

There, she'd said her piece. She put down the flat iron on the top of the range. She had a blanket folded over on the table and an old piece of cloth next to it to wipe off the smuts that clung to the iron's base. She was ironing the long white nightgowns Eli wore. He had quite a little wardrobe of clothes now, most of them larger than necessary so that he could grow into them.

'We can't both be here all the time, how will we live?' Gladys was the other side of the table grating up a tiny bit of cheese, hoping to make it stretch to sandwiches for the lunch tins.

'I've worked out that with the promised money that Eli said he would make sure was taken from his wages at source and sent to us regularly, and if we both work part-time and take extra shifts, we could do it. We'd also save the money we pay Ada for babysitting. I just want to spend more time with him.'

Gladys's voice was wistful. 'He ain't going to stay a baby long.'

'Exactly.'

'I'll have a word with Mr Scrivenor.'

'You're a love, Gladys.'

'Time was a bloke would be putty in my hands, but now . . .'

'I've never known you not get a feller to do what you want,' said Goldie. She tossed her long hair back from her shoulder and picked up the iron with a cloth then spat on it. It sizzled; she wiped the bottom of the iron by running it over the folded cloth. Satisfied it was clean, she began to iron one of Doll's blouses.

Gladys put her fingers beneath her breasts and breathed in sharply.

'What's the matter?'

'A bit of indigestion, I think.' She laughed. 'Don't look so worried, I'm not ready for the knacker's yard just yet.'

'Probably all that Christmas stuff that Will gave us.'

Goldie thought back to the packages of food they'd been given. It had been a quiet Christmas working different shifts at Priddy's. The war didn't cease just because it was a special day, but they'd spent an evening at the Rainbow and the music and dancing and chat with Marlene and Mac had been wonderful. The high spot had been the gifts from Doll.

It had been decided not to give presents, as money wasn't that plentiful. Gladys, Goldie and Doll had clubbed together and given Solly back the five pounds he'd paid for the baby. But on Christmas morning Goldie had found a pretty brooch in the shape of a bird, wrapped in paper, on the kitchen table. Gladys unwrapped a blue short-sleeved jumper. Solly had a pair of cufflinks shaped like half-moons and the baby had knitted clothes, a tiny pair of cotton shoes, a silky pillow and matching quilt set, and a patchwork cat. All courtesy of Jane from Priddy's, who sold items she made at home in her spare time.

Gladys was the first to notice Doll no longer wore her gold watch. It didn't take long to realize the girl had sold it to buy the gifts.

'Doll, you shouldn't have done that,' Gladys had said.

'Why not? That old watch is just a thing. My present from all of you is a proper family and a new life. You've given me something I've never had before and I value that much more than gold.'

Gladys had turned away so the girl wouldn't see her cry.

Gladys asked Goldie, 'You answered Eli's letter?' She glanced up towards the mantelpiece.

Goldie said, 'I will.' She hung Doll's blouse across the back of a chair. Gladys had finished the sandwiches with the aid of a jar of paste and was shutting the lids on the Oxo tins they both used as lunch boxes when voices were heard and the front door was opened. Goldie heard the key swing back against the wood. A blast of cold air swept into the kitchen along with Doll and Solly.

'Shut that door!' shouted Gladys. Then to Solly, 'Ain't you got no home to go to?'

'My mum's gone round her friend's house and Dad's out, so there's not much point in me going home to an empty house then coming back to take Doll to the Rainbow.' He looked wounded. 'You don't have to feed me, but I've got a present for you.' He held out a bag. 'Be careful.'

Gladys took the paper bag and looked inside and counted.

'Five eggs!' A huge smile lit her face; she counted again. 'Five real eggs!' Gladys hadn't seen so many eggs for ages. She looked at Solly.

'A friend gave them to me. I mended his shed. He's got chickens.'

'I think you deserve to stay to tea.' Goldie put the iron down in the hearth to cool. Then she folded the blanket once more and put it in the sideboard. 'We've got potatoes, cabbage and apple pie from Siddy for afters, and we'll divide the chops. A couple of eggs with grated onion and milk will make omelettes. It'll be a feast.'

'She's had a letter from Eli,' said Gladys, butting in.

Goldie saw Solly's face fall. 'You going to answer it?'

'Yes,' she said. A frown crossed Solly's face.

'Oi! Don't you start him off,' Goldie shouted as Doll picked up baby Eli and started making him laugh.

'I don't know how we managed without this gorgeous baby,' sang out Doll.

Goldie smiled, thinking of the change in the girl. She

didn't mind changing his nappies or feeding him, even when he insisted on spitting his food out all over her. It gladdened her heart to watch Doll play peekaboo with him. Gladys, too, had changed. She'd put on weight and was definitely happier now that she knew Will was interested in her. Maybe, thought Goldie, that was one of the reasons Gladys was happy to talk to Scrivenor about changing their hours. Not only would it give her more time to spend with Siddy, who had been neglected lately; it would also give her more time to go down to the Rainbow.

'I'd better go and sort out the meal,' said Gladys. She began to rise from the chair while still holding tight to Mogs.

'Sit still,' said Goldie. 'The last time you made an omelette you burned it. These eggs are precious; I'll do it.' She looked at Solly. 'You can lay the table.'

She saw Gladys sink back on the chair, smoothing Mogs's fur, and Goldie smiled.

Later that night Goldie sat in the old armchair, leaning an upturned tray on her knees, and with paper and pen at the ready she reread Eli's letter.

*Dear Goldie,*
*Your letter telling me of how you braved Mrs Brooks and calmly walked away with little Eli gladdened my heart. I'll*

provide funds so you'll not be out of pocket by looking after him. My parents, in their letter to me, showed no emotion about Rebecca's sad demise. My father quoted, 'As ye sow, so shall ye reap.' He didn't ask me about her baby. Of course, I've no idea what was said at the funeral. I'm sure my father will never recognize little Eli. He was always hard on Rebecca and myself growing up, yet he was always gracious to outsiders. The Bible featured greatly in our lives.

I have a great favour to ask. Could you visit Rebecca's grave at St Mary's churchyard? If you could place flowers there occasionally, it would make me so happy. I don't want her to be forgotten. I will of course reimburse you.

Another great favour? Would you mind if I wrote from time to time for news of little Eli? It's a lonely life here. I had a girl, but she was killed in a bomb blast. When eventually I am granted leave I would very much like to come and visit the boy, if I might?

Jamie and I were good friends. I miss him. Thank you for naming his son after me. I feel it is a great honour. I'm sure, because of your generosity, the little boy will grow into a fine man.

Sincerely,

Eli

Goldie began to write.

## Chapter Twenty-One

'Gladys!' On hearing her name she turned. It was her week for babysitting and she was pushing the pram through the market. She came face-to-face with Mac.

'Hello.' He stopped her. 'I'm glad I've caught you before you read about it in the *Evening News*.'

She stared into the detective's handsome, craggy face.

'What's the matter?'

He removed his trilby and scratched at his red hair.

'Two boys found a body washed up on Stokes Bay beach. It wasn't a pretty sight.'

Gladys opened her mouth, but he hushed her.

'The body is Rene Watts, the woman who worked with Doll's brother, Fred Leach.'

'Oh, my God! Are you certain?' Her knees had gone to jelly and she was glad of the pram to lean against.

'There was enough of her to do tests to confirm it. She

was also found with some cheap jewellery that one of the girls working at the Blue said she wore.'

'What did Fred say?'

'That she'd disappeared about the time his sister ran off and he'd thought they'd gone together.' The baby was stirring, so Gladys pushed the big pram back and forth, hoping the movement would calm little Eli.

'Did he ask you about Doll?'

'Don't worry, I dig for information, I don't give it out.' She smiled at him gratefully and took a deep breath. The smells from the market flooded her senses.

'How did she die? Drowning?' The woman had been a good friend to Doll; without her help the girl wouldn't be living with Gladys.

'There was a hole in her skull.' He bent forwards. 'I shouldn't be telling you this, but it looks like she'd been tied up.' He put his hand on her arm. 'Someone put her in the sea.' He moved from one foot to the other. 'I thought you'd like to tell Doll before it all comes out.'

Gladys nodded. 'That's really kind of you, Mac.' She felt shaken. 'Me and Doll had promised each other so many times to pay her a visit, but we never got around to it. What with her being scared of Fred . . .' she added.

'Doll's safe enough working for Will.' He leaned forward and looked in the pram. 'Meeting you has saved me a visit to Alma Street. Your latest addition is growing.' He put his hand towards the child and little Eli curled his fingers around Mac's thumb. Gladys could see it made Mac emotional.

'You and Marlene, no sign of a little one?' She knew it was their dearest wish to have a child between them. Marlene's girl was at school now. She had struggled for years as an unmarried mother before meeting Mac. He adored Marlene, who was one of Gladys's oldest and most trusted friends. She'd taken little Eli round to visit and naturally had told her the truth about Rebecca and Jamie.

'So, Priddy's has allowed the two of you to work different shifts so you can spend more time with this little one?' He extracted his finger and stood up straight.

'No one was more surprised than me,' she said.

Baby Eli obviously didn't like it that Mac had taken his finger away and let out a lusty yell.

'That's a good set of lungs,' said Mac. 'Look, Gladys, a word of warning. Keep Doll away from her brother; there's no telling what he'll do if and when he finds her. I'd bet my life he had something to do with that poor woman's death.'

Gladys nodded before she picked up the crying child and laid him against her shoulder. Little Eli stopped crying, comforted by her closeness. She was overwhelmed by a rush of tenderness and the feeling of a terrible responsibility that she and Goldie must care for this perfect creature. It was both horrifying and quite wonderful.

Doll pulled the key through the letter box and opened the front door, then squeezed past the pram that was practically blocking the passage. She was cold after the long walk back from Priddy's and was thankful the kitchen was like an oven. Since baby Eli had come to live with them, the place smelled different. Talcum powder, soap and sweet-fragranced creams. The baby was lovely, she thought. As soon as she bent over him after taking off her coat and boots and slinging everything on a kitchen chair, he gave her a big grin, showing his two pearly bottom teeth.

Gladys wasn't so happy. She was about to feed the baby. 'Sit down, love, I want to talk to you.'

Doll looked expectantly at Gladys.

'I met Mac in town today and he wanted to tell us something before it was in the paper.'

'What?' It must be pretty serious, Doll thought. Gladys had tears in her eyes.

The baby snuffled and went on feeding.

'A woman's body was washed up off Stokes Bay. It's Rene.' She looked at Gladys, but before she could say anything Gladys added, 'Mac says they're sure.'

'It was Fred.' Doll felt her anger rise.

'Hush! You don't know that.'

'Oh, yes I do. He hurt her because she helped me.'

'I thought he cared about Rene?'

'If someone crosses the line, it don't matter whether he likes them or not.' Her tears were falling now. Why didn't she go and see Rene?

'Doll, sit down here and finish feeding baby Eli for me; I've got things to do.' Gladys got up with the child in her arms and passed him over to her. Doll moved herself over to Gladys's vacated chair. The child was agitated. Cross because he'd been contentedly sucking at his bottle and it had been taken from him. Doll gave him back his feed.

'Thank you,' she said. She knew Gladys had given her the task of finishing feeding him to stop her being upset. She looked down at the little boy she loved so much. Gladys always seemed to know what to do and when to do it. 'Fred's my brother,' Doll said. 'But it doesn't stop me hating him.'

Gladys stood watching her, then went down the passage. When she returned she had her coat and boots on and a scarf around her neck.

'I meant it when I said I had something to do. I need some Beechams Powders. I got heartburn something terrible. You can sort his lordship out, can't you?'

Doll nodded. She knew Gladys hadn't been herself just lately.

'Don't worry about our dinner, I've peeled the potatoes and I'm going to the fishmonger to see if they've got something nice.' She looked down at Mogs twining himself around her legs. 'I hadn't forgotten you.' She bent down and patted his sturdy body.

The wireless was on and big-band music was playing. Doll was happy to have the baby to herself. He'd drained his feed and his eyes were flickering, so she knew he was ready for his bed. Gladys had already bathed him and Doll bent her head, breathing in the sweetness of him. She put him to her shoulder and rubbed his back until he burped, getting rid of the wind that had accumulated. She took him upstairs to the back bedroom, where Gladys had left a hot-water bottle in his new cot.

One-handed, she transferred the bottle to Goldie's bed and settled little Eli. He was a good baby and had already started to sleep through the night.

The cot was freshly painted. Solly had brought it round to the house one Sunday morning. He said he'd found it on a bomb site. A couple of the struts had been broken, but he'd gone to Wheelers and bought some dowelling, and after he'd painted it, it was as good as new. Baby stuff was practically a non-starter in the shops. It really was a case of make do and mend, which is what they did with the mattress. Gladys and Goldie had cut up clean jumble-sale clothing and stuffed a huge bag. The finished product was a big improvement on the drawer that Eli was now too big for.

Doll couldn't get Rene's face from her mind. Oh, how she wished she'd done as she'd promised and gone to Southsea to visit her. Tears began to roll down her cheeks.

As she flicked off the light switch, she heard the front door open then the clatter of the key as, job done, it banged against the back of the door. Doll went downstairs.

'Anyone in?'

'Shhhh!' Doll put her finger to her lips. 'I've just got him off.' She raised her eyes towards the stairs and looked at Solly, who had just divested himself of his overcoat and thrown it across the pram. He took off his trilby and ran his fingers through his hair that, once freed, fell across his forehead. Doll's tears increased.

'Whatever's the matter?' He was standing near the open door to her room. He held out his arms and she leaned into them. Her teary face snuggled against his chest and she allowed her sobbing to continue.

She began telling him between her tears about Gladys's meeting with Mac.

'I should have gone to see her,' she cried. The lamp on the pavement outside the house shone through her window, sending fingers of yellow light to brighten the room. They made the silk coverlet on her bed glisten.

'You couldn't have known what would happen,' he said.

He smelled nice. Of Brylcreem and something woody and masculine. Solly was stroking her hair as though she was a little girl, and it was comforting. Doll had never had a man's arms around her. Dancing was different, of course a male partner held her close, but this felt special. She'd cared about Solly from the first moment they'd met and she loved being alone with him in the car when he collected her or took her to the Rainbow. She always felt that it was their special time together. It was true he had never touched her; he'd always treated her with respect. But she wasn't a child any more. She went to work. She danced on a stage.

She pushed against him and he stumbled backwards onto the bed. She fell with him, her face closer to his than it had ever been before. His mouth opened and she stopped his words with her lips.

Never before had Doll kissed a man, and though at first his lips were unyielding, slowly he melted against her. She put an arm around his neck to hold him close and could feel the heat coming from him as she traced down the front of his shirt with her finger until she felt the warm skin on his chest.

Solly groaned. He made to move away, but she used her weight to keep him pinned to the bed. He was breathing heavily but she wouldn't let him turn his head away from her probing tongue.

It seemed so natural to her, what she was doing. She was amazed that without any previous experience she knew exactly what to do.

She could feel the beating of his heart. Doll was drowning. She moved her tongue between his teeth and she felt certain he responded. Doll was practically weeping with pleasure, carried to the highest of heights, but his arms stiffened and he thrust her body away from him.

She heard his one word, 'No!'

She didn't hear the front door opening. But she heard Goldie's voice as the electric light bloomed.

'You little tart!'

She was pulled away from Solly and the slap that landed on her face hurt so much. It was such a surprise that she cried out.

'Solly, get in the kitchen.' Gladys's voice was hard and cold, so very cold. Solly rolled from the bed and practically fled down the passage.

'All the street could have walked by and seen this spectacle, it's like a knocking shop!' Goldie swung the curtains closed. 'Whatever did you think you were doing?' she shouted.

'I think that's pretty obvious,' Gladys said. Then, 'You'd better get to bed, missy. We'll talk in the morning!'

She pushed Goldie out and slammed the door shut. Doll heard them stomp down the hallway. The kitchen door banged and two minutes later she heard footsteps climb the stairs, as someone had gone to look in on the baby.

Doll undressed and got into bed. Her brain was whirling.

Solly hadn't disliked kissing her, of that she was sure. But oh, how wonderful it would have been if it was him pushing her down on the bed!

Tears filled her eyes, for herself, and for Rene found floating in the cold, cold Solent.

In the kitchen Solly was getting the third degree.

'But why did you allow yourself to go along with it?'

'Because, Gladys, he's a bloke like any other and if it's handed to him on a plate, he'll take it,' Goldie answered for him.

Solly looked crestfallen.

'I'd only been gone five minutes.' Gladys said.

'I'm sorry. I didn't start anything and I think deep down you believe that, else I wouldn't be sitting here. But you're right, Goldie, I'm a bloke and she's a very attractive girl. But that's all she is, a girl. I can only repeat, I'm sorry. Look, I didn't kiss her back. It won't happen again.'

'Bloody right it won't!'

'All right, Goldie, that's enough. Anyone would think him and you was . . .' Gladys searched her face. 'You're jealous!'

'Don't be stupid!' Goldie spat out the words.

Gladys watched as Solly rose from the kitchen chair. 'It's not a night Doll goes to the Rainbow, so why are you here?'

'For God's sake, I didn't plan it.' Solly moved to the door and went into the passage. The springs of the pram complained. He returned with a large square package. 'I got these down the market and brought them round. I know you're short.' He put the package on the table. 'I left them in the pram.'

Gladys ripped open the brown paper. A dozen white terry-towelling napkins tumbled out. She looked at him. 'What can I say?'

'Thanks might be nice.'

Gladys looked sheepish. 'Thanks,' she said.

Solly stared down at Goldie, who was on her knees on the rag rug, riddling the fire. 'Do you want me to do that?'

Goldie pushed back her hair, leaving a sooty mark on its blondness. She got up and handed him the poker. 'Go on, then.'

Gladys said, 'I'll pop in and have a word with Doll. Trouble is, she's growing up, and fast.'

# Chapter Twenty-Two

'Look, it's French, a Longoni with drop handlebars.' Gladys had pushed through the crowd and was bending down to look at the racing cycle. She had a dreamy look on her face as she touched the chrome handlebars and fingered the shiny gears.

'He reckons he's going to get fit for the New Year,' said Maisie Robbins.

'Well, it's a tidy ride from Lee-on-the-Solent for ol' Scrivenor,' admitted Henry Williams. 'Nice machine, though. You can't just buy a bike like this in the shops, he must have had it on order for ages and ages.'

'With his money, it stands to reason he can afford the perks.' Mary Thomas stared at it. 'I ain't been on a bike for yonks.'

'I've never ridden one with drop handlebars,' said Gladys. 'I used to ride an old boneshaker when I was younger. It's been my dream to ride a racer.' Her eyes were wide with wonder.

The bike, shiny and new, stood against the wall in the enclosure. Other bikes were lined up nearby. Many of the workers cycled to Priddy's, as it was easier and cheaper than hanging around waiting for a bus.

'Let's go in and get changed,' said Goldie. Mr Scrivenor had requested that Goldie come in for the next couple of days as there was a special rush job on. Luckily their neighbour hadn't minded taking baby Eli. Neither Goldie nor Gladys could refuse, as Scrivenor had already been so kind to them. Doll was in the changing room putting her own clothes in her locker and changing into her navy-blue dungarees and white turban, the uniform of Priddy's female workers.

The weather was bitterly cold, but a thin sun shone and early daffodils were already showing their tips in the long grass near the woodland full of glistening white snowdrops.

'Come on,' urged Goldie, she took the brown carrier bag containing their Oxo tins and flasks from Gladys and began to walk away.

'Go on, girl!' a voice urged.

Goldie looked back. To her horror she saw that Gladys had wheeled the bicycle from its spot near the wall. She was riding it, wobbling around on the cobbles.

'I never been on such a bike in all my life,' she shouted, a daft grin on her face. 'I always wanted a go on a racing model. Now my dream's come true.'

Goldie shouted, 'Get off! Put it back! There'll be hell to pay—'

She didn't get any further, for Gladys was picking up speed, her feet only just reaching the pedals. The crowd was urging her on, laughing and cheering, Gladys loving every minute. Goldie could see she had great difficulty in looking where she was going while hunched over the drop handlebars.

The scraping crash told Goldie the sad truth that the thin wheels had caught between the stones.

She left the carrier bag on the ground and ran towards Gladys.

'C'mon, get up!' Goldie, cross, put her hand beneath her friend's arm and tugged, trying to free her from the bicycle.

'I can't. I fell on the bleedin' bar, my fanny hurts something terrible!'

The crowd around them were laughing and making inane remarks.

'If Scrivenor catches you, you'll be hurting in your wage packet! He'll give you the sack!' Goldie said.

'That's his pride and joy,' said Mary Thomas.

Gladys glared at her and attempted to climb out of the

metal. Her face, shrouded in agony, told of her pain. Finally she stood up, unsteady, but nevertheless upright.

Jake Allen, a big man from the packing department, bent down and picked up the bike. 'It looks all right,' he said, eyeing the cycle all over and testing the brakes. 'Maybe them Frenchies knows how to make 'em scratch-proof.' He looked at Gladys, then at Goldie. 'Better take her to the nurse,' he said. 'You don't know what damage she might have done to herself.'

Mary Thomas cried out, 'Especially there!' And she pointed to her nether regions. The dwindling crowd laughed. Jake said, 'I'll put the bike back, maybe ol' Scrivenor'll never know.' He had a smile on his weather-beaten face as he wheeled the cycle away back towards the sheds.

'It don't half hurt,' said Gladys. 'Thanks, Jake,' she called. He waved back at her.

'Serves you right,' said Goldie, 'acting like a girl at your age.'

Gladys sniffed. 'I always wanted a go on a bike like that,' she repeated, 'I just couldn't help myself.' Then, 'I could do with a cuppa.'

Goldie looked across the cobbles. 'Someone's taken our lunch tins in. You'll have to wait for a cup of tea. We'd better get changed first, then I'll come with you to see the nurse.'

The changing room went quiet as they entered, with

Gladys still moaning. Slowly the hum of noise increased again. Mae Elliott checked them over for missed hairgrips, cigarettes and matches, which were naturally forbidden, and she made sure they'd changed into the special boots provided by Priddy's.

Goldie walked along the corridors with Gladys hobbling at her side and grabbing hold of her arm.

'Hurry up,' urged Goldie as Gladys, moaning, started to lag behind. Eventually they reached the nurse's office. Gladys was still tucking her hair beneath the hated turban when the door opened and Anna Windsor urged them in.

The room smelled of antiseptic and Gladys wrinkled her nose. It reminded her of hospitals and she hated hospitals.

'I don't need to ask you why you're here. I was watching you through the window. You hit that crossbar with a wallop.'

'Oh, dear, I hope Scrivenor didn't see . . .' Gladys pulled a face.

'You'll have to wait and find out, won't you?' There was kindness in the older nurse's words. 'Get undressed and sit up on the couch,' she said. She pulled a curtain aside to reveal a leather bed. 'Put your clothes on that chair.' She pointed to a chair in the corner. Then she looked at Goldie, who'd turned away and was staring out of the window.

'I'm not watching you fiddle with her lady-bits. I'll stay this side of the curtain.'

Gladys said, 'Daft, this is, I only just got dressed after getting undressed and now I'm undressed again.'

'Be quiet while I examine you,' the nurse said, and with a swish the curtain enfolded the two of them. 'Just take down your knickers,' she added.

Gladys lay there, hardly daring to breathe. The nurse's fingers seemed to find all the tender bits and a couple of times Gladys yelped, only to receive a glare from Nurse Windsor.

Every so often Gladys was treated to a smile, but all she could think of was how soon she could get out, because Scrivenor would wonder where she was as she hadn't reported to him, and she wasn't at her overseer's desk if he came round.

'Okay, you can sit up now.' Nurse Windsor smiled at her. 'There's bone bruising that will go soon but as far as I'm concerned little likelihood the baby's been harmed. Pull your knickers up.'

'What?' The disembodied voice came from Goldie.

'I beg your pardon?' Gladys's voice was shaky. Her hands began to tremble and her head was swimming.

'I assume you know you're over five months pregnant?'

Gladys knew what she was hearing, but it didn't make sense. Then the fainting spells, the tiredness, the sickness and her weight gain all added up.

'Drink this.' The nurse was handing her a glass of water.

Goldie had pulled back the curtain and was watching her, aghast. 'Look,' the nurse said, 'I'll go along and wangle some tea from somewhere, while you two have a chat. Priddy's needs its workers to be on the ball, and I can see you've both had a shock.'

Gladys was staring at Goldie as if she'd never seen her before.

Goldie came and sat on the edge of the couch. 'You didn't know, did you?'

Gladys shook her head. 'I've been having funny turns but I thought I was going through an early change.'

'Too bloody early,' said Goldie. 'Is it Siddy's?'

Gladys shook her head. 'No.' Goldie was staring at her. 'I know you'll think I'm a tart, but I don't know who the father is.' The words tumbled from Gladys's lips.

Goldie pursed her mouth. Gladys saw she was assimilating the news.

'I've only ever had one kiddie an' that was my Pixie. When she died in that bomb blast I never thought I'd have any more. It wasn't for want of trying.' Why, oh why wouldn't her body stop shaking?

Goldie suddenly leaned across and put her arms around her. 'What are you going to do?'

'Do? Whatever do you mean? I'm well over the safe time for getting rid of it even if I wanted to . . .' Gladys disentangled herself from Goldie. 'You know, I don't want to get rid of it. I'm getting all excited now. Imagine me. A baby? This is a little sister or brother for baby Eli . . .'

There was a moment of quietness.

'If you're excited, then so am I,' said Goldie with a grin from ear to ear.

'How do you feel?' The nurse's blue uniform was swishing with the starch in it as she entered the room. She put the tray with three cups of tea upon her desk and then passed one over to Gladys. Gladys took it gratefully. Her heart was beating fast. She was happy, she really was.

'I'll write a letter for you to take to Blake's Maternity Home at Ham Lane. But go and see your own doctor first.' The nurse passed Goldie her tea. Then she sat down and began scribbling. Gladys drank her tea, which was like nectar. Then she finished dressing. The excitement inside her wouldn't go away. She hoped it never would. After a while the nurse handed her an envelope.

Goldie was smiling at her. She didn't have to ask her friend if she really was pleased about the baby; she could see she was. Every baby was a gift from God. As Gladys opened the door and said her goodbyes, the mournful wail of the air-raid siren cut through the air and all hell was let loose.

'I have to get to our workshop to check the girls out,' Gladys shouted. She stuffed the envelope given her by the nurse into her dungarees pocket and, half hobbling, half walking, made her way along the corridor with Goldie close on her heels.

Once in the workshop, she saw the girls at their places waiting for the shift to start. They looked worried because of the siren and there was no one to tell them what to do. Obviously, they'd been on time but she hadn't, so the machines were a non-starter. Gladys breathed a sigh of relief as she grabbed her worksheets. She had no idea who hadn't turned up for work but she could certainly make sure those that had hurried to safety. Luckily she knew her girls well, so could tell none were missing. They filed out into the yard and away from the dangerous materials in the workshop. Goldie hadn't left her side.

'You got to look after yourself now,' she shouted. The sky darkened with planes.

Through the windows Gladys could see the flashes and hear the terrible noise of bombing as Portsmouth seemed to take the brunt of the battering.

'We have to find Doll,' Gladys shouted back.

'Solly will take care of her.' Gladys admitted to herself that as he was in charge of Doll's workshop, he would indeed make sure the girl had taken cover.

Gladys was happy the rage she'd felt when first she'd discovered Doll on the bed with Solly had abated. Solly had become like one of the family and she liked having him around. It had been extremely hard for her to admit to herself that he had pushed the girl away, but she had seen it happen. The more she thought about the incident the more she realized she could hardly blame the girl. Solly was a good-looking man. Besides, how could she go on thinking ill of Doll? Her father couldn't care less about his daughter and Fred hadn't been a good example of a man to admire. She wasn't exactly a good example either, was she? Especially now she was expecting and had no idea who the father was.

Goldie had dragged her to the abandoned railway arches. They fought for space with the other workers. It wasn't long before the dreaded putt-putt sound could be heard, then the long cigar shape came into view with flames billowing from the rear. Goldie grabbed Gladys's hand but the bombing machine flew out of sight. Then came the terrible noise of its landing.

It seemed as if everyone had opted for silence. They all knew the risk they were taking. It only needed one bomb to hit the armament factory and Priddy's and her workers would be no more. Even the small bombs, incendiaries, caused fires. They had to be extinguished immediately. Gladys could feel Goldie's nails biting into her flesh. She knew Goldie was worrying about baby Eli. Would he be safe?

Ground fire was hammering the skies and the air was

filled with the smell of cordite. A thin mist of smoke had drifted over the stretch of water from Portsmouth and Gladys could see flames shooting up to the sky from one of the buildings on the Hard. Then a tin mug of tea was shoved into her hand. The smell immediately raised her spirits. It was dark brown, the way she liked it.

'Get that down you, girl,' Eddie Saunders, one of the packers, said. 'We're a lot better off than those poor buggers they found in Auschwitz; at least we stand a chance.'

'I read about that in the *Evening News*,' Gladys said. 'Piles of bones, a death camp with the remainder of its inmates near to death. How can those Germans be so bloody cruel?'

No one answered her. They were probably all thinking of their own mortality, she decided. Then the all-clear sounded. This raid had seemed very short. Sighs of relief could be heard.

'You think Scrivenor'll let us take the rest of the day off?' Gladys heard Mary Jackson ask.

'I bloody hope not,' Gladys said. 'We got a war to win.'

# Chapter Twenty-Three

She squeezed her hands around her waist and then turned sideways, so that she could see herself in the mirror. She was definitely rounded, but didn't look pregnant. Gladys had been tiny when she'd given birth to her daughter all those years ago and it looked as if she'd be able to go another couple of months before it became obvious that she was with child.

The wireless was on, Frank Sinatra crooning away. Gladys liked the skinny Italian singer. She'd gone off Bing Crosby. She began to hum along with the music, while throwing blouse after blouse onto her bed, pulling them out from the wardrobe. Doll had given her a message from Will that he'd like to see her. Doll didn't say why.

Gladys had already decided to wear her black skirt, as it had always been generous around the waist, and now she was looking for a blouse that didn't have to be tucked in. She decided on a silky cream one with a pussy bow at the neck.

As soon as she was dressed she went downstairs and looked out at little Eli, who was still fast asleep in his pram outside the front door. He was well wrapped up against the cold, but the fresh air would do him good, she'd decided.

Today and the rest of the week was her turn to be with the child, and she relished every moment.

Scrivenor had taken her aside and told her he'd asked Ida Reynolds to take her place as overseer on her days off. Gladys had been happy about that. She loved her work at the munitions factory, but it was only fair to the girls that there was someone else they could refer to. She'd never felt indispensable.

In the kitchen, she shoved a disgruntled Mogs to the floor and took his place sitting in the old armchair beneath the window.

'Don't you look at me like that!' The cat stuck his tail up straight and went out to investigate his food dish in the scullery. Gladys propped her chipped mirror on the arm of the chair and began her make-up.

She pencilled in her eyebrows, then using her finger smoothed blue eyeshadow on her lids. Not too much; some women made themselves look like clowns. Then she used her finger again to wipe pan stick carefully beneath her eyes to hide the shadows. Some women at Priddy's smothered their faces with the creamy stick, hoping it would be a barrier against the yellowing of the skin caused by the poisons they worked with. After much spitting on her little brush and wiping it on the block of mascara, her eyelashes took on a darker hue. She'd given up wearing false eyelashes for everyday because she frequently lost one or both. The bright-red lipstick completed her desired look. It was said Hitler hated red lipstick, so out of defiance bright red was the favoured colour of English girls, when they could get it.

She thought of Fred not allowing Doll to wear make-up. Of course, some men believed make-up on a woman meant they were a tart, but that was mainly the older generation, who were set in their ways. Fred had stopped Doll from wearing make-up because it was all about control. He didn't want anyone to see how pretty she could be with a little paint and powder. Gladys sighed. At her age the girl needed to be experimenting with clothes, hairstyles and everything else that was part of the growing-up process.

Gladys put her make-up back in the cotton drawstring bag that was its home, and began to take out the wire curlers from the front of her hair. A good brushing, a glance in the small mirror to check the back of her hair in the mirror over the mantelpiece, and she was ready to change little Eli, put on her high heels and black swing coat, and go.

It was a cold, clear day and as she walked along Forton Road she noted the gaps like pulled teeth where bombs had destroyed houses. Their gardens were filled with plants growing in the rubble as though no one had told them they weren't needed, and for some reason that made her feel very sad.

The market was in full swing. She waved or spoke to friends she met and at the fishmonger's stall she purchased some cod to make a fish pie for tea, and some scraps for Mogs. George was heavy-handed with the scraps.

'You look nice today, Glad.'

'I bet you say that to all the women.'

'I don't, because they aren't called Gladys!'

She laughed at him, put the fish he'd wrapped in newspaper in the bottom of the pram, and walked on.

Gladys loved the market. The colour, the noise, the smells and the cheeky banter from the stallholders; even the war couldn't take that away.

Eventually she arrived at the Rainbow, on the front facing the Ferry Gardens. She looked in despair at the steps leading up to the entrance. She didn't want to leave the baby in his pram outside. Prams were hard to come by. She started to heave the heavy thing up the stone steps.

'Hang on, leave that to me.'

Mac came bouncing down the steps and took the handle from her. She smiled her thanks and looked up to the open door to see Will standing there. He gave her a big smile and her heart flipped.

With the pram beside a table, Will told her to sit down. He yelled across to a girl wiping down one of the counters to bring a pot of tea. Glancing around, Gladys saw that the place was spotlessly clean, and it smelt of polish. It wasn't yet open for business.

Mac stood next to Will and Gladys compared the two men. Will, boyish with his dark curls, and Mac with his shock of red hair. His trilby was on the table and his long raincoat was over the back of a chair. Gladys guessed they had been chatting about business before her entrance, and it wasn't yet resolved.

'I can't do anything without proof,' said Mac, 'and even then it wouldn't look right to my superiors if I got entangled in black-market squabbles . . .'

'You wouldn't call it squabbling if your livelihood was being taken from you.'

'I agree, mate, but your goods come into this country by illegal means.' He gave a huge sigh. 'Her brother wouldn't risk coming over here, not even for Doll.' He looked down at Gladys, then back at Will, who'd picked up an old cardboard beer mat and was shredding it to pieces. 'He knows all about you and your past and I wouldn't say he's shit-scared, but he's playing it safe.'

'So I can't expect any help from the police?'

Mac shook his head, then bent down, picked up his coat and shrugged himself into it. 'Like you, I think it's him. If something happens to the toerag, the coppers at South Street would turn a blind eye.'

He leaned in close to Will and said, 'I also believe he killed that woman. But can I do anything about it? Can I bleedin' hell!'

He looked down at Gladys. 'Sorry about the language, Gladys.' His face had reddened with embarrassment. She laughed. Then he added to Will, 'I just wish someone would give him a dose of his own medicine.'

Mac buttoned his overcoat. A young girl was trotting across the parquet flooring with a tray filled with tea things. Mac walked over to the pram and, leaning in, pulled back the covers. 'He's a smasher, ain't he, Gladys?' He looked back at her. 'You're one in a million, you are. Not many would take in a child like you and Goldie have.' He pulled the covers back over the sleeping baby. 'And now you're going to have one of your own. I'd give anything for a houseful of kiddies.' He put his hat on and nodded goodbye to Will. Too late, Gladys had seen the sadness in his eyes.

Will had gone quiet. He was looking at her as if he'd never seen her before. The girl was busying herself pouring out tea. Will said sharply, 'Leave that.' The girl looked at him, opened her mouth to say something, then obviously thought better of it and walked away on her high heels, her bottom swaying.

Gladys could see that Will was watching Mac walking lightly down the steps. Then he turned to her.

'I suppose it's that long streak's kiddie?'

Gladys knew he meant Siddy. She had no intention of telling the man before her anything about the child she was carrying. She was cross with Mac for blurting out her private business. She'd told Marlene, as the woman was one of her dearest friends. She'd also asked her to keep quiet about it. But the head that shares the pillow shares the secrets and of course Marlene had told Mac and just like a bloke he'd blurted it out.

She didn't answer him. She stirred milk into her cup, and then held up the little jug to ask him if he wanted milk. He nodded. Then he sighed. 'I should congratulate you,' he said. He looked towards the pram. 'You are going to have your hands full.'

'The more the merrier,' Gladys said. Let him think the child was Siddy's. Better that than tell him it might belong to one of the men she'd given more than a farewell kiss, before they went overseas to fight. Of course, she would have taken precautions if she'd had any idea she might conceive again after the birth of her daughter so long ago. But after not becoming pregnant over the years, her precautions had relaxed. She pushed his cup and saucer towards him.

Siddy. She hadn't told him yet!

She was angry with herself. Siddy was one person who ought to know. He was overjoyed about little Eli and sat for ages cuddling him, as long as the child was happy, mind. One cry and Siddy went back next door to his own house.

'I've always wanted children.'

Gladys put down her cup. 'Have you?'

'I'd have thought you'd have guessed that, the way I often have young Ronnie and Reggie raising hell down here.' He pointed across the room and as Gladys followed his arm she could see through the window the two boys, with an upturned bench and a blanket over it, on the grass in the Ferry Gardens.

'That's a tepee,' Will said. 'I had to make two bows and arrows out of branches from that willow over there.' Again he pointed.

'Aren't you scared that play-fighting will make them into thugs later in life?'

She could see one of them with a pretend knife jabbing it into his twin's back.

'That's a load of rubbish,' he laughed, showing his white teeth. 'Look at me.'

Now it was her turn to laugh. Then she remembered why she was there.

'Doll said you wanted to see me?'

He nodded then ran his fingers through his curls. 'It's to do with Doll.'

Gladys's heart began to beat fast.

'I know you're trying to keep her out of trouble and that Solly picks her up to take her home, but in this place it's difficult to keep her away from men.'

Now her heart was thumping so hard she was sure he could hear it. 'Go on,' she said.

'I got a lad humping crates around in the cellar. He should be at school, university, he calls it. He's training to be a vet, but any moment now he's expecting his call-up papers, so he's working for me.'

'Why are you telling me this?' Gladys wanted him to get to the point.

'He's taken a shine to Doll. I think she likes him, an' all . . .'

Gladys could feel the worry rising from her beating heart and flying out the window.

'I know she wanders down to chat with him when she's not on stage and he often comes up and stands watching her dance. The thing is, I know you're worried about her getting in with a bad lot because that brother of hers,' he practically spat the words out, 'kept her a virtual prisoner—'

'Leave them alone.' Her words practically shot from her mouth.

He looked relieved. 'He's a nice kid,' he said.

Gladys put her hand across the table and touched his arm. 'You don't know what a relief this is. I want her to have friends her own age; boys as well.'

'But what if they . . .'

'With someone her own age, it's natural.' She thought of Solly and how the girl had practically pinned him to the bed. He wasn't right for her; he was too old and with a bit of luck Solly would end up with Goldie, she hoped.

'So you don't mind them being together? Not that it's been going on long.'

'Mind? I'm pleased as Punch.' She felt his hand cover hers. 'Thank you for looking out for her. I always knew I could trust you,' Gladys said.

Almost as if on cue, the baby began to grizzle.

'I've brought a bottle with me. Do you mind if I feed him now? If I don't, he'll scream all the way home.' Gladys was on her feet, untangling little Eli from his warm bedding.

'He's bigger than I thought,' said Will. 'Could I hold him?' His words came out hesitantly.

Gladys stared at him. 'What? You'd like to?'

'I told you, I like kids.'

Gladys held the crying bundle and sniffed. 'I'll change him first, then you can have him, with pleasure,' she said. 'Oh, I do like a bloke who likes kids.'

# Chapter Twenty-Four

Will buttoned his fly and turned to leave the gents lavatory of the Blue. The place stank of stale piss. He went to wash his hands at the stone sink, but no water came from the tap. Trying to avoid the questionable wetness on the cement floor, he opened the door and went out into the corridor and came face-to-face with two men exchanging money. He saw one put notes into his wallet. Will turned his head; he had no desire to know what they were up to. He could guess.

He thought of the bright young girl who danced in his club and tried to imagine her here, on the tiny stage so close to the punters they would have been able to touch her. He shuddered. Thank God Doll was with Gladys and had a better life now.

Thinking of Gladys, he remembered the very pleasant time he'd spent with her before his club's opening time the other morning. They'd chatted and laughed and he'd found it so easy to be in her delightful company. That kiddie was something else. Will's lips formed a smile, remembering how he'd made the little boy laugh and dribble and show off his newly acquired teeth.

All the women he'd had over the years, all the money he'd spent on them – even set up a few in nice flats – yet not one of them had wanted to spoil her figure by giving him a son and heir. Bitches! All of them, out for what they could get from him. Now he could sleep with any woman he wanted just by snapping his fingers, but the only one he really wanted had tied herself to a skinny streak of misery who looked and acted more like a bleeding poofter than a man.

Of course, he could ask her to marry him.

But she was pregnant with the old codger's kiddie. He couldn't break that up, could he? Though wasn't she fair game until the bloke put a ring on her finger? Could he take her, with all her commitments and two children? Of course he could. And she wasn't too old to have another child, by him.

He hadn't liked to ask her when the new baby was due. No doubt it wouldn't be long before the finger-pointing and the tongue-wagging began. Neighbours could be cruel. She was such a caring person; everyone had applauded her for taking in that poor little homeless Eli, but they wouldn't be so nice when they found out she was about to be an unmarried mother.

He walked into the dull light of the club, where in the corner men were sitting at a table playing cards. At another table, a roulette wheel was turning. On the stage was a practically naked girl playing with a snake. It was disgusting, and not even titillating enough for him to go on watching.

'Cigarettes?'

The voice intruded on his thoughts. A blonde girl stood in front of him wearing fishnet stockings and a very short skirt that showed her suspenders. She tried again. 'Cigarettes, sir?' He caught a whiff of strong, flowery perfume. He looked down into the tray she carried in front of her. His hand strayed to a packet of Kyriazi Frères.

'How long you been selling these?'

'Not long. The boss gets them in special for discerning customers.'

'How much?'

When she told him the price he almost gagged. Nevertheless, he handed over the money for a packet of his own cigarettes that had been in the hold of a hospital ship, the *Jupiter*, two weeks ago. He'd bought tins and packets of the colourfully boxed cigarettes. They were made in Cairo and on the face of the cartons showed a lion smoking, with a woman snuggling up to the animal.

'Can I get you anything else, sir?' Will knew exactly what she meant, but he didn't want any of it. He smiled and shook his head. He thought he'd ask a few questions to see what answers she gave him. He put his hand on the box to stop her wandering away.

'Is Rene about?'

The girl looked around before answering vaguely. 'She doesn't work here any more.'

'Oh, why's that?'

She shrugged. 'She left a goodish time ago, never left a forwarding address.' Will guessed from her answer that she and probably the rest of the staff had been told the same story. 'What if I told you she'd been fished out of the Solent with a hole in her skull?'

For a moment the girl stared at him. Then her face drained of colour and she moved quickly away. She was swallowed up by the crowd. He knew she'd tell Fred.

Will threaded himself through the sweat-stinking crowd, who were still watching the girl with the snake, and walked quickly through the lobby and out onto the street. He'd seen enough. Mac had hinted that Fred was responsible for Rene's death, but he couldn't prove it. Mac had also suggested it was Fred who was robbing him of his black-market goods. Will could see Mac's reasons for not wishing to implicate Fred. To follow up on Fred's theft of Will's goods, which were themselves illegally sourced from Cairo, Mac would have to implicate both Fred and Will. They were mates. But hadn't Mac said if Fred disappeared it would be no great loss?

The rain was falling softly as he walked along the main road leading to Clarence Pier. He took the box of cigarettes from his pocket and stared at it.

Ioannis the Greek's ancestors had built the factory near the Souk El Tewfikia in Cairo in 1873. Will got a good deal because of their long-standing friendship, otherwise they would have been far too expensive to import. Will knew it was highly unlikely Fred had come by these cigarettes any other way than by stealing them from the *Jupiter*. With the popular brands like Players and Woodbines difficult to come by because of the war shortages, Turkish-style cigarettes, though an acquired taste, were greatly preferable to no cigarettes at all.

Will was fed up with being taken for a fool by scum like Fred. It was time he did something about it.

'What did Will want to talk to you about?'

'That's for me to know and you to find out.'

'Oh, Gladys.' Doll banged the bowl containing baked apples down on the table.

'Oi! Mind my crockery!'

Doll made sure the big bowl wasn't cracked. The cooked

fruit, courtesy of Siddy, smelled delicious, especially with the cores cut out and the fruit filled with honey, also courtesy of Siddy.

'Is there any of that Carnation milk left?' Goldie looked up from the chair beneath the window. She was knitting a matinee jacket for Gladys's forthcoming baby.

'I think so.' Gladys took three tea plates from the cupboard, put them on the table and began dishing out. 'C'mon, Goldie, get up to the table.'

Goldie put down her knitting, got up and went over to the table where she pulled out a chair and sat down. Doll was already in her place.

'Don't it smell nice?' The apple flavour filled the kitchen. Gladys smiled at her.

'If you must know, Will wondered how much longer it would be before Solly stops collecting you from the club. He says Fred won't dare come near the Rainbow, so you're pretty safe to come home on your own, unless there's someone else who could bring you back safely.'

Doll paused, with her filled spoon halfway to her mouth. 'Actually, there is a boy, he's ever so nice, you'd like him.' It all came out in one breath. Doll stared at Gladys.

'Well, that's all right, then.'

Doll looked amazed. 'You mean you don't mind me being with Joe?'

'Should I mind?'

A big smile passed over Doll's face. 'Gee, thanks!'

'Oi! Not so much of that American slang in here. We're English, we are.'

Goldie looked at Gladys and they grinned at each other. Goldie finished scraping her plate. 'That was lovely.'

'I need to pop round and see Siddy.' She looked at the clock on the mantelpiece. 'I was thinking of asking him, among other things, if he'd like to come round this evening. We could play a game of whist?' She looked at Doll, then at Goldie. 'Unless anyone's going out?'

They shook their heads. 'Right,' said Gladys. 'I think it's about time I told Siddy about the baby, don't you?'

Goldie sat on her bed. It had been a bad day today for her. She'd dreamed of Jamie last night and this morning, on waking, the realization hit her anew that he was dead.

Well-meaning people told her that 'time heals'. She hoped they were right.

The little boy looked like him. His large questioning eyes with their long fair lashes reminded her every day of Jamie. Never once had she regretted bringing him home from that dreadful woman's house.

A letter had arrived from Jamie's parents, telling her about his death and commiserating with her. They'd known how much she'd loved their son. There were no details of how or when Jamie would be brought home, if indeed he would be. The letter had traces of tears; well, she supposed they were tears, on the paper. She thought how distressing it must have been for them to write it. It had been extremely sad to read. She decided she would visit them later and take flowers.

Goldie and Gladys had discussed telling them about little Eli, but had decided to let them grieve for their son before hurting them with the news that he had gotten a young girl pregnant, who had then committed suicide. Jamie's parents weren't young and he was their only child. Everyone fell in love with little Eli and his cheeky smiles. It would be wonderful for him to have grandparents. They were good people, and Goldie had no doubt little Eli would bring them joy. After all, the little boy had given back Goldie her reason for living.

She went over to his cot, looked down at him and a great well of love flooded her body. She smiled.

# Chapter Twenty-Five

Siddy was sitting in front of the range, his feet propped up on the fender. He looked up in surprise at her entrance. The wireless was on and just as she was about to speak he put his finger to his lips, admonishing her to silence. 'Don't forget the diver', the catchphrase from the Tommy Handley show *ITMA*, came over the airwaves and Siddy chuckled, showing his false teeth.

'Makes me smile every time,' Siddy said. 'D'you want a cup of tea?'

'Not yet.' Gladys sat down on a little leather stool at his feet. It was warm and cosy in front of the fire. She smiled up at him. 'We had the apples baked,' she said. 'A right treat. I tried to feed baby Eli a little bit all mashed up, but he wasn't sure whether he liked it or not.'

'There's a few more Bramleys up in the rafters,' he said. 'Turn off the wireless; I guess you've got something to tell me.'

Gladys frowned, wondering how he knew. But she rose, went to the sideboard and switched off the set. She settled herself at his feet again.

'Who's the father?'

His question took her by surprise. 'How d'you know . . . ?'

'I'm not senile, Gladys. I know every bit of you and I've seen the pounds pile on in the right places. I was waiting for you to tell me.'

'Sometimes I believe you know me better than I know myself.'

'Am I the last to know?'

Gladys shook her head. 'I've been trying to keep it a secret until the busybodies start pointing their fingers.'

'And they will,' he said. 'Going to be hard with two little ones in the house.'

'You can say that again.' Gladys blew out her cheeks. She looked into his eyes.

'I wish it was mine.'

She sighed. 'To tell the truth, Siddy, I wish it was yours too, but I don't know who the father is.' She watched his face for any signs of disgust at her words and when his expression didn't change she knew he hadn't judged her. 'Of course, I got a few suspects in mind. But the main thing is this little one is mine.' She put her hands protectively across her stomach. 'Now the surprise is over, I'm as pleased as Punch.'

'Have you thought how you're going to manage?'

'I've tried not to think about it. As you know, me and Goldie are doing split shifts at Priddy's to look after baby Eli, but I can't work to full term because of all the poisons. I don't want to harm the little blighter before he's born, do I?'

'How about I keep you?'

Gladys thought she'd heard him wrong, but he was staring at her, waiting for an answer.

'That'll give the neighbours something to chew on,' she said. Then she shook her head. 'I don't think so, Siddy.'

'We could get married.'

Gladys really thought she'd misheard him this time and laughed. 'I thought you said married!'

'I did.' He tapped his hand on the arm of the chair. 'I'm quite harmless, you know. If you married me, the baby would have a name and you'd be well taken care of. I've got a bit put by . . .'

She was staring into his face. He meant it. He really did.

'I wouldn't ask anything of you that you weren't prepared to give and I do love you,' he continued.

Gladys rose from the stool. Her head was whirling. She made her way out to his scullery and lit the gas on the stove. She shook the kettle, checking there was enough water for tea, then set it on the flame.

She'd come next door to tell him about the baby and here he was proposing to her!

She put her head around the kitchen door. 'I'm not head over heels in love with you, Siddy.'

'You don't have to be. I got enough love for the both of us. You've got a big heart, Gladys. I want to be part of your little one's life. All men have ever done is take from you. I want to give. There'll be no restrictions. Your life will belong to you. I don't want you to change in any way, except for you to be my wife.'

The kettle was boiling. She made the tea. She thought of all the times when she'd been upset and she'd let herself into this house at night and crept into bed beside Siddy. She hadn't come for the lovemaking, she'd come for the way she'd felt safe with his arms around her.

'Gladys.'

She answered his call by poking her head back around the door. He continued, 'There is one thing I'd like to suggest, and that is that I keep this house on. Of course, we'll be together more, but I'm too old to be woken a hundred times in the night by the cries of little ones. I'll have a sort of bolthole to escape back to my books. You come and go as you please. That's if you say yes.'

More thoughts ran around her brain as she set the cups on a tray. The offer of a name for her child was tempting.

She knew how cruel people could be to fatherless children, but did she care enough about Siddy to marry him?

Suddenly, Will's face flashed momentarily in front of her. He was exciting. He was the sort of man that made her go weak at the knees. But Gladys needed security, not only for her baby, but for herself. Will was an unknown quantity. There was no doubt that marriage to Siddy would enable her to do her best for Goldie, little Eli, Doll and the new baby.

Her mind made up, she picked up the tray and took it into Siddy's kitchen, setting it down on the table. Gladys knelt down on the rag rug in front of her friend. She looked into his eyes.

'Yes, Siddy,' she said. 'I'll marry you. Thank you.'

Gently, he smoothed her hair and bent forward to kiss her forehead. 'That's made me so happy,' he said.

'And me, love.' Gladys got up, stepped over to the kitchen table and picked up the brown earthenware teapot. 'A cuppa to celebrate?' Then she remembered. 'I forgot, we need a fourth to play whist.' A smile lit her face. 'Coming round?'

'I don't mind if I do,' Siddy said in a comic voice. 'That's another catchphrase from *ITMA*.' Then, more seriously, he asked, 'Have you got any of that kiddies' orange juice?'

Gladys was stirring his tea. 'Yes.' She handed him an

enamelled mug. Baby Eli was allowed the orange juice for the vitamins in it.

'Well, if you look in my sideboard you'll find a bottle of gin. We can celebrate as we play cards.'

Gladys pursed her lips and repeated, 'I don't mind if I do!' Siddy laughed.

Doll was thinking about Gladys and how much she admired the woman for taking everything in her stride. She was like a mother to her as well as being her friend. They'd walked to work together this morning, as it was Goldie's turn to look after little Eli.

Doll had never been happier. She had a good job here at the factory, she loved dancing at the Rainbow and she and Joe were going to the pictures this evening to see *Meet Me in St Louis*, with Judy Garland, at the Criterion picture house. She was hoping they'd sit in the back row.

1945 had started out as a very good year. She'd stopped looking over her shoulder all the time, though Doll still felt sure Fred was the cause of Rene's death. She was certain Rene had been killed because she had helped her leave the Blue. Through Mac she'd learnt the police couldn't pin Fred down as her killer.

Gladys's baby was due in April. It would be lovely with two kiddies in the house. She only hoped she could finish knitting the baby bootees she'd been toiling over in time. Goldie had taught Doll how to knit, but the white wool was becoming very grubby.

The wireless was on in the factory and above the noise of the women talking, the Mills Brothers were belting out 'You Always Hurt the One You Love'. Doll was working on a lathe and keeping her eye on the drill in case it broke. If it did she'd have to call Solly over to sort out the machine.

He was a good supervisor. Easy for the women to get on with, and of course they all fancied him, with his blue eyes and blond hair. She'd felt ashamed for a long while about the night she'd pulled him down on the bed and started to kiss him. He'd never talked to her about it, simply went on coming to the house as though nothing had happened. He was still carrying a torch for Goldie.

She stared into the machine. Doing the same thing continually made her eyes itch and tiredness set in. The long room was hot and stuffy and the smell and taste of burned metal ground by the machines seeped deep into her throat. The work was exacting and she had to be precise in her movements. Luckily her hands were very steady.

'*Eeeeow!*' The scream rent the air.

A sudden, unexpected hush from the women filled the room. Then the sound of the screaming woman sent chills down Doll's spine. She looked away from her lathe and saw

Marie Jenner bent over her drilling machine. Momentarily she wondered why she was looking into the works and then it suddenly hit her. Her hair was caught up!

Churning, twisting and thumping, the girl's head was being drawn into the bowels of the chomping machine.

'Solly, turn off the machines!' Doll's harsh voice cut through the music and noise. She ran to the end of the line and stared at the girl in horror. Other workers were screaming and crying. Doll shook the shoulder of the frightened woman next to her. 'Run for the nurse, Jacky, tell her we need an ambulance.' When Jacky didn't move, Doll shouted, 'Fuckin' now!' The woman pushed her way through the gawping onlookers and ran. Thankfully the machines stopped, grinding to a halt. The cries from the girl caught in the machine's jaws sounded even more terrible.

Some of Marie's hair had been pulled out, taking a large flap of scalp with it. The slice of skin with hair clinging to it dripped blood that was flowing everywhere. The metallic smell almost eclipsed the stink of the oily machine. Marie was trying to stand up straight, but couldn't move because she was trapped. She was making a heart-wrenching noise.

'Get out of the way!' Doll pushed a woman aside and reached for the heavy industrial scissors lying on the wooden bench. With one hand on Marie's shoulder to steady her, she shouted, 'Shut up! Don't move!' With her other hand she cut the hair that was twisted around the drill. The sight of the swinging skin filled Doll with disgust. But now with both arms around Marie she helped the girl to lift her head out of the oil and blood. Marie began to scream again as soon as she saw the mess in the cogs of the machine. Doll grabbed her hand before she put her fingers to the flesh hanging from her head.

The nurse had arrived and was pushing through the crowd. Doll was holding on to Marie, cuddling her, trying to shield her from the prying eyes.

Marie cried, 'I can't stand . . .' Doll had to bear her weight as Marie fainted. Her blood was fast soaking into Doll's dungarees.

'You've done well.' Solly looked at Doll and nodded. Then he picked up the girl and, with the nurse running alongside him, carried Marie away to meet the ambulance. Mr Scrivenor had just appeared and he nodded at Doll before accompanying Solly and Marie.

Doll looked down at the long swathe of fair hair in the machine and sat down on the bench, putting her head in her hands. She suddenly felt very sick and wished all the women would go away. Vaguely, she heard Gladys shouting.

Women began to file out of the workroom. Gladys had given them an early break. Still Doll sat alone. No one spoke to her. Gradually the workroom became silent except for the wireless. She realized Bing Crosby was singing.

'Here, get this down you.' A mug was being held beneath her nose. Automatically, she took the tea.

Gladys said, 'They've taken her to hospital. You did well, Doll. I'm so proud of you.' Gladys sat down beside her on the bench and at first Doll sipped at the tea, then she gulped it gratefully. She bent down and put the empty enamelled mug on the floor. Drops of blood were congealing on the parquet flooring. She sat up, laying her head on Gladys's shoulder, and sobbed.

# Chapter Twenty-Six

Fred checked his large office safe. It contained little money. Profits were down. He knew it was because he couldn't afford to pay decent artists to appear at the Blue. He couldn't afford extra for speciality acts, so night after night the women gyrating on his stage were little more than prostitutes, who supplemented their wages by taking clients round the back. Of course, extras had always been on the Blue's menu, but the nubile young girls had been replaced by haggard older women.

He missed Rene. She had hired and fired the girls and taken the ones who needed help under her wing. But Rene was no more, and as long as he had someone, anyone, on the stage, he was reasonably content to open each day.

He was angry with himself. Rene's body should never have got free of the bindings he'd used to secure her to the buoy. He'd been banking on her not being discovered for a long while. She'd have been unrecognizable by then. He could do without that red-haired detective breathing down his neck. Still, the coppers had nothing on him.

The gambling was where he made some profit.

His croupiers were crooked. A sleight of hand, a foot beneath the table on the pedal that stopped the roulette wheel from turning, and money dripped into his coffers. Not as much as he'd have liked, because after all, you can't cheat a cheater and extra money went into the croupiers' pockets.

His beer and spirits, when he could get them, were watered down. His cigarettes, cigars and menu were courtesy of Mr Hill from Gosport.

He closed the safe. There was hardly any point to locking it. It was time for him to hijack another boatload of food and cigarettes.

Thoughts of Doll crossed his mind.

His little princess was not living in Portsmouth or Southsea. His searches had yielded nothing. All he'd ever done was try to keep her safe, to keep her away from the riff-raff in his club and on the streets.

A punter had let slip that she was appearing in Hill's Gosport club, the Rainbow. He'd been told she looked good and was well. It was in his own interests to keep away from Hill. It only wanted one snotty grass to let slip that he was stealing from him and he'd be a goner. But trusting

Hill's blokes to keep him in the loop about when and where his black-market goods were arriving meant another payout.

He missed Doll. The house wasn't the same without her. He sighed.

Doll threw her arms around Joe. 'I like you walking me home,' she said.

Joe disentangled himself, stared at her then smiled. 'It's lovely being with you,' he replied.

'Would you like to come in and meet Gladys?'

'It's late,' he said. 'I don't want to put anyone to any bother . . .'

Doll slid her hand through the letter box and pulled out the key. The moon was bright, the stars glittering and she felt as if she could conquer the world. Dealing with Gladys and possibly Goldie would be easy after the terrible experience she'd had with Marie Jenner that day.

Complete strangers had come up to her during the day, admiring her speed and quick thinking in saving the girl from more pain. Even Mr Scrivenor had called her to his office and congratulated her. Doll said she hoped the workers would now understand the importance of wearing headgear. She herself hated pushing her long hair out of sight beneath the itchy turban, but better to suffer than to risk losing her hair. She'd asked after Marie and where she'd been taken, but he either didn't know or didn't want to tell her.

Once in the warm passage, Doll could hear the wireless playing. Gladys was sitting in the armchair changing little Eli, who was gurgling away happily. The sweet smell of talcum powder filled the kitchen.

'Gladys, I'd like you to meet Joe, from work.'

Gladys smiled at him, 'So you're the new boyfriend, eh?'

'Don't make him blush! Can I make him a cup of tea?'

'Of course. Just go easy on the tea leaves, it'll be Saturday before I can get any more.' Gladys snapped the curved pin shut. 'I'm so fed up with the rationing, Joe.'

Doll had already taken off her coat and offered to take Joe's raincoat, which she took out to hang on the hooks near the front door.

'Sit down, lad.' Gladys waved towards a kitchen chair.

Out in the scullery, making tea by putting in one very small spoonful over the old leaves in the brown teapot, Doll could tell by Gladys's tone that she'd made a snap judgement and liked Joe.

She heard the key in the door, and voices and cold air announced Goldie and Solly. They both came into the kitchen.

'Smell the teapot, did you?' Gladys laughed, then asked, 'Enjoy the picture?' After looking after the baby all day,

Goldie had allowed Solly to treat her to the film at the other local picture house, the Forum.

'*To Have and Have Not*. The things Humphrey Bogart and Lauren Bacall say to each other. A right cheeky pair,' said Goldie.

Solly was looking at Joe.

'Doll's feller,' Gladys said.

Solly reached out to shake hands. 'Haven't seen you around the armament factory,' he said.

'No, you wouldn't, because he works for Will,' Doll said.

'You were brilliant today,' began Solly, talking to Doll.

'Shut up! I'm sick of hearing about it. Anyone else would have done the same.' Doll disappeared back into the scullery. Gladys looked at Goldie who made a face at her.

Solly coughed and blushed. He turned to Joe. 'You must be due your call-up papers . . .'

Joe got up from the chair and walked over to the scullery door. He looked at Doll busy at the stove. 'They came today. I've been trying to tell you all evening, Doll.'

Gladys felt Mogs brush against her legs. With great difficulty, she bent down and picked up the cat. He immediately started to purr. He still slept in her bed at nights. She began to wonder how the animal would take to the new baby being in her bedroom with them.

Gladys's ankles were puffy. That wasn't helped by her still working at Priddy's and being on her feet all day. Her dungarees had to be exchanged for a much larger pair to accommodate her blossoming body. She found the work tiring now and appreciated the fact that she did split shifts with Goldie. Siddy had told her to give it up. He said he couldn't understand why she wouldn't take money from him now, before they married. But she'd made a promise to herself that she wouldn't live off him until the ring was on her finger, so Siddy started showering her with even more gifts.

She remembered a couple of mornings ago, just after Goldie and Doll had left the house. A big thump on her back door had frightened the life out of her. She was in the scullery making a bottle for little Eli and had nearly dropped the National dried milk tin on the floor. Through the window she could see a big man with a knitted hat wearing blue overalls.

'What d'you want?' She had on her dressing gown and didn't like to be caught unawares by men in her back yard.

'Make us a cuppa?' He put his face to the window and smiled a toothy grin.

'Bugger off, I'm not dressed,' she yelled back. 'What are you doing in my garden anyway?'

'Open the door an' I'll tell you.'

Little Eli was squirming in his wet nappy and yelling for

his bottle. Gladys remembered now that she'd seen the bloke knocking at Siddy's house a couple of days ago. She opened the door.

'He's got a strong voice, hasn't he?' He nodded towards the little boy.

'Never mind the baby, why are you banging at my back door?'

'Where d'you want the opening?'

She slammed the kettle on the stove. 'What you on about?'

'He wants a back door facing your back door.' The man nodded towards Siddy's house. For a moment she stared at him, convinced he was mad, then she remembered. Siddy had said that when they were married he didn't want the neighbours counting how many times he went out of his front door and into hers. So he'd arranged to have a door set in his scullery wall, opposite her back door. Then they could come and go as they pleased without nosy neighbours being able to see.

Gladys picked up little Eli, who was mollified and stopped crying. 'Didn't he tell you where to put it?' She began preparing the bottle one-handed.

'He said he'd leave it up to you.'

Gladys shook her head. Siddy was too kind and wanted her to make decisions that suited her. No man had ever been that generous to her before. Sometimes, as now, it annoyed her.

'Does it matter?'

'Got to be careful of gas pipes and electric cables.'

'Well, put the door where they ain't.' The kettle began to boil. She shoved the wet baby into his arms and said. 'You want a cuppa, you got to work for it. Hold him while I do only two jobs at once.'

She made a fresh pot of tea and finished the baby's bottle. Then she took the child back and said, 'My name's Gladys. What's yours?'

'Percy,' he replied.

'Well, Percy, isn't Siddy in?'

'He was. He gave me the key to his front door and said he was off to buy an engagement and wedding ring.'

'Did he now?' Gladys smiled at Percy. 'Do I get to choose the colour of the door?'

'So, when are they expecting you to go?' Doll sat on Joe's lap. She'd been dreading talking about his call-up, but it couldn't be put off any longer.

The bench in the Ferry Gardens was cold and there was a wind off the sea. She could smell soap from where he'd washed his hands while waiting for her to finish her spot on the dance floor.

'The end of February.'

Doll slowly let the air out of her cheeks. 'So soon?'

He took off his jacket and put it around her. She liked it that he made these small gestures. It made her feel loved and wanted. She snuggled into his jumper.

'I don't have any say in the matter. Will you write to me?'

'Do you want me to?'

He sighed. 'I think I love you.'

'Only think?'

He nibbled at her ear. She liked his warm breath on the side of her face.

'I know I love you,' he said. 'I haven't known you for long, but there is such a thing as love at first sight.'

The sea was hitting the wall and making waves that splashed loudly. She thought of how cold it would be in the water. She could see the ferry boats moored for the night, moving in the sea as though trying to escape from the roped bollards.

'Do you care at all for me?' His words were measured. How could she tell him she wanted him? He knew nothing about the life she'd been forced to lead with Fred, that she'd only ever known real kindness afterwards, sharing a house with Gladys and Goldie and, of course, darling little Eli. Joe came from a nice, loving family. How could he possibly understand that she was scared to tell him she loved him? What if she confessed her love and then he became like Fred, keeping her away from other people, locking her up, telling her what to do, how to behave?

The only people she felt completely safe with were Gladys and Goldie.

She was also safe at the Rainbow, Mr Hill made sure of that. She was safe at Priddy's. Of course there were dangers from bombs lurking around every corner there, but not from people.

Doll took a deep breath. 'I think I love you, but in a way I'm glad you're going away, because it will give me time to make up my mind if what I feel for you and you feel for me is a good kind of love.'

There, she had said it. Would it be enough for him?

From across the road came music, noise. A laughing crowd surged from the Rainbow, spilling out into the night.

He had lifted her head and was looking into her eyes. 'We've got all the time in the world, you know that, don't you?' he whispered and bent forward. She closed her eyes and felt his tongue loosen her lips so they could taste each other. He was irresistible to her and she felt as if she was floating on air, as light as thistledown. Doll wanted more, much more. She'd never had a proper boyfriend and she closed her eyes so he wouldn't see the pleasure he was giving her.

Joe had never made a move on her except a goodnight kiss. She'd begun to think he didn't fancy her. But now they were both trembling and the kiss that had started slow and lingering was rising to a frenzied passion.

She felt his hand move down to her breasts and he caressed them tenderly. She opened her eyes to see the stars shining brightly and she felt like crying for no reason.

Then he moved away and broke the spell.

'I want to, you want to, but not here, not like this. I want it to be special, to mean something. I want to go away to the army and remember, to know you're thinking of our first time together too.'

'What if you don't come back?' Her voice was small.

'I'll come back. I love you,' he said.

# Chapter Twenty-Seven

Will sat amongst the tombstones of the dead from the Royal Victoria Military Hospital at Netley, his eyes fixed on the horizon, waiting for HMT *Longmerton* to appear from the English Channel into the Solent waters. It was surprising how many captains of ships returning from hot countries could be persuaded to do his bidding with a bit of financial incentive.

The weather was calm, the air strangely balmy for the beginning of March, though the forecast had promised bad weather later. Daffodils urgently showed their buds. The living amongst the dead, he thought, looking around the graveyard.

He could see the landing stage where the troopship would halt and spew out her broken military personnel to be hauled up to the main building. Now, though, several American jeeps were parked alongside ambulances for those too incapacitated to walk to the hospital.

Many troops were offloaded at Southampton and brought to the hospital by road, because the waters here were shallow and large ships often ran aground.

Passing time, he flicked idly through the pages of last night's evening paper. The front page was claimed by the devastation of Dresden, after a day and a night's relentless bombardment from our planes and those of the Americans. Casualties of 400,000 and as many as 130,000 people dead. Would this war never end? Would life ever get back to normal? No, nothing would be quite like the times he remembered; never again.

Dusk was overtaking the day by the time the ship neared the jetty. He watched the stream of broken men leave, brought down the gangway by helpers. Nurses and doctors were nearby at the ready. Then he strolled down to the jetty and introduced himself to the captain.

Will had decided not to divulge his plans. He was hoping to discover which of his men he could no longer trust, who was stealing from him the goods he brought into the country illegally. Names were already in his mind, but he needed absolute proof.

Handshakes, a chat about the wounded, the weather and other pleasantries, and Will was escorted down to the hold where boxes, baskets and crates were labelled and tied down to prevent them sliding about during the voyage.

He spotted his own contraband almost immediately and noted that it was intact. But he counted again to be sure, before going upstairs to the captain's cabin and joining him in a drink. On several boxes he had chalked crosses.

'Ever thought of taking your load off the ship here?' the bewhiskered man asked, swirling the golden liquid around in his glass, while the ship chugged through the waters down to Portsmouth. The cabin was untidy and smelled of oil. A large solid table was covered with charts, some rolled up, some laid flat and secured by the decanter of spirits.

'Easier to offload at Portsmouth or Gosport; my premises are near the ferry. But I'll unload wherever is easiest for the vessel carrying my stuff.'

His answer satisfied the captain, who nodded. 'I don't usually ask questions.' He understood the man's meaning. His job was to deliver contraband to a specified destination, and what happened to it after that was nothing to do with him. He wasn't paid to load or unload, merely to ferry the goods.

Will shook his head to the offer of more alcohol. It was acknowledged that he would melt into the darkness before the ship docked at Portsmouth, to observe the handling of his cargo. To all intents and purposes, tonight Will wasn't there.

A short, sharp knock on the cabin door and a whisper.

'I'm needed,' was all the captain said as he closed the door behind him, leaving Will alone.

After his goods were delivered onto his own small craft, he would travel with it to the storage facilities at the back of his club. When it was locked away, and only then, would he go upstairs to his apartment and have a well-deserved drink. That was his intention; that was the envisaged easy part.

It was dark outside. The portholes showed only the navigation lights in the water. Rain, or the residue from waves dashing on the portholes, made it difficult for Will to see. It looked as though the weather forecaster had been right after all. Every so often the lights were blotted out; Will could only guess that the ship was passing obstacles, other craft, in the channel.

The movement of the ship made him sleepy, but he knew he wouldn't allow himself the luxury of a nap. Instead, he thought of his club and the money it was making, fast being eroded by the goods that regularly disappeared.

He had thought his men were loyal, but now he couldn't trust anyone until the thief or thieves were apprehended. All he wanted from his men – and women – was honesty – of a kind.

His girls were Gosport's finest. Nothing sleazy or tacky about them. Of course, what they got up to outside his premises in their own time wasn't any of his business, as long as it didn't reflect on him. The waitresses and dancers could look after themselves and fend off the punters, if that was what they wanted. His prostitution racket was a different kettle of fish. He made sure his girls were cared for.

The only dancer he made certain wasn't subjected to the men's bawdiness was Doll. She was bright, fresh and perhaps a candidate for one of his London clubs. He'd maybe have a word with Gladys about that, later.

Thinking of Gladys made him frown.

He was angry with himself for offering her an afternoon reception at the club as a magnanimous wedding gift. But it was done now. She'd accepted and he wouldn't go back on his promise, even though he wished she wasn't marrying that thin streak, Siddy.

His frown changed to a smile as he remembered Gladys, huge in her maternity smock, helping the twins fit jigsaw pieces together while the baby slept. She had no idea how motherhood and pregnancy made her such a desirable woman. Violet Kray had taken a fancy to Gladys and the two women had made a corner of the club their own during the quiet afternoons. The boys, Ronnie and Reggie, adored her. He laughed aloud, thinking of the way Gladys hid her eyes as the boys boxed against each other in his gym attached to the club.

'We'll be docking soon.' The captain poked his head around the door.

Will rose from the seat, suddenly alert at the news. The time had passed quickly. He patted his chest and felt for his flick knife, always secure in his top inside pocket. He never carried anything on him in the way of identification. If anything went wrong and he dropped, say, his wallet, his identity and whereabouts could easily be discovered and he didn't want that. He pulled his cap down low over his forehead, and wrapped the thick scarf around his throat. The navy woollen jacket he wore was similar to any sailor's coat.

Once up on deck and hiding behind a lifeboat, Will was able to look down to the choppy waves and watch a motor torpedo boat come alongside the HMT *Longmerton*, which had anchored in the deeper water at Portsmouth.

He looked about the deck. Conveniently, the captain and his crew had disappeared, leaving only a couple of men helping to tie the ropes, securing the smaller vessel below. Then they too left. The smaller craft, the MTB, wasn't one he recognized.

But it was his goods that were now being delivered to the MTB by the men who had boarded the bigger ship via a rope ladder. The rain hadn't had time to wash off the chalk marks on the boxes. He recognized very few of the half-dozen or so men handling the cargo. One was Baz Bowen, a man he thought he could trust, and another was Doll's brother Fred. He'd suspected Fred Leach all along, but had never thought of Baz as being anything but a true friend as well as a good employee.

Another small vessel was coming up alongside the *Longmerton*. The wind and rain made visibility difficult, but he saw it was his own boat. The men in the second craft seemed agitated and unwilling to join the men already unloading cargo. The wind blew oaths from his men in his direction.

He crouched, secure in the knowledge he wouldn't be discovered, and looked down at Baz issuing orders. Well, he supposed they were orders; the actual words were whisked away. However, it was plain to see his men were reluctant to board either the *Longmerton* or the MTB.

He did a headcount, memorizing the employees who were under his instructions to unload his goods from the *Longmerton*. He saw his cargo being transferred to the MTB by their crew, while his men did nothing. He wondered if fear had stopped them.

Then a couple of boxes were lowered to the smaller vessel. One of his men, Costello, took charge of them and put them down in the bottom of his boat. He remembered his last consignment had also yielded only a couple of boxes. Perhaps this was some kind of sick joke?

Baz Bowen was still holding forth to the MTB's crew and

Will saw preparations being made to let go of the ropes holding the craft. It was time for him to come out from his hiding place and mingle with the crew of the MTB. He realized how difficult this might be, considering the low body count.

What he saw next made his blood boil. Baz Bowen was paying off his crew. Standing on the deck of Will's craft, handing out notes that were being passed to his men.

Two men in particular appeared very friendly toward Bowen. He could see them laughing and joking as the money changed hands.

The unloading was almost at an end; he could tell by the number of boxes stacked on the deck of the MTB. But one man wearing a furry Cossack hat pulled low over his forehead was climbing the rope ladder to the *Longmerton*. He appeared on deck and went down into the hold, reappearing later with a large carton. Will waited until both the man and his package were out of sight of the crew of the small boats.

He emerged from the shadows, grabbed the man and with a quick fist landed a punch to his face. Astonishment and pain buckled the man's legs, causing him to drop the box and fall against the ship's railing. Thinking quickly, Will snatched at the man's hat. Then, horrified, Will saw him slide beneath the ship's rail and fall. His arms went forward to save him but with barely a splash the man had slid into the rough sea. Grabbing the package before it too rolled over the side, he gazed at the roiling waves, but there was no sign of the man. His heart dropped. That was not meant to happen.

Then, exchanging his hat for the Cossack one, Will walked as quickly as he could and began climbing down the ladder, glad the package he was carrying probably contained cartons of cigarettes. It was light enough to require only one hand to hold it, leaving him able to use his other hand to grab tightly at the swaying rope ladder.

The box was taken from him as he dropped into the MTB. The ropes holding the boat were freed. His was the last collection of the black-market goods.

Notes were pushed into his fist as he crumpled onto a seat close to a wet, dishevelled man. In the dark he'd been mistaken for the man he had knocked overboard.

Angry voices from the smaller vessel cut through the bad weather and reached his ears. The crew had no doubt realized there was no more stock for them. Baz Bowen, on Will's craft, was yelling orders to the men and handing out more money.

Mosely, an elderly man who often helped Will in his gym, was remonstrating with Baz Bowen. It was obvious he wasn't happy about the MTB arriving at the troopship first and unloading what wasn't theirs to take. He threw the money back at Baz Bowen while uttering oaths.

Bowen pushed him aside. Mosely, trying to regain his footing after losing his balance, stumbled and fell over the side and into the heaving sea. Will felt his hands clench. He wanted to save the man, but if he moved or showed concern, his identity would be discovered. On his own he was no match for Fred Leach and his men. He gave an inaudible sigh of relief as Mosely was pulled from the sea and back into the boat. A coat was thrown over him for warmth. He was safe; another of Will's men was attending to him. Will recognized the man who had pulled Mosely from the water as Ralph Dodson.

Baz Bowen climbed back into the MTB. Will thought he was an idiot to risk his life jumping from one craft to another in the heaving sea. The boat, with Will aboard and now free from the *Longmerton*, was soon racing across the stretch of water from Portsmouth, heading towards Gosport.

This surprised Will, as Fred's business venture was in Southsea, on the borders of Portsmouth, so why was the MTB heading towards Gosport?

The other boat, his craft, which was lighter and faster, was now ahead of them in the stormy sea. When its lights disappeared from view, Will could only imagine it was being returned to the moorings at Ferrol Road.

The rain was stinging his face now. He daren't go inside the cabin, out of the bad weather, in case he was recognized. The craft seemed to be heading towards the car ferry and the smaller boatyards near Haslar Bridge.

The other men sitting around him were talking and passing round a half-bottle of brandy. He took his share, as did the others, but didn't join in the banter. He watched the lights of the shoreline grow brighter.

Fred Leach was up in the wheelhouse, staring straight ahead. Once the boat docked, the lighting on the pontoon would show Will up as an impostor. He had to make a move before it was too late; he had a job to do. There was no time for sitting and watching for the alcohol to return.

He rose, mumbling to the man squeezed at his side, and walked alongside the dimly lit cabin, careful not to slip on the wet teak and holding on to the metal rail. Two men stood at the wheel with Fred. The noise of the engine was throaty and spray hurled itself at the cabin's windows and into the boat.

He wasn't noticed by them, of that he was certain, for they were still sharing a joke. He moved from the doorway to inside the wheelhouse, standing behind Fred. Fred was concentrating on guiding the boat, looking ahead at the fast-approaching jetty and listening to the men.

Will carefully extracted his knife, keeping it hidden

beneath his coat. He pressed its button, a small sound that was lost with the engine noise. His finger guided the blade.

Will didn't like violence, but Fred had murdered Rene in cold blood, of that Mac was certain. Hadn't Mac intimated the world would be a safer place without Fred Leach? And if Will didn't stop the man from thieving from him, who else would?

With a single jerk of his arm he felt the knife pierce and enter the man's lower back. Before Fred or anyone else had time to realize what had happened, Will was back standing in line to receive another hit from a bottle, this time whisky. He prepared for the inevitable collision by holding fast to the boat's railings.

The MTB, wheel spinning, was knocked off course as Fred slumped to the floor of the wheelhouse. The boat drove into the jetty, hitting the landing stage with force and scraping along the buoys hanging from Gosport's pontoon. The crash and splintering of wood was muffled by the heavy rain.

Good-natured jibes were hurled into the air as the men dragged themselves up from where they'd been thrown about the craft.

Then, 'Fuck me! He's copped it.'

One man jumped from the boat to the jetty and legged it up the gangway, closely followed by a couple more. Will almost smiled to himself; the first sign of trouble and men became cowards.

Will jumped, almost stumbling, but he righted himself and followed the running men. He made for the darkened, closed ticket kiosk where he waited, breathing heavily, pressing himself into the blackness of the doorway. It wouldn't do for him to be discovered now.

Footsteps, running, passed him. When he was sure there could be no one left on the MTB he came slowly out into the lamplight.

He badly needed to pee. The lavatory at the Ferry Gardens was still open. After relieving himself, he stared at his reflection in the fly-specked mirror. He was looking at the face of a killer. He didn't like what he saw. There was no way the man who had fallen overboard could possibly have survived. Two men had died tonight at his hands. It was a dog-eat-dog world. He didn't get to where he was today by not protecting his assets, but nevertheless, what had happened didn't lie easily with him.

His assets? They now included a sleazy club and a ramshackle boat, smashed and lying at the ferry pontoon. The Blue, he knew, was owned outright by Fred Leach. The boat, he guessed, had also been his property.

Of course, by rights those assets, such as they were, belonged to Doll.

But he'd already made himself a sort of godfather to her, hadn't he?

The girl couldn't run a club; she could barely look after herself. Though in years to come she would be a feisty woman, he knew that by the way she reacted to danger at the armament factory.

He would take over the Blue, pay off the debts it had accrued – he knew there were plenty – and get it up and running, taking any profits he made for himself, of course. After all, he wasn't a bloody charity, was he? But then when she was older he would hand the club over to Doll so she'd be set up for life. He winked at himself in the mirror. Yes, that's what he'd do.

Doll, after being controlled by her brother, deserved better than the mental intimidation she'd been subjected to all her young life. And if running a profitable club wasn't what she wanted, he would buy it from her. By the age of twenty-one she'd know what she wanted out of life.

But now he had other things to think of.

He took off the Cossack hat and threw it in the wire mesh rubbish bin, then ran his fingers through his curls.

What he had to do next needed to be done immediately. Tomorrow would be too late. The coppers would be all over the MTB like flies on shit. It wasn't every day boats crashed into Gosport's pontoon.

Once outside the public urinals, he stared across the stone platforms where the buses drew in and looked at his club. The lights and the faint noise of music showed he was still doing business. He smiled contentedly.

But before he could go inside the Rainbow, he wanted the goods he'd paid for safely locked away.

A lone dog walker passed him.

'Evening,' the man said. Will answered him, then walked away. Dog walkers and kids were nearly always the first on the scenes of crimes.

How long it would take someone to find the MTB with the body on board and the black-market goods was anyone's guess, which was why he needed to act quickly.

He made his way back past the ticket kiosk and down to the pontoon. Amazingly, someone had tied up the boat and turned off the engine. He looked at the front and side of the vessel and scratched and frayed paintwork stared back at him. The rotten landing stage had taken the brunt of the hit. The MTB's teak boards had caved in, but the buoys had done their job; despite some broken planks floating in the water the damage was above the waterline. If the craft's engine wasn't damaged, she'd be watertight to move.

After looking carefully about him and making sure there was no one around, he boarded her and went straight to the wheelhouse. To his surprise, the key was in the ignition. As he turned the key, she started. He sighed with relief. There was blood on the floor but no body. He decided someone had kindly pushed Fred overboard. He searched the thirty-foot boat. His goods were all over the place but it looked as though very little had been stolen.

He cleaned up the blood with a rag. He drew the line at standing in another man's blood. As he worked he thought of the dog walker; maybe he'd noticed the MTB. Maybe he'd already reported it.

It might prove difficult to explain to the law what he was doing with a boat that wasn't registered to him. Though he doubted very much Fred had got around to registering the craft. There was no name on the side. Perhaps Fred wasn't even the legal owner? But with black-market goods on board it was better that he move the boat to safer moorings immediately.

He wondered about the boat's origins. Maybe the sturdy little vessel had been used to ferry men back from France?

He took her round past the daily ferry craft moored for the night, the *Ferry Fairy* and the *Valdane*.

Upon reaching the boatyard at the bottom of Ferrol Road, he was pleased to see his own small vessel moored in its usual place. He tied up beside his boat.

The boatyard was dark. Craft on stilts being repaired looked like monsters from another world with their shadows lengthened by moonlight. The bad weather had abated. The moon was bright when it wasn't hidden by cloud. Once aboard his own craft, he saw she was clean and tidy. And empty. He wondered which of his men was responsible.

Tomorrow he'd have a chat with the owner of the boatyard. Maybe get him to paint over the damage where the MTB had crashed against the buoys. Possibly renew the teak planking; she was a nice little craft and deserved better. The rain had eased right off now and the stars glinted in the darkness.

He put the key in his pocket, happy that the remainder and bulk of his goods were locked inside the MTB. He began to whistle as he stepped from one wooden walkway to the next, then onto the pier and the shore. A rat disappeared into a pile of wooden decking.

Then he began the short walk through the cobbled streets to the back of his silent club, in darkness now except for a ground-floor passage light. He pushed open the door, wondering what to expect, but all he found were the two small boxes standing on the wooden floor.

Time enough to sort out everything in the morning, he thought.

But memories wouldn't go away. Again he felt bad about the man he'd caused to fall overboard. If Fred Leach had gone into the sea, then the body would surely wash up, as would the other man's remains.

There was no doubt that Fred was dead. Will knew how to handle a knife.

That slimy toerag would steal from him no more.

But how to tell Doll? He decided there was no need to say anything until the body turned up.

There was also the problem of the men he had thought he could trust, especially Baz Bowen.

## Chapter Twenty-Eight

Will used the crusty bread to mop up the runny egg and tinned tomato juice, then pushed his plate away. Young Diane, who had prepared his full English breakfast, was quite the little cook, he thought. Sometimes it was nice to have the club full of young women eager to do his bidding and sometimes it made him angry that there wasn't one amongst them he could pour out his heart to. He really must stop comparing every woman with Gladys Smith, the one he couldn't have.

Earlier he'd given orders for his men to assemble in the kitchen at nine. Before that he'd handed the keys of the MTB to young Joe and told him to take some of the men, unload his goods and bring them back to the room at the rear. He'd given Joe an envelope containing a sweetener for the owner of the Ferrol Road boatyard. Should the police go round there for any reason, his knowledge of how the boat came to be moored there would be sketchy. But he'd instructed the boatyard owner to tell them that the craft now belonged to William Hill.

He knew exactly how he was going to deal with the aftermath of last night.

He walked across the club's polished dance floor and entered the kitchen, nodding a greeting to the ten or so men standing about. There was worry on a few faces. Will guessed they were anxious about being interrogated over the loss of his goods. And no doubt word had got round about Joe unloading the bulk of the cargo early that morning.

The smell of baking filled the air, but as he'd just eaten he could appreciate the aroma for what it was, bread rolls tantalizingly rising in the large oven, made by his chef for the lunchtime trade.

'Mosely, go down to the gym. The twins will soon be here and ready for your excellent coaching.' Will remembered how the elderly trainer had remonstrated with Baz Bowen and been dipped in the sea for his trouble. Mosely was leaning against the scrubbed wooden table. He seemed none the worse for his swim in the Solent.

The grey-haired man nodded and left, with no questions asked. Years ago, Mosely had been a professional heavyweight boxer. Too many punches caused him to give up the sport, so now he trained lads who fancied their chances in the ring. Reggie and Ronnie worked with him and he had told Will the twins showed promise.

Will praised his chef, told him he didn't need him for a while and that if he felt like a smoke to go out into the yard. Will had one rule about smoking in the club – never in the kitchen. Will was certain of Eddie's loyalty. The man hadn't been anywhere near the fiasco that was last night.

He then moved on to Joe, who sat on the side, his long legs swinging against a cupboard door.

'When you leaving us, Joe?'

'Three more days, Mr Hill.'

Will nodded. 'You'll be missed, especially by Doll. I know you'll get leave from – where is it? Aldershot, the training barracks?'

Joe looked morose but nodded.

'Take her out on Sunday. I'll get another of the girls to fill her spot. Might even put a bit extra in your wage packet,' he laughed. There were smiles, for he paid them in cash, not a wage slip or packet in sight. Joe's eyes shone. 'Get out of here,' Will said good-naturedly.

Three more men were treated in a jocular manner and left the kitchen, smiling.

Will spoke to another man he'd spotted on the boat, one who'd remonstrated with the ringleaders along with Mosely and had rushed forward to help pull him from the sea. Ralph Dodson stood a few feet away from Will.

'How's the wife?' Will knew they were both mourning the sudden cot death of their second child. Dodson normally cleaned the Rainbow and did odd jobs around the place. Will listened as he apologized for being late that morning; he'd been to the doctor's surgery with his wife and was finding money tight because her medical costs seemed endless.

Will said, 'Get home to your missus, mate, but just for today, mind.' The man looked relieved and, as he passed Will, muttered his apologies again. Will pressed a note into the man's hand and said, 'Buy her some flowers, take her to the pictures.' He watched as Dodson closed the kitchen door behind him. He was sad he could do no more than offer a picture house treat for the couple.

Three men remained with Will. Baz Bowen and two men he now knew to be especially close to him.

Will took his flick knife from his inside pocket and clicked it open. He enjoyed seeing the startled look on all three faces.

'Bit jumpy this morning, boys? Had a late night?' Will stared long and hard at each of them in turn. 'I'm going to tell you three a little story.'

Will leant against the warm oven and stared at Costello. He knew he didn't have long, for his chef would return at any moment to take the browning rolls out from the oven.

'I've worked hard all my life and I don't expect to be defrauded by my own men. Men I thought I could trust.' Will was busy cleaning his nails with the sharp knife. He could practically smell the fear emanating from the men. 'Last night was quite an eventful time, what with boats cluttering up the harbour, men going overboard . . . Some even lost their lives.' He paused. 'If I ever hear talk of last night there will be more lives lost. You know exactly what I mean, don't you?' He didn't wait for a reply, but carried on. 'Last night was also the very last time you will ever steal from me.' Will looked at Baz Bowen. His thin face was sheet-white.

'You're all extremely lucky I'm sick and tired of all this killing business. But I'm sad to say, fellers, the other blokes appear to be all the staff I require for the moment. I have to let you go. You're getting the sack.' Will began to laugh.

The men looked at each other, frowning.

The shame of dismissal would follow them. They were now has-beens who'd have to depend on any menial work that might come their way. For no boss would dare to cross William Hill and employ them. Smart suits, silk ties, good food and access to pretty girls had been taken away from them. In an instant.

Not one of them spoke. Nor did they look at each other.

William Hill was a powerful man. Will knew each of them was wondering whether it might have been better if he'd knifed them on the spot, instead of handing each of them the slow death that was surely coming.

'It's called, in this business, "keeping your nose clean". You didn't do that. Now, get out of my club.'

Will watched as the men shuffled out. He'd sorted out his own problems. But then he always did, didn't he?

His chef bounced in, picked up a tea towel and opened the oven door.

'Done to a turn, Boss,' he said.

'My sentiments exactly,' said Will.

'I've done you a picnic lunch for when Joe collects you,' Goldie said. 'Do you know where he's taking you?'

'Not really, but I know it involves a train journey.' Doll flicked the blouse over so she could get at the collar more easily. She pressed the still-hot iron into the corners of the blue cotton material, then turned and set the flat iron on top of the range. Doll looked at the neat pile of pressed garments on a kitchen chair, then at the remainder of the clothes on the old armchair. 'I'll be glad when I've finished this lot,' she said to Goldie, whose turn it was to look after little Eli despite Gladys having a day off. 'I'll get washed and changed then.'

Gladys was still working at Priddy's, loath to hand in her notice. Soon it would be too dangerous for her to continue breathing in the fumes, as she'd be putting the child inside her at risk, if she hadn't already. Her feet and ankles had puffed up, but that apart, she felt fine. She was also glad that Goldie's skin complaint had cleared up.

Doll had two days off. She wasn't dancing at the club until the day after Joe was leaving to do his National Service.

'I'm going to miss Joe. Do you miss Jamie?'

Goldie was about to leave the kitchen but she stopped, turned and stared at her.

'Do you know you are the only person who has asked me that? Everyone has been obsessed with what a horrible man he was, but nobody has asked me how I feel about losing the man I loved.'

Doll used the iron holder to lift the iron, then wiped off the smuts on a rag. She began to attack the white nightgowns that were becoming too small for the fast-growing little Eli.

'I had loved him for what seemed forever. To be removed from that love with such finality hurt me. Knowing a man has hurt you doesn't mean you can cut him out of your life easily.'

'It must have been hard for you. Still is, I suppose,' Doll said.

Goldie remembered how difficult it had been trying to disguise her tear-streaked face in the mornings. How she'd been unable to sleep, trying without success to work out why she hadn't been enough for Jamie, why he'd strayed. Had it been her fault?

'I sometimes wonder, if he was still alive, whether we could still make a go of it . . .'

'You couldn't trust him! He's hurt you once and he would do it again.' Doll was adamant, her voice rising sharply.

'Possibly.' Goldie paused. 'But like I've said, you can't switch love off just like that, it's not a tap.'

'I think I love Joe,' Doll said. She folded the nightgowns. Her neck had reddened with the secret she'd just shared.

Goldie was watching her. Then she smiled. 'You be careful, girlie. Joe's going away. Don't let him leave you with more than happy memories!'

Doll left later in the morning on Joe's arm.

Goldie put the little boy down for a sleep, tucked him in with a big kiss and went down to the kitchen to sit in the old armchair and read the copy of *Woman's Weekly* that Gladys had brought home.

'Aren't you going to read that letter?'

Goldie stared at Gladys, then looked to the mantelpiece where an envelope was leaning.

'I didn't know that was there.'

Gladys shook her head, then passed her the letter so that she didn't need to get up.

Dear Goldie,

Thank you for the letter and information about young Eli. I am longing to see him, but when, I cannot say. None of us has any information regarding leave. I have pinned his photograph on a board inside the Churchill tank where some of the other men keep a few mementoes. He's a handsome little chap.

We saw a heavy attack by our bombers this evening and need to stay here another night, sleeping under the tank. We are at a place called Wezel, a rich farming area. There are so many hens that we have a few in the tank! The Germans were here. They've only just been driven out and there are bodies in the fields.

The place is full of mines, so it's not safe to wander from the road. There are bomb craters but most of them from our own aircraft.

There are rumours of the bridges beyond Wezel being demolished by the Hun. Our next orders depend on the enemy. If the Germans have withdrawn there is nothing for us to do here, west of the river Rhine.

I hope you'll find the time to write back with news of little Eli.
Best wishes,
Eli

'Will you write back?'

'I don't see why not. He's sending money and has a right to know how his nephew is faring.' Goldie passed the letter to Gladys and sat down again in the big chair.

'Yes, he should have a father figure in his life. Eli seems a decent bloke. But it must feel funny writing to someone you've never seen or met? What will you say when the child wants to know why the other kids have fathers and he doesn't?'

'I shall tell the boy the truth – that his daddy died for his country, a hero.' Goldie was trying to hold back her tears. 'There's going to be a lot of children who'll be fatherless.' Life went on, she thought.

She looked at Gladys standing next to the chair, then leaned forward and put her arms around her huge stomach, her ear close to her belly.

There was silence except for the wood crackling in the grate.

A load of logs had been delivered to Gladys while Siddy had been out. They were helping eke out the coal. If it wasn't for the child the house wouldn't need to be kept so warm; extra layers of clothing would suffice. The logs had been brought up the alley and dumped outside the scullery, a gift from Siddy. Unfortunately, they'd been dumped right in front of Siddy's new door! Unless they moved the logs

– and neither Goldie nor Gladys fancied doing that in the cold – entry to and from Siddy's house at the back was not possible. Siddy's good idea had fallen flat, for a while at least.

'I reckon you're going to give birth to a footballer.' Goldie smoothed Gladys's bump then let her hand drop. 'Thank goodness the wedding is this weekend, otherwise the baby'll be there with us.'

## Chapter Twenty-Nine

The sea was a long way out and the mud felt soft beneath her toes. A light, cold wind had risen, but surprisingly for the time of year it was warm. Doll could feel the tightness of her skin and knew her cheeks would be pink because she wasn't used to the sun's heat. She took a deep breath of the salt-laden air. The breeze lifted her cotton skirt and she pulled her hair away from her face.

'This is one of the happiest days of my life.' She slipped her hand into Joe's. 'But I have to push away the thought that you'll soon be gone.'

'It's just the same for me,' he said. He had his grey flannel trousers rolled up and a Fair Isle pullover covering his collarless shirt.

'No.' She shook her head. 'Your life will be full of new things; I'll be in Gosport being reminded of you at every turn. I'll be the lonely one.'

She looked beyond the stony Littlehampton beach to the remains of the picnic eaten earlier on the grass, the blanket they'd sat on and a souvenir postcard in a bag along with a novelty egg timer as a small gift for Goldie and Gladys. There was a stick of rock for baby Eli. She knew he couldn't eat it, but he was good at sucking things.

The place was deserted, with marram grass growing where the stones gave way to sand. Way over to the right, beach huts stood lonely and neglected, their shutters broken and roofs showing the results of past winter storms.

'I shall write as often as I can. I don't suppose I'll be allowed home before training ends, but hopefully they'll let us have leave before we're shipped out . . .' His voice tailed off and he looked apprehensive.

Joe stopped, bent down and picked up a small dead crab. Doll squealed and began running towards their belongings, with Joe in hot pursuit. She was fast on her feet and laughing as she slipped out of his grasp and then crying out in pain as she ran across the stony beach. She was still ahead of Joe as she collapsed, laughing once more, onto the old blanket.

He fell beside her and scooped her up in his arms, kissing her face, her neck, and then dangled the white shell of the dead crab in front of her.

'Ooh!' Doll grabbed at the fragile shell and hurled it as far as she could away from her. Then they kissed once more, but this time she could hear her pulse rushing in her ears almost as loudly as the waves meeting the shoreline.

'Are you cold?' he asked, lifting his head and looking into her eyes. The sun had disappeared behind dark clouds.

'Not really.' Though Doll actually felt as though she'd been thrown into the icy sea, she didn't want to tell him she was cold, or he would insist on leaving the beach and the day would be spoiled.

He kissed her again, harder this time, almost bruising her lips. Doll ran her hands down his broad back.

'I could kiss you to death, eat you up,' he whispered into her ear. He began with soft little kisses from beneath her chin, down her neck, and as he undid the top button of her blouse, he made her shudder with expectation as he trailed his tongue between her breasts. Undoing its other buttons he tugged aside her blouse and made butterfly kisses down to her waist. He looked down at her lying beneath him.

'You are so beautiful,' Joe said, his voice husky with emotion.

He pulled away her skirt and his hand moved slowly up her leg. Doll didn't want him to stop. Goldie's words were echoing in her ears. Stop, stop, her head was urging, but her heart was saying, go on, go on.

'I'm scared,' she whispered.

She felt him searching in his pocket.

'Don't be,' Joe said. 'I've got something. But if you don't want me to, I won't.'

He moved his wallet into the sunlight, leaning back so she could see what he was doing. He pulled out a small square packet.

'What's that?' Doll sat up and looked at him, then at the packet that he had torn open. He was handling the piece of creamy-coloured rubber with care.

'It's a condom.'

Doll put out a finger and touched the rubbery softness. 'What's it for?'

'It goes over my thingy so you won't have a baby.'

She gave out a long, deep breath. Doll had never seen a penis before, let alone an erect one, and she'd never seen a condom. Joe guided her hand to the front of his trousers. She almost drew back in alarm but curiosity overcame her fear. His hardness made her feel strangely excited.

'It's better if you put it on,' he said.

'But I've never, I don't know . . .'

'All you have to do is fit it over the end, then roll it along.'

Doll stared at him. 'You know an awful lot about it. Have you done this before?'

'Good lord, no!' He pulled her close to him. 'I bought these—'

'These!'

'They come in a packet of three.' He pushed the condom into her hand. 'I've never bought anything like this before. I had to go into four different barber shops before I had the courage to ask for them.'

'Did you have four haircuts?' She couldn't help giggling.

'No, thank goodness. But the last barber said you get them free in the army. He also said most of the soldiers don't use them for what they're made for, but to keep the ends of their guns dry! I didn't know if that was some kind of joke.'

'Well, I never,' said Doll.

'We won't be able to use it at all if we don't stop chatting. Come here, my gorgeous girl! It takes two, you know.' He wriggled closer to her. 'Touch me again.'

Doll could see his penis straining against the flannel of his trousers. Tentatively she put her hand over the bulge.

Joe moaned with delight, then kissed her again, this time with his mouth open. She could feel his tongue searching and gave herself up to his kiss. His hand went to her breast, kneading and squeezing. She felt as if she was on fire as his hands stroked her bare legs then up to her knickers and began slowly to peel them down. When they stuck at her knees Doll pulled them away, excited as a rush of air touched her bare skin.

'Now, put it on now,' he urged. He guided her hand, fitting

the condom onto the tip of his penis. Doll could hardly take her eyes away from the huge, long, ridged member, their fingers touching as he and she, together, unrolled the thin rubber over his penis.

Then she was lying on her back with her knees apart, waiting for him, for it to happen. The smell of his body was filling her senses: cologne, sharp and tangy, soap and something else, that musky scent that was his maleness.

Doll was panting, as a feeling of overwhelming desire engulfed her, tormenting her with the longing to feel him inside her. Slowly she raised herself up to accommodate him. He entered her, and at first she imagined it was too tight; then felt a sharp pain before she began automatically to move with him.

Joe was moaning and calling her name over and over again, while Doll wondered why she had waited so long for this blessed joy.

Her desire was at a peak when, with his kisses smothering her, he groaned, tensed his body, and then a strong involuntary contraction of his muscles left him gasping and once more he was calling her name over and over again.

Doll felt as though she was drowning. She came up for air, weeping and struggling for breath but extremely happy.

'Let's get rid of this.'

Doll knew he was removing the rubber but she couldn't

be bothered to watch; she was drifting off, drowning sleepily in her love for him.

He pulled her clothes back decently about her, then lay alongside her, his head on her breast.

'Thank you,' he whispered. 'That was my first time.'

'Oh, I've had plenty,' Doll said.

Joe sat up and she opened one eye to see the consternation on his face. She pulled him down, 'Only pretending,' she said.

# Chapter Thirty

'Sorry to come at an inappropriate time, especially on your wedding day, Gladys, but I'm on official business.'

Gladys ushered Mac into the house. She was in the process of removing her curlers, so half of her head was covered in tight sausage-like curls. She pulled out a kitchen chair for the red-haired detective and said, 'Don't stand on ceremony with me. What's happened?' Mogs looked up from his sprawl on the rag rug, but soon settled again.

Mac took off his hat and put it on the table. 'I thought it better to let you know now, instead of at the register office this afternoon, or indeed the do down at the Rainbow. I thought as Siddy'll whisk you away for a couple of days on honeymoon, the mess wouldn't be cleared up until . . .'

'Get on with it. I'm jumpy enough without you making things worse.' She put her hands on her hips and glared up into his eyes.

'We've another body, actually two bodies, washed up on the town shoreline. One hasn't been identified yet, but the other one is Fred Leach, Doll's brother.' He looked about him.

'She's not here, she's gone to get my bouquet.' Holding on to the back of a chair, Gladys eased herself down. 'Soon there'll be more bodies than fish in those waters.'

'He was knifed, Gladys, very recently.'

'And you're telling me so I can impart the news to Doll.'

He nodded. 'I can wait for her to come back and tell her myself, but I thought you might prefer to do it in your own time, as today's a special day. I didn't think you'd want me to send a policewoman around to do it.'

She shook her head. 'He was nothing to me. Not that I'd wish ill of anyone.' She gave a long sigh. 'It would be better coming from me.'

She began to fiddle with a flowered hat that she intended to wear, which was lying on the table.

'You'll still be there, along with Marlene, at the club?'

He nodded, got up and said, 'We'll not be looking too hard for his killer. He was a nasty piece of work, Gladys.' He put his hand on her shoulder. 'You've done wonders with that girl since she moved in here. She was a right little madam at first, wasn't she?'

Gladys sniffed. 'She's grown, and not just in years. I

love her like she was my own.' Gladys sighed and put sad thoughts of her own daughter, Pixie, from her mind. Today was her wedding day. 'Leave it with me, Mac,' she said. 'Don't forget your hat,' and she pushed his dark felt trilby towards him.

Gladys stood outside Fareham Register Office with her arm through Siddy's. He looked at her and smiled. She thought of all the men she'd had, but this was only the second time she'd married. Her first wedding when she was barely more than a girl had produced Pixie. Or rather, Pixie had caused the wedding. Both her husband and her daughter were memories now. The husband she didn't want to remember, and her daughter was locked in that safe place inside her heart forever. She smiled back at Siddy and waited for Goldie to take the photograph. A train rattled by on the overhead viaduct railway line, its smoke billowing down onto the road, smelling warm, like hot mist.

Gladys stepped from one foot to the other; her shoes were pinching her. The bunion on her big toe was giving her gyp. It was March, but the cold wind didn't affect her; instead she felt hot in the enormous maternity smock with the sailor collar. Her matching navy-blue skirt was stretched to its utmost and she wished more than anything that she could go to her own wedding reception in her candlewick dressing gown and pom-pom slippers, the only articles of clothing she felt comfortable in.

'One more photo, in case it doesn't come out,' pleaded Goldie. Doll grabbed hold of the camera and stepped in front of a man and woman walking by.

'Could you take one of us all, please?'

After much explaining about which button to press, Goldie and Doll stood close to Gladys and the stranger snapped them all for posterity.

In Siddy's car, driving towards Gosport, Gladys looked at the two rings on her finger. Siddy had presented her with the engagement ring only a few days ago. Gladys had never had one before. The single stone shone and glittered.

'Thank you for making an honest woman of me,' she said. She thought she could smell mothballs on Siddy's suit.

'Don't know about you, but,' Siddy said. 'I'm shattered.'

'What, shattered already and tonight's your wedding night?'

He looked alarmed. She grinned at him and patted his hand. 'Don't worry, love, I'm only teasing.'

'Thank goodness for that, Mrs Butler.'

'That'll take some getting used to,' she said with a smile. 'I've been a Smith forever.'

Doll had been overwrought ever since Gladys had told her about Fred.

'She's trying to put a brave face on things,' said Gladys, expecting Siddy to know what she was talking about.

Luckily, he did. 'It was better to tell her immediately than to have the news hanging over our heads all day.'

'Exactly what I thought, but I expected her to break down when I told her that her brother was dead.' Gladys was happy about Siddy's reassurance that she'd done the right thing in telling Doll sooner rather than later. 'I don't like the girl acting as though it doesn't matter.'

'Deep down it'll be different, you mark my words.' He paused. 'What about Goldie catching your bouquet?'

'I think she could do with a good man in her life. Let's hope it comes true that she'll be the next to be married, but I'm going to stay in her life with little Eli for as long as I'm required.'

He turned his eyes away from the road and smiled at her.

'You keep your eyes on the road, husband dear, or else we'll be having an accident.'

Siddy did as he was told, but he continued speaking. 'I've already seen my solicitor and made sure you and the new arrival are well cared for. And I know you'll look after those around you . . .'

'Shut up, Siddy! Anyone would think we'd just come from a bleeding funeral, not a wedding!'

'Seriously, though, you must help me remember I haven't

335

only got myself to think about now.' He tapped his fingers on the steering wheel. 'I quite forgot about cars to take the rest of your family to the register office – all I thought about was driving us there and back in my own car—'

'Siddy, stop it. You are one of the most generous people I know. Is that why you phoned for a taxi at Fareham?'

He nodded. 'I've lived alone for so long I've got quite selfish and self-centred in my ways. I need you to tell me where I go wrong. Promise?'

'Oh, Siddy, you been giving me food all through this war, that's not being selfish.'

She could see him thinking. 'If you say so,' he said finally.

Eventually they got to the ferry and Gladys was amazed to see a painted banner hanging outside the club saying, 'Congratulations Siddy and Gladys'.

'Oh, isn't that nice?' Gladys was overjoyed. 'Thank goodness it hasn't rained, else the colours would have run.'

Siddy dropped her at the door so that she didn't have to walk too far carrying her extra weight, and for this she was grateful. Will came down the steps and helped her up into the club, while Siddy went off to park the car.

'Welcome, Mrs Butler,' Will said. Gladys smiled back at him and gasped when she saw what he'd done for her inside the club.

Tables were set out with chairs surrounding them and on

each was a long vase with a single flower. She wasn't sure what kind they were, only that from their freshness he'd obviously bought them from a shop and not the market. At the side, near the kitchen, was a long table spread with food.

'I haven't seen so much to eat in one place for ages,' Gladys said. She eyed the tinned ham, tinned peaches, tinned pineapple and the assortment of cakes, bread and pies made by Will's chef. There was even a wedding cake on a stand. Then she remembered that the last time she'd seen a feast such as this was also here at the club.

'Good. I want to give you a good send-off to married life.'

She looked into his eyes and wondered why, somehow, she didn't believe he really meant the words.

'Considering you know so little about me, that's a lovely thing to do,' she said.

'I know enough, Gladys Butler.'

Gladys felt a shiver run down her spine. She felt like running her fingers through his glossy curls and hugging him for his generosity, but she controlled herself.

He led her to a table where a tall microphone stood on the floor. 'That's there for the groom to make a speech . . .'

'Oh no, Siddy won't do that!' She knew she was looking horrified.

'Well, there are always speeches at a wedding.' He waved an arm expansively. 'I've sat Mac and Marlene here, quite near you, and I've left a seat for myself opposite. Is that all right?'

'That's lovely,' she said. Though she wondered how she was going to feel, having to look at Will for most of the afternoon. Oh, how different it would be if she had married him . . .'

Then she berated herself for thinking such terrible thoughts as Siddy came into the club. He was perspiring with the effort of the steps. She could understand that, they'd nearly defeated her in her pregnant state.

'Over here, love,' she called out.

'How much do you need for doing all this, Will?' Siddy was fiddling inside his jacket for his wallet.

'I'm doing it as a favour,' said Will. 'I don't want your money.'

'But . . .'

'But nothing, Siddy. It costs me little and besides I had a windfall this week with stuff coming from abroad, so I'm happy to help you and Gladys. The only thing is, this is a club I run to make money, so later when darkness falls and no doubt all your family and friends have left, it'll be back to business as normal. Of course you're welcome to stay on, but no doubt by then you'll all be exhausted . . .'

'Will there be music and dancing for me?' Gladys's face lit up with girlish happiness.

'Of course, you can't have a reception without a band and dancing! Siddy, you got to take Gladys round the floor for the first waltz.'

'Oh, no! I don't dance.' Siddy looked horrified.

'Well, may I have the honour instead?'

Gladys had to remind herself to close her mouth. 'You wouldn't feel ashamed dancing with a barrage balloon?'

'I would be honoured.'

Siddy looked relieved he didn't have to make a fool of himself. Gladys's heart was thumping like a drum.

# Chapter Thirty-One

'Gladys. Gladys, love.' Siddy's insistent voice woke her.

It took a moment for her to realize that her husband was sleeping in her double bed with her. Today had been her wedding day and after the wonderful time she, and she hoped everyone else, had had at the Rainbow, she had fallen asleep tucked up spoon-like with Siddy.

'Gladys.' His voice was insistent. He didn't usually sleep with her. It was she who sneaked into his house next door when she was feeling down.

'Just a moment,' she said, moving with great difficulty towards the bedside lamp and switching it on. Gladys blinked at the glare, then began the effort of rolling round to see what he wanted. She listened carefully. The house was quiet. There had been a kerfuffle at about ten o'clock when little Eli had woken up, wet, hungry and angry. But Gladys knew Goldie would soon sort the little boy out.

Siddy had been bewildered.

'Go back to sleep, love,' she'd said. 'You'll soon get used to his noise.'

He must have heard the child crying before, Gladys thought. After all, the walls weren't that thick. But now there wasn't a sound in the house apart from Mogs's contented purring, which Gladys found comforting.

'Oh!'

The eyes that peered at her were slits in a swollen red face, and frightened the life out of her. Siddy was scratching at his neck, which was angry-looking and striped with blood where his nails had pierced the skin.

'Gladys,' he said weakly. His voice was croaky, as if it was difficult for him to speak.

'Oh, Siddy, whatever's the matter, are you ill?'

'Not ill,' he said. He wiped away the water running from his eyes and sniffed. 'It's your cat. I think I must be allergic to it.'

'I'll go and get you some water,' she said, struggling to get out of bed. She looked at Mogs, curled in a ball on the pillow between the two of them. Mogs opened one eye, then closed it again, but the purring went on.

'No, don't bother with the water.'

'I'll put the cat outside, then.'

She slipped her hand beneath the warm, furry body, but was unable to remove the fat animal because he stuck his claws in the pillow like fish hooks and her pillow lifted along with the cat.

Siddy stilled her. 'No, don't worry about that.' He looked sheepish as he struggled up. 'Would you mind if I went back to my own house? This happened to me before, when I was younger.'

'Oh, Siddy, it's our wedding night.' She knew she sounded peevish. She tried again to disengage the cat, who kicked out with his back legs and caught her arm. 'You little bugger,' she said. The purring stopped. Gladys rubbed the blood away from her skin. Mogs now lay full length across the pillow, not purring, but flicking his tail. 'He's used to sleeping with me,' she said, trying to defuse the problem.

Siddy was pulling back the covers. His long, thin white legs disappeared over the side of the bed as he sat up. 'I'll go to my own bed.'

'Shall I come?'

She hoped he'd say no, for his house would be cold and she was loath to move from her comfy bed.

'No,' he said. 'But I'll borrow your dressing gown, if I may?'

When they'd arrived back at number fourteen after the do at the club they'd simply tumbled into bed. As Siddy lived next door there'd been no need to bring his things, as he could just as easily get them in the morning.

'You take what you like, love.'

He shrugged himself into her pink candlewick gown and bent over the bed to kiss her.

'Do you need me to put some ointment on you, or something?' He looked really bad, all swollen like that, she thought.

'I'll have a wash when I get in and by the morning, hopefully, it'll be gone. I don't want you to worry yourself about anything. I'll pop round in the morning so we can check our lists for what we need for Pagham.'

She thought about the holiday he'd arranged by the seaside. He'd wanted two weeks away, but she insisted on only a couple of days in case the baby decided to make an appearance.

She heard him go downstairs and waited to hear the front door open. Instead, she heard the scullery door creak. Then she heard a thump. Then a swear word. Siddy had forgotten the logs were in front of the new doorway into his scullery. Gladys hauled herself to the side of the bed. She didn't want to call out in case she woke little Eli again. Just as she was waving her feet around beneath the bed, searching for her slippers, she heard footsteps going along the passage, the front door opening and closing and then silence.

Gladys abandoned the hunt for her slippers, switched off the light, and rolled back into bed alongside Mogs, who was still stretched out and purring again.

She dreamed someone was crying. Gladys woke and realized there was someone sobbing downstairs. The noise was soft; nevertheless in the quiet of the night it had woken her.

She switched on the bedside light, heaved herself out of bed and found her slippers, which took her a while to get into now that her girth prevented her from bending easily. She looked for her dressing gown then remembered Siddy had worn it back to his house. She smiled to herself, thinking how cross he'd be if someone had seen him coming from number fourteen wearing her pink dressing gown.

She thought about the remaining logs outside on the concrete blocking access to his house and resolved either to do the job herself or to ask Solly to pile the wood beneath the window, out of the way.

All these things she was thinking as, one step at a time, she descended the stairs towards the kitchen and the sound of tears being shed.

In the light from the range, she saw Doll sitting in the big old armchair, her legs curled beneath her, a mug of tea on the floor and a handkerchief held to her eyes.

Gladys moved towards her. 'Whatever are you doing, love?' She pulled the handkerchief away to reveal Doll's tear-stained face. 'It's Fred, isn't it?'

Doll nodded. 'I didn't mean to wake you . . .'

'Doesn't matter. I'm awake now and here, so you can tell me all about it.'

Doll got up and said, 'You sit here.' She picked up her untouched tea and put the mug on the table. Gladys sat in the armchair.

'You've been so good all day,' she said. 'Acting like his death didn't bother you. I've been waiting for you to break down.'

Doll looked at her. Her eyes were glittery with the wetness of her tears. Gladys shifted to the side of the chair. 'Sit with me, there's room for a little one on this big old monster.'

Doll squeezed in beside her and laid her head close to Gladys's cheek. Gladys could smell cigarette smoke in Doll's hair from the party at the Rainbow. 'I know you had feelings for him, love. He was your brother.'

Doll sniffed. 'I keep thinking about when I was younger and he was the only one who ever took any notice of me. He'd buy me little gifts out of the money he earned. Sherbet dabs, liquorice sticks, a clip for my hair. Fred always listened to me.'

'No one's all bad, Doll.'

'No, that came later. Though the more I think about it, how he allowed his life to become what it was, the more I think it was because he had no one to care about him, so he poured all that caring onto me. Maybe he didn't go about it the right way, treating me as if I was some porcelain dolly to be kept in a box. But I think he did care, Gladys.'

Gladys patted Doll's knee. All that acting as though she didn't care that her brother was dead was just that: an act.

'Of course he cared. But like most men, he thought if he kept you in a little box and put you in his pocket, didn't allow you to mix with anyone, you'd be safe.' Gladys sniffed. 'He didn't realize what harm he was doing to you. A lot of men are like that with their wives. Practically keeping them under lock and key, always asking where they've been, who they've talked to.' Gladys felt a sudden pain slice into her side. She groaned and saw Doll's eyes widen with fear.

'Stop that, it's nothing. I shouldn't have been dancing me feet off in that club.'

Doll looked satisfied with Gladys's explanation of the pain.

'See, blokes don't realize women need a bit of freedom, otherwise we feel trapped.' She could see Doll was thinking about her words.

Then the girl said, 'When they let his body go and he can be buried, Will said he'd pay for the funeral. I told him I'll pay him back, but he won't hear of it.' She paused. 'I did care about Fred, Gladys. I even thought about going to see him to let him see I was all right . . .'

'No!' Gladys's voice rose. 'That wouldn't have worked at all.'

Doll was nodding her head. Because of the tight space the two occupied it seemed as if the whole chair was shaking. Doll moved her arm to encircle Gladys's neck. Gladys realized just how much she cared for this wayward girl.

'You looked good dancing with Will.' Doll had changed the subject. Gladys remembered how she'd felt in his arms and, God forgive her, wishing she wasn't pregnant because she could have got closer to him. 'I think he cares for you.'

Gladys laughed. 'He cares for a lot of women.' She remembered the musky smell of his skin, the feel of his hands on her body.

'No, that's where you're wrong. He's a bit of a loner, actually. There's no woman in his life. He goes off on his own, but comes back alone. Business, he calls it. Mind you, he's happier than he was, there was some problem about his wholesalers, so he said. But apparently it's sorted now.'

'You do realize he often sails close to the wind?' Gladys said. 'Not everything he does is honest.' She felt she had to warn the girl that William Hill wasn't a saint.

'Of course. But if it was that much against the law then that detective, Mac, wouldn't be mates with him, surely?'

Gladys wanted to tell Doll she had a lot to learn. But Will had obviously won her over, so who was she to put a spoke in his wheel? And Doll was right. Mac wouldn't hang about chatting and drinking with him if he was such a bad criminal.

'There's two sides to everyone, just like there was with Fred. I don't think Will is a bad man. I think he cuts corners.'

'He always asks me how you are.'

Gladys was happy to hear that. 'Does he?'

'Oh, yes, and he really likes it that you get on so well with Violet Kray and them two boys of hers.' Suddenly Doll yawned.

'You should get back to bed, missy. But first let's see if that tea you made is still hot.'

'Never mind me, you should get back upstairs to Siddy. It's your wedding night. He'll worry if he wakes up to find you're not there.'

Gladys gave a little laugh and pushed Doll aside so she could wriggle her way out of the chair and go and feel the teapot. She began to tell the story of Mogs – and Siddy's affliction.

Pretty soon they were both laughing. Doll closed the kitchen door in case the noise they were making woke Goldie and little Eli.

## Chapter Thirty-Two

Gladys walked hand in hand with Siddy along the stony beach at Pagham. The sharp wind stung her face, yet the day itself was clear and sunny. She'd been in a happy mood since waking despicably early after a disrupted night. She looked at Siddy. His face had almost returned to its normal size, but with puffiness still remaining beneath his eyes. Every so often she had to warn him against scratching his neck.

'Makes you look like you were out on the razzle last night,' she said.

'I told you once before that your life is too exciting for me and that I'd never fit into your household. I didn't expect to be ousted by a cat, though.' He squeezed her hand. Then he put his other hand to his back and groaned. 'Moving those logs this morning didn't do me any favours,' he said.

She let out a small giggle and he pulled her round and

enfolded her in his arms as best he could with her bump in the way.

'Siddy, it's come between us,' she said, laughing louder.

'Mrs Butler, I love you,' he said, before kissing her on the forehead. 'How about a spot of lunch in that little café over there?' On the corner was a small restaurant with a noticeboard on the pavement.

'Sounds good to me,' Gladys said. The walk had given her an appetite. They'd booked into a hotel near the beach and had already unpacked their belongings before embarking on a walk. Bed and breakfast at the Swan's Nest left them free to go where they wanted during their short stay. Siddy said he had enough petrol to go to Littlehampton, if she desired.

'Wait just a moment.' Siddy paused at a bench near the yacht club. He sat down and motioned for her to sit as well. 'Look, love, I meant what I said some time ago. I really am going to stay in my own house next door to you. Bloody Mogs can sleep where he wants, then.' He said it kindly, so she knew he wasn't really cross. 'Besides, what with the little one coming,' he added, eyeing her bump, 'there isn't the room or the quiet that I'm used to. I'm used to leaving books down on the floor and papers spread out on tables. With two kiddies soon crawling around, taking over and picking up this and that, I'll get cross. I'm too crotchety for change.'

Gladys opened her mouth to challenge him, but realized he was tired. It wasn't the years that divided them, but all he'd been through in Germany and the fact that he'd lived a solitary celibate life since then.

'It'll make me wonder why you married me, Siddy.'

'Because I love you. Besides, my money will go to the state when I die, unless there's someone to leave it to. I'd rather you had it. I keep telling you that.'

Gladys thought that sounded mercenary, but she knew full well what he meant.

'I can still come and cuddle into you, can't I?'

He looked into her eyes. Gladys saw the love and kindness there. 'You'd better,' he said. 'And as often as possible, before that new baby takes up all your time.'

'Oh, Siddy,' Gladys said. 'I do love you.'

'And you don't know how much I wish I could show you I love you too,' he said. Too late, she saw the tears in his eyes.

'Goldie, you can't go on working as much as you do.'

Gladys put her hand on Goldie's arm. She'd been waiting for her to come home from Priddy's so that she could talk to her. She carried on, 'It's good of you to go back to putting in as much time as possible so we won't be short, moneywise. But when little Eli wakes in the night and you have to get up to see to him as well as rise early for work, it wears you out.

We're back at square one: you're not getting to see as much of the little chap as you'd like during the day.'

'I don't mind . . .'

'I do,' Gladys cut in. 'We've all got to pull our weight for this war, I know that, but Siddy's giving me cash now every week for housekeeping and what with the money from big Eli and Doll's wages we'll be fine.'

'But Siddy gives you money for you, not to keep us.'

'All for one and one for all.' Gladys pulled out a kitchen chair and bade Goldie sit. 'If you don't like taking my money, how about going in to the armaments yard for a few evenings a week? Little Eli'll be in bed then. I can sort that out with Mr Scrivenor; would that make you feel better?'

Goldie swung back her hair. 'Yes,' she said. 'And you're right, I'm feeling like little Eli's milestones in growing are passing me by. Look at when he sat up for the first time – I wasn't here to see it.'

Gladys gave a sigh of relief. 'Settled?'

'Settled,' said Goldie. She made to get up.

'Stay there. I've already started the dinner; well, peeled the potatoes. You've been on your feet all day. Have a cuppa first.' Gladys managed to get to her feet. She put her hand near her groin. 'This little bugger is getting heavier and heavier,' she said.

Out in the scullery she stirred half a teaspoon of tea

into the dregs in the pot and hoped it would be strong enough.

She thought about the funeral of Doll's brother at the weekend.

They'd all gone to pay their last respects. Doll had written to her father but the letter had come back with 'address and name unknown' written on the envelope. Doll hadn't said anything to her, but Gladys knew she was upset she hadn't been informed of her father's new address. When Goldie discovered this from Doll, she said she was determined to find out where the pair had gone. Will arrived as they were about to go into the chapel at Ann's Hill Cemetery. His sleek Jaguar always took Gladys's breath away.

Will arrived alone, stood at the back for most of the service, and left before the interment with only a nod of recognition. He made an exception for Doll, who he chatted to for quite a while. Gladys couldn't help but think how suave he looked in his dark suit, dark overcoat and trilby hat. Little Eli wasn't enamoured of the cold chapel and started to cry. Gladys was surprised when Will took the boy from Goldie's arms and went outside with him, returning a short while later with the child quietened to hand him back to Goldie.

Gladys thought he had taken a shine to Doll, but in a fatherly way.

Now she finished making the tea and took in a cup to

Goldie, who had moved from the kitchen chair to the old armchair and sat with her feet curled beneath her.

'I'm tired, but not tired enough for bed: besides, it's too early. I wish something nice would happen,' Goldie said.

As if in answer to her plea, a voice called out, 'Cooee, it's only me.'

Solly came into the kitchen.

'Doll's not dancing tonight, is she?' Gladys put her hand to her head as though she'd forgotten something.

'No, I just came to ask if you'd like to go and see *Old Mother Riley*, the picture's on at the Criterion.' He looked expectantly at Goldie, who promptly started to laugh.

'Well, you got your wish,' said Gladys to Goldie. Solly looked at them and frowned.

'I'm not ready and I've not eaten,' moaned Goldie.

'What if I buy fish and chips; I saw Stacy's are open? You could get ready while I'm gone.'

Gladys stretched upwards towards the mantelpiece and took her purse from the shelf.

'Ooh!' She clutched her back, dropped the purse and Goldie jumped up, her arms out ready in case Gladys fell. 'I'm all right, it's just a twinge. It was all that walking I did at Pagham.'

'That was days ago, before the funeral. I'm going nowhere until I'm sure you're all right.'

Solly gave Gladys the purse he'd picked up.

'Thanks, love.' She took out some money and made to give it to him, but he waved her hand away.

'For goodness sake, you do enough for me. I think I can afford to get us fish and chips.'

Still rubbing her back, she said, 'Me, you, Doll, Goldie.' She was counting the people needing a meal.

'What about Siddy?'

'He's gone off for a couple of days, something to do with business . . .' Gladys's voice tailed off.

Then Solly asked, 'Will you be all right on your own?' He blushed. 'I mean, what with the baby an' all?'

She said sharply, 'You'd better get down to Stacy's before the fish is all gone. The boy's asleep.' She raised her eyes towards the bedroom overhead. 'Doll will be home soon, and she's not going anywhere tonight, so I won't be alone.'

Solly picked up his hat from the table, jammed it on his head, and it wasn't long before Gladys heard the front door close.

'He likes you,' she said.

Goldie wriggled out of the chair. 'I like him. But only "like". He's a good friend, but that's all he'll ever be.'

'You could do a lot worse,' muttered Gladys. 'Drink your tea.'

*

'Old Mother Riley is a man dressed up as a woman.'

'Of course she is, that's what makes it funny.' Gladys looked at Doll. Why was everything always so black and white to young people? Stop being such a misery, she told herself. She couldn't settle. She cursed Siddy for making her walk when she wasn't used to walking. Bing Crosby was singing 'Don't Fence Me In'. He was everywhere, she thought. Every time she switched the wireless on it was Bing Crosby. 'You're making a mess of that wool.'

'I can't do right for doing wrong,' said Doll. She put down the white knitting and got up. 'I'm making a pot of tea and I'm using fresh tea leaves, so put that in your pipe and smoke it.'

Gladys put down the book she was trying to read, *The Lady in the Lake*. Normally she liked reading and Raymond Chandler was a good writer, but for some reason she couldn't make sense of the words. She'd read to the bottom of the page then had to go back and read it again, for the story had gone completely from her head.

'I think there was something wrong with that cod.' Gladys tapped her fingers on the cover of the book. 'Maybe it wasn't fresh.'

'Well, mine was fine and nobody else complained,' came the shouted reply.

Just then the siren sounded.

'I can't believe it! We go ages without anything happening . . .' Gladys hauled herself to her feet and went down the passage to the front door, behind which the electricity meter sat. Then she came back into the scullery and said, 'I can't get right down on the floor beneath the copper to switch off the gas, you'll have to do that.'

Doll said, 'Wait a minute until the kettle's boiled.' They glared at each other. Gladys let out a deep sigh.

'Go and get in the Morrison. I'll fill the flask and bring you in a cuppa, maybe that'll cheer you up,' said Doll.

'Where's Mogs? I ain't getting in no shelter without him.'

Mogs was asleep on the rag rug. Gladys bent as best she could and picked him up, cuddling his warm body against her cheek.

The pain that shot through her groin made her shout out, 'Oooh!' The cat jumped from her arms. Belly flat on the rug and tail swishing, he glared at her.

Doll came in with the steaming kettle in her hand. 'What's the matter?'

Gladys felt the wet rush down her legs and soak into her slippers. 'The baby's coming.'

## Chapter Thirty-Three

'Will you be all right while I go and phone for an ambulance to take you to Blake's?'

'Put that bloody kettle down and I'll tell you.' Gladys held on to the arm of the chair, bent over with the spasm that was circling her middle.

Doll turned and went back into the scullery. Gladys heard her stir the teapot after setting the kettle on the stove.

Outside there was the unmistakable sound of a doodle-bug. Gladys held her breath as it came nearer.

'Please God, no, not now. No one's had the chance to get to a shelter.'

The terrible silence as the bomb cut out. She held her breath.

The noise was earth-shattering. The house quivered and dust fell down like snow. 'Get in the shelter,' Doll cried. A creak and a scraping sound and the cream-and-green kitchen cabinet toppled over. It was only the table that stopped its descent to the floor.

The first thing Gladys noticed was the huge cobweb on the wall behind the cabinet. She shook her head; that was the least of her problems.

There was the sound of running feet and people shouting and the smell of burning. Strangely, she could smell rubber and petrol.

'I don't know what to do first, get you to hospital, get into the Morrison or look out the door and see who's copped it. That doodlebug was very near to us.'

Doll was right. The V2 rocket had landed too close for comfort.

Another spasm took Gladys by surprise. She clung to the table for support. The cabinet's pull-down door had fallen open and butter, milk and condiments had slid to the lino. 'Pick up that butter, Doll, can't waste that.' Yet another jolt of pain gripped her. 'I don't think I'll make it to Blake's. The pains shouldn't be this close.'

Through the curtains the sky was changing colour with the searchlights. Although there was no electric light on, it was bright enough in the kitchen. The range gave both heat and firelight. The logs sparked and sizzled.

Doll ran along the passage and tentatively opened the front door. Gladys, close on her heels, asked, 'What is it?'

Despite the door being slammed shut almost immediately, the smell of burning came in swiftly.

'It's the garage! Hutfield's at the end of the road has copped the bomb!'

The two women stood staring at each other. Hutfield's had tanks of petrol below ground. The bomb obviously hadn't reached the flammable liquid, but it could, at any moment. Only luck had stopped it from landing directly on the tanks.

'There's petrol . . .' Gladys put her hand over her mouth. Her heart was pounding. 'That'll go sky-high, taking us with it!' Just then, the sound of sirens told her that relief vehicles had arrived; fire engines, possibly ambulances. Gladys was muttering a prayer for the victims and rescuers that they'd keep safe.

'We won't be allowed out of Alma Street to go past that lot,' Doll said. She put her hand on Gladys's arm. 'Come and get in the shelter.'

Gladys put both hands beneath her stomach. It felt as if she were bursting, like a ripe tomato. 'You'll have to help me.' Another pain gripped her. 'Ohhh!'

Doll's mouth fell open. 'I ain't never attended a birth before,' she said.

'Well, you're going to now.' Gladys's eyes fell on the cup

of tea on the table. She drank it back, bits of dust and all. She looked at the fallen cabinet. 'It'd help if that wasn't in the way. We'll need to get into the scullery.'

Doll lifted and closed the drop-down flap and gripped the cabinet where one of the drawers had fallen out. The light object was soon upright again. Gladys didn't want to think about the stuff inside it, probably broken and mess all over the place.

'I didn't want my baby to come into a dirty house,' said Gladys, glad the cobweb was obscured from her view.

Doll slid in a drawer. 'Better now?' She didn't bother to hide her sarcasm.

Planes flew overhead and ground fire sounded. Another huge bang startled Gladys. She suspected it was from the garage. She grabbed at Doll's hand.

'Go and get towels out of the cupboard in my bedroom,' she said. As she spoke, she heard the thin wail of little Eli upstairs grow into a full-blown yell. She looked at Doll. 'I'd forgotten all about him!' She put her hand over her mouth and giggled.

'And me!' Doll was blushing. 'I'll go and bring him down. Shall I put him in his pram?'

'No, put him in the shelter. If we go, we all go together.'

'So you're still a misery?'

As she went out of the kitchen, Gladys threw a teaspoon at her. It missed because another pain had gripped her and her aim wasn't straight.

When Doll came downstairs again with the little boy in her arms she was also clutching nappies, muslin squares, and an all-in-one that Eli had taken to being dressed in, having grown too big for the nightgowns.

Gladys was holding on to the table again, her teeth clenched, her eyes closed.

'Hello, Poppet,' she said, as soon as she could speak. The little boy had a snotty nose where he'd been crying. He put out his arms to go to Gladys. 'No, Nanny can't hold you, Nanny's got a tummy ache.'

'You do know he doesn't understand a word—'

'Yes, he does. And he stinks!'

Doll put Eli on the rag rug. Mogs glared at the child but defiantly didn't move. Gladys watched as Doll wheeled in the big pram and left it in front of the cabinet. 'Just in case we need it,' she said.

'I could do with another cuppa.'

Doll waved her hands in the air. 'Look! One pair!' She gathered together cream, nappy and liner and cotton wool. A few minutes later, the air smelled of soiled terry-towelling.

'You going to put that in soak?'

'No, Gladys, I'm putting it in the china cabinet!'

Gladys made a face at her, then wrapped her arms around herself as though hugging her body, and swore. 'That was a big one,' she said moments later. As the pain eased she watched Doll put the child in the shelter. His arms and legs began to wave, as the little boy gurgled contentedly to himself.

'Doll, go and see what's happening at the end of the road.'

Obediently, Doll went down the passage and opened the door. More noise and cordite smells greeted her and Gladys, who, amazingly, was close behind her.

Fire engines were spraying a sort of foam and shovelling sand onto the building, and seemed to be getting the fire under control. The whole of the semicircular office building at the front was a still-smoking ruin covered in what looked, from where Gladys was standing, like snow.

'Thank God they didn't get the petrol tanks,' Doll said.

Gladys said, 'Look, there are coppers making sure that people don't pass and telling that lot to go away. I told you, Doll, you'll have to be my midwife.' Doll looked stricken with fear at the prospect. 'C'mon, let's get back indoors.'

Gladys couldn't make it back to the kitchen without bending over in an effort to still the pain.

'Shall I go and make your bed ready?'

Gladys said, 'I'd rather stay downstairs in front of the fire.' Doll looked at her in amazement, but didn't speak.

A whizzing sound could be heard and Gladys said, 'Not again.' Louder and louder came the noise, then nothing. She held her breath. The crash was not close.

'Poor buggers.'

Gladys shook her head at Doll's words. 'We're going to win this war,' she said, brightly.

'I only wish I had your faith,' Doll answered.

'I got to lie down,' Gladys said. 'Will you help me take my clothes off?'

'Won't you let me phone Blake's?'

'Not much point. You've seen the end of our road; nothing'll get through that lot. I'm not leaving you and little Eli alone either.' She put out her arms so Doll could pull her clothes over her head. 'Is there any hot water left in the kettle?'

Doll nodded.

'I'd like to try to have a bit of a wash.'

Doll went out into the scullery and Gladys heard water going into a bowl.

'Want me to help?'

Gladys shook her head. 'I'll do it.'

Doll went upstairs and came back with a clean nightdress and Gladys's dressing gown. She put them on the table in the scullery. Gladys was scrubbing at her body, every so often stopping to pant and puff. Doll opened the flask and poured out tea. Gladys, bent over with pain, hobbled into the kitchen. She looked at Eli, but he'd gone to sleep, oblivious to the commotion around him. His arms were above his head and he looked as if he didn't have a care in the world. Mogs had crept in beside him and eyed Gladys warily.

'I've been saving old newspapers, they're under the sink. Can you spread them on the floor? Better roll the rag rug up first.'

Doll did as she was told. Then she ran upstairs and came back with an old sheet to spread over the papers. Gladys was sitting on the edge of the chair, moaning with pain. 'Sorry,' she mouthed. Doll handed her the tea and Gladys drank it back, practically in one gulp.

There were dull thuds coming in from outside where far-off planes were dropping their loads. Gladys hoped they wouldn't come nearer. She ran her hands through her hair. It felt sweaty and greasy.

'I don't remember it being this bad with my Pixie,' she confessed. 'Mind you, that was a while back.'

The sweat was running down the sides of her face and even with her teeth clenched together, she still managed an ear-splitting scream. She looked at Doll. The poor girl was scared out of her wits.

'I haven't done anything like this before,' Doll said again.

'Well, it's just as well I have, then.' Gladys gave a sort of strangled smile. 'I'd better warn you, I might swear and say things I normally wouldn't, but please don't worry, it's quite normal – well, it was for me . . .' Gladys gritted her teeth. She slid down in front of the fire. 'Just hold my hand and tell me I'm doing fine from time to time and remember women have been doing this for years and years. Ohhh.' When the pain had subsided once more she said, 'Maybe you'd do better to put little Eli in the pram and wheel him into the passage? I don't want to frighten him. Ohhh.'

Doll went and did as she'd suggested. Eli, fast asleep, didn't wake.

Gladys leaned her head back on the old armchair in exhaustion. She was going to need all her strength.

And then she was disappearing into a world of pain and excitement and screams until her head swam and she couldn't think straight. All she was aware of was Doll wiping her face and neck and breasts with a damp cloth and saying, 'You can do this, come on.'

Vaguely she heard the 'all-clear' and tried to speak, to say, Thank God. Another raid was over. But her mind wouldn't allow her body to do anything else except try to push the child out of herself and into the world.

Time held no meaning. She gripped the arms of the old chair, using them as a lever while she screamed.

'You're nearly there, push!'

'What d'you think I'm doing?'

Just when she thought she couldn't push again and the baby would have to stay where it was, an enormous urge engulfed her and she panted and grunted and pushed. She felt the child slide from her body.

Doll cried, 'It's a little girl.' Gladys saw her lift the waxy, bloody baby that seemed extraordinarily long and thin. She looked at the cord attached to herself, through which she'd kept her baby safe these past months. Gladys's heart lifted as the baby was placed on her body.

'I have to cut this?'

That sudden surge of energy that comes after the birth inspired Gladys to yell, 'Scissors, in the knife drawer. Dressings are in the cupboard.'

The rattle of cutlery produced scissors and Doll took a deep breath while searching for the first-aid box that usually contained very little.

Gladys kept her hand on her daughter while the scissors went through the slimy cord, leaving, as she had dictated, just enough to eventually shrivel and fall away in a couple of weeks' time.

A large dressing that looked incredibly big on the small stomach made Gladys nod her head happily.

Doll had thought to put a bowl of water on the table and Gladys saw her smooth the crying child's face with wet cotton wool, before she placed the little one back in Gladys's arms.

The crying increased. Tears of happiness were rolling down Gladys's face.

'She's beautiful.' The words were said in wonderment. Whatever misgivings Gladys might have had about the father's identity were quashed as she cradled the naked baby. A huge surge of love flowed from her towards this small being, who was her own person, regardless of her parentage.

Doll was now rolling something in newspaper. Gladys hadn't felt the placenta leave her body. Doll used the metal lever to lift the top off the range and put in the paper parcel, pressing it down.

'Give her back to me and you can have her when you're both cleaned up.'

Gladys, totally exhausted, tried to sit up using the front of the chair as a backrest. The all-consuming love that had come with the child would stay, forever. Gladys wouldn't change this moment in time for anything. She gazed at Doll and said, 'Make us a cuppa, love?'

# Chapter Thirty-Four

'That girl's a marvel!' Gladys couldn't stop praising Doll. 'When I think what a spoiled brat she was when I first took her in! Whoever would have thought she'd turn out to be such a wonder?'

Violet Kray smoothed back her blonde hair. 'I knew she was special when I first saw her dance on that stage there.' She pointed to the parquet flooring in the Rainbow. 'Funny how a brother and sister could be poles apart, isn't it?' Gladys didn't answer immediately, so Violet went on, 'Take my two. Reggie is the sensible one and Ronnie is inclined to jump to conclusions too quickly. It's always Reggie who calms him down.'

'Fred was a bad man,' Gladys said, nodding agreeably at Violet's description of her boys. 'Did they find out who done for him?' She glanced through the window towards the ferry, where a boat was disgorging passengers. Ronnie and

Reggie were playing football near a notice that said Keep Off The Grass. They were sturdy, well-built boys, polite to Will and to Gladys, and loved Violet to distraction.

Violet shook her head. 'When you get someone as evil as that I don't think the coppers care one way or another who gets rid of him. They're just glad he's gone. Less bother for them.'

'I suppose so,' said Gladys. She picked up the child from her lap where she had been bottle-feeding her and lifted her across her breast, rubbing the little one's back with circular motions.

'I'm surprised you're not breastfeeding.'

'Broke my heart when I found it wasn't working,' Gladys sighed. 'That's the curse of being an older mother.'

'You're not old.'

'Late thirties is old these days. Still, what with orange juice, cod liver oil and malt, I'll make sure this little one stays bonny.' Gladys seemed to have bloomed since the birth. She had quickly fitted back into her costumes with their tight skirts and neat fitted jackets, and now she wasn't working at Priddy's, her hair shone, her skin was a creamy pink and her energy was boundless.

She usually brought both kiddies with her when she visited Violet at the Rainbow, fitting them both into the big Silver Cross pram. But Goldie was home and wanted little

Eli with her. Gladys was going shopping in the market after she'd left her friend and the club. She needed some vegetables to make a nice stew with the breast of lamb the butcher had saved for her. Siddy liked her stews.

He adored the baby. Gladys had named her daughter Sydney, for him. Siddy spent a lot of time at number fourteen, but always went home to his own house to sleep. He kept a wary eye on Mogs. The cat tried hard to jump on Siddy's lap whenever he sat down. It was as though Mogs had some personal vendetta against Siddy.

'She still writing to that lad?'

Sometimes, Gladys thought, she needed to be a mind reader to follow Violet's butterfly mind as she flitted from one subject to another.

'Doll and Joe are like a proper couple. Yes, they write to each other all the time. He's in Germany, Berlin. He said they're not allowed to fraternize with the Germans. Montgomery said that.'

Violet nodded. 'I meant that tank bloke and your Goldie. And anyway, I don't know who'd want to have anything to do with them Germans, some of the things they've done.'

Gladys went on rubbing her daughter's back. 'Yes, but it's all platonic. She sent him a photograph of Eli.'

'What's he look like? The bloke? Good-looking?'

'They haven't exchanged photographs of themselves. It's not that kind of relationship.'

Violet's answer to that was drowned by Sydney's burp, which was loud and clear. Violet laughed. The kitchen door opened and a pretty young girl came out with a tray.

'Mr Hill says it's teatime.' Violet and Gladys looked at each other and smiled. A small cake stand contained fancy cakes and pieces of shortbread. On the tray, two cups and saucers and two plates plus cutlery sat with a small teapot, steam curling from its spout. Milk was in a jug and sugar in a bowl.

'He likes you,' said Violet knowingly.

'Hitler's dead!' Solly rushed up the hallway and burst into the kitchen, dragging a young woman with dark hair and wearing spectacles. 'Hitler's dead!' he said again.

Gladys looked at him in amazement. 'Don't be silly,' she said and put down the copy of *Woman's Weekly* she'd been thumbing through, which had been given to her by Goldie. Goldie had gone to town with little Eli on the bus.

He turned to the girl at his side. 'Isn't it true? Tell her, Patsy.'

The girl said, 'It's on the news. Hitler shot himself in his bunker. His Eva's gone as well, she poisoned herself.'

'Well I never,' said Gladys, still not sure if she believed the news.

'He reckoned everyone had deserted him, including his own men. He blamed the English and Americans for turning the tide of the German people's affection for him.'

'Well I never,' repeated Gladys. She sat down heavily in the old armchair, hardly daring to believe it could be true. 'What a turn-up for the books!'

'How can the Germans fight a war without a leader, Solly?' The strange girl looked at him.

'I don't think they can. I suppose it means the war's over bar the shouting.'

'Do you really think so?' Her eyes shone with excitement, looking up at Solly.

'And who might you be?' Gladys looked at the young woman in her sober outfit of belted raincoat, black shoes and shoulder bag.

'Sorry, Gladys, this is Patsy Winters, she works in the office. Mr Scrivenor is her uncle and he's asked me to look after her.'

Gladys eyed their still-entwined hands. 'I see you're doing that very well.' She said to the girl, 'Would you like a cup of tea?'

'Oh, yes, please. Is that your baby asleep outside the door?'

'Yes, that's my little girl.'

'She's lovely. I hope you don't mind, I had a peek at her before I got dragged in to see you.'

Gladys decided she was a nice girl. Solly was watching Patsy's every move. Gladys thought he looked besotted. The fragrant smell of lavender wafted over to Gladys.

'Are you sure about Hitler?'

Both Solly and the girl said yes, at the same time, looked at each other and then laughed. Gladys said, 'Sit yourselves down, I'll put the kettle on. Patsy, why don't you tell me all about yourself?'

'I wish I'd met her.' Goldie was undressing little Eli, who didn't like it much and was grizzling.

'You know Solly, he'll bring Patsy round again if it's serious. She seems a nice little thing. Have you heard about Hitler?'

'Everywhere I went in the market they were on about it. They say he was round the bend at the end.'

'Round the bend at the beginning to start the blinking war, if you ask me.' Gladys was folding washing brought in from the line. 'I heard on the wireless that there's more concentration camps full of dead and starving people than we ever knew about. Mussolini and his fancy piece have been shot and hung up as an example to people. Makes you wonder what's going to happen next, doesn't it?'

Goldie sat Eli in the high chair that Siddy had got hold of. She pushed a hard crust of bread into his hand and he quickly found his mouth. She gazed at him adoringly.

'If the war ends, what will happen to Priddy's?' Goldie asked.

'There will always be a need for arms. Priddy's will probably still make armaments for the forces. Can't have an army and navy without weapons, can we? In any case, even though the war may possibly be over in Europe, we still got to sort out them Japanese.'

'You're probably right. But I expect they'll cut down on the number of people who work there and there won't be overtime.'

'Don't worry, I doubt it'll happen overnight,' said Gladys.

A small cry came from the hallway, where the pram held Sydney.

'That's my little girl,' Gladys said. 'Mummy's coming.'

'And they say every child should know its father,' Gladys said, watching Siddy carefully bathing the tiny girl. 'I think love is more important.'

Normally his hands shook – remnants from his treatment at the hands of the Nazis – but Siddy held the baby firmly as he soaped her. 'She's a miracle and she's going to grow up in peacetime,' he said.

'Hang on, Siddy, we still aren't sure what's happening.'

'The government will make an announcement at three this afternoon, you mark my words. They said so, so they will.' Siddy had finished rinsing the child in the enamel basin on the table in front of the range. 'Pass us a towel.' Gladys handed him a warm, clean towel from the fireguard and watched entranced as he carefully patted the child dry, then enfolded Sydney in another dry towel and passed her to her mother.

Gladys said, 'C'm'ere, little one, Daddy doesn't want you any more.'

'You're much better at fitting tiny arms into tiny clothes,' he said. 'I'll take this and put it down the sink.' He disappeared into the scullery with the bowl of water. 'Where's Goldie?'

Gladys said, 'She's gone round to Priddy's with Eli. Solly told her Mr Scrivenor is having a talk with all the workers, so she thought she'd better be there.'

She looked down at her child. 'You're going to a party this afternoon.'

Will was hosting a get-together at the club so they could listen to the special broadcast on the wireless.

Already the streets were festooned with bunting, and festivities had started immediately upon hearing of Hitler's death.

'I think we deserve a celebratory drink.' Siddy, back in the kitchen, had taken a half-bottle of whisky from his pocket. He was busy pouring measures into two glasses.

'Where did you get that from?'

Siddy's answer was to touch the side of his nose. He drank back the draught after pushing a glass across the table towards her.

'I don't want a drink this early, I'd rather have a cup of tea,' Gladys said, buttoning a white knitted matinee coat onto Sydney. Siddy drank hers as well, then went back out to the scullery and she heard the pop of the gas beneath the kettle.

A loud knock at the door made her jump. Most people just slipped the key through the letter box, opened the front door and came in.

'Can you get that, I want to finish dressing Sydney?' She'd already picked up the small hairbrush and was making a quiff in the little girl's hair.

Siddy shuffled down the passage and Gladys heard him speaking to someone, then the words, 'You'd better come in.'

Gladys had finished prettying her daughter and was now smoothing the sheet in the carrycot with one hand while holding Sydney beneath her other arm. She'd decided to take the carrycot to the Rainbow, in Siddy's car. Little Eli was in the big pram and after seeing Mr Scrivenor at Priddy's, Goldie was walking down to the club.

'I hope you don't mind me calling unannounced,' said the tall, blond man, who was in uniform and wearing a beret. 'I take it you are Gladys Smith?' He seemed to fill the room.

'Gladys Butler, actually. I've remarried.' She nodded towards Siddy, who was escaping to the scullery to finish his teamaking. 'You are?'

'Eli. I'm Rebecca's brother.'

'Oh, my God,' said Gladys. She put down her daughter in the carrycot and covered her with a light blanket. 'You've got leave?'

'Not before time.' He had a deep voice, a tanned skin, white teeth and almost took Gladys's breath away with his broad shoulders and the bluest eyes she'd ever seen. 'I've been writing to Goldie . . .'

'And kindly sending money for the lad.'

He smiled at her. Gladys liked dark-haired men, but she knew she could easily change her preference to blondes. She smiled back at him.

Siddy came in from the scullery with a tray and mugs, teapot, milk and sugar and put it down on the table. 'Or would you prefer something stronger to celebrate?'

He showed the man his bottle but it was declined.

'Maybe later, thanks. I came to see my nephew. Tea is fine,' Eli said.

'Aha,' Gladys said. 'We got a slight problem. We've been

invited to a party this afternoon, in the town. Eli is with Goldie and we won't be seeing her until we get there.'

His face fell.

Siddy said, 'Why don't you come with us, in the car. It'll be a lovely surprise for her.'

'I can't go to a party, I haven't been invited.' Eli looked disappointed.

'Yes, you can, I'm inviting you. You'll be very welcome, I can assure you of that.' Gladys was looking forward to seeing Goldie's jaw drop when she set eyes on Eli.

'Too right,' said Siddy. 'We wouldn't be having a party if it wasn't for all you lads giving us something to celebrate. We couldn't fight a war without brave men. I'll pour you a cuppa. I'm Siddy, by the way, you can come and sit down and tell me about your experiences; only if you want to, mind. Gladys will take a while to put on her best bib and tucker, you know what the ladies are like. I'm very pleased to meet you, lad.'

Siddy began to pump Eli's arm and Gladys escaped upstairs to get ready. As she passed by Eli she automatically pulled in her stomach, pushed out her chest and treated him to a wide smile.

# Chapter Thirty-Five

'You sit in the front, Eli. Gladys, get in the back and I'll put the carrycot beside you. Eli, do you mind having the bag with the baby's paraphernalia down by your feet? Babies come with a lot of baggage for beings so tiny. The boot's full of little Eli's stuff.'

Siddy sorted out the car and they set off. Gladys was amazed how much bunting had been put up, strung across the streets and round doors and windows. Almost everyone was wearing red, white and blue of some description, apart from the uniformed. The very air felt full of promise, thought Gladys. She wound down the window so she could hear the people in the streets singing, dancing and generally having a good time now that the threat of falling bombs was a thing of the past.

A kiddie adrift from her mother ran in front of the car, making Siddy brake.

'Watch it!' Gladys put her hand down to stop the carrycot

from sliding along the seat. On the pavement the little girl looked shamefaced as her mother scolded her. 'There's people everywhere,' said Gladys.

The weather was dry but overcast. Gladys wondered if it might rain later. She sat behind Eli taking stock of him. She'd already asked him about sweethearts, but he'd told her his girlfriend had died in a raid. It had taken him a long while to get over her death, he said.

'After spending so much time with the regiment and then being unhappy about what happened to my sister, I haven't bothered about girls,' he said.

Gladys stared at his wavy blond hair, longing to run her fingers through it.

Siddy managed, with difficulty, to drive into the town. The streets of Gosport were packed with people. Men and women were spilling out onto the pavements from the pubs and almost everyone was waving flags. There was a barrel organ opposite Woolworths and Gladys thought it sounded lovely, especially with all the people singing along to its music.

Near the bus station Siddy pulled up and said, 'Look, you two go on in. Eli, will you carry the baby in the cot? That'll leave you with the bag, Gladys. I'll bring little Eli's stuff, after I've found a space to park.'

They both agreed as Gladys said, 'Normally you can park

outside the club on the road but there's too many people about.' Eli was looking around him. He held the carrycot by folding the two handles together. Sydney was fast asleep.

Gladys said, 'I've got the bag.' She watched Siddy drive off. 'He doesn't like being in crowded places,' she said. 'His nerves sometimes get the better of him.' She didn't say anything else, because her breath was taken away in amazement by the Union Jack flags and all the coloured bunting draped outside the club.

'This is a nice place,' Eli said, looking about him.

'It's run by a Londoner. He's a good friend to us all.'

Once inside the Rainbow, Gladys heard a woman call her name above the sound of the dance music. It was Violet Kray. The air inside was sweaty and filled with cigarette smoke. 'I've saved two tables, Will put them together and you're the last to arrive.' Violet waved a hand at the seating arrangements, then stared at Eli. She put her hand to her mouth and whispered to Gladys, 'Cor!'

Gladys said softly, 'You can say that again.' Then, 'Where is everyone?' She looked around her and into the crowd at the same time as introducing Eli to Violet. Violet was wearing a flowered dress with puff sleeves and a sweetheart neckline and looked summery. In her hair she had a real flower. Gladys wore her black dress and pearls; she knew she looked good in black. Then she asked Eli to put the carrycot on a chair while she went over to the pram near the wall. She motioned him to follow.

'There's little Eli.' She pulled back the quilt covering him to expose his chubby legs splayed out and his arms way above his head. He was fast asleep. His cheeks were pink and his hair was practically the same colour as his uncle's.

Eli stood in wonderment. Gladys could see tears in his eyes as he said, 'He looks so like Rebecca.' He began to trace the sleeping child's face with his finger. He looked at Gladys and said, 'I can never thank you and Goldie enough for looking after him.'

Gladys decided to leave them alone, and taking a deep breath to help dispel the emotion she was feeling, she returned to the table and foraged in her handbag for her handkerchief in case she cried.

'Oi! You! Leave that baby alone! What d'you think you're doing?' Goldie pushed her way in front of Eli and smacked his hand away. 'That's my baby, leave him alone!'

Gladys looked back at the pram in amazement. Goldie stood in front of the man in uniform. Her hands were now on her hips, and she looked as if she meant business. She was wearing a tight baby-pink short-sleeved sweater and grey flared-leg trousers. She looked very fierce, even though she only came up to his chest.

Eli stepped back in surprise. Gladys could see him staring

at Goldie. Her hair had come unpinned because of her frantic dancing and its blondness glittered beneath the electric lighting. Gladys quickly moved across to shield Eli from Goldie's temper.

'This is Eli!'

'I know it's baby Eli! I don't want any old serviceman thinking he can touch what don't belong to him!'

Gladys held on to the fist Goldie was shaking. 'Goldie, it's Eli, Rebecca's brother!'

Goldie was suddenly speechless. Her face reddened and she put her hand to her mouth, which had fallen open in surprise. She was like a deflated balloon.

Eli began to laugh. It was a big, deep laugh and made Gladys and Violet laugh along with him.

'You must be Goldie,' he said. The red-faced young woman looked at the floor, embarrassed.

'Sorry,' she mumbled.

'I'm not,' Eli said. He put out his hand and said, 'I'm very pleased to meet you at last.'

'You're not going to take my baby – I mean – little Eli, away, are you?' She touched his fingers.

The words came out all in a rush. He shook his head. 'No, no. I can't look after a little one. It looks like you're doing a brilliant job. He's so bonny. And he's so like my sister.'

Gladys saw Goldie relax. The look on Eli's face told her

he would be happy to talk to Goldie all night about the little boy. Goldie was smiling at him now. Gladys turned away and left them to it. The smile on her face was practically from ear to ear.

People were packed into the club like sardines in a tin.

Violet said, 'Have you seen my twins?' She raised the glass of gin and orange to her lips. The two women spent a while discussing the scene between Goldie and Eli, the boys forgotten until Gladys reminded her and said.

'Them two boys are never where they should be.'

'God knows what they'll be like when they grow up,' admitted Violet. She took another sip of her gin and orange. 'Will's been out a dozen times to ask where you are, Gladys. He's doing a roaring trade with booze. He said we're not to pay for any of our drinks, they're on the house.'

'I like the sound of that,' said Gladys. She began to drink her gin and orange.

'He's a bit of all right, isn't he?' Violet was still looking at Eli. He'd taken off his black beret and pushed it through a loop on the shoulder of his blouson top. 'He suits that tank regiment uniform.'

Gladys nodded and took another look at Goldie and Eli, who seemed to be alone in a sea of people. She sighed contentedly. 'They make a nice couple with all that blonde hair. She could do with a good man, could our Goldie.'

Gladys could see Mac in a dark suit and Marlene wearing a green dress that set off her fiery hair. She waved and Marlene waved back. Gladys then spotted Solly, standing looking out of the window across the harbour with his arm around Patsy. She hoped they would make a go of it together. She seemed besotted with him.

Doll pushed through the noisy crowd and put her arms around Gladys. She smelled of Californian Poppy and the red dress she had on suited her to a T. Gladys hadn't seen the dress before.

'Where'd that come from?'

'All the girls got presents of dresses. Will bought rolls of silky material from India.' She paused. 'Came by boat about a week ago; he got the woman that mends our costumes to make them. I didn't say anything to you before because I wasn't going to wear it if I didn't like it. What do you think?' She twirled as best she could amongst the mass of people around her.

'It makes you look grown-up.'

The dress was knee-length with buttons down the front and puffed sleeves.

'I'm not a child!'

Gladys thought how cool and calm Doll had been when she'd given birth to Sydney. No, she thought, Doll wasn't a child any longer. 'It's a beautiful dress and you look lovely.'

Doll was pleased. 'I've had another letter from Joe. He'll be getting leave soon. He's still in Germany but he said the Germans are hungry and crushed.'

'Well, we didn't start the war!'

'No, we didn't, Gladys,' said Siddy, coming up behind her. He had a tray of drinks in one hand, which he put on the table. 'Compliments of Will. He said he'd be over soon. I'd have been here sooner but I couldn't find a space to put the car.' He sat down heavily on a chair next to Violet and tucked a bag of little Eli's stuff under the table. He looked around and saw Eli talking to Goldie.

'They look like they're getting on all right together. I'll go and ask them if they'd like a drink.'

Gladys stopped him as he rose from the chair. 'Oh, no, you don't. Leave them two alone. They're getting on all right without you interrupting them.'

Siddy sat back down again, reached forward and took his drink from the tray. 'Bottoms up!' he said, downing the whisky in one. 'It's too noisy in here for me,' he said. 'I won't be staying for long, Gladys.'

'Who's that?' Doll had spotted Eli with Goldie.

'That's Eli, Rebecca's brother,' Gladys told her. 'You can keep your eyes off, you've got Joe.' Sydney began to grizzle.

'Pass me the big bag, Violet, I'll go into the kitchen and get them to warm her bottle up,' said Gladys. She watched

Violet drag out the bag then forage in it and produce a baby's bottle ready made up with milk.

Gladys elbowed her way through to the kitchen and almost ran into Will, who was coming out. She showed him the bottle.

'Give it to me,' he said. She thought how smart he looked in a dark suit. She followed him towards the big gas stove, where he took down a small saucepan from the shelf above and put some water in it to warm the bottle of milk. He lit the flame beneath the pan. 'You look very nice this afternoon. Did you get the drinks I sent over?'

'Thank you,' Gladys said. She wondered why she was almost always tongue-tied when he was near him.

'Everything all right?' His eyes held hers. She knew she was blushing, but she managed to blurt out, 'Yes, thank you.'

Again the silence. Then he said, 'That Eli seems a nice bloke.'

'Goldie seems to think so,' she said.

'I'm going to get everyone to shut up soon. It's nearly three o'clock and we should listen to what Churchill's got to say.' He took out the bottle, shook it, and let the milk fall on his wrist. 'Just right,' he said, handing it to her.

'You've had some practice,' Gladys said.

'There's a lot you don't know about me, Gladys Butler. I could teach you a thing or two, one day.'

She stood there, holding the bottle of milk, while he leaned in very close to her. So close that as he bent his head his curly hair brushed against her forehead. She could smell his lemony cologne. Her heart began beating fast, so loudly she thought he might hear it.

'I bet you could an' all,' she whispered. She couldn't seem to take her gaze away from his beautiful deep-brown eyes.

Then common sense took over and she shook the bottle of milk and said, 'A hungry little girl to feed.'

He nodded, looked at his watch. 'It's almost three. I must quieten down that crowd out there so we can listen to the speech.'

He held the door and she sailed through it, click-clacking in her high heels towards Sydney, who was crying in earnest now in the carrycot.

Gladys lifted her and snuggled the little girl into her breasts. With the teat in her mouth the baby sniffled once and then sucked contentedly.

Will was now at the microphone and his deep voice came over loudly, making the noise of the packed club cease almost immediately.

'We're about to hear a speech, so let's all make sure we don't miss a word.' The wireless was loud as the speech began, and Gladys, cuddling her little girl, felt the tears spill as the beloved voice of Churchill stated, 'Hostilities will end officially at one minute after midnight, Tuesday, 8th May, but in the interests of saving lives, the ceasefire began yesterday to be sounded all along the front . . .'

Gladys used one hand to wipe her nose, but it was as if she had no control over her feelings as she listened carefully to the rest of Churchill's words and allowed the tears to fall unchecked.

When the cheering erupted, Sydney quivered violently and spat out the teat. Her frightened scream cut through the sounds around her like a siren.

Gladys knew she'd not had enough bottled milk to satisfy her. Sydney wouldn't sleep, but would become a very grumpy little girl. She tried again with the teat. Sydney moved her head away, still scared by the noise, and wailed.

'Can't blame her, she's unsettled.' Gladys jiggled her against her breast.

'I think I'd like to go back to the house, Gladys,' Siddy said. 'This is a bit much for me.' He drank back another whisky, then got up from his chair.

Will had now joined them, a broad smile on his face. 'I've got one of the girls to bring over more drinks. We've got to celebrate.'

'I couldn't drink another thing,' said Gladys.

Siddy put out his arms and bent towards Sydney. 'Why don't I take her home with me. I can feed her and change her and she'll sleep better at home than in her cot in here. It's much too noisy for the little mite.'

Gladys hesitated, but then said, 'If you're sure?'

'Never been more sure.' An understanding look passed between them. What Siddy was saying was, 'Have a good time, Gladys, let your hair down, come back when you're ready and don't worry about the little one, she'll be safe with me.'

Gladys passed the squirming baby to Siddy, got up from the table, collected the carrycot and picked up the bag containing her stuff. 'I'll come down to the car with you.' They began to thread their way through the noisy bar room.

'Pheew, I didn't realize how smoky it was in there until I got out here,' Gladys said, taking deep breaths of fresh air after she'd negotiated the steps.

'That doesn't do the little one much good, does it, Gladys, all that nasty smoke?' He handed her the child. 'Look, love, wait here and I'll bring the car round, no need for you to carry everything to where I've parked it.'

She nodded and moved aside as a drunken man wobbled past her. Out here was a continuation of what was going on in the Rainbow. Dancing, singing, cheering.

She smiled at a line of girls, arm in arm, who were trying to do the Palais Glide but not succeeding very well and falling over with laughter.

Gladys stood by the kerb and looked across to the Ferry Gardens, where more people sang and danced. She thought she caught a glimpse of the Kray boys, but wasn't sure. Violet spoils those boys, she thought. A man sitting on top of a lamp post waved to her and nearly toppled off. She thought of baby Eli, sound asleep in the big pram inside the club, and smiled. That lad would sleep through anything, she mused. She'd tell him about all this when he was older. She hoisted Sydney up over her shoulder and patted her back, wishing she'd stop her crying. Still, when Siddy put her in the car the movement would send her to sleep; it always did.

# Chapter Thirty-Six

Siddy looked at his shaking hands holding the steering wheel. The noise, the feeling of euphoria, was almost more than he could take. There were still poor souls in concentration camps, dying of the cruelty the Germans had put them through. And he knew all about cruelty. His life had been taken away by cruelty. Oh, he could still function as a man, almost, but not as a husband for his beloved Gladys. Nor as a lover. When he caught a glimpse of a beautiful boy: the turn of a male cheek, a sun-bronzed hand running through dark curls, a glistening body covered in drops of sea water as a youth ran up the summer beach, his feelings recalled his time in treatment.

But it was Gladys who made his heart ache. He could give her presents, he could be kind to her, but he couldn't be the husband she needed.

She understood, she said she'd had her fill of men who

loved her and left her. But Gladys needed what he couldn't give her.

Loving, he thought, always comes as a surprise, taking your breath away, like a sunrise. Loving Gladys made him desire her, especially when she was curled into his back. And yet he could do nothing.

He stopped the car outside the club, got out and took the child from Gladys. When Sydney was tucked into the carrycot, he marvelled that so small a child could make so much noise. He slid the cot onto the passenger seat, so that he could keep an eye on her and try to soothe her. He put the bag on the floor. He kissed Gladys and told her to get back inside the club.

He watched through the open passenger window as Gladys pushed through the revellers and climbed the steps at the front of the club, turned and waved, then was gone.

Siddy swung the car carefully out to the middle of the road. A Provincial bus had trouble cutting through the revellers and honked its horn. Siddy went first, turning right by the tobacconist, Findley's, and gathering momentum past the Dive café. It seemed as if the crowd had thinned on the pavements here, in an effort to be where the most excitement was, at the Ferry Gardens. He put his foot on the accelerator.

It was at that very moment one of the twins – who could tell the difference between them? – ran out onto the road.

Siddy swerved. 'Oh, no!' The words hung in the air.

The car mounted the pavement, hit the closed glass door of Woolworths, smashed its way inside the shop, then embedded itself in a counter before finally coming to a stop.

Siddy felt an intense pain in his chest as the steering wheel sandwiched him to the seat. Then he was aware of something missing. The crying of Sydney had suddenly stopped. Then darkness descended.

'My baby, my baby, where's my baby?

The ambulance men wouldn't allow Gladys near the car. The mangled metal steamed. She could see the top of Siddy's head pressing against the front windscreen, which miraculously wasn't broken. Blood ran from his nose and from the one ear visible to her. She couldn't see into the car, but she had been assured the only person it contained was her dead husband.

'There's no baby, madam.' The fireman's face was grave.

Someone put a blanket around her shoulders and she threw it to the floor of the shop. 'Where's my baby?' Her cry rang out and she pushed away the arm that had encircled her shoulder.

'What happened?' Will's voice shot arrow-like into the crowd.

A voice from the bystanders: 'He crashed into Woolworths.' As if Gladys couldn't work that out for herself.

She had known nothing until Reggie Kray had run into the club and started pulling at her dress as she danced and went on tugging until she noticed him. And now her husband was dead, her child gone.

Reggie stood with his twin at the rear of the crowd surrounding the car. The boys, dressed identically in grey jerseys, grey flannel shorts, grey knee-length socks and black shoes, looked away the moment her eyes found them. She realized immediately that the boys knew something.

Mac was coming towards her. 'Come and sit down, we'll find the child,' he said.

But Gladys ignored him and pushed through the bystanders. She looked at the twins, alike as two peas in a pod. She could smell sticky sweets, and the fronts of both boys' jerseys were dirty.

'Thank you for coming to tell me about the accident,' she said quietly. One boy was frowning, his hand clenching and unclenching; nervous, Gladys thought. 'Your mum'll be here in a moment, so you mustn't be scared. Want to tell me what happened?'

'He nearly ran me over.' The boy's words came out clearly, but in a rush, as though he was expelling a secret.

'But it was you came to get me?' She addressed the other lad. He nodded.

'So you saw what happened?'

Sensing she wasn't a threat, both boys began talking at once.

'Slow down,' Gladys said. She felt a presence and looked up to see Will. 'Go away,' she said clearly. She didn't want the boys to become ill at ease; she needed to gain their confidence. Will's dominant presence could halt that. Will frowned, but he turned away, walking back to the police and their notebooks.

Gladys saw the firemen lifting Siddy's body on to a stretcher, a blue blanket covering him completely. Her heart dropped. He really was dead. A tear fell; another began a trail down her face. The nearest boy put out a hand and touched her wet cheek.

'The baby's all right.'

Gladys stared at him, hardly able to believe what he'd just said. Then she pulled him close. 'Where is she? Ronnie,' she said, 'tell me.'

'Reggie,' he corrected, and dropped his grubby hand from her face.

'Tell her,' demanded his twin.

The boy tried to wriggle away.

'Please?' she begged, unsure whether she'd be better holding him tighter or letting him go. She loosened her grip and stood up. He stepped back, opened his mouth and it all poured out.

'We looked in the car, saw the man was a goner. The baby was crying. I sent him,' he nodded towards his brother, 'to get you. I thought the baby might be hurt. I couldn't see her. She was screaming and the covers were all on top of her so I pulled the carrycot through the window and took her back there in case anything fell on her and she got blowed up. We saw this picture where everything got blowed up. Planes was blowed up. It was called something about Tokyo. Anyway, that Van Johnson was in it.' His voice carried on about the film, gaining momentum with his excitement at what he'd seen. Then he stopped and pointed over towards the firemen now using a small crane to tow back the vehicle from the shop out onto the road so they could secure the store. 'Things like that got blowed up.' Gladys sighed, then took a deep breath.

'So where did you put the baby so she'd be safe?' Convinced now that they had taken her daughter to safety and were telling the truth, she said quietly, 'No one is going to tell you off.'

'Over there.' They spoke as one, pointing towards the rear of the store.

'Show me?'

She had to move quickly to keep pace with the boys. They ran down to the deserted end of the store, to the counter where all the brooms and brushes, dustpans and pokers were laid out for sale. From behind the counter one of the boys dragged the carrycot into view.

'Oh!!!' At the sight of it, Gladys cried out.

'We thought the baby would be safe here.'

Gladys grabbed the handles and pulled the cot out into the aisle. The silence was excruciating. Gladys, her heart in her mouth, lifted back the covers.

The baby slept on.

Gladys threw the blanket on the floor and picked up her child, examining her head, her face, her arms, her legs. The child quivered, woke, opened her tiny mouth, squeezed her eyes shut and began to cry. Gladys rained kisses on her, talking all the time, senseless words, her heart overwhelmed with relief.

'Thank you, boys,' she cried. 'You did well.'

Violet arrived, puffing and panting. 'I thought one of you got run over.' She was cross and Gladys could smell the sweat where her exertions had overheated her body. 'You little buggers, you'll be the death of me . . .'

Gladys interrupted her. 'They kept the baby safe. They saved her.'

Now she had her child back, she didn't want the boys punished for what could have been an accident. Siddy had been drinking. Possibly his reactions weren't as quick as they could have been. If that was so, he'd paid a heavy price for his whisky.

'Let's get out of here,' she said. 'Why don't you take them back to Will's place?' She looked at the boys, then at Violet. 'Get Will to give them some ice cream.' Grins formed on the boys' faces.

With the child in her arms, she walked to the front of the store. Violet and her twins followed. Reggie had picked up the carrycot and Ronnie and he were swinging it by the handles.

At the smashed counter a policeman in uniform was waiting for her. There was broken rubbish on the floor, but the vehicle had gone.

'Where have you taken my husband?' Gladys asked. Her body felt heavy, her words difficult to form.

'To the War Memorial Hospital. He'll need to be identified.'

She nodded. 'I'll go as soon as I can.'

'You found her, then?' The policeman looked at Sydney. 'I'll arrange an ambulance for you and the baby.'

She shook her head. 'No need.' She walked away, through the remaining sightseers, her heels clicking on the hard surface.

Waiting by the smashed door and broken window were Will and Mac.

'I sent Violet and the twins back to the club,' Will said. His face was sombre. 'There wasn't anything they could do here. They want to comfort you. Is the baby all right?'

Gladys nodded. A wave of exhaustion hit her.

'I'll see they get home safely,' he added.

'Too many people get in the way,' added Mac. 'I expect you'd like a bit of peace and quiet?' He opened his arms and drew her into them. 'I am so sorry about Siddy, Gladys. If it's any consolation, death would have been practically instantaneous.'

She allowed herself to be comforted, then pulled away. Mac's closeness was smothering her and her baby. She nodded. 'Thank you.' It seemed the right thing to say. She felt so very tired.

It was dusk now and revellers were still dancing in the streets. It was noisy with singing and laughter, and across the water fireworks were spurting in the air and showering Portsmouth with golden stars. It seemed wrong for all this excitement to be going on when her Siddy, who never hurt anyone, was gone.

Gladys said, 'I want to go home. I want to be by myself.'

'I'll take you,' Mac said.

# Chapter Thirty-Seven

Gladys sat in the old armchair. The house was empty apart from herself, little Eli asleep in one bedroom and Sydney asleep in her big cot in Gladys's room. Mogs was sleeping on the arm of the chair, his legs dangling down. Idly she smoothed his fur. He opened one eye but didn't move.

There was a smell of cooked food lingering in the kitchen. They'd eaten bacon bits and fried tomatoes for tea.

Doll was at the pictures with Joe. He'd taken her to see *Thirty Seconds Over Tokyo* at the Criterion picture house. Gladys had no idea whether it was an A- or U-rated film, but recognized it as the picture the twins had seen, probably by climbing through the window of the gents lavatory. It was hard to keep up with the boys and their exploits.

They'd stayed away from Siddy's funeral, though. Violet hadn't come down to Gosport from London; Will hadn't liked the idea of the boys running riot in the churchyard.

The funeral had been tasteful, but Gladys had lost her best friend as well as her husband. Siddy would have a piece of her heart forever.

Goldie and Doll had announced their intention to find their parents. The motive behind this was the death of Fred and then the untimely death of Siddy. Gladys was pleased about this. 'Life's too short and family means everything,' she'd told them.

'He's at rest now,' Gladys told Mogs. She meant Siddy. Mogs flicked his tail. 'He would have liked the white roses. For Peace,' she added.

She picked up her cup and drank deeply. Will had given her four caddies of tea. There were Indian girls on the tins in filmy clothing, but the tea tasted fine.

Goldie had gone dancing with big Eli, who was still on leave, along with Solly and Patsy. The four of them had travelled across on the ferry to Kimbell's Dance Hall at Southsea. The girls had looked a treat in their summer dresses, flowers pinned in their hair.

Big Eli had asked Gladys if it would be appropriate to ask Goldie to marry him. Since the girl did nothing but bore the knickers off anyone who'd listen to her going on about how wonderful he was, Gladys told him it was very appropriate.

This afternoon she'd been summoned to the solicitor in Gosport's High Street.

That was after the morning had been spent listening to Mr Scrivenor at Priddy's telling all the workers for the second time that the armament yard would continue making shells and cartridges. The war in Europe was ended, but the Japanese needed to be stopped. He also warned the women that men would be returning from the war and priority had to go to them. Some of the women might lose their jobs.

Already Gladys had seen a man in his brand-new demob clothing. The pin-stripe suit, complete with braces and a trilby, looked very smart. Scrivenor had promised that although some women would lose their jobs, hopefully orders would come in from the government to supply arms for the forces and he'd do what he could to keep most of the workers on.

The solicitor's office had smelled of furniture polish.

She'd arrived early, but promptly at two she'd been shown into an office filled with dark, shiny furniture.

'Good afternoon, Mrs Butler,' the grey-haired gentleman had said, shaking her hand. He bade her sit down and then started flicking through the pages in front of him that had been tied with ribbon.

'I'm sorry about your husband's untimely demise,' he said. 'Did you know he had property in Gosport?'

She wanted to say of course I did, we didn't have any secrets. But apparently Siddy did have secrets.

'There are three houses.' She racked her brains: two properties in Alma Street, but where was the third? Wasn't there a house near Brockhurst?

'There's also a shop in the High Street.' He passed over the deeds to the shop. She saw it was near Bemister's Lane and currently a shoe shop. That was a surprise. Now she was looking at the deeds of the three houses. Two in Alma Street and one at Brockhurst, currently let out.

'You are quite a wealthy woman, property-wise; there's no outstanding mortgages.' Suddenly it hit her that she owned her own house and would never need to pay rent again.

The solicitor put a bank statement in front of her. She gasped when she saw the total balance.

There were forms to sign, documents to fill in. She decided to leave all the deeds with the solicitor and requested that he carry on working for her now Siddy was dead.

She wanted to go home, let everything settle in her head and cuddle her baby.

Walking down to the ferry to catch a bus, she started to cry. She had no idea why the tears were falling and felt rather silly, because people stared as she passed them.

Before she caught the bus she walked through the Ferry Gardens. Bright flowers filled the immaculate beds. The light wind ruffled her hair and she could feel the heat of the May sun. She watched the squat beetle-like ferries cross the expanse of water between Gosport and Portsmouth. The car ferry, too, clanked through the sea on its chains.

Gladys looked across at the Rainbow but didn't intend to visit. She would be made welcome, but she wanted to be alone.

And now it was evening and she was by herself.

She thought of all that had happened to her, the unhappiness, the happiness. The war was over. It hadn't been all bad.

She was determined to be the best mother she could be to Sydney – the child she'd named after the only man in her life who gave her everything, including his name, yet took nothing.

She ran her fingers through Mogs's silky fur. She looked at her empty teacup. The wireless was playing softly and the music made her smile, thinking of the dances she had gone to, the fun she'd had. The men she'd kissed. It was hard for her to realize that the siren, Moaning Minnie, wouldn't start up its mournful shriek at any moment. Soon would come the clearing-up, the aftermath of war. Blackout curtains finally removed, sticky tape scraped from windows. In Gosport, rebuilding of the bombed premises would begin and no longer would the streets look like mouths with gappy teeth. No more searchlights. No more crowding into air-raid shelters. The men would return to their families. Broken men would need time to heal, in mind and body. This time last year she was alone, but even though she'd lost Siddy, now she had a family: one she would cherish, love and look after.

Mogs was purring. Gladys stared at the pile of ironing needing to be done, and ignored it. She wondered what the future would bring.

A smile lit her face as she thought of Will.

# Acknowledgements

Thank you to my hard-working class at St Vincent. Thursdays wouldn't be the same without you. Thanks especially to Norman, who I can depend on to set me right; to Martin for his help and common sense; to Maureen, a kindred soul, and to Ollie, for being Ollie. And if I haven't named you, that doesn't mean I don't appreciate you or your talents. You all enrich my life.

Many places, street names and topography are real and I apologize for liberties taken to suit the storyline. The characters, however, are pure figments of my imagination.

# Discover

# ROSIE ARCHER

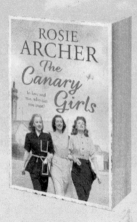